Praise for the Marked Trilogy

"Exhilarating adventure in an edgy world of angels and demons highlights the opener of Day's Marked trilogy. Dynamic and vibrant, Eve is an impressive protagonist, and her fierce spirit and determination to make the best of her circumstances will keep readers enthralled."
—*Publishers Weekly*

"Day, a.k.a. multitalented author Sylvia Day, explodes onto the urban fantasy scene with a new twist on the Cain and Abel story. It's dark, gritty, and sexy to the max, so readers can be thankful the next chapter in this pulse-pounding series is only a month away!"
— *RT Book Reviews*

"Great characters and terrific storytelling in a hot-blooded adrenaline ride. A keep-you-up-all-night read."
—Patricia Briggs,
#1 *New York Times* bestselling author

"*Eve of Darkness* is a sizzling, heart-pounding urban fantasy that thrilled and fascinated me from beginning to end. Eve is a smart, spirited heroine I won't soon forget!"
—Jeri Smith-Ready,
award-winning author of *Wicked Game*
and *Bad to the Bone*

TOR BOOKS BY S. J. DAY

Eve of Darkness
Eve of Destruction
Eve of Chaos

EVE *of* DESTRUCTION

Sylvia Day
writing as S. J. Day

A TOM DOHERTY ASSOCIATES BOOK
NEW YORK

EVE OF DESTRUCTION

A Tor Book
Published by Tom Doherty Associates
175 Fifth Avenue
New York, NY 10010

www.tor-forge.com

Tor® is a registered trademark of Macmillan Publishing Group, LLC.

ISBN 978-1-250-16591-6

Our books may be purchased in bulk for promotional, educational, or business use. Please contact your local bookseller or the Macmillan Corporate and Premium Sales Department at 1-800-221-7945, extension 5442, or by email at MacmillanSpecialMarkets@macmillan.com.

Second Mass Market Edition: September 2018

Printed in the United States of America

0 9 8 7 6 5 4 3 2 1

To all our soldiers serving in the United States military: Thank you. You are respected and deeply appreciated.

For those of you on foreign soil: Come home safe. We love and miss you.

• •

My time in the military was deeply enriched by the soldiers who crossed my path. From Foxtrot Company, 229th Military Intelligence Battalion: Oglesby, Frye, Antonian, Doughty, Anderson, Edmonds, Calderon, McCain, Slovanick, and Pat.

Christine: You will always be the sister of my heart.

I love you, guys. Never Quit.

My deep gratitude goes to:

My editor, Heather Osborn, for giving me the time I needed and for all the cheerleading she does behind the scenes to support this series.

Nikki Duncan (www.nikkiduncan.com) for the McCroskey name and enthusiasm over *Eve of Darkness*.

Jordan Summers, Karin Tabke, Sasha White, and Shayla Black for always being there for me. *You rock, ladies!*

Melissa Frain at Tor for loving the first book enough to clamor for this one.

Seth Lerner for breaking one of his cardinal rules. I'm honored.

Denise McClain and Carol Culver for assisting me with the French dialogue.

Giselle Hirtenfeld/Goldfeder, whose first name I gave to a nightmare in this book. The real Giselle is actually a dream to work with.

Susan Grimshaw of Borders Group, Inc., whose last name I appropriated for an alpha werewolf. Far from being villainous (like my Alpha turns after the loss of his child), Sue is one of my heroes. *Thank you, Sue, for all the support you have given to me and my books over the years.*

My father, Daniel Day, for his help with the Italian dialogue. *Thanks, Dad!*

Therefore whosoever slayeth Cain, vengeance shall be taken on him sevenfold. And the Lord set a mark upon Cain, lest any finding him should kill him.

—GENESIS 4:15

Anno Domini 2008

Class R4AD08

Student/Origin:
Callaghan, Kenneth: Scotland
Dubois, Claire: France
Edwards, Robert: England
Garza, Antonio: Italy
Hogan, Laurel: New Zealand
Hollis, Evangeline: United States
Molenaar, Jan: Holland
Richens, Chad: England
Seiler, Iselda: Germany

Number of Graduates:
CLASSIFIED

Number of Casualties:
CLASSIFIED

Status:
PENDING INTERNAL REVIEW

CHAPTER 1

Evangeline Hollis woke to the scents of Hell—fire and brimstone, smoke and ashes.

Her nostrils flared in protest. She lay on her back, unmoving, willing her brain to catch up with her circumstances. Licking her lips, she tasted death, the bitterness coating both her tongue and mouth in a thick, immovable wash. Her muscles shifted in an attempt to stretch and a groan escaped her.

What the hell? The last thing she remembered was . . .

. . . being burnt to a crisp by a dragon.

Panic assailed her with the memory, quickly followed by her mind lurching into full awareness. Eve jackknifed up from her sprawled position, sucking in air with such force it was audible. She blinked, but only inky darkness filled her vision. Her hand reached up to her arm and her fingertips found the raised brand there. The Mark of Cain—a triquetra surrounded by a circlet of three serpents, each one eating the tail of the snake before it. The eye of God filled the center.

The mark burned whenever she took the Lord's name in vain—which was often—and whenever she lied, which was less often but useful on occasion. When dealing with Satan's minions, playing dirty leveled the playing field.

Where the fuck am I? In her upright position, the smoky stench in the air was magnified. Her nose wrinkled.

Maybe I'm in Hell? As a longtime agnostic, she still struggled with facing the reality of God. Heaven, Hell, souls . . . They were concepts that couldn't be explained with reason.

Besides, if there was a merciful God and a Heaven, she'd be there. She had only been cursed with the Mark of Cain for six weeks and she hadn't yet been properly trained in how to kill Infernals, but during that short time she had eradicated a tengu infestation, killed a Nix, and managed to vanquish a dragon. She'd also helped put a lid on a major new threat to the good guys—a concoction of some sort that allowed Infernals to temporarily hide in the guise of mere mortals. *And* she'd managed to get Cain and Abel to work together for the first time since they were kids.

If all that wasn't enough to save her soul, she would take her chances with the Devil. Maybe he'd have a better sense of fair play.

As Eve's mind struggled to catch up with her present, the sound of singing penetrated the fog of her thoughts. She couldn't understand a word, but it was familiar all the same. The language was Japanese; the voice, her mother's.

The idea of sharing Hell with her mother was oddly both comforting and chilling.

Eve's hands clenched tentatively, testing the soft surface beneath her, attempting to discern where she was. She felt satin, like the sheets on her bed. A cool breeze touched her brow and Eve's vision exploded into living color. She jerked violently in surprise.

She *was* in her bedroom, sitting atop her king-size bed. As if her senses had been muted, the steady crashing of waves against the Huntington Beach shoreline increased in volume. The soothing rhythm drifted down the hall from her living room balcony and brought welcome relief.

Home. As her tension dissipated, Eve's shoulders relaxed. Then, a brief glimmer in the periphery of her vision made her turn her head.

Lifting her arms to shield her eyes from the blinding light, she barely made out the silhouette of a winged man standing in the corner between her bleached pine closet doors and her dresser. Eve blinked back an unusually thick wash of tears. She risked another glance at the angel and found that, once again, her mark enhancements knew what to do even when she didn't. Her arms lowered. She could see him now without damage to her vision.

The angel was tall, with brawny arms and legs displayed by a knee-length, sleeveless robelike garment. The gown was white and belted with a tan braid. The black combat boots with wicked spikes running up and down the outside were a surprise, as was the impossible perfection of his features. His jaw was square and bold, his hair dark and restrained in a queue at his nape. His irises shimmered like blue flame, and he had an air about him that warned her to keep on his good side.

His gaze lowered to her chest. Hers followed. She was nude.

"Yikes!" Grabbing the top sheet, Eve yanked it up to her neck.

Miyoko Hollis appeared in the doorway, buried in an armful of laundry.

"Hey, you're awake," her mother called out, her voice flavored with a Japanese accent.

"I guess so." Eve was so happy to see her mom, her eyes burned. "It's good to see you."

"Eh, you say that now." Striding toward the bed with the brisk stride of a retired nurse, Miyoko was a compact whirlwind of energy, a tornado that often left Eve feeling exhausted. "You didn't move a muscle for a while. I nearly thought you were dead."

Eve *had* been dead, that was the problem. "What day is it?"

"Tuesday."

Another noxious breeze assaulted her nostrils and Eve waved a hand in front of her face. Her gaze found the source on her dresser—an incense stick.

"Whatever fragrance that is," Eve muttered, inwardly reeling that she had lost two days of her life, "it stinks."

Miyoko moved to the end of the bed and dumped the still-warm pile of clothes onto the comforter. She wore Hello Kitty pajamas—pink flannel pants and a T-shirt that had a giant Hello Kitty face on the front. With her black hair in pigtails and her unlined face, she looked more like Eve's sibling than a parent. She also acted as if she owned the place, which she didn't. Darrel and Miyoko Hollis lived in Anaheim—home of

Disneyland, California Adventure, and Eve's childhood. Still, whenever her mother visited, Eve found herself fighting for her place as alpha female in her own house.

Eve watched her mother walk right past the angel without batting an eye. Standing with crossed arms, widespread legs, and folded wings, he was impossible to ignore . . .

Unless you couldn't see him.

"Aromatherapy aids healing," Miyoko pronounced.

"Not when it smells like shit. And why are you doing my laundry again? I wish you could come over and just relax."

"It's not shit. It's jasmine-chamomile. And I am doing your laundry because it was piled up. Can't relax in a messy house."

"My house is never messy." Her mom did laundry every time she came over, despite the fact that at twenty-eight years of age Eve was perfectly capable of doing her own. No matter how spotless her condo might be, her mother cleaned it—rearranging everything to her liking in the process.

"Was, too," her mother argued. "You had an overflowing basket by the washing machine and a sink full of dirty dishes."

Eve pointed at the boxer briefs, men's shirts, and towels in the pile. "Those aren't my clothes. The dishes aren't mine either."

She wondered what her mother would do if she learned that she was washing Cain and Abel's clothes. The brothers went by the names Alec Cain and Reed Abel now, but they were still the siblings of biblical legend.

"Alec has been using all the towels and leaving his

clothes on the bathroom floor." Miyoko's tone was starkly chastising. No man was good enough for Eve. They all had some flaw in her mother's eyes, no matter how small. "And both he and your boss get new glasses every time they have a drink."

"Alec lives next door. Why doesn't he go mess up his place?"

"You're asking me?" Her mother snorted. "I still don't know why Reed spends so much time at your house. It's not natural. Or why your boyfriend is CEO of a corporation like Meggido Industries, but I've never seen him in a suit."

The thought of Alec in a suit made Eve smile. "When you run the place and you're good at it, you can wear whatever you want."

Eve stretched gingerly, wincing at the lingering tenderness in her spine. Then, she hollered, "Alec!"

"Don't yell."

"It's my house, Mom."

"Men don't like to be yelled at."

"Mom . . ." She heaved out a frustrated breath. "What do you care, anyway? He leaves towels on the bathroom floor."

It was a pet peeve of Eve's, too, but she didn't think it made a man unsuitable for marriage.

"It's inconsiderate," Miyoko groused. "And unhygienic."

Eve glanced at the angel, embarrassed to have him witness their squabbling. His burning gaze met hers, then his nose wrinkled.

"Mom!" Eve's tone was more urgent. "Put that incense out, *please*. I'm serious. It stinks."

Miyoko grunted, but moved to tamp out the incense stick. "You're difficult."

"And you're stubborn, but I love you anyway."

"You're awake," Alec interjected, walking through the open bedroom door. He stared at her with fathomless eyes, his gaze darting over her in search of any cause for concern. "You scared me, angel," he said gruffly.

Angel. It was a pet name only he ever used. Every time she heard it, her toes curled. Alec's voice was velvet smooth and capable of turning a reading of Hawking's *A Brief History of Time* into an orgasmic experience.

Dressed in long shorts and white tank, he looked hotter than most men did in a tuxedo. His black hair was a little too long and his stride boasted a bit of a swagger, but no matter what he wore or how casually he moved, he looked like someone you didn't want to piss off. It was the hunter in him, the predator. Alec killed for a living and he excelled at it.

He was the reason she'd been marked. He was also her mentor.

His brother Reed entered the room behind him. Their features were similar enough to betray them as siblings, but they were otherwise as different as night and day. Reed favored Armani suits and sharp haircuts. Today he wore graphite gray slacks and a black dress shirt open at the throat and rolled up at the wrists. He was her superior.

Every Mark had a handler, a *mal'akh*—an angel—directly responsible for assigning them to targets. Reed had once likened the mark system to the judicial system. The archangels were the bail bondsmen, Reed was her dispatcher, and she was a bounty hunter. She wasn't a very good one . . . yet. But she was learning and trying.

In the meantime, Reed was responsible for her assignments and for peripherally ensuring her safety. As her mentor, Alec's sole responsibility—under usual circumstances—was keeping her alive. But God had been unwilling to lose the talents of his most established and powerful enforcer. Alec cut a deal to be with her, and the result was that Reed often had more liability where she was concerned. Considering the festering animosity between the two brothers, the setup was fucked all around.

"Welcome back to the land of the living, Ms. Hollis," Reed greeted. He smiled his cocky smile, but his dark eyes held an uncertainty Eve found endearing. He had no idea what to make of his feelings for her. Since she was in a relationship with his brother, she couldn't help him with that. She tried not to think about her feelings for him. It was just too complicated. Her life was already a disaster of biblical proportions.

Both men spotted the angel in the corner, who stood unmoving. They bowed slightly in deference.

Because Miyoko was too busy glaring at Eve, she failed to catch the gesture. Eve used her job as an interior designer as an excuse for Reed's frequent visits. As far as her family knew, she worked from home most days and if Reed wanted to see what she was up to, stopping by was the best way to do it. But Miyoko didn't believe the lie. She assumed all male interior designers were gay and Reed was most definitely *not*. Eve had no idea what her mother thought was really going on, but she knew the obvious animosity between the two men was fodder for suspicions.

Alec's smile warmed her from the inside. "How are you feeling?"

"Thirsty."

"I'll get you some ice water," Reed offered.

She smiled. "Thank you."

Alec bent and pressed his lips to her forehead. "Are you hungry?"

"A banana would be nice." She caught his wrist before he could draw away. "I had a dream. A nightmare. I was killed by a dragon."

"Your subconscious is trying to tell you something," her mother interrupted. "But you couldn't have dreamt you died. I heard if you die in your dreams, you die in real life."

"I think that's a myth."

"There is no way to know," Miyoko argued as she folded laundry. "If it happened to you, you would be dead and couldn't tell us."

Alec sat on the edge of the bed, watching Eve with an alert gaze. He knew she couldn't say what she meant while her mother was in the room.

"It's over now," he soothed. "You're safe."

"It was so real . . . I don't understand how I'm sitting here now."

"We'll talk later, after you've had a chance to eat." He squeezed her hand. His expression held the softness he showed only to her. "Let me get you that banana."

He left, and her mom returned to the side of the bed. Leaning over, Miyoko whispered loudly, "He fights with your boss. About *everything*. You would think they were married. Too much testosterone in those two. Not enough brains."

The angel made a choked noise.

"Mom . . ." Eve glanced at the corner. He looked pained. It was an expression her father wore often.

Miyoko straightened and gathered up the now-folded clothes. "A *thoughtful* man would carry sunscreen to the beach. He wouldn't let you get burned."

Sunburned at the beach. Eve snorted at the excuse. If only she'd been bedridden for something so simple. "I can count on one hand the number of guys I've seen carry sunscreen."

"A good man would," her mother insisted.

"Like Dad?"

"Sure."

"I've never seen Dad with sunscreen."

"That's not the point."

"I thought it was."

Eve loved her father, she really did. Darrel Hollis was a good ol' boy from Alabama with an even-keeled temper and a gentle smile. He was also oblivious. Retired now, he rose at dawn, watched television or read, then went back to bed after dinner. The most unexpected thing he had ever done was marry a foreign exchange student (and Eve suspected her mother hadn't given him much choice in the matter).

"Stop dating pretty boys," Miyoko admonished, "and find someone stable."

Eve shot a beseeching glance at the angel in the corner. He sighed and stepped closer. His voice had a soothing resonance no mortal could create.

"You want to replant the flowers in the pots by your front door," he whispered in Miyoko's ear. "You will go to the nursery, then home, where you will spend the rest of the afternoon indulging in your passion for gardening. Evangeline is fine and no longer needs you."

Her mother paused, her head tilting as she absorbed

the thoughts she assumed were her own. The gift of persuasion. Eve hadn't mastered that one yet.

"You should get a spa pedicure, too," Eve added. "You deserve it."

Miyoko shook her head. "I don't need—"

"Get a pedicure," the angel ordered.

"I think I'll get a pedicure," Miyoko said.

"With flowers painted on your big toes," Eve went on.

The angel shot her a quelling glance.

Eve winced. "If you want," she amended quickly.

Alec returned with the banana. Standing by her bed, he peeled it, arresting her with the sight of his flexing biceps.

"I'm going home," her mom said suddenly. "The laundry is done, the dishes washed. You're fine. You don't need me."

"Thank you for everything." Eve intended to stand and hug her mother, but remembered that she was naked between her satin sheets.

Miyoko waved her off and headed toward the door. "Let me change first and get my stuff together, then I'll say good-bye."

Reed's voice rumbled down the hallway and swept over Eve's skin like the warm caress of the sun. "Let me help you with that, Mrs. Hollis."

Eve looked at Alec, who resumed his seat on the edge of her bed. Then, she glanced at the angel. "Hi."

"Hello, Evangeline." He stepped forward, his heavy boots making no sound on the hardwood floor. He had an inordinate number of feathers and appeared to have three pairs of wings. He was beyond impressive; he was the most perfectly gorgeous creature she had ever seen.

"Who are you?" she asked before taking a bite of

the fruit. The first chunk was swallowed almost whole, followed immediately by another. Her stomach growled, reiterating that the mark burned a ton of calories and she was expected to keep up by eating frequently.

"Sabrael."

Chewing, she glanced at Alec again.

"He is a seraph," he explained.

Her eyes widened and she chewed faster, embarrassed to be naked in such company. The seraphim were the highest ranking angels, far above the seven archangels who managed the day-to-day operations of the mark system here on Earth. Alec was a *mal'akh*—the lowest rank of angel—as was his brother. Eve was a lowly Mark, one of thousands of poor suckers drafted into godly service for perceived sins. They worked for absolution by hunting and killing Infernals who'd crossed the line one too many times. A bounty was earned for every successful vanquishing, indulgences that went toward the saving of Mark souls.

"Can I get dressed?" she asked, wiping her mouth with the tips of her fingers.

Alec stood and took the empty peel from her. "Sabrael won't leave until he speaks with you. Celestials have a different view of nudity than mortals do. Tell me what you need and I'll get it."

Eve directed him to a beach cover-up that hung in her closet. It was made of pale blue terry cloth and sported a hood, short sleeves, and a pouch in the front. Alec dropped it over her head, and she shoved her various body parts through the appropriate openings.

"Okay, Sabrael," she began, brushing her hair back from her face. "Why are you here?"

"The better question would be: Why are *you* here, Evangeline? You should be dead."

She bit back a groan. Another riddle. It seemed all the angels spoke in them, except for Alec and Reed. Those two spoke so bluntly she'd be perpetually blushing if not for the mark, which prevented her body from wasting energy. "I thought I was."

"You were. But Cain claims you have knowledge we need."

Eve looked at Alec. "You brought me back from the dead to grill me for information?"

Sabrael's arms crossed in front of his massive chest. "You were going someplace where we would not have been able to ask you. It was the only way."

Her gaze moved heavenward. "You're not winning any brownie points with me," she called out.

"It is not your place to demand Jehovah prove himself to you," Sabrael said in a terrible voice.

"You said we missed something in Upland," Alec prompted, his fingers lacing with hers.

She thought back to her last assignment—vanquishing an Infernal in one of the men's bathrooms at Qualcomm Stadium. Alec had taken her out on their first "date"—a Chargers versus Seahawks football game. Reed had come along and said it was time to parlay her classroom instruction into the field.

"A wolf," she murmured.

"What?"

"I assigned her to a werewolf," Reed said from the doorway. He approached the opposite side of the bed and passed a chilled bottle of water across the expanse to Eve. "A kid. Easy pickings."

"Only it wasn't a wolf," Alec retorted. "And it sure as shit wasn't easy."

"But there was one there," Eve explained. "One of the kids we spotted in the convenience store in Upland."

Upland. She'd never think of the town the same way again. They had been sent there on an investigation. Just as Marks bore the Mark of Cain on their arms, Infernals bore "details" that betrayed what species they were, and what their rank in Hell's hierarchy was. Sort of like military insignia. They also reeked of rotting souls, which made them easy to detect. When Eve stumbled across an Infernal who bore no details and no stench, she and Alec had been tasked with discovering how that was possible. They'd found that a masking agent had been created, a concoction that could potentially tip the balance between good and evil enough to set off Armageddon.

The operation had been run out of a masonry in Upland. The place was gone now, blown to smithereens when Eve shoved a water demon into a fired-up kiln. But it appeared the original problem still remained to be dealt with. The dragon had been odor-free, a condition made possible only by the mask.

"He said the Alpha sent him," she went on. "They wanted me dead as retaliation for the death of his son."

Alec's face took on a hardened cast that chilled her blood. "Charles."

"The bigger issue," she said quickly, "was that the dragon he brought with him didn't stink or have any details."

"There has to be more of the masking agent somewhere," Reed said. "A stockpile or a new batch."

"Perhaps the mask is permanent?" Sabrael suggested.

"No, it wears off. I saw it happen."

The seraph's gaze moved to Alec. "You did not smell the Infernal either?"

"I told you, I didn't pay attention." Alec continued to focus his attention on Eve. The muscle in his arm twitched just below the mark, as if it pained him, and she knew immediately what he was doing—he was lying. The mark burned when sins were committed.

Turning his head to look at Sabrael, Alec said, "I haven't been trained as a mentor. I don't know how to focus on both the target and Eve at once. I only know how to hone in on her."

To bring her back from the brink of Hell, he'd lied to someone in power. A seraph. Or maybe God himself. Alec would pay for that . . . somehow, some way. And now he was lying again. For her.

Her grip on his hand tightened until she was white knuckled, but he didn't complain.

Miyoko bustled back into the room, her gaze narrowing at the sight of the two men on either side of Eve's bed. "Okay, I'm ready to go."

Alec stood so Eve could get out of bed, but he held her back when it became clear that she was too dizzy to complete the effort. She held out her arms for a hug instead.

"When did you get your scar removed?" her mother asked as she bent over.

Her fingers brushed over the Mark of Cain. All of Eve's childhood scars had been removed with the mark. Her body was a temple now. It ran like a well-oiled machine—precise and without deviations such as sweating, a racing heartbeat, or labored breathing. Except when sex was involved. Then everything worked in full mortal fashion. It made orgasms as addicting as a drug, since it was the only time a Mark could get "high."

Eve frowned when her mother didn't say anything about the mark on her deltoid. Her younger sister Sophia's first tattoo had been lamented with the statement, "You used to be such a beautiful baby."

"I get a tattoo," Eve said dryly, "and you're worried about a mole?"

"You got a tattoo?" her mother screeched. "Where?"

Eve blinked and looked down at her arm. She glanced at Alec who shook his head.

Her mother couldn't see it.

Sadness settled over Eve, weighing her down. The barrier between her and her old life wasn't just metaphorical.

"Just kidding," Eve husked, her throat tight.

"That was terrible," her mother complained, pushing her gently in recrimination. "I almost cried."

They hugged, and her mother straightened. "I made some *onigiri*. It's in a container by the coffeemaker."

"Thank you, Mom."

Reed moved to the door. "I'll help you carry your things down, Mrs. Hollis."

Miyoko beamed. Eve's condo was on the upper floor and the carport was subterranean.

"Kiss ass," Alec muttered, as they left.

Eve smacked him. "She needs help."

"I was going to help her, if he hadn't jumped all over her."

Sabrael cleared his throat. "You will hunt the Alpha wolf, Cain."

There was a long moment of stunned silence, then, "Eve is in training."

"And she will remain that way," the seraph assured.

"The classroom is the safest place for her to be, but you must go."

Alec shook his head. "No way. You can't separate a mentor/Mark pair."

"Charles Grimshaw is connected to the Infernal mask. His son was at the masonry where the concoction was being manufactured and the masked dragon that killed Evangeline was sent at his behest. Time is of the essence. He must be put down before he causes more damage. Your agreement was that you would still perform individual hunts as well as your mentored ones."

Alec ran both hands through his dark hair. "Once it becomes known that she's still alive, they will hunt her. She'll need me nearby to protect her."

"Raguel has full use of his gifts at the moment. I doubt even you can offer better protection than an archangel in full regalia. Also, don't forget that you are earning double indulgences for every vanquishing. Killing an Infernal of Grimshaw's prominence will advance you by years."

Alec's jaw tightened. "And I'm just supposed to say, 'Sorry, angel. I'm off to save my own ass, so you're on your own'?"

Eve winced.

"I'll be okay," she reassured, her thumb brushing soothingly over his palm. "Shouldn't be any trouble at all. You and Reed can go about your business without worrying. We all know Gadara won't allow anything bad to happen to me, since he needs me to bully you two."

"That doesn't mean," Reed drawled as he returned, "that we're not going to worry. You always manage to find trouble."

She almost argued that Gadara liked to shove her face first into trouble just to irritate Alec, but that wouldn't make them feel better.

"I especially don't like that this week is field training," Alec said, glancing at Reed. "It's one thing to be in Gadara Tower. It's another to be out in the open."

"Fort McCroskey is a military base," Sabrael said.

"A *closed* base."

"It still has a military presence, and Raguel will travel with his entourage of guards."

Eve frowned at all three men. "What are you talking about?"

Reed explained. "Raguel is taking your class up to Northern California. There's a former Army base there that he likes to use for field exercises."

Eve groaned inwardly. A week-long trip with a class of newbie Marks who resented her for having the infamous Cain as a mentor and the equally revered Abel as a handler. She figured the coming week would be as much fun as a Brazilian wax.

"Doesn't the Alpha live in Northern California?" she asked.

Alec nodded. "A couple hours north of the base. Fort McCroskey is near Monterey, the Grimshaw pack is nearer to Oakland."

"A couple of hours' drive is quite convenient," Sabrael pointed out. "You could have been sent on assignment to the other side of the world."

"You can't make me like this," Alec bit out. "But I'll take Eve up to Monterey, then continue on."

Reed grinned. "I'll keep a close eye on her while Cain is busy."

"You have an Infernal to classify," Sabrael reminded

him. "You both must trust that Raguel will see to Evangeline's safety."

Eve sighed. "Anyone want to switch places?"

"Sorry, babe," Reed said. "Mark training isn't a place to play hooky."

"She's not your babe," Alec snapped.

Reed held both hands up in a gesture of surrender that was belied by the mischievous twinkle in his eyes.

Their feud wasn't helped by her past intimacy with Reed. That happened before Alec had reentered her life, so he didn't hold it against her. But to say that he didn't trust his brother to be within a mile of her would be an understatement.

Alec looked at Eve, his features softening. "You'd rather hunt real demons than pretend to?"

"Maybe I was resurrected with a different personality," she suggested. "Like *Invasion of the Body Snatchers.*"

"Or maybe you're pissed off at getting killed, and want a little payback."

Her mouth tilted at the corners. How well he knew her.

"But if you are a pod person," he continued, "you have great taste in bodies."

A tingle moved through her. His wink told her he knew it.

"Four more weeks, angel. Then we'll tear 'em up."

Four more weeks of class, one of which was a camp-out. Eve sighed. She was definitely back among the living.

Hell would have more direct means of torture.

CHAPTER 2

I'm sorry about Takeo."

Reed glanced at the Mark who entered Gadara Tower beside him. "Thank you, Kobe."

Kobe Denner scrubbed a hand over his face and cursed in his native Zulu. "He saved my life once. I still owed him one. He was a good Mark."

"My best." Avenging the Mark's death was at the top of Reed's to-do list. But first he had to classify the Infernal who did the deed, then he needed to learn how best to vanquish it.

"I heard some unknown demon-type did it."

"Yes, that's true."

"Must have been a badass to take out Takeo."

"I've never seen anything like it." The graveness of the situation was evident in Reed's somber tone.

"Shit." Kobe's dark eyes were sad. His features were kept youthful by the mark, but nothing could hide the weight of experience that burdened his five-foot ten-inch frame. Killing demons took a terrible toll on the soul. "It's already bad out there."

"We'll find and kill it. We always do." Reed was grateful to sound more confident than he felt.

Kobe paused beside one of the many planters that decorated the lobby atrium. "Do you think Takeo got in?"

Reed inhaled deeply, contemplating the best answer to the question. It was a common one among Marks. They were working for absolution and all wanted to know if they would be granted access to Heaven if they lost their lives before collecting enough indulgences.

"He deserved to," Reed answered.

It was the best answer to give that wasn't a violation of the Decalogue, but it clearly wasn't the answer Kobe wanted to hear.

Still, the Mark accepted it with a grim nod. "If you need me for anything, let me know."

"I will." Reed shook the Mark's hand, then they separated. Kobe headed toward the tucked-away bank of elevators that led to the subterranean floors, an area that was restricted to Marks and Infernal allies and prisoners. Reed crossed the bustling lobby to reach the private elevator that would take him directly to Raguel Gadara's office.

At least one hundred business-minded pedestrians congested the vast space. Fifty floors above them, a massive skylight illuminated the atrium and served as an architectural invitation to God's blessings. The steady hum of numerous conversations and the industrious whirring of the glass tube elevators testified to both the effectiveness of the design and Raguel's widely lauded business acumen. On the surface, all was well at the headquarters of the North American firm. Mortals conducted business here in blissful ignorance of Gadara's true purpose—the oversight and control of thousands of Marks.

The seven archangels were responsible for funding their firms in a secular fashion. Raguel had a knack for real estate, which had created a multibillion-dollar empire and a notoriety that rivaled Donald Trump and Steve Wynn. Gadara Enterprises owned properties the world over, from resorts in Las Vegas and Atlantic City to office buildings in Milan and New York. As a handler assigned to Raguel's firm, Reed had traversed the various halls so often he could do it with his eyes closed. But ever since he had marked Eve here, he could no longer do so comfortably.

Without volition, his gaze moved to the stairwell door that concealed the landing where he'd taken Eve. Memories hit his brain in a rapid-fire series of graphic images. The recollections were so vivid, he could feel her lush curves beneath his hands and smell her perfume. His dick hardened and he adjusted himself for comfort.

"Damn you," he growled, as much to Cain and Eve as to himself. He needed her to advance his ambitions, but he didn't need to admire her. Or covet her.

Entering the elevator, Reed stabbed at the lone button on the panel. There was a long pause as the camera in the corner focused on his features, then the security guard on the receiving end of the feed set the lift in motion. It shot up the thirty flights to the penthouse in a matter of seconds, but Reed could have shifted across the distance in the blink of an eye. Teleportation was a blessing given to all *mal'akhs*—except for Cain, who'd had the gift stripped from him. Reed chose to take the slower secular route today in order to gain the time needed to get himself under control. By the time the doors opened, he felt ready to deal with Raguel.

He exited into the massive, well-appointed office as if he owned it. An intricately carved mahogany desk was angled in the far corner, facing the bank of windows on the opposite side. Two brown leather chairs faced the desk and an eternal fire crackled in the fireplace. Above the mantel, a portrait of the *Last Supper* as imagined by Da Vinci brought God into the space, as did the crucifix adorning the wall behind Gadara's chair.

The archangel himself stood at the windows with his back to Reed. His hands were shoved in his pockets, and his bearing was regal and relaxed. The contrast between his cream-colored garments and his coffee-dark skin enhanced both beautifully.

"How is Ms. Hollis?" he asked, without turning his head.

Adjusting his slacks, Reed settled into the chair before the archangel's desk. "Recovering and putting on a brave face."

"Cain is not capable of arranging Ms. Hollis's resurrection alone." Raguel pivoted away from the Orange County vista. "You must have helped him."

"Help Cain? *Me?*" Reed's mouth curved slightly. Whether he had or hadn't was for him alone to know. The ambitious archangel didn't need any more ammunition.

The mark system had been built to work cohesively and, at one time, it had. Now, however, the race to please God better and more often than their counterparts had led to dissension and subterfuge among the archangels.

"Not that I mind, of course," Raguel assured. "It would have been a tragedy to lose her."

"It's a miracle it hasn't happened sooner, considering the deviations from protocol that she's suffered through."

"She has to be put through her paces. She has to be better than her peers, tougher and quicker. Unafraid. Her work with Cain will always make her the target of Infernals like Charles Grimshaw."

Reed's fingers curled around the ends of the armrests. Raguel was using her to further his own ends . . . and to aggravate Cain. "She became a target because we had her waving in the wind."

It was a coup for the archangel to have Cain on his team, and that was possible only because Eve was assigned to the North American firm. If anything happened to take Eve from Raguel's power, Cain—and all the prestige he brought with him—would be lost, too. Which was why Raguel was dragging Reed into the whole mess. He hadn't counted on Eve throwing a wrench into his plans.

"What does not kill her will make her stronger."

Reed's gut twisted with the memory of her scorched and broken on the bathroom floor. "She's already been killed once. Guess it can't get any worse."

"Your sarcasm is ill placed."

"What do you expect, Raguel? You ask if she's okay when you're the reason she was dead in the first place."

The archangel exhaled audibly, a soft but chastising sound. He was in his element while class was in session, the only time an archangel was given free use of his celestial gifts. Power thrummed through the air around him and divine radiance burnished his appearance with a golden glow. If he chose to, he could extend gold-tipped wings to a thirty-foot span. But he only had four weeks left before his students would graduate and he would once again be trapped within his temporal guise.

The training of new Marks took seven weeks, and the archangels rotated the duties so they could each enjoy their God-given power. The rest of the year the Lord *suggested* they live mortal lives. He believed the archangels would be more sympathetic to His beloved mortals if they suffered the same inconveniences.

The archangels could choose to disregard the suggestion, of course. Jehovah was a strong proponent of free will. But there was a price to pay for every transgression. Considering the heat of the competition between the archangels, they were loath to incur even the smallest setback.

Raguel changed the subject. "We have to find the Infernal who killed your Mark."

"Yes, we do. Has there been word of further sightings?"

"One possible. In Australia."

Raguel moved toward his desk. Elegant in build with coarse black hair liberally sprinkled with gray by design, the archangel didn't age as mortals did, but he was forced to simulate the passing of years in order to allay suspicion. Eventually, this incarnation of Raguel would have to die and he would be reborn as someone else. Sometimes slipping into the role of a descendant was possible. At others, a full reinvention was the only viable way.

"Was another Mark lost?"

"Yes."

A chill swept through Reed. He would never forget the manner of Takeo's death. There had been nothing left of the Mark but skin clinging to forest branches and fluttering in the night air. "You can't mistake this Infernal's signature for any other's. If it's the same demon, it will be obvious. Was there a witness?"

"Yes, the handler was present at the time."

Mariel, another handler under Raguel's purview, had heretofore been the only celestial to glimpse the demon. Only briefly, but long enough to bring a haunting terror to her eyes when she spoke of it.

It crawled inside my Mark, she'd said. *Disappeared in her. She c-could not c-contain it.*

What remained was an explosion of tissue and skin in quantities not sufficient to make up a body. Where did the bones and blood go?

Reed exhaled harshly.

Raguel leaned one hip against the front of his desk. "Perhaps you and Mariel should go to Australia and question Uriel's handler yourselves."

"I want the Infernal, not reports of it."

"It will not take you long. A few hours, at most."

"If you insist, I'll go. Otherwise, I don't see the point." But Reed's outer capitulation came with inner doubts. Aside from having lost a Mark to the beast, he had nothing to offer in the way of assistance. Hands-on investigative work was the duty of Marks. His job was simply to know the strengths and weaknesses of those under his watch and to assign them to hunts where they had the best probability of success.

"You do not seem pleased," Raguel noted. "I thought you would be."

"Why? Because I want retribution for Takeo's death? It won't bring my best Mark back. I can only pray that my testimony was sufficient and he is with God now."

"Something else is troubling you, then. What is it?"

"This whole thing troubles me. Violence is escalating. Now there's a mask Infernals can hide behind and a new class of demon that's tipping the balance."

"We do not know that there is more than the one."

"It's killed three Marks in three weeks," Reed bit out. "One is enough. How long do you think it'll be before Sammael deems the trial run a success and makes more of them?"

The Fallen One was always eager to exploit any advantage.

"Jehovah never gives us more than we can handle. The Infernals are not the only ones who are improving."

Reed pushed to his feet. "That knowledge isn't helping me at the moment."

Raguel opened the humidor on his desk and withdrew a cigar, placing it between his lips uncut and unlit. He didn't smoke, but he enjoyed the act of holding a cigar in his mouth for reasons Reed had never grasped.

"Are you having a crisis of faith?" the archangel asked, his words spoken around the cigar.

"If this Infernal continues to murder Marks at a rate of one a week, we'll need to step up recruitment, training, mentoring—just to maintain our numbers. And if it keeps taking out our best and brightest, we'll soon be left with only novices."

"You paint the direst of pictures, Abel, as if this demon will charge through our ranks unchecked."

"It's my job to anticipate and prevent."

"Which is why I think you should accompany Mariel."

"I'm going." Reed stood. "I'll call her and we'll head out."

There was more behind Raguel's request than preventive measures. The archangel wanted his firm to be the one responsible for the identification and vanquishing of this new demon. He didn't want Uriel to take that honor, or any of the other archangels.

"I will be assembling the class and taking them to Fort McCroskey this evening. Report your findings to me there."

"Fine. Keep an eye on Eve."

Raguel withdrew the cigar from his smiling mouth. "Of course. She is my star pupil."

"Is that because she's already good? Or because you want her to be?"

"She is passably proficient." Raguel shrugged. "She could be brilliant, if her heart was in it. As it is, only determination drives her, and that is not enough to achieve the heights she might be capable of."

"How many new Marks have their heart in it? They're all drafted into service." Reed ran a hand through his short hair, reminded again that Eve was not at all the sort of mortal who usually became a Mark. She was/had been agnostic and she hadn't committed a crime of sufficient severity. Her only offense was being a temptation to Cain; the shining, delicious apple in his garden of demons and death.

"Ms. Hollis is different," Raguel said, his resonant voice rolling gently through the air. "Marks always come to us with varying degrees of faith within them. She has none at all, and she is hindered without it. Other Marks find strength in their desperation to save their souls; she lacks that edge and that deficiency might be the death of her."

If Raguel didn't see to that first. "Are the other Marks still hostile toward her? She might be 'dumbing down' to avoid further antagonism."

"I have never witnessed any hostilities."

Reed's mouth curved wryly. "That doesn't mean they're not there."

Because Eve was paired with Cain, a legend in the field for both his 100 percent kill rate and his autonomy, she was tormented by those who were jealous of her "good fortune." They assumed Cain did the lion's share of the work and she stood around looking pretty. They didn't bother to learn how wrong they were.

Cain had also pulled strings to keep Eve close to her family. Marks, as a rule, were transplanted to foreign firms. They were mostly loners, those who had either distanced themselves from family and friends or didn't have any for a variety of reasons. Their lack of strong emotional ties facilitated their acclimation to the life of a Mark. It also created a divide between them and Eve that was undeniable.

But Raguel blindly—or conveniently—ignored how the other Marks treated her.

"Just keep her alive while I'm gone," Reed said. "That's not asking too much."

"Keep *yourself* alive, Abel," Raguel returned. "We have a great deal of work ahead of us."

As if Reed could forget that.

Armageddon. It was coming. Sooner, rather than later.

Alec pulled Eve's Chrysler 300 into her assigned spot in the subterranean garage of Gadara Tower. Turning off the engine, he glanced at her, noting her set jaw and taut posture. Her long, dark hair was pulled back in a ponytail and her slender body was dressed in a black cotton tank top and khaki shorts. He reached out to her, kneading her tense shoulder muscles. "Are you okay?"

She nodded.

"Liar," he murmured.

"Let's just say I would prefer to go camping with a different crew, if I had a choice."

His hand wrapped around her nape and pulled her closer. He nuzzled his nose against hers. "I'll miss you."

An impatient thumping upon Eve's trunk shook the car and drew his attention to the rear window.

"No place for muckin' aboot!" a masculine voice shouted.

Alec pushed up his sunglasses, noting that the heckler was one of a group of three people walking by. He was tanned, blond, and looked to be in his early thirties.

"That's Ken," Eve said with laughter in her voice.

Ken's eyes darted between them, widening with horrified recognition. He quickly retreated, holding both hands up in a gesture of surrender. He had a duffel bag draped over one shoulder and teeth white enough to blind. "Sorry, Cain. I didnae ken it was you."

"Smooth move, arsehat," one of his companions muttered, shoving him.

"Ken, huh?" Alec grinned. "I was just thinking he looks like a Barbie doll."

"Don't let that pretty-boy exterior fool you. He's the best in the class."

Alec climbed out of the driver's seat and rounded the trunk. Opening the passenger door, he helped her out and asked, "What's his nickname?"

Eve had assigned names to all the Marks in her class. He thought he knew why. A nickname could serve two purposes: it could dehumanize a subject or it could personalize them. Alec suspected Eve's use of nicknames was due to both reasons.

"Just Ken," she said, "since he does look like a Ken doll."

Catching her elbow, Alec led her toward the elevators.

She shot him a wry glance. "You know, Gadara isn't going to like me riding up to Monterey with you instead of with the others."

"Gadara could use one of his planes to transport you all up there. Since he doesn't want to make life easy for you, we're not going out of our way to make life easy for him."

"You keep breaking rules for me."

He shrugged it off.

She looked at him in a way that made him want to take her back to bed. "The wolf in the bathroom told me you made a deal for my life. Then broke it."

"You believe everything an Infernal tells you?" He didn't want her gratitude. Not when he was the reason she was marked to begin with, and certainly not when he was hoping she would learn to like being a Mark.

"Thank you," she said softly, killing him.

They rode the elevator up to the atrium level.

Eve's nose wrinkled. "I don't think I'll ever get used to the smell of so many Marks in one enclosed space."

"You have to admit, it's more pleasant than the stench of rotting Infernal souls."

"Yeah, but it's too much. Makes it hard to breathe."

The lush vegetation in the atrium planters created

a humidity that intensified the sweet smell created when a hundred-plus Marks gathered. The effect was pleasant to Alec, as was the surge of power he felt whenever he was surrounded by Marks. Stepping into a firm was always a heady rush, no matter which firm he visited or where it was located. His blood thrummed with energy and his heart rate lurched into an elevated rhythm, as if the other Marks shared their energy with him. But Eve's senses were still very sensitive. He wondered how long that would last. Since he'd never mentored before and had yet to be trained for the task, he had no benchmark to compare her to.

They crossed the marble lobby to a recessed hallway where a private set of elevators would take them to the bowels of the building.

"What do you know about this fort we're going to?" Eve asked. "Anything?"

"Fort McCroskey was closed in 1991. There are some services still available—a commissary and some family housing for the students of a nearby military school—but otherwise it's a ghost town."

"Why are we going there?"

"There's enough infrastructure left to facilitate training. The Army still uses it for that reason on occasion and since our purpose is the same—the defeat of an enemy through force—it serves our needs just as well."

"Fun."

Alec linked his fingers with Eve's. The next week would be rough for her. "I'll be back before you even have a chance to miss me."

The cast of her features changed from disgruntlement to worry. "I'm an idiot. Bitching about learning how to defend myself while you're on assignment."

"I'll be fine. You just take care of yourself."

Eve eyed him carefully. "But it's not going to be easy, right? He has subordinate wolves to protect him; you're alone."

"It's no fun when it's easy."

"I wish I felt that way." She leaned against the metal handrail that surrounded the elevator car and crossed her arms. It was her *you-are-not-going-to-bullshit-me* pose. "Have you done this before? Gone after an Alpha while he's home with his pack?"

"Piece of cake."

"Now who's lying?"

Alec grinned and took in the view from the top of her head down to the combat boots on her feet. Eve was the type of exotic beauty people looked more than twice at. Creamy skin, inky dark tresses, red lips. His own paradise, his refuge from the rigors of his life.

It had been lust at first sight ten years ago and nothing had changed since then, despite being apart the entire time. She was his apple, his temptation. He was her downfall. Talk about a shitty foundation for a relationship. They had baggage, hurt feelings, regrets. Eve was the kind of woman a man married. White picket fence, kids, and a dog. Alec was aiming for advancement to archangel and heading his own firm.

The elevator doors opened and they stepped into the training center. The entire floor was dedicated to creating the best fighting force of Marks possible. There were classrooms with desks as well as dojos, indoor firing ranges, weight rooms, and fencing studios. Alec sometimes stayed to watch the instructions, impressed with the level of efficiency. As the original Mark, he'd been forced to survive by the skin of his teeth.

Some said he was born to kill, built for it, and he agreed.

Eve led the way to a glass-enclosed conference room. As they entered, the conversation died and all eyes turned toward them. There were a handful of people in the room, ranging in age from late teens to middle age, male and female. Some sat around the long table that dominated the center of the room, others sat atop it with their legs dangling over the sides. Ken was pouring himself a glass of water from the silver pitcher on a nearby console. They all looked at Eve, then glanced furtively at Alec except for a nearby blonde who assessed him boldly from head to toe.

"How are you feeling, Hollis?" asked a dark-haired Hispanic man in jeans and a button-down flannel shirt.

"Good. Thanks for asking."

As Alec joined Eve in the far corner, he returned every stare. Eve hopped onto the widow ledge, her lithe legs dangling and her fingers curled around the lip. They were white knuckled, betraying her unease. The tension in the room was thick and it pissed him off.

He leaned back and crossed his arms, facing the room dead-on. Uncomfortable shuffling ensued, then a return to the previous discussion.

Ken cleared his throat. "I cannae wait to get started."

"You're two sammies short of a picnic," a petite redhead said derisively, flipping her hair over her shoulder.

"Well," Alec murmured for Eve's ears only. "The girls are easily pegged with their nicknames, I think. 'Goth Girl' especially. I'm assuming the redhead is 'Princess,' since she's covered in glitter."

Eve smiled. "I am so high school, aren't I?"

"It's not your fault they're easily identifiable.

Besides, I liked you in high school," he purred, alluding to the ill-fated tryst that led them to where they were today. He couldn't regret it, and he took every opportunity to remind her of why she shouldn't regret it either.

Eve bumped her shoulder into his. "Can you guess which one is 'Mastermind'? That one's a bit harder."

Alec looked around. There were seven people in the room besides themselves. Since he had already identified four of the Marks, he quickly ruled them out—Ken, the red-haired princess with her glitter mascara and lip gloss, the Goth girl with her pale blonde hair and pixie-perfect features, and the "Fashionista" whose height and rail-thin figure were the stuff of supermodel dreams. The remaining occupants were the guy who greeted Eve when they entered, a wan and slightly portly teenage boy in a nylon jogging suit, and a gray-haired gentleman in dress slacks and polo shirt.

"The old guy?" he guessed. "He kinda has that Magneto vibe."

"You're older than he is," Eve reminded. "And no, he's 'Gopher.' His name is Robert Edwards."

"Okay. Then it's the guy in the jeans."

"Nope."

Alec's eyes widened. "The kid? You're shitting me."

Laughing, she said, "No, I'm not. He's older than he looks. Early twenties. Name is Chad Richens. He and Edwards are both from England, so I'm guessing that's one of the reasons why they gravitated toward each other. The other is that Richens can come up with schemes, but he doesn't like to do the dirty work."

"Like what?"

"Like the time he had Edwards swap out everyone's bayonets with dull ones from the previous day. We all worked twice as hard as he did that session, because he and Edwards were the only ones to have freshly sharpened blades. It was Richens's idea, but Edwards was the one who actually made the switch. Claire freaked when Ken figured it out. I thought she was going to give herself an aneurism."

"The fashionista?"

"Yes, Claire Dubois, from France. Isn't she gorgeous? She says she wasn't before the mark. Apparently, she used to be a meth addict. She burned her apartment down and killed her boyfriend in the process, which is why she was marked. She's still very high strung and fidgets a lot."

Alec studied the teenager. "How is Richens doing in the physical portion of the class?"

"Not good. Even with the help of the mark, he has trouble with the combat training, which is why I think he tries to get through the sneaky way. He's a video game junkie and strategy is his strength, not his fists. He also has a short fuse." Her voice lowered. "Edwards told me Richens's dad was abusive. I think he carries some of that around with him."

It didn't escape Alec's notice how well Eve had researched her classmates in order to better understand them. It was a sign of a natural hunter. Killing wasn't merely a physical act. It was also cerebral. "There must be some potential in him, or he would have been assigned to a nonfield position."

"He killed someone. I don't know the details. He won't talk about it."

"Murderers usually end up with field work automatically."

"Stupid," she muttered. "I think his being here is a major screwup on someone's part."

"Watch it." Alec shot her a chastising glance. Eve's beliefs were her own and he respected her right to have them, but sometimes she voiced her opinions in a way that was too irreverent to be safe. "So, that leaves us with the dark-haired guy. He's 'Romeo,' I take it."

Eve nodded. "Antonio Garza, from Rome. But that's not why I call him Romeo. He's got a thing going with Laurel . . . and being discreet isn't his strong suit."

"Which one is Laurel? The princess?"

"That's the one. Laurel Hogan. Romeo wooed the Goth girl first, but she says he's too much of a gigolo for her tastes. He's better off with Laurel anyway. If you ask me, Izzie is missing a few tools in the shed."

Alec studied the petite blonde with a calculating eye. She was slender, pale, her blue eyes rimmed with thick kohl and her mouth painted a dark purple. He would describe her as "delicate," despite her spiked collar and cuffs. "Why do you say that?"

"Izzie's pulled a Bowie knife on damn near everyone in this room at some point or another. She doesn't like any of us."

"That's an odd name."

"It's short for Iselda. Iselda Seiler. 'Izzie' suits her more than 'Goth,' I think. Like the other girls, her nickname is more of a description than anything else."

Alec noted the guarded way Eve watched the other woman. Not that he blamed her. The blonde had been mad dogging him since he entered. "You don't like her."

"I don't mind her," she corrected. "But she sure seems to have a problem with me. More so than the rest of the class, and that's saying something."

"Is there anyone here you get along with?"

"Well . . ." Eve shrugged. "I don't *not* get along with

anyone, but I haven't made any friends either. I just keep a low profile and stay out of the way."

Alec turned to face her. He asked her about her experiences in class every day, and every day she found a way to redirect him to another topic. Their present conversation was the most she had shared to date.

"How does Raguel feel about that?" he asked. "I bet he wants you front and center."

Her nose wrinkled. "Sure, so he can pick on me and point out all the ways I'm doing things wrong."

Alec's jaw clenched. When he was done with Charles, he would deal with Raguel. Eve had innate talent. It was a travesty that she didn't know it because the archangel withheld his praise.

As if Alec's thoughts served as the archangel's cue to appear, Raguel entered the room by floating through the glass door, displaying for one and all a small portion of his power. He was dressed casually in loose-fitting indigo linen pants and tunic, but the intensity that radiated from him belied the outward appearance of leisure.

A brief nod passed between Alec and the archangel, then Raguel looked around the conference room. His lyrical voice rolled though the room like smoke, "Good afternoon."

"Good afternoon, *moreh,*" the class greeted in unison, using the Hebrew word for "teacher."

Raguel frowned. "Where is Molenaar?"

"He hasnae shown his face yet," Ken answered.

Alec glanced at Eve, trying to remember which classmate was absent.

Her lips formed the words, *the Stoner.*

Nodding, Alec wondered at the composition of students in the class. Two former drug addicts, a teenager with poor motor skills, and an elderly gentleman most likely set in his ways. Marks came in all shapes, sizes, pasts, and temperaments. But only select Marks became hunters rather than behind-the-scenes personnel with occupations like personal assistant or travel coordinator.

It was Dubois and the absent stoner who most disturbed him. Addicts had the hardest time acclimating to the mark. In addition to the loss of their homes, family, and friends, they also lost their crutch. The mark was an instant cure, changing the body so that mind-altering substances were no longer effective. Some novice Marks went crazy facing reality. They hadn't been capable of functioning without drugs in their ordinary mortal lives. It was impossible for some to cope with sobriety in an extraordinary world filled with demons who wanted them dead.

"We will leave on the hour," Raguel said, "whether Molenaar is present or not."

Eve raised her hand. "What is the purpose of this field trip?"

Raguel widened his stance and crossed his arms. He raked the room with a sweeping glance. "All of you carry fear. You must face it and learn to see past it. You have been tasked with eliminating the vilest of Hell's denizens. The horror movies you enjoyed in the past are nothing compared to what you will face daily. I am taking you to a place where fear will be your closest companion. You will learn to function at your best when confronted with the worst."

Alec felt Eve shiver.

He reached for her hand and tugged it from the lip

of the window ledge. His fingers linked with hers, a silent offer of comfort. To say he felt shitty for his part in her marking would be an understatement, but that wasn't the worst of it. He couldn't change what happened in the past. He could, however, change the future. But he wasn't working as hard on that as he should be.

Eve wanted him to help her shed the mark and he'd promised that he would. But her desire to be free competed with his need to keep her around long enough to learn the mark system from the ground up. It was the best way for him to position himself as the most obvious choice to head a new firm. The Infernal threat was growing and more Marks were needed. Alec wanted to step into position as soon as expansion was finalized. He couldn't do that as the outsider he'd always been. The wanderer, cursed to roam. Through Eve, he was finally established in one place, watching Marks from their inception. Once he completed mentor training, he would have hands-on experience with every aspect of the system. No one would be better suited to lead than him.

"You will learn to work together," Raguel went on. "You are not in competition with one another, although some of you act as if you are. You are a team; your goal is the same. The loss of one weakens all of you. By the time we are done, you'll have become accustomed to both surviving and helping your brethren survive as well."

"Sounds flash," the princess—Ms. Hogan—said.

"*Sì.*" Romeo winked at her.

Richens shifted uncomfortably. Izzie yawned.

Edwards, however, drummed his fingertips into the tabletop. "I've been to Fort McCroskey. The place is a dump. Overgrown with weeds and crawling with vermin."

"Eww." Laurel's nose wrinkled. "I've changed my mind."

"I will protect you, *bella*," Romeo drawled.

"You will all protect each other," Raguel corrected.

Ken rubbed his hands together. "We can do this."

"Is there Wi-Fi?" Richens asked.

"Of course." Raguel smiled indulgently. "All the modern conveniences. I do not want to completely isolate you. The intent of this exercise is to simulate actual field situations."

"Simulate?" Eve's fingers tightened on Alec's. "Are the Infernals we're hunting simulated, too?"

"In a fashion. Your prey will be real Infernals. There's nothing on Earth capable of reproducing their scent, so we have to use actual demons."

A ripple of laughter moved through the room.

"But they work for me," Raguel went on.

"A pity that," Ken muttered. "I was hoping we'd finally get to kick some demon arse."

"All in good time, Mr. Callaghan. Gather around the table, please. Let us pray for success in our endeavors before we depart."

The students stood, forming a motley group that made Alec ponder the future of the mark system. Eve freed her hand from his grip and slid off the ledge.

His brows rose.

"I'm going to step outside," she whispered.

Izzie approached. "I'll join you."

"I would prefer you two remain," Raguel called out, having picked up their exchange with his celestial hearing. "Whether you join us in prayer or not is moot. We need to act together in everything."

Alec caught Eve around the waist and drew her back against him. He said a prayer for both of them. With the way their luck had been so far, he knew they needed all the help they could get.

CHAPTER 3

As her car approached the unguarded entrance of Fort McCroskey, Eve took in her surroundings. In the glow of the setting sun, the signage delineating the end of public land shimmered from a recent coat of fresh paint. The road beneath her tires darkened as she crossed the threshold, compliments of a new layer of asphalt. Ahead, lights attracted customers to the commissary, the parking lot of which boasted more than a few cars.

"It doesn't look abandoned to me," she said. "Maybe I have an overactive imagination, but I pictured this place looking a lot different. Cobwebs and tumbleweeds. That sort of thing."

Alec glanced at her from the passenger seat. "You haven't seen the best parts yet."

"Oh, great. Something to look forward to."

"Look forward to me coming back," he purred, giving her one of his looks. He was, quite simply, ferociously sexy. And he knew it, which made him even more dangerous.

She jerked her attention back to the road. "You're going to get us into an accident. It's hard to drive when your toes are curled."

Eve slowed to maintain the distance between the front of her car and the white van carrying the other Marks. The white Chevy Suburban behind her carried six of Gadara's personal guards, as well as a week's worth of provisions and all of their equipment.

Occasionally, some of her classmates looked back at her, but never with any show of friendliness. She probably should have ridden with the group to foster solidarity, but she didn't have the energy. She didn't know if coming back from the dead was supposed to feel like killer PMS or not, but she was seriously cranky and sluggish.

They drove down streets lined with homes whose architecture ranged from 1950s duplexes to 1980s single-family dwellings. The residences were all well lit, with cars in the carports and large manicured yards. She'd done some research on the place and learned that it had been established in 1917, became an official fort in 1940, and closed in 1994. Nowadays, it still served a variety of uses, both civilian and military. The homes they passed now were occupied by married soldiers attending the nearby Defense Language Institute and the Naval Postgraduate School.

Eve lowered the window and let the crisp, salt-tinged air into the vehicle. Although the base hugged the same Pacific Coast as her condominium, the northern climate was very different. The temperature was cooler, the sky more overcast, and the trees were pines instead of palms. She wished they were riding Alec's Harley instead, but the seven-hour ride would have been tough even for a mark-enhanced body.

"I bet the soldiers who were stationed here loved it," Alec said.

"It's a shame it's closed. I had a friend whose brother was stationed at Fort Leonard Wood, Missouri. He called it 'Fort Lost in the Woods, Misery.' I'm sure he would much rather be here."

"No doubt."

They followed the van around a bend in the road. Eve caught sight of a building with boarded-up windows and butterflies took flight in her stomach. She told herself it was a mental thing—her body wasn't supposed to react to stress—but that didn't help. She was nervous and scared. "So . . . Do you know anything about the training that goes on here?"

He reached over and squeezed her knee. "I checked around while they were loading up the Suburban. Raguel has only used McCroskey a couple times so it was difficult to find anyone who has been through the experience. The two Marks I spoke with said it was a pivotal assignment for them, one that changed their perception of everything."

"For the better?"

"So they say."

"Only two Marks?" She swallowed hard. "What happened to the rest of them?"

Alec shot her a wry look. "They're out in the field, doing their job. They're not dead."

Eve exhaled in a rush. "Good to know."

"I *will* get you out of this before it kills you," he vowed, looking grim and determined. "You're not going to end your days marked."

Her reaction to his promise was so mixed, Eve

couldn't decide how she felt about it. Three weeks ago, her reply would have been, "You bet your ass." Now, she was ambivalent. She had never in her life quit something because she didn't like it. She made it to the end before saying she'd given it her all.

"You know," she began, "I've gone through this training with a 'one-day-at-a-time' attitude."

"That's not a bad attitude to have, angel. Sometimes, it's the only way to get by."

"Yes, but in this case, I think I need to see the bigger picture."

Alec pivoted in his seat. His movement was fluid despite his size. At six feet four inches and two hundred and twenty pounds of lean, mean muscle, Alec had a body that was coveted by both men and women. Even with the mark—which made him preternaturally powerful—he worked out regularly to maintain his prime physical condition. He took his work very seriously and she admired him for that, even as she chastised herself for being far less committed.

"And what would you do with the bigger picture?" he asked.

"Hell if I know." Her shoulders lifted lamely. "I just can't help feeling as if throwing myself headfirst into the whole marked business makes it easier for God to keep me here for a while."

His fingertips stroked down her forearm. "Jehovah doesn't recognize easy or hard. He does what he thinks is best."

"Well, *I* recognize easy and hard," she retorted. "And what used to be hard is becoming easier and sometimes it's not so bad. But then sometimes—like dying in a dirty men's restroom—it's really fucking awful."

"So try it out this week," he suggested. "Give it your all for seven days and see what happens."

Eve's fingers wrapped tighter around the steering wheel. "I don't want to like this, Alec. I don't want to become comfortable."

The van turned a corner, taking them into a less-populated area. The homes on this street were dark, the yards yellowed. The sun was setting, adding shadows to the mix. Suburbia faded into desolation and Eve shivered.

"What do you want, angel?"

"I want normal. I want marriage and kids. I want to grow old." Eve glanced aside at him. "And I want you. Most of the time."

When the van pulled into one of two parking spots in front of a darkened duplex, she stopped in the street and stared at the home. The Suburban passed her and took the remaining space.

Alec's head turned away from her. "I don't come with normal," he murmured.

"I know."

The van rear door slid open and Ken leaped out, stretching. Then he set his hands on either side of the frame and leaned in, appearing to listen to instructions passed along from someone inside. He glanced at Eve idling in the street and gestured for her to park at the curb.

She sighed. "Here goes."

After parking the car, Eve climbed out of the driver's seat and joined the others. The rest of the group poured out of the van. Gadara stood between the two vehicles and waved his arm in a sweeping motion. The exterior lights blazed to life.

"Brilliant," Laurel said, popping her chewing gum.

Shedding some light on the situation didn't ease Eve's discomfort. Instead, it brought the disrepair of their living quarters into stark relief. Paint peeled from the siding and trim, cracks marred the cement walkway, and the asphalt in the drive was crumbling. A cockroach ran between the two cars and Laurel screamed.

Izzie rolled her eyes and stomped on the bug with her Dr. Martens. "It is dead," she said in a tone made gruffer by her German accent. "You can quit screaming now, please."

"I am not staying in a place infested with bugs!" Laurel cried.

"I told you this place was cocked up," Edwards said. "I brought some insecticide."

"We do not kill God's creatures," Gadara admonished.

Claire snorted. "Are you certain they aren't Infernal creatures? I believe cockroaches and mosquitoes are demon spawn."

"They are moving out, Ms. Dubois. Give them a few minutes and they will find another home in the area to occupy."

Richens shoved his hands into the front pouch of his hooded sweatshirt. "We're truly holing up here?"

"Yes, we truly are. Gentlemen in the duplex on the left, ladies to the right."

"I hope none of you snore," Izzie muttered.

"Why can't we stay in the nicer neighborhood?" Laurel asked.

"For the ladies' benefit?" Romeo added.

"And scare the noobs with our mad ways?" Ken scoffed.

"Mr. Callaghan is correct." Gadara walked to the

rear of the van and opened the back doors. "Our hours will be erratic, we will often be armed, and we are an eclectic group. We want to attract Infernals, not mortal curiosity."

"I wish I could stay," Alec said. "Sounds like fun."

Eve looked at him. He offered a reassuring smile and she made an effort to return it. Although she had never in a million years imagined the scenario she presently faced, there was no point bitching about it. It was what it was. She would just have to make the best of it.

"Yeah, right," Richens grumbled, picking up his backpack and hefting it over his shoulder. He hit the back of a guard who was unloading equipment from the Suburban. "Sorry, bloke. Unintentional."

Ken collected his duffel. "Yer a lot of feartie-cats. I'm chuffed o'er this holiday."

"Of course you are," Claire said. "You are insane. Hand me the burgundy bag, *s'il vous plaît.*"

Returning to her car, Eve hit the trunk release on her remote and rounded the back to get her duffel bag. Alec beat her to it, whipping around her and catching the handle before she could.

His gaze met hers. "You know I always have my cell on me. Call me anytime, no matter what the hour."

The last thing Alec needed while moving in for a kill was to be distracted by a phone call. She shook her head. "Don't worry about me. You just take care of business and come back in one piece."

"You gonna miss me, angel?" he purred.

She smiled in answer. She felt the same way about Alec as she did about her training—she was afraid to commit herself too fully to either. Lose one, lose them both. He was a fixture in her life only as long as the mark was, and keeping the mark wasn't an option. Marks lived outside the normal order of man. They couldn't die of natural means and they couldn't create life. Eve wasn't prepared to accept that.

But those were concerns for another day. Right now, a man she cared deeply for was heading into danger.

"Of course I'll miss you," she said. "Be careful."

"Listen." He set his free hand atop her shoulder. His eyes were hot, his mouth firmly set. "You're a natural. I know Raguel hasn't bothered to tell you that, but you are. You have an innate talent."

"I got killed!"

"But not before you sent the dragon back to Hell," he reminded. "You know how few Marks can make that claim? I'm probably not supposed to tell you this. In mentor training, they'll most likely tell me to tell you to follow the rules. But I'm telling you to follow your gut, you hear me?"

Eve stared up at him, arrested by his intensity. "Follow my gut?"

"Yeah." Alec tapped a blunt fingertip against her temple. "And your head. You're a smart cookie, angel. Fuck the rules and go with your instincts."

She nodded. He kissed the tip of her nose. "And miss me. A lot."

A moment later, he was pulling away from the curb and she was left alone with her classmates. Eve trudged up the drive, steeling herself for a week of being emotionally isolated.

Ken was shutting the rear doors of the van when she joined the rest of the group at the end of the driveway.

"Divide by gender," Gadara said, "and begin preparing the homes for habitation."

"Where are you going?" Laurel asked, frowning.

Gadara's brows rose at her tone, but he replied calmly, "To the commissary."

"You need to be military to shop in the commissary," Edwards advised.

"I have clearance, Mr. Edwards."

"He's an archangel," Izzie muttered, "not an idiot."

"Sod off."

Eve smiled at the exchange, but her merriment faded when she caught Gadara's gaze.

"Ms. Hollis. Please ensure that things flow smoothly in the women's quarters. There are air mattresses over there." Gadara pointed at the pile of equipment in front of the garage.

Laurel scowled. "Why is she in charge?"

"She is the only one of you to have actual field experience."

"Yeah, and she got the shit kicked out of her."

The class didn't know that she had died, Eve realized with some surprise, which made her wonder if her resurrection was a big secret.

Gadara's dark eyes took on a warning gleam. "Humor me, please, Ms. Hogan."

Laurel shot an arch glance at Eve. Romeo set his arm around her waist and murmured in her ear.

Eve's chin lifted. Of course Gadara would stoke the animosity. From the beginning, he'd made her marking as difficult as possible. It was his way of keeping Alec under his thumb.

"Mr. Edwards." The archangel turned away. "Please oversee the arranging of the men's quarters, especially the kitchen. We will begin dinner preparations when I return."

"Are we hunting tonight?" Ken asked.

Gadara shook his head. "No. Tonight is about settling in and preparing for tomorrow."

"Then we better get started," Eve said before heading toward the ladies' side. The other women fell into step behind her.

The sun was dipping low on the horizon, streaking the sky with jeweled hues. The view was breathtaking, and Eve paused on the small cement porch step to take it in.

"Maybe it won't be so dodgy here after all," Laurel said.

"Maybe," Eve agreed, hoping that was true.

The comfortable stillness was shattered by the howl of a wolf in the distance. A chill coursed down Eve's spine.

"There are wolves at the beach?" Claire asked in a whisper.

"*Were*wolves," Izzie corrected grimly.

As the color of the sky took on the hue of blood, Eve's enjoyment in its beauty fled. The evening air took on an ominous, oppressive weight.

They were out there. Infernals. Waiting, as the Marks were, for orders to kill. They passed their time toying with mortals, leading them to the edge of Hell, then shoving them over.

Eve pushed open the unlocked door and gestured for the others to enter to safety before her. "Let's get inside."

"G'day, mates."

Reed smiled at the Aussie greeting. "It's past midnight."

"Sorry to keep you waiting," Les Goodman said, gesturing them into his small but well-kept house in Victoria Park. As the Australian handler who'd witnessed the most recent attack by their mystery Infernal, he was the reason Reed and Mariel were Down Under. He'd been tied up with the formalities that followed a Mark killing and had finally called Reed to come over about thirty minutes ago.

"I wanted to record my report while everything was still fresh in my mind," Les explained as they moved into a comfortable living room furnished with brown leather furniture and sturdy wooden pieces. "Not that I will ever forget, mind. I'll have nightmares about what happened to my Mark forever."

"Thank you for agreeing to see us, Mr. Goodman," Mariel said. "We wish we were here under happier circumstances. We're very sorry for your loss."

"Thank you. Call me Les, please."

Mariel wore a loose floral dress and coordinating blue sweater, which gave her a casual and approachable air. Her wild flame-red hair, however, was pure seduction, but Les didn't appear to be affected as most single men were.

"You know Abel, of course," she said.

Les extended his hand to Reed. "Yes, of course. Welcome, Abel. It's an honor to have you here."

Reed accepted Les's handshake, noting the strength and confidence conveyed by the *mal'akh*'s grip. Les was blond, his skin darkened and weathered by the sun, his appearance arrested to look as if he was somewhere in his midforties. Grief weighed heavily upon his broad shoulders and bracketed his mouth and eyes with deep grooves of strain. Such physical manifestations of emotion were rare in *mal'akhs* and were only caused by the loss of a beloved. Les's Mark had meant a great deal to him.

Affairs sometimes formed between Marks and their handlers, since they shared a connection that transcended the physical. A Mark could share fear and triumph and a handler could reassure and offer comfort across many miles. Also conducive to work-related romance were the isolated lives led by Marks and the lure of their Novium, which was brought on by the thrill of their first hunts. Even *mal'akhs* weren't immune to a Mark awakening to full power.

"We appreciate you taking the time to answer our questions," Reed murmured, thinking of Eve and his own growing connection to her. God help him when her Novium hit, which would happen soon after she finished training and began hunting in earnest.

He glanced at his Rolex. It was early evening in California. She would be in Monterey now. By the end of the week, she would be three weeks away from graduation.

Les's jaw tightened. "I'll do anything necessary to catch that demon. I've never seen anything like what happened to Kimberly. I pray I never see anything like it again."

"Did you see the Infernal?" Mariel asked in a soothing voice.

"Yes." A haunted look came to the handler's blue eyes. "It was built like a brick shithouse. Nearly six meters in height and two meters wide at the shoulders."

Reed looked at Mariel with both brows raised. She had described the demon far differently.

The high-pitched whistle of a teakettle came from

the back of the house. Les motioned them to follow him.

"Come along." His booted steps thudded heavily across the hardwood floor. "We'll talk in the kitchen."

They settled around a scuffed linoleum-topped table. Les turned off the gas stove and poured boiling water into a waiting teapot. His domesticity contrasted starkly with his rugged appearance—worn flannel shirt, faded jeans, and large belt buckle.

"The Infernal I saw," Mariel began, "was a little over seven feet tall, nowhere near as large as the one you describe."

Les set the pot on the table, then returned to the counter to retrieve a paper bag. He shook the contents—scones—onto a plate.

"Well, here's the thing." He glanced over his shoulder at them. "It wasn't that big before it killed my Mark."

Reed's cell phone vibrated in his pocket. He withdrew it quickly. He normally kept the damn thing off, but with Eve in training he wanted to be accessible. Glancing at the caller ID, he cursed silently. *Sara.* He hit the button that sent the call to voicemail.

Sarakiel was both an archangel and his ex-lover. She helmed the European firm, her flawless angelic features fueling the sales of the multimillion-dollar Sara Kiel Cosmetics empire. She was also on his shit list, so he had been avoiding her calls for the last few weeks. That wasn't going to change right now.

"You're saying the Infernal grew in size?" Reed asked, returning his full attention to the conversation.

"Yes." Les set out three teacups, then pulled out a spindle-backed chair for himself.

"Did you witness the attack?" Mariel asked.

"Just barely. If I'd blinked, I would have missed it. The blooming thing was fast. Impossibly fast. It rushed at Kim in a blur. Ran on all fours—fists and feet to the ground. Almost like an ape, but graceful like a canine. Kim screamed and the Infernal leaped into her open mouth, just disappeared inside her. I couldn't believe it. By the time I figured out what happened, it was over."

"What did happen?" Reed asked the question, but he already knew the answer.

"She . . ." Les swallowed hard. "She *exploded.* But it was wrong. All wrong. What was left behind . . . there wasn't enough. There wasn't enough *of her*. No bone, no blood . . ."

"Just muscle and skin," Reed finished, declining Les's silent offer of tea.

"Yeah, that'd be right. So where does everything else go?" Les poured two servings of tea, his hands visibly shaking. After he set the pot down, he looked between Mariel and Reed. "I think the Infernal absorbed the rest. That's how it grew."

Mariel accepted the cup Les handed to her. "Were you responding to a herald?"

A herald was an instinctive cry for help from Mark to handler that was so powerful it was sometimes felt by mortals. A sixth sense, some called it. The sensation that something was "off," something they couldn't put their finger on.

Les shook his head. "I didn't wait for it. I'd sent her after some *Patupairehe* faeries that were causing trouble for tourists. They were her specialty, so when I felt her fear, I knew something was wrong."

Reed leaned back in his chair. "Raguel didn't say anything about the Infernal growing larger."

"He doesn't know." Les broke off a piece of a scone. "Uriel wanted to keep the news to himself until he could figure out what to do with it."

"This is not the time for the archangels to be territorial," Mariel protested.

"My thoughts exactly, which is why I'm telling you. There is something else." Pushing away from the table, Les twisted around in his seat and collected an item from the counter behind him. He set it down in front of Mariel.

She picked up the zippered sandwich bag and examined its contents. "It looks like there's blood on this rock."

"There is. Open her up."

Mariel did as directed. Instantly the honey-sweet smell of Mark blood filled the air. It was unusually robust and Reed found himself breathing through his mouth to diminish the potency of the scent.

"Your Mark's blood," she noted. "Why are you keeping it?"

Les's lips thinned. "That's the Infernal's blood. I put a hole in the thing when it came at me."

"If your scene is anything like the one I saw," Reed muttered, "that could be Mark tissue. There was nothing within three yards that wasn't completely covered with gore."

"I shifted some distance away before I discharged my pistol," Les said. "That blood didn't come from my Mark, because we were at least a kilometer's distance from where she was killed."

"How did the Infernal know where you were shifting to?"

"That's the question, isn't it, mate? My theory is that the Infernal absorbs not only the blood and bone of the Marks it kills, but also some of the connection to the handler. I'm guessing it's only temporary. Before I finished emptying my clip, it became impervious to the bullets. Could have been some kind of warding or could have been acquired vulnerability from my Mark that faded when the connection did. The Infernal certainly had no idea I was going to shoot it."

"Even temporary is too long." Reed's foot tapped against the floor. "How much information can it absorb? How long does it retain what it learns? We need to know if your theory is right."

Mariel carefully closed the bag. "Can we go to the scene? I'd like to take a look for myself. I'm the only one who's seen all the locations of attack. I would like to see if a usable pattern emerges."

"Of course." Les drank his tea in one swallow. "The area is remote. Stick close during the shift."

He disappeared.

Glancing at Mariel, Reed stood. "Let's go."

CHAPTER 4

Reaching around Izzie—who refused to move—Eve set a large bowl of salad on the makeshift dining table. They had combined three folding card tables into one larger table in the men's dining room. Seating was still cramped, but Gadara insisted they eat together. Eve understood that he was trying to foster a familial connection between the Marks, but after three weeks of sharing lunches at Gadara Tower, she couldn't see why it would work now when it hadn't before.

"I hate tomatoes," Laurel griped, looking into the bowl. "Couldn't you have kept them separate?"

"Feel free to help," Eve retorted.

Gadara entered the dining room from the adjacent kitchen. He carried a fresh-from-the-oven pan of lasagna—without the safety of gloves.

Glaring at Eve, Laurel tossed her strawberry-blonde hair over her shoulder with a practiced flick of her wrist. She was in her early twenties, her skin freckled in a becoming way, her eyes a pretty cornflower blue. She was a couple of inches taller than Eve, slightly more slender and less athletic, and gifted with the ability to complain about nearly everything. Eve had no idea how that proclivity had gone over in her homeland of New Zealand. Here in America, Laurel's charming accent softened the annoyance factor some. She was one of the classmates Eve wondered about. What could Laurel have done to end up marked? Her self-preoccupation was annoying, but otherwise she struck Eve as innocuous enough. And she seemed like the type who needed a lot of friends, not a loner.

Gadara looked at Eve with a questioning glance and she shook her head, silently telling him not to worry about it. She was having a hard time adjusting to the new image of the archangel she was forming. Before she'd been marked, she had held Gadara in high esteem for his secular talents. Donald Trump aspired to be Raguel Gadara when he grew up. As an interior designer, Eve had applied to Gadara Enterprises for a job, hoping to be a part of the redesign of his Mondego Hotel and Casino in Las Vegas. Now, she was working with him—just not in a way she could ever have imagined.

Of course, their association wasn't happenstance. Alec swore nothing was a coincidence and everything followed a divine plan. If that was true, the loss of her virginity to Cain and her subsequent marking had both simply been a matter of time. Therefore, working for Gadara had also been inevitable.

To her, the whole thing was wack.

Richens appeared from the kitchen. He skirted Gadara and set a plate of store-bought garlic bread on the table. "I'm starved. Let's eat."

"Who will say grace?" Gadara looked at Eve.

Her brow arched.

"I will." Claire stood, towering over the table.

The Frenchwoman's brown hair was super short and looked as if she had cut it herself. Her skin was porcelain perfect, her lashes thick and dark behind cute black-framed glasses that were worn for aesthetic reasons only—the mark cured myopia and every other imperfection. She was so beautiful it was hard not to stare, yet she didn't pay much mind to her looks. She wore no makeup or hair products. However, she did have a weakness for clothes. For this short trip, she had brought a duffel almost as big as she was.

The moment the short prayer was finished, the group settled elbow-to-elbow at the makeshift table and began passing the food around. It wasn't gourmet cuisine, but it was still pretty good. For a while, everyone was too busy shoveling food to talk—sating the need to refuel often and in large quantities—then excited discussion about the week's upcoming events kicked into high gear.

Eve ate mechanically, feeling disconnected from the boisterous atmosphere by a fuzzy sensation she called a "brain cloud." She felt as if she was coming down with a nasty cold. She was exhausted and suspected she was running a mild fever. Since the mark prevented illness, she was more than a little concerned. As soon as she had a moment alone, she planned to call Alec about it. She didn't feel like discussing any weakness in front of the others.

"So what's on the agenda for tomorrow?" Ken asked, always ready to leap in headfirst.

"My training plans are a closely guarded secret, Mr. Callaghan," Gadara said, smiling. "Besides, in actual field conditions you will have to think on your feet."

"What should we do to prepare?" Eve asked.

"Dress in layers. It is chilly in the morning here and depending on how well you progress tomorrow, we may be out until evening."

"That is when the ghosts come out and play," Izzie said in a deliberately affected low and dramatic tone, followed by a *bwa-ha-ha* bark of laughter that sounded even funnier with a German accent. "Maybe they will visit us tonight."

"Don't make jokes," Claire muttered. "Real Infernals are bad enough."

"Who says I'm joking? I watched a television show on this place just last week. One of those ghost hunter series."

Richens nodded. "We have similar programs in the U.K."

"What are you talking about?" Claire asked.

"There are people," Edwards explained, "who go to allegedly haunted locations and try to find proof of supernatural activity. They record their activities for television."

"*Vraiment?*" Claire's brows rose. "With what type of equipment do they search?"

Ken laughed. "A camcorder and a torch. Mostly all you see is screaming in the dark."

"Yes," Izzie agreed. "That is what I saw. It was strange that they waited until the middle of the night to 'investigate.' They deliberately turned the lights off, too. What is the reasoning behind doing that? If there are Infernals in the place, they don't give a shit if the lights are on or not."

"Torches?" Eve asked.

"Flashlights," Gadara explained.

Claire frowned. "What is the purpose?"

"Entertainment," Richens muttered.

"For whom? The persons screaming in the dark? Or the television viewers?"

"I don't get it either," Eve said, figuring she could contribute at least that much to the discussion.

Everyone looked at her, then resumed speaking.

"So are there truly Infernals in this place?" Claire asked. "Or just overactive imaginations?"

"There are Infernals everywhere," Gadara reminded. "But what fuels these shows are rumor and conjecture. However, if there are Infernals nearby when the shows are filming, they sometimes play along for their own amusement."

Eve pushed back from the table and stood, taking her plate with her. "I need to make a call before it gets too late."

"To Cain?" Laurel's smile was brittle.

"Who I call is none of your business."

"You are fortunate to have someone to answer you," Romeo murmured, rubbing his fingertips up and down Laurel's spine.

Eve knew her situation was rare. She couldn't decide if that was a blessing or not. Did her lingering connection to her family mean she didn't have many indulgences to earn to gain her freedom? Or was her connection to Cain so valuable that her family ties were worth overlooking?

Setting her plate on the counter by the sink, Eve exited out the kitchen door and sat on the cement stoop. Above her, the sky was a gorgeous midnight blue. An inordinate number of stars twinkled between rapidly moving clouds. In her hometown, pollution created a charcoal gray night that hid much of the universe's celestial beauty, but Eve would gladly trade being there for here.

She punched in Alec's number. As the phone rang, Eve brushed her hair back from her damp forehead. She became dizzy if she moved too quickly, and her breathing was coming fast and shallow. The mark only allowed such reactions when arousal or a hunt was involved. Stress and illness weren't factors.

So what the fuck is wrong with me?

Her physical acclimation to the mark had been screwy from the get-go, fading in and out like someone twisting the volume knob on a radio.

"You've reached Alec Cain. Leave a message or call Meggido Industries at 800-555-7777."

The sound of Alec's voice made Eve's throat tight. "Come back in one piece," she told his voicemail. "And call me when you can."

Feeling in need of some fussing, she speed-dialed her parents and waited impatiently for one of them to pick up. They would check the caller ID first, since they never answered calls from numbers they didn't recognize—

"Hey, darlin'."

Eve smiled at the sound of her father's familiar drawl. "Hey, Dad. What are you doing?"

"Watching television and telling myself to go to bed. How about you?"

"I'm up in Monterey."

"Oh, that's right." The smile was evident in his voice. "Your mother told me you had some work up there."

"Yes. Work."

"Well, take some time to see the aquarium."

"I'll try."

There was silence for the space of a few heartbeats, but Eve was used to it. Her father was the master of silence—companionable, awkward, and disapproving. She could handle screaming shrews and bellowing assholes, but Darrel Hollis's wordless disapproval could make her feel smaller than an ant.

Usually she'd try to fill the void with inanities, but tonight she was just glad to have an open line to someone who loved her.

Her father cleared his throat. "Your mom isn't here right now. She went to her tanka group."

"That's okay. I'm fine with just talking to you."

"Is something on your mind? Are you having trouble with Alec?"

"No. We're good."

"You both should come over for dinner when you get back into town."

"Sure. We'd like that."

Another stretch of silence, then, "Are you having work trouble?"

Not that she could share. "Nothing's wrong, Dad. I just called to say hi. I miss you."

"I miss you, too. Looking forward to having dinner with you." He yawned. "I'm going to call it a night, honey. Don't work too hard."

Eve sighed, wishing they were capable of doing more than making small talk. "Say hi to Mom for me."

"Of course. And find a way to the see the aquarium. You can't go to Monterey without seeing the aquarium."

"I'll do my best."

"Night, Evie."

She snapped the phone shut just as the kitchen door

opened behind her. As she pushed to her feet, a hand settled on her shoulder and urged her to stay down.

Eve looked up. "What's up, Richens?"

"Stick around," he said, joining her on the small step. "I could use the company; this place gives me the screamin' abdabs."

"Is that like the creeps?"

"Yeah."

It was the first real overture any of the Marks had made to her, so she stayed.

She slid over a little to give him more room. "Me, too."

"Is that why you called home?"

"Kinda." She was keeping her health to herself.

"Your old man isn't very chatty, eh."

"Didn't anyone tell you that eavesdropping is rude?"

"No. So what's your sin?"

Glancing at him with arched brow, Eve was struck again by his youth. He'd been a pudgy teenager when she met him just three weeks ago. He would retain that youthful appearance until he lost the mark, but the baby fat was gone. The mark made the body too efficient to carry around extra weight. His acne had cleared up, too, and the scars from them. What remained from the transformation was a young man of average height and build with somber features and wily gray eyes.

"Is that like 'what's your sign?'" she queried.

Richens shook his head. "I wouldn't piss off Cain by hitting on his girl. Besides, you're a bit long in the tooth for me."

"Ouch."

He shrugged. "So, what did you do to end up here?"

"Cain."

"That's it?" He scowled. "You're here for shagging?"

"So I'm told."

He muttered something under his breath.

"Sorry to disappoint," she said.

"It's okay," he said magnanimously. "It can still work out."

"What can still work out?"

"My plan. I killed people. Two of them. That's why I'm here."

Eve blinked. "You?"

She'd pegged him as the type of kid who drank too much soda, ate too much junk food, and played too many intricate, complicated video games. Murder, however, did not become him.

"Don't act so bloody startled." He shoved his hands in his sweatshirt pouch. "The owner of the store where I worked was an arseface. I was doing his job, too, but not getting paid for it."

"You should have quit, not killed him."

"I didn't kill *him*."

"Oh. Sorry."

"It was supposed to be a simple robbery. I knew how much money came in and when it went out to the bank. I'd helped to select the security system for the place, so I knew all the codes. The scheme was aces. I was to work the counter and play the victim, and my girl's cousin was to pull off the heist."

After her initial surprise, Eve didn't find the tale too unbelievable. Richens was so detached, so cerebral. He would have viewed the whole thing as a game. "Something went wrong, I take it."

"I was swizzed," he bit out. "That's what went

wrong. The bloke wasn't her cousin at all, she was banging the git. They thought they'd hie off with *my* share of the spoils? Not bloody likely."

Eve didn't know what to say to that, so she said nothing at all.

"Then the blighter shot a kid dead," Richens continued, his voice rising along with his temper. "Wasn't no more than ten years old, I'd guess. Buying some chocolate. That's when I pulled the gun out from under the counter and shot *them* both dead."

"Why are you telling me this?"

"Because I think teaming up is the way to get ahead." He looked at her. "Like that television show *Survivor,* I think working together in small groups is the way to win."

"But we're not trying to eliminate each other in order to win a prize."

Richens's gaze narrowed. "So? We can still help each other. You're the brawn, I'm the brains. Better to be at an advantage than at a disadvantage, wouldn't you say?"

"Why me? What about Edwards?"

"Edwards is in with us. He has his reservations, of course, because he doesn't want to irk Cain, but he'll come around. It's easier to work with girls. Less chest thumping. He'll see that."

Eve laughed. "You could have approached Izzie. She's brawnier than me."

"She's also 'round the twist," he scoffed.

"Aren't we all?"

He stood. "If you're not interested, just say so."

She noted his short fuse for future reference.

"I'm all for working together," Eve murmured. "I could use some friends around here."

His smile was nothing less than charming. It transformed his features and brightened his eyes. He held out a hand to her and helped her to her feet. "We've got a deal, then."

"Sure." The coming week was going to be interesting.

Richens opened the kitchen door, which swung inward, and stepped inside, completely foregoing the "ladies first" rule. Eve shook her head and was about to enter behind him when the low growl of a canine rumbled through the evening air. Chills raced down her spine.

Pivoting on the narrow stoop, she blinked and engaged the nictitating lenses that allowed her to see in the dark. She searched the nearby area, the heat of her already fevered skin rising.

But she saw nothing. No gleam of moonlight in malevolent eyes, no betraying movement. She sniffed the air and smelled the sea.

Still, she knew something was out there.

The bushes dividing their yard from the neighbor's rustled. Eve leaped to the yellowed grass and landed in a crouch. A tiny puff rushed out at her and she caught it, lifting it by the scruff and drawing her fist back to strike.

Hold it, sweetie! the toy poodle cried, flailing its tiny legs.

Eve paused midswing, her marked senses retreating as quickly as they'd come, taking the overwhelming urge to kill with it. The mark created power and aggression in highly intense quantities. The sensations were base and animalistic, not at all the elegant sort of violence she might have expected the Almighty to use in the destruction of his enemies. The surge was brutal . . . and addicting.

Don't punch the messenger.

"Jesus—ouch!" Eve winced as her mark flared in protest. Since she wasn't a pet owner, days could go by without any animals speaking to her. She often forgot that the mark had given her new senses, such as the ability to converse with all of God's creatures. "What are you doing running at me like that?"

I'm in a hurry. Put me down. This isn't dignified.

Eve set the little creature down and watched as the obvious stray shook herself off. Despite the filth that darkened the poodle's cream-colored fur to a café au lait color, the dog was adorable. "Why are you growling at me?"

Not at you, doll face. The teeny poodle pranced daintily and looked at Eve with somber, puppy-soft eyes. *At those around you. You feel it, too. You're smack dab in the middle—*

An explosion rent the air. Eve jerked in surprise, then found herself splattered with gore and fur.

"What the hell?" she screamed, leaping to her feet.

Izzie stood in the doorway with a gun. A second later, the light from the kitchen was blocked by the number of people crowded behind her.

Eve looked at the carcass on the ground and the mark's potency rushed through her. "You idiot! What did you do that for?"

"It was attacking you," Izzie said, shrugging.

"It was the size of my shoe!"

Gadara materialized on the stoop and held his hand out for the gun. Izzie passed it over.

The archangel looked at Eve. "Are you okay, Ms. Hollis?"

"No." She looked down at the blood on her clothes. "I'm really fucking far from okay."

"What happened?"

"A stray wanted some dinner scraps." She glared at Izzie. "And ending up getting blown to smithereens instead. What the hell caliber pistol is that?"

Gadara turned his attention to the gun, then to Izzie. "This is yours?"

"Yes."

"You were told to come unarmed. I will provide everything you need."

Izzie's purple stained lips thinned stubbornly. "I told you, I saw that ghost program on television. I could not come to this place without protection."

"You have no faith," he said, eyeing her with a narrowed gaze. "You have no belief in me. I am here to help you rebuild you life and attain the skills to live it to the fullest."

"And there are millions of demons prepared to end it," she argued.

The archangel hovered above the stoop, his silence as condemning as shouted rebukes. Even Eve shuffled nervously and she had done nothing wrong.

"What happened?" Ken yelled from the back of the kitchen.

"Seiler shot something."

"What? Let me by."

"It was only a dog," Izzie muttered, looking mulish.

"A dog?" Ken scoffed.

"Everyone back in the house," Gadara ordered, his voice resonating with celestial command.

The persuasion was so forceful, it was nearly tangible, and Eve took an involuntary step forward. She forced herself to stop by supreme effort of will.

"Why were you packing heat right now anyway?" she asked Izzie. "And where did you hide it?"

Izzie turned on her boot heel and shouldered her way back into the house.

Eve quickly moved to follow her. She didn't feel sick anymore, at least not physically. Sick at heart, yes. And so furious with Izzie she wanted to strangle her.

Gadara caught her arm as she rushed by. "Leave her."

"Her problem is with me."

"And now it is with me." His dark eyes burned into hers, taking on a golden sheen. "You suffer from lack of faith, too, Ms. Hollis. It is why you often find yourself in situations such as these."

She opened her mouth to protest, then snapped it shut again. They both knew what was really going on. Reiterating wasn't necessary. "I want to know what answers she gives you."

He smiled indulgently, his teeth white against his brown skin. "You assume I mean to question her."

The cryptic reply was so like him. So like all the angels actually.

Gadara gestured toward the driveway. "Take Dubois and two guards with you back to the other side of the duplex. You can clean up and prepare for bed."

"I don't feel . . . right," she said, surprising herself. She wasn't quite sure why she was telling Gadara that when she didn't trust him.

He studied her. "In what way?"

"I'm hot."

His brows rose.

"Hot flashes. Intermittent fevers. That sort of thing."

"That is impossible."

"Tell that to my body."

"You are under stress, Ms. Hollis, and experiencing dramatic and rapid change. It is not surprising that your mind would expect your body to have physical responses to such extreme pressures . . . even to the point of phantom maladies."

"Which is just a convoluted way of saying it's all in my head." She dismissed him with a frustrated wave of her hand. The *persuasive* undertone in his voice wasn't lost on her, but it wasn't effective either. "My on-the-fritz brain and I will just run along now."

He dismissed her as easily, turning his back to her and levitating over the remains of the stray. As he spoke a foreign language in a low tone, his arm made a wide gesture over the gore, turning it into ash, which sank into the earth.

Eve was depressed by the waste and tantalized by the tiny bit of information the poodle had managed to impart before dying.

. . . those around you. You feel it, too. You're smack dab in the middle—

Smack dab in the middle of what? And what did the people around her have to do with it?

CHAPTER 5

Alec made it as far as Santa Cruz before he pulled off Highway 1 and secured a motel room. He didn't want to travel any farther in Eve's car. The Alpha had obviously sent his dogs to track her, hence the attack at Qualcomm Stadium. Alec would need to switch to a rental to avoid being recognized before he drove into Brentwood—the Black Diamond Pack's den.

As he pushed his key card into the door lock, Alec thought about Eve at Fort McCroskey. Frustrated by circumstances he had long ago lost control over, he pushed the door open with undue force. She wouldn't be the same person by the end of the week. The experiences that came from being marked changed people in both drastic and subtle ways. He loved who Eve was and that wasn't going to change, but he also missed the eighteen-year-old girl who'd given her innocence to him. That was one of the penalties for his sin, the same penalty his parents had paid when they gave in to temptation—you can take what you shouldn't, but in the end you still won't get what you wanted.

I'm coming for you, Charles, he thought, looking around the motel room with distaste. *If you had left well enough alone, I wouldn't have to be here.*

Unfortunately, the Alpha's death would set off a chain of events that could ripple outward, affecting other packs and creating room for new—possibly more dangerous—Alphas.

"Better the demon you know," Alec muttered.

When Charles was gone, his Beta would step up. Pack members would scatter, reinforcing other packs or creating new ones. Charles, for all his many faults, was familiar and—previously—fairly cooperative. His demise would most likely give birth to greater threats, since the inheritance of power was often accompanied by an initial display of force, not goodwill toward the enemy.

Alec stepped deeper into the room. The door shut behind him. For years he'd lived on the road like this. A new town every few days. A different motel room. Another forgettable girl to screw when the need to do so distracted from the hunt. There had been no one to worry about him and no one for him to look forward to going home to. He'd spent thousands of nights lying in the dark, watching the glare of vehicle headlights drifting across unfamiliar ceilings. Nowadays, he had a sweet condo on Pacific Coast Highway, right next to his dream girl, and he resented having to settle for less.

Eve was in his life full time now, and he spent many of his nights in her bed. Sometimes she sent him home, but he knew she wanted him to stay. She hoped it would make it easier to say good-bye to him if she practiced doing it now. But Jehovah's intent was to make choices difficult and nothing she could do would change that.

Restless, Alec hit the streets on foot. He needed an Infernal. Or more accurately, he needed an Infernal's blood. He had to find a cocky, stupid one who would throw caution to the wind and want to brawl. There was at least one in every town. He just had to find it. Sometimes the search took hours; other times he was lucky and stumbled across one fairly quickly. Tonight he didn't care how long it took. He wasn't heading into Brentwood until the morning and he knew worry over Eve would keep him awake most of the night.

He strolled over to the downtown area of Santa Cruz and the bustle of Pacific Avenue, whistling all the way. Boutiques and sidewalk cafés commingled with music and bookstores and countless restaurants. Pedestrians were attired in a wide spectrum of styles ranging from business suits to torn fishnets paired with Dr. Martens.

Perfect. Alec smiled. Infernals loved crowds. More mortals to play with.

His first stop was at a coffee/smoothie shop where he ordered a cherry-laden concoction because it reminded him of Eve. The girl at the counter was mortal, pretty, and a flirt. A month ago, he would have arranged to meet her after work. No promises, no entanglements, and he'd sleep hard in reward. Not any longer. Tonight he'd exhaust himself with a different kind of exertion. His biceps flexed at the thought.

There was no steady pump of adrenaline, as would accompany a sanctioned hunt, but it would come later. Marks weren't vigilantes; they couldn't attack Infernals at will. The loophole was that if a Mark was endangered, he had free rein to defend himself to the death. There was always a back door, if you knew where to look.

As Alec moved leisurely through the milling shoppers, he stayed watchful. There were Infernals all around him, the scent of their rotting souls competing with the smells of food, hot beverages, and human perfumes. He was in search of any demon who could be goaded into a fight, one whose blood would create his signature fragrance—*eau de Infernal*—a scent that would disguise his and give him the cover he needed to penetrate a den full of wolves.

He knew the moment he'd found what he was looking for.

She stepped out of an Irish-themed pub several feet ahead of him. As suited her Norwegian heritage, the Mare was fair skinned and blonde. Her demonic blood made her willowy and stunning, an irresistible lure to most men. Someone, however, had turned her down, if her scowl was any indication. She was irritated, agitated, and tense. Everything about her screamed "end of my rope," which hinted that the right amount of goading might provoke her to overlook both the rules and his identity.

Mares were shape shifters who thrived on nocturnal torment. Chest pains, horror-filled dreams, tightness of breathing . . . The blonde bombshell in front of him fed off the distress she created in her sleeping prey. Her class of demon was the reason the term "nightmares" had come into wide use, and they were easily riled when denied a particular target. Correction: they were easily riled, period. Any sort of dispute created the negative environment they craved.

As he approached, he grinned. "Crash and burn?"

She bristled visibly. "Go away, Cain."

"What turned him off? Did you push too hard?" He studied the dark circles under her eyes, bags carefully hidden beneath expertly applied makeup. His focus altered from confrontation to curiosity. "You've waited too long to feed."

She attempted to pass him.

He sidestepped into her path. "A gorgeous Mare like you should have dinner crawling all over her. Why leave empty-handed?"

"I'll scream," she warned.

"Do it," he goaded softly, his smile fading. "Let's see what happens."

Fear added an acrid tinge to her scent. The cheekbones he'd admired from afar were prominent due as much to gauntness as to breeding. With proximity, she appeared to be famished. That went against a Mare's very nature. They tormented sleepers for both sustenance and pleasure. Even if she didn't need the former, she wouldn't deny herself the latter.

Her crimson sheath dress left her arms bare. Circling her forearm just above her elbow was a moving band of twisting vines and veined leaves—her detail, proclaiming her a servant of Baal, the demon king of gluttony. Another reason she should be well fed.

"What do you want?" she asked crossly.

"I wanted to brawl. Now I want to know why you haven't eaten." Alec gestured at the throng around them. "There's no lack of food."

"Why do you care? Go pick a fight with someone else."

He stepped out of the way. "Fine with me. You don't

look capable of giving me the stress relief I'm looking for."

The Mare remained unmoving for the length of several heartbeats, clearly suspicious of his easy capitulation.

"Go," he ordered. "You're boring me."

She departed with swiftness, her stilettos clicking impatiently down the sidewalk. Men watched her walk, looking for any sign that an advance would be welcomed. But her posture rejected any overtures and the aggressive set of her frail shoulders caused other pedestrians to clear the way.

She reached the corner of Locus Street and glanced back. By then, Alec had moved to the short wrought-iron fence that surrounded the patio tables of the pub. He sat on the railing and lifted his smoothie cup in toast.

As soon as the stoplight changed, the Mare bolted across the street.

Alec took off, too. He raced across Pacific Avenue with preternatural speed, dodging the moving cars with such dexterity the drivers never saw him. From the opposite sidewalk, he shadowed the Mare, using the crowd for cover. Music poured out of a busy coffee shop and a group of slightly tipsy women tried to detain him, but Alec kept pace. He watched the Mare withdraw a cell phone from her purse. She paused at infrequent intervals, looked backward, sensing his pursuit but unable to confirm it visually.

Fucking complications.

Nothing came easy for him. All he'd needed was a pint or two of Infernal blood. Now he was chasing a desperate Mare and facing the possibility of being outnumbered. If she had anyone in her corner, she'd be calling for reinforcements.

As if he didn't have enough on his plate with Charles.

Walk away.

His mark wasn't burning. She wasn't a target. She'd refused to take the bait. He couldn't hunt her.

Alec growled and the couple in front of him leaped to the side, clinging to each other.

He could no more back off now than he could resist Eve. When his attention was caught, it was firmly snared. Until he knew why a Mare was killing herself—starving while surrounded by an all-you-can-eat buffet—he couldn't let it go. Someone or something was exerting enough pressure on her to make eating unpalatable. Her survival instincts had goaded her to hit the clubs in search of a meal, but fear had prevented her from taking a victim home.

It didn't make sense for a higher ranking Infernal to order a minion to commit suicide, so why had her superior done that to her? Infernals wanted to rule the world. The greater their numbers, the better. If they wanted something dead, they killed it and made sure the deed was done. They didn't leave it to chance, such as waiting for starvation to take its final toll.

The Mare reached the end of the downtown section of Pacific and rounded the corner, heading into a somewhat quieter area of town. The foot traffic began to subside and the businesses changed from high-end and trendy establishments to smaller, less affluent merchants. As the energy of the surrounding venue changed, a new atmosphere descended, swirling around Alec like an evening mist—damp and chilling. He hadn't sensed it on the other side of town, but here it was prevalent.

Something wicked this way dwells.

Alec shot an accusing glance heavenward. It wasn't a coincidence that he had exited the highway at this particular destination.

He watched the Mare turn into the delivery bay of a hotel. Unlike the serviceable but amenity-less lodging he was staying in, this was a full-service establishment with a dozen stories worth of rooms. He noted the gargoyles rimming the roof of the building and a grim smile curved his mouth. Ever since he and Eve had investigated a group of tengu demons masquerading as grotesques, he knew to be on his guard. As long as Infernals had a way to mask their scent and details, everything was suspect.

Increasing his gait to a lope, Alec reached the mouth of the alleyway. Beneath the smell of motor oil and rotting garbage in Dumpsters was the stench of Infernals. More than one. Rolling his shoulders, Alec limbered up for the battle ahead. The demons were desperate and frightened; he could smell their disquiet. That made them more dangerous. When you had nothing to lose, there was no reason to hold back for safety's sake. He knew that from centuries of personal experience.

Alec walked into danger without preamble or stealth. There was no point. They smelled him coming.

There were a half dozen of them, four men and two women, one of whom was the Mare. They were a ragtag bunch, their clothes and hairstyles as varied as the downtown crowds. They faced him as a unit, arranged in a half-moon formation. And they all looked emaciated.

Their weakened states evened the odds considerably, but deepened the mystery.

"Are you hunting Giselle?" the other girl asked.

It was a reasonable question. If the Mare was an assigned target, nothing could save her. But if his pursuit was due to any other reason, they might be able to bargain her out of trouble.

"No." Alec stepped forward. "I just didn't want to miss the party."

"Leave her in peace," one of the men rumbled. He held a fat cigar between lips hidden by an unkempt beard. A kapre. He was a long way from his native home in the Philippines. The protective stance he adopted in front of the second girl—whose Baphomet amulet betrayed her as a witch—offered a possible reason why. Kapres followed their loves for the entirety of their lives.

"Make me," Alec said.

"We're no threat to you." But the kapre's voice lacked conviction and his eyes shifted nervously.

None of the Infernals would look Alec in the eye.

A frisson of warning skated down his spine. His Mark senses burst into full acuity in a brutal rush of power. Giselle's gaze darted to a spot just over his left shoulder.

Confirmation of the impending ambush came with the whistle of a blade. Alec dropped to a crouch. As the katana sliced through the space where his neck had been a split second before, the kiss of a breeze told him how close he'd been to decapitation.

Twisting at the waist, Alec lunged at his attacker. His shoulder rammed into the Infernal's diaphragm. They hit the ground with jarring force, Alec on top, the winded demon pinned beneath him.

In the blink of an eye, Alec noted the demon's mask

and head-to-toe black attire. He registered his assailant's small stature, then the pillow of breasts against his chest.

A female.

For Alec, fatal battles were as familiar as sex and just as fluid. He was a creature of instinct and homicidal precision. He didn't plan or panic, he didn't flinch or hesitate. When his life was in danger, he didn't think twice. And he loved the hunt. Every minute of it. Predation created a high that couldn't be replicated. Only another hunter would understand the allure. The hunger. The dark need that was both savage and seductive.

Alec drew back his fist and swung. Two rapid blows to her covered face. The crush of bone echoed in the semienclosed loading bay, as did the clattering of her sword to the ground.

The Infernal grappled to regain her weapon. Her fingernails pierced through her gloves, shredding the skin on the back of his hands. She tried to knee him in the balls, but he shifted, absorbing the blow with his thigh. She lost necessary purchase with the miss, he took the advantage.

He wrestled the hilt free, then bit out, "It's been fun."

Aiming at the tender spot between throat and arm, Alec thrust the length of the two-foot blade diagonally into the demon's body, bisecting her chest cavity from left shoulder to right hip. His aim was perfect, nicking the heart. Instantly she exploded into a pile of sulfuric dust, and Alec dropped to the ground, prone. He rolled to his back, then jumped to his feet, brandishing his new weapon with affected insouciance. The fact that none of the other Infernals had tried to join the fray while he was distracted was puzzling. Demons played dirty, always.

The witch standing beside Giselle crumpled to the ground, her multiplicity spell broken by the death of her warrior half. A moment later, she burst into ash, unable to survive without the part of herself Alec had killed.

The kapre bellowed in agony. It turned and leaped to the brick wall that enclosed the end of the bay. Punching through the facade with fingers and toes, he crawled halfway up the building. Then he threw himself from the sixth floor and hit the oil-stained cement in an explosion of ash.

"What the fuck?" Alec was stunned.

In centuries of hunting, he'd witnessed only a handful of suicides. Infernals would rather go down fighting. It was the best way to ensure Sammael didn't hold their demise against them . . . too much.

But he quickly shook off his astonishment in favor of saving his own ass and getting what he needed from the remaining demons—blood and information.

"So . . ." The word was drawled, the mark regulating his breathing and heartbeat so that they remained as steady as a ticking clock. He brushed at the ash on his shirt and jeans with the back of his free hand. "Did you draw straws? Or should I just pick one of you to vanquish next?"

Someone was going to answer his questions and someone was going to give him some blood. The only question was: which one?

The male on the far right volunteered. With a roar that drowned out the sounds of the city around them, he leaped forward and bared his fangs. A vampyre.

"I just had a smoothie," Alec said. "I should be extra sweet . . . if you can manage to get a bite."

The demon withdrew a stake from the small of his back. Alec beckoned him closer with a wriggle of two fingers and a cocky smile.

"*Servo vestri ex ruina!*" the Infernal snarled.

Alec raised his sword. "*Dei gratia.*"

The vamp thrust his weapon deep into his own chest and exploded into dust.

Another Infernal pounced from the depths of the ashy haze that filled the air. The third male. This one tilted his leonine head back and howled at the moon. A werewolf.

"It's my lucky night," Alec muttered. "I got a mixed bag of nuts."

The wolf was short and stocky. His barrel chest and thick forearms and thighs warned Alec that this particular tussle was going to take some effort.

Or it would have, if the wolf hadn't put a gun to his temple and blown his brains out.

"Holy fucking shit."

If Alec hadn't seen it with his own eyes, he wouldn't have believed it. As the report of the shot reverberated around him, he wondered if his smoothie had been spiked. In his reality, mass suicides among Infernals were unheard of.

When the ash from the third Infernal took too long to clear, he widened his stance and adjusted his grip on his blade, prepared for a charge. But nothing rushed at him from the depths of the churning cloud. It only grew bigger, more opaque, as if being continuously fed.

Were the others checking out, too?

Alec's gut knotted. The order of his existence—so

damn repetitive he had begun to think he was living his life on a loop—had been thrown completely out of whack since Eve had been marked.

As the floating debris in the compact delivery area finally began to dissipate, his suspicions were confirmed. There was nothing left of the Infernals. No one remained to explain what the hell was going on.

Disturbed and disgusted by the waste, Alec tossed the katana into one of the Dumpsters and exited back out to the street. Every step he took away from the scene was heavy with reluctance. Leaving empty-handed went against his very nature, but what choice did he have? Without an Infernal to pursue, he had no leads to follow.

Raguel, he called out.

Yes? The archangel's voice was as resonant in thought as it was in reality.

You need to send a team of Marks to Santa Cruz. In explanation, Alec relived his recent memories through his connection to Raguel.

There was a moment's stillness, then, *Call me.*

What? Why?

A jolt caused Alec to stumble mid-stride, followed by the silence of a severed communication.

Raguel?

He reached into his rear pocket for his cell phone, cursing when he realized it was still in his backpack in the trunk of Eve's car. He had tossed it there before they left Gadara Tower, figuring that the only person he was interested in talking to would be sitting right next to him. Now he'd have to wait until he reached his room to call Raguel, a delay that was too lengthy. What game was the archangel playing? Raguel needed to send a team of Marks out here immediately. Someone had to figure out what the hell was going on, and it couldn't be Alec because he had places to go and a wolf to kill.

Two blocks away from his hotel, Alec knew he was being tracked. He veered off the sidewalk and entered a convenience store. Skirting his way past the public restrooms, he ducked into the employees-only area. Within moments, he was exiting out the rear service door and rounding the building to catch his shadow unaware.

But it was he who was caught by surprise.

She hid in an unlit corner of the lot, her shoulders hunched forward and her Nordic appearance hidden under the glamour of a dark-haired Latina beauty. The red dress, however, was unmistakable.

Alec slipped along the low cement block wall that bordered the edge of the parking lot and came up on her from behind. The Mare was functioning so far below normal she didn't scent him until he was a few feet way.

"Cain." She faced him. Her face was tear-streaked and her mouth bracketed with lines of strain.

"Giselle." His arms crossed. "You change your mind about that brawl?"

"It was the only way," she whispered. "They have to believe I'm dead or they'll find me. They'll kill me."

"Who?"

Her blue eyes, so hard and wary earlier, were soft and pleading now. "Take me with you when you leave Santa Cruz. Then I'll tell you everything."

Eve was tired of staring at the water stains on the ceiling. It was driving her nuts to lay unmoving in her bed when she felt so restless and sticky with heat. On the opposite side of the room, Claire's steady, rhythmic breathing illustrated the other Mark's continuing slumber.

Lucky, she thought grudgingly.

Sighing, she tried closing her eyes to see if that would put her to sleep. She had spent the last two hours ruminating over the same questions in a frustrating loop.

Why hadn't Alec called her back?

What did Richens really want?

What had the dog intended to tell her?

What the hell was wrong with Izzie?

Something was rotten; that was all Eve knew for certain. And speculation over what it could be was keeping her awake.

The dog smelled something I'm not picking up. And no one else was catching it either. How was that possible? She could understand her classmates being behind the curve, since they were all still growing accustomed to their new "gifts." But what about Gadara? And his guards?

Eve slid her legs over the side of the bed and pushed her feet into a waiting pair of flip-flops. Her flannel pajama bottoms and matching top had seemed like a good idea that morning. Now that she was suffering from a low-grade fever, she inwardly cursed her choice. She'd never be able to fall asleep when she was too hot for comfort.

As she picked her way to the bedroom door, the hardwood floors creaked and groaned despite her best efforts at a stealthy exit. Claire mumbled in her sleep and rolled to her side, facing away from the disturbance that Eve was creating.

When she gained the hallway and closed the door behind her, Eve exhaled her pent-up breath with relief. Izzie and Laurel were in the master bedroom, which shared a wall with the room she occupied but was farther away from the common areas. Lack of window coverings allowed plenty of moonlight to illuminate the empty living room, delaying any need for her nictitating lenses.

Pausing in the center of the main living space, Eve shook off the feeling of a ghost walking over her grave. The men's half of the duplex was on the other side of the master bedroom walls and the three other females were only feet away. Yet her body was tense and her stomach was knotted. Every creepy, awful horror flick she'd ever seen was brought to life by the musty smell and unfamiliar noises of the house and surrounding exterior. The illusory perception of some homicidal maniac standing behind her made her want to shiver . . . if only the mark would let her.

"Damned sadistic imagination."

Eve. The rumble of Reed's voice hit her as the sensation of a hot summer breeze—a warmth drenched in the darkly erotic scent of his skin—engulfed her.

She reached back to him, grasping for the thin thread of awareness that flowed between handlers and their Marks. She'd heard that some Marks were able to share whole thoughts with their handlers, but she didn't have that ability. For her, it was only distant echoes of emotion. She secretly wondered if that was her fault, if she was afraid to let him in because of Alec.

Or maybe . . . due to more personal misgivings.

Feeling too exposed, Eve retreated both mentally and physically, stepping out of the shaft of moonlight and into the shadows. As she withdrew, she felt Reed lunge for her. She froze, startled by his vehemence. His concern and apprehension were so strong she felt them as if they were her own. Something was wrong wherever he was, something that had him checking on her and assuring himself of her safety.

Eve rolled her shoulders back. Alec and Reed had their own burdens to bear. They had more experience, but their jobs weren't any easier than hers. She was a big girl and she needed to take care of herself.

I'm okay, she told him. *Don't worry—*

A group of dark forms moved through the moonlight, arresting her in midthought. Their shadows raced across the patch of light she'd just vacated.

Frightened, Eve's gaze shot to the window and out to the view beyond. The street was eerie in its lifelessness. The streetlights were dim, the houses across the way were dark, the road was empty of cars.

"Just a flock of birds," she whispered, wishing she was one of those people who weren't afraid of anything. "You need sleep, that's all."

A large hunchback shape lumbered across the lawn toward the men's side of the duplex, moving in the opposite direction of the shadowy figures.

"Christ," she breathed, then winced as the mark on her arm burned in chastisement. Her mark enhancements woke with a start, stealing her breath. Her fever returned with a vengeance, but instead of wiping her out with exhaustion, she was possessed by a wild, edgy energy. She'd ridden on a roller coaster once that had made her feel much the same. The car had shot from the station like a bullet, building speed with every second, hurtling her toward a towering precipice framed with a ring of fire.

Eve sprinted to the front door and opened the locks. She looked outside, engaging her nictitating membranes to see. The two guards who had been stationed at the front and kitchen doors were already in motion, running stealthily around either end of the hedge fence that bisected their property from the neighboring one.

But they were still heading in the opposite direction of the hunchbacked form.

Her gaze lifted beyond their retreating backs. There *were* other unwanted visitors out there. She could see what looked to be half a dozen tall and lean forms moving rapidly in a disjointed pack. Their presence prevented her from calling out to the guards or even whistling.

She glanced down the hallway at the other bedrooms and considered waking the girls. But Infernals had hearing as good as hers and trying to keep quiet would eat time she didn't have. If that lumbering thing was after Gadara, she couldn't allow it to get any closer.

Threats are to be neutralized, not minimized, the archangel had taught. *Do not prevaricate. They learn with every confrontation and you do not want to give them the chance to ambush you in the future.*

"Go," she muttered to herself grimly. "You can scream for help *after* you stop it."

Locking the door behind her, Eve took off around the front of the house. Blood lust spurred her stride and her muscles flexed in anticipation. Her senses were so acute she could hear the faint sounds of a television show coming from an occupied house a couple of blocks away.

Usually archangels were ensconced in buildings

filled with Marks who acted as an early warning system. It was impossible for a stinky Infernal to sneak past all of them and get to an archangel. At least it *had* been impossible before the creation of the Infernal mask. Now, all bets were off.

Gadara had only four guards to protect him and a class of newbie Marks who couldn't even smell whatever the poodle had detected.

Kicking off her sandals, Eve ran barefoot across the coarse dead grass that covered the shared lawn. Ahead of her, the bulky creature rounded the front of the duplex and disappeared down the cement pathway that led to the entrance of the men's side. A light was on in the living room, but a sheet had been draped over the window, blocking the view of the interior. As Eve ran past, she heard Gadara speaking. The resonance of his voice betrayed his power, creating a potent lure to an ambitious Infernal.

You can do this. She deliberately ignored the size of the Infernal she hunted. The demon was easily six and a half feet, with massive shoulders and a protruding back. Eve had no idea what class of Infernal fit that description or what its specialty might be. It could have razor-sharp teeth and claws, or it could spit fire like the dragon that killed her on Sunday. Or perhaps it had some other, deadlier talent.

Don't think about it. She swiped strands of her hair off her hot and sticky forehead.

The demon stood on the unlit porch. The far side of the stoop was enclosed by a thin wooden partition that blocked the moonlight. It loomed as a large void before her, drenched in shadow, the finer details of its form indiscernible even with her enhanced sight. There was only the massive back and disproportionately thin legs. Nothing else was defined. The scent of it was unusual, more bitter and acrid than rotting. It was an anomaly, which frightened her, but the power of the mark goaded her to leap first and ask questions later.

Eve lunged, tackling the beast and shoving him through the partition. The shattering of the wood was like a thunderclap in the still of the night. They crashed to the ground on the other side of the step, tangled with splintered rubble and each other.

"Help!" Eve yelled, grappling with the unwieldy beast. It was softer than she expected and oddly unresisting.

"Help!" the Infernal screamed.

She froze.

The porch light came on, and men tumbled out of the duplex.

CHAPTER 6

"Help!"

Eve blinked rapidly, startled to recognize the thickly accented voice. She gaped down at her capture. *"Molenaar?"*

Like an overturned turtle, the Mark wobbled precariously atop the military-style rucksack on his back. "You're insane, Hollis!" he screeched. "A maniac!"

"Ms. Hollis." Gadara caught her beneath the arms and hefted her up as if she weighed nothing. "What are you doing?"

Eve watched Romeo help Molenaar to his feet. A large shawl was tangled around the man's neck, but it had previously been wrapped around his head, shoulders, and backpack, giving him the hunchback appearance. "You stink," she accused.

"So you thought I am a demon?" Jan's blue eyes looked ready to pop out of his head. "I was forced to hitchhike to here after I was left behind. The driver I traveled with did not care about his odor."

The girls came charging around the corner of the house—Izzie in pigtails, Claire sans glasses, and Laurel sporting a green beauty mask caked to her face.

"What is happening?" Claire demanded, eyeing the gathering with arms akimbo. "When did you arrive, Molenaar?"

"I wish I had not come now!" He glared at Eve.

"You shouldn't be sneaking around in the middle of the night," she argued.

Gadara turned his head to look at her, his gold hoop earring catching the light and glinting. "Were you defending us from a perceived threat?"

"It's dark. With that thing on his head and back, I couldn't tell what he was. And where the hell are your guards?"

"Right here." A dark shape appeared from around the corner, his stride surefooted and confident. Eve recognized the voice as belonging to Diego Montevista, Gadara's chief of security and one badass Mark. "Chasing down some delinquent teenagers. But there should be two guards here."

"On point, sir," Mira Sydney replied from her position on the stoop. As large and forbidding as Montevista was, Sydney was the polar opposite. Fair to his dark, petite to his bulk. But she was his lieutenant, and it was clear they had developed a strong affinity. "When you went after the trespassers, we closed ranks and moved inside."

Gadara stepped closer to Eve. He pressed his wrist to her forehead and his gaze narrowed. She looked back at him with a challenging tilt to her chin. She felt as if she was burning up and knew he had to feel it, too.

"Well done," he said. Nothing more.

"Excuse me?" Molenaar protested. "She almost killed me!"

"You should not have been tardy this morning, Mr. Molenaar," Gadara dismissed. "Then this misunderstanding would not have happened."

Laurel spun on her heel and stomped away. "This is ridiculous," she tossed over her shoulder, "and I'm tired. Good night."

"I will walk with you, *bella,*" Romeo offered, jogging after her.

Richens snorted in disgust. "That's devotion if he can still shag her with that shit on her face."

"Mr. Richens." Gadara's voice was disapproving, as was his frown. "You will keep such vulgar thoughts to yourself. Please show Mr. Molenaar into the house and help him settle in."

"I'm hungry," Molenaar said, shrugging off his rucksack.

"You're always hungry," Ken scoffed.

Claire yawned. "I am returning to my bed." Her gaze settled on Eve. "Please do not wake me when you come in."

Eve's return smile was forced.

A cell phone with a Handel's *Messiah* ringtone rang inside the men's quarters. Her brows rose.

Gadara smiled. "That would be mine, of course."

"Of course." Archangels with cell phones, such was her life. Ready to crawl under a rock, Eve offered a brief wave, then moved around him. "I'm calling it a night."

"You should wait a moment, Ms. Hollis," he suggested. "Cain will insist on speaking with you."

"How do you know—" Eve stopped. Of course he would know, he was an archangel.

"Because I ceased communicating with him when we heard the disturbance out here." His dark eyes were bright with amusement. "And I told him to call."

"Oh. Right." As if Alec took orders well.

"Come in where it is warm."

"I'm not cold. I told you that." And the fact that he wouldn't acknowledge her condition made it even more suspect.

Still, Eve followed Gadara to the men's side of the duplex. Edwards was pouring himself a glass of milk in the kitchen. Richens was leaning against the counter and speaking in rapid, heavily accented British English that was unintelligible to her. He acknowledged her with a jerk of his chin, then looked back at Edwards, who was examining her with an assessing glance.

She fought the urge to flip them the bird.

"Everything is as it should be," Gadara said into the phone. "Yes, there was a disturbance . . . Fine. In fact, she is extraordinary. I am quite impressed . . . Yes, I told her you would. Just a moment."

The archangel held the phone out to her. Accepting it, Eve moved to the far corner of the living room where a massive spider web occupied much of the space.

"Hi," she said in a subdued tone that made her feel better but wouldn't prevent mark-enhanced eavesdropping.

"Hey." The sound of Alec's gruff, purring voice filled her with relief. "You're not answering your phone."

"I had to turn it off so it didn't disturb my roommate."

He growled. "Put it on vibrate and keep it on you."

"I tried that, but then I left the damn thing under my pillow when I couldn't sleep."

"What's going on, angel? Are you hurt?"

"I'm fine."

"Raguel cut me off, and you weren't answering. Scared the shit out of me."

"It was a stupid misunderstanding."

"Couldn't have been that stupid. You impressed Raguel."

"What can I say?" She shrugged. "He's easily amused."

"Does he have you training already? It's after two in the morning."

"I told you, I couldn't sleep."

"You miss me." There was a smile in his voice.

"That, and it's too hot to nod off."

"Hot? In Monterey at night?"

Eve rubbed at the space between her brows. "I think I'm coming down with something. I'm pretty sure I have a fever."

There was a long pause. "You can't get sick."

"You have to believe me, I'm not giving you a choice. Gadara won't listen to me and—"

"I'm going to take a shower."

She stiffened at the sound of a woman's voice in the background on the other end of the phone. It was throaty and seductive, as if the speaker had just woken up . . . or just had a screaming orgasm. "Who is that?"

Alec groaned. "A mess."

"Sounds like a woman."

"She's a Mare."

Eve's foot tapped against the hardwood, her earlier feelings rushing to the fore. "She doesn't sound like a horse to me. I bet she doesn't look like one either. Where are you?"

He laughed, the low rumble as enticing when she was mad as when she was completely besotted. "She's a Mare, as in *night*mare. And I'm in my room. It's the middle of the night, where else would I be?"

"You have a naked woman in your room in the middle of the night."

Edwards gave a low whistle. Eve turned around and flipped him the bird.

"She's not naked yet," Alec said calmly.

"Well, I don't want to hold you up so I'll let you go."

There was a pregnant pause, then, "Tell me you're kidding."

"Sounds as if the joke's on me."

"Give me a fucking break."

Eve pinched the bridge of her nose. "Ignore me. I'm not feeling well."

"She's an Infernal."

"I'm not rational."

"She's not you."

"Got it."

"Nothing to worry about. Understand? And anyway, you don't strike me as the jealous type."

"I'm not jealous of you, I'm jealous of her. She's naked with you. Call me back when I'm shacked up in a motel with a naked guy and see how you feel about it."

"I'm not shacked up, and she's not naked within eyesight. But . . . point taken."

A reluctant smile curved her mouth. "Why do you have an Infernal taking a shower in your room?"

"Bad luck?" He exhaled his frustration. "Something is really screwed up around here. She offered information if I'd get her out of the area."

"Like Hank?"

The Exceptional Projects Department—located in the subterranean floors of Gadara Tower—housed Infernals who worked for the good guys. Some did so by force, others were defectors from Hell. They all used their various talents to further the Mark cause.

"Yes. Like Hank and the others."

"How will creating nightmares be helpful?"

"Mares see into dreams. Sometimes that helps in learning what Infernals have planned."

"Subconscious eavesdropping?"

"Exactly. They can also make subliminal suggestions."

"What about the Alpha?"

"Giselle will have to tag along." Alec's tone was blunt and uncompromising. "I'm not interrupting my hunt, it's keeping me away from you."

Eve forced herself to ignore his use of the Mare's first name. She knew it was nothing. *Knew* it. But her agitated emotions were seeking any outlet. "Can you trust her?"

"You worried about me, angel?" he asked softly.

"You know it."

"I'll make you a deal: I keep myself in one piece and you do the same."

"You're on." She yawned against her will.

"Go to bed," he ordered. "I need to finish talking to Raguel, then I'm crashing, too. I want an early start."

"Listen," she looked over her shoulder at the rest of the room's occupants, then lowered her voice, "a dog tried to talk to me earlier."

"Oh?" The rise in his interest was palpable. "About what?"

"That's the thing, I don't know. She said something was fishy around me, then Izzie shot her."

"*Shot* her?"

"Yeah, for no other reason than she felt like it, as far as I can tell."

"The dog is *dead*?"

Eve winced. "Yes."

"How do these things happen around you? I've only been gone a few hours!"

"Hey," she said defensively, "I didn't do anything."

Molenaar yelled from the kitchen, "You attacked me, *krankzinnige vrouw!*"

"Why is he calling you a crazy woman?" Alec asked. "And why did you attack him?"

"Ignore him." She crossed the living room and exited the house for privacy. Due to lack of heating, the house wasn't much warmer than the outside, but the addition of a breeze helped cool her overheated skin.

"Shit."

"Not my fault. Besides, you're supposed to take my side. You're my mentor."

"Okay." He exhaled with deliberation. "Let's take it from the top. The feverish feeling is probably just your body's adjustment to the changes it's going through. You remember how it was when you went through the first part of it."

Oh yeah, she would never forget. She had felt as if she was on fire from the inside out and the need for sex had nearly driven her insane. Who would have thought God would tie two such disparate concepts as killing and loving into the same event? Then again, Eve had always thought the Almighty had a sick sense of humor.

"Probably?" she persisted, picking up on his slight hesitation. "What else could it be?"

"Well . . . there is the Novium."

"The Novium?"

"It hits Marks right before their mentoring ends and they've achieved some autonomy."

"So it can't be that."

"Right. It's way too soon. So you're adjusting, that's all."

She kicked at the ground. "Sucks."

"I bet. As for you jumping your classmate . . . He apparently didn't like what you did, so it's not sexual. Since that's the only thing I would give a shit about—aside from you hurting yourself—we'll just chalk that up to you being you."

"I hope you're not expecting a warm welcome when you get back," she muttered.

"Hot and sweaty, actually. Can't wait." A seductive purr rumbled across the cellular waves.

Eve's mood changed from hot and irritable to hot and bothered. "Better be nice to me, then."

"I'll be very nice to you, angel. You've never had any complaints. Now about the dog incident . . . I admit, that bothers me. What is Raguel doing about it?"

"Nothing that I can see. He told me to let him handle it."

"There must be a reason why he's not pressing the issue."

"Apathy?"

"I know you don't trust him, so trust me. He's got it covered."

Eve's free hand went to her hip. "You aren't here, Alec. He didn't even blink when Izzie killed that poor dog."

"As an archangel, he's closer to God. I'm guessing the connection is similar to trying to watch television and carry on a conversation at the same time. He's distracted, not careless."

"So you say."

"When I'm called to stand before Jehovah, I lose all sense of everything—time, feelings, reality. It's very . . . serene. I can't imagine how the archangels make it through their days with that connection open all the time."

"Regardless, I'm watching my own back." She looked around, making sure she was still alone. "I can't help but think that it's a little too convenient that Izzie acted when she did."

"I know you can't stay out of trouble, but can you please keep yourself safe?"

"Ha. So says the man with a naked demon in his shower."

The door opened behind her. Eve faced it. Montevista gestured her back with a jerk of his chin.

"I'm being summoned," she said, as she moved toward the house.

"Phone on you at all times. Got it?"

"Hey, I tried to call you earlier and you didn't answer."

"Won't happen again." Alec's voice softened and filled with warmth. "I am here for you, angel, even though I'm not there."

"I know."

"Try and get some sleep. It'll help you with the side effects of the transition."

"Will do." She passed Montevista, who held the door open for her, and entered the house. "Stay safe."

"Back at ya."

Gadara leaned elegantly against the old kitchen countertop, his appearance flawless despite the late hour. She held out the phone to him.

He traversed the distance between them in the blink of an eye. His fingers wrapped around hers, cooling her temperature with a single touch.

"Thank you," he murmured, his dark eyes filled with an age's worth of knowledge. "Your concern on my behalf pleases me greatly."

Although it was contrary to her desire to get her old life back, Eve appreciated the archangel's praise. "You're welcome."

They shared a brief smile. Gadara took the phone and resumed his conversation with Alec. Eve stepped into the kitchen for a bottle of water before she headed back to the girls' side of the duplex.

"Stick close tomorrow," Richens said, watching her from his position by the sink.

"Okay." The whole covert association thing was weird to Eve, but she'd play along at least until she figured out what was going on.

Edwards grunted. "And try not to be all over the place."

"I hope I'm not the only one of us who would have acted first and asked questions later," she shot back. "With that backpack and shawl over his head, Molenaar didn't look human. And he was heading toward Gadara."

"I am touched," Gadara called out.

"Stop eavesdropping." She glared at him, peeved to find him grinning. It made him look boyish and almost . . . cute. And Gadara wasn't cute. He was ambitious and blessed with celestial gifts she could only wonder at. He was also on a power trip where Alec was concerned, and she bore the brunt of his machinations. Eve didn't want to like him. She certainly didn't want to like his adorable grin.

"I think your superpowers are messed up," Edwards muttered.

Eve grabbed a water bottle from the stash on the counter and headed out. "See you guys in a few hours."

Leaving the house with Sydney in tow, Eve headed back to the girls' side. They rounded the corner and found Izzie waiting in the driveway at the front of the duplex. Without her usual cosmetics, the blonde looked startlingly young and delicate. Her skin was as pale as cream, her features finely wrought. She was as short of stature as Eve, but much less curvy. It looked good on her, as did her rainbow-striped knee-highs and black baby-doll pajamas. Izzie had the appearance of a pixie with a Goth edge.

Eve eyed her warily. Her inner warning bells went off whenever Izzie was near.

"Hello." Izzie straightened from her leaning position against the front of the Suburban.

"What are you doing out here, Seiler?" Sydney asked.

"Waiting for Hollis."

Both of Eve's brows rose. Two overtures in one day? After three weeks of cold shoulders? "Did you need something?"

"Can we talk?"

"I'm listening."

They continued forward. Sydney deliberately fell behind.

"He asked me, too, you should know," Izzie said.

"Who asked you what?"

"Richens."

Eve's steps faltered, then she realized she wasn't all that surprised. "Really."

"He did not tell you?" Izzie sighed dramatically. "He said I was the only female in our class worthy of asking."

Ignoring the dig, Eve asked, "Do you know what he's thinking?"

Izzie shook her head. "I do not care. There is something wrong with him."

There was something wrong with all of them as far as Eve was concerned. And the fate of the world rested, in part, in their hands. How scary was that? "Why are you telling me this?"

"I thought you would wish to know."

"You haven't told me much of anything yet."

The blonde sighed. "Also, I thought perhaps we should join forces, too."

"*We?* As in you and me?"

"Yes." The word was said with exasperation, as if Eve was slow to catch on. "Richens has a purpose for why he wants his own group. If we could understand, it would be of use to us."

"'We' as in *me,* right," Eve murmured wryly, "since you turned him down?"

Izzie smiled, but it didn't reach her blue eyes. "Right."

"If you want to know what he's up to, why didn't you play along and find out?"

"Patience is difficult for me." Izzie glanced aside with a slight smile, her short pigtails swaying in the damp evening air.

Eve wished she'd been a fan of the reality show *Survivor*. She might have picked up some tips about how to backstab, a skill she suspected her classmates had long ago mastered. "How old are you, Izzie?"

"Thirty. Why does that matter?"

Eve would have guessed that she was younger. She shrugged. "Just curious."

"You don't wish to know why I was marked?"

"Sure. Are you going to tell me?"

"No." Izzie climbed the short steps to the front door and opened it. Her loosely laced Dr. Martens thudded onto the hardwood of the living room. Sydney brought up the rear, locking them inside the house while another guard kept watch outside. Four guards, two for each duplex.

The moon had drifted farther along in the sky, shining less light into the space and creating more shadows. Eve was suddenly exhausted and a giant yawn escaped her.

"Tell me why you are here," Izzie said, kicking off her boots.

Eve headed down the hall to her room. "Not tonight, I have a headache."

"We can help one another."

Eve paused at her door. "How exactly are you going to help me?"

The blonde shrugged. "I will think of a way."

"Don't hurt yourself." Stepping into her room, Eve shut the door and crawled into bed. She was asleep almost as soon as her head hit the pillow.

Festive tropical music poured from hidden speakers while a warm ocean draft gusted through the open French doors of Greater Adventures Yachts, the manufacturer of the multimillion-dollar boats that funded the Australian firm.

Reed feigned the appearance of examining the photos of various ships on the wall, but in truth, he didn't see any of them. Instead, he saw the horror of the night before—the blood splattered over acacias and broken melaleuca trees, the wide circular depression in the wild grasses, the skin of Les's Mark torn from the missing body. Caught on various twigs, the flesh flapped in the evening breeze as a macabre banner, taunting them with their helplessness.

What the hell were they dealing with?

"Are you all right?" Mariel asked from her position beside him.

"Not really, no."

"If it's any consolation, you're good at what you do because you let the shit get to you."

He managed a slight smile. "Flattery will get you everywhere with me."

"Abel!"

Reed turned at the sound of the familiar, jovial voice. Uriel approached with his ever-ready wide grin and bright blue eyes. Sans shirt, the archangel sported only tropical shorts and flip-flops. His skin was tanned mahogany and the ends of his longish hair were bleached by the sun.

Bowing, Reed showed his respect and appreciation for the courtesy Uriel paid him by allowing him to investigate on Australian turf. As he straightened, the archangel clapped him on the shoulder.

"It is good to see you again," Uriel said.

"And you as well."

Uriel accepted Mariel's extended hand and kissed her knuckles. "Let us go up to my office."

They left the large waiting area and ascended a short flight of steps up to an expansive loft. A glass-topped, white wicker desk faced another set of open French doors. The stunning view of the beach beyond was a bit like the vista Eve's condo enjoyed. However, the water in Huntington Beach was a dark bluish-gray. The water here was bluer. Beautiful. Reed found himself wishing Eve were here to see it.

Dropping into the chair behind the desk, Uriel said, "It is unfortunate that you are not here under more pleasant circumstances."

Mariel took a seat.

Reed remained standing. He noted a small rack on a nearby console that held several bottles of wine. He crossed over to it and carefully lifted one, reading the brilliantly colored label. "Caesarea Winery?"

"A new venture," the archangel explained.

"I hope it does well for you."

"It always pays to be cautious and plan for contingencies, which is why I invited you to come out here."

"We appreciate the invitation," Mariel murmured.

"Where's Les?" Reed asked. "I would like him to be present, if you don't mind."

"On the beach. He will be up in a moment." Uriel's features were grave. "He is taking the loss of his Mark very hard. I told him to hit the waves for a bit and clear his head. Everyone needs to be focused on the puzzle at hand."

"It's a terrible puzzle." Mariel's voice was soft and filled with sadness. "Something truly heinous."

As if on cue, Les entered through the balcony doors,

dripping wet and sprinkled with sand. No one missed the catch in Mariel's breathing, least of all the handsome Aussie, who gifted her with a slight smile. "Hello."

Uriel launched into the discussion without hesitation, looking between Reed and Mariel. "What did you determine last night? Is this situation similar to what you both experienced with your Marks?"

"Yes." Reed returned the wine bottle to the rack. "The same."

"So you believe it is the same Infernal?"

"Or the same *classification,*" Mariel said. "We don't know if this is one demon or several."

Uriel looked at Les, who nodded his agreement. "It's a possibility to consider."

"Three attacks in three weeks." Reed thought back to the order he'd received to vanquish a tommy knocker causing trouble in a busy Kentucky mine. The faeries were Takeo's specialty; the Mark had vanquished many of them. "For a new class of Infernal, there seems to be no learning curve. This demon has jumped straight into killing on a mass scale. And it's not attacking defenseless mortals or novice Marks; it's taking out our best and brightest."

"I sent Kimberly after *Patupairehe,*" Les said grimly, "but we never saw any. So I'm wondering what happened to the original assignment."

"Perhaps this Infernal is killing other demons, as well as Marks?" Uriel suggested.

Reed crossed his arms. "Or the seraphim are vulnerable in some way. Either erroneous information is leaching into the system or our lines of communication aren't sacred. An Infernal could be intercepting the assignments as they're sent down to us."

"How would that be possible?" Mariel breathed, clearly horrified by the thought.

Uriel leaned forward with his forearms on the desk. "Marks graduate from their mentors every day. Killing one established Mark a month barely puts a dent in our numbers. It hurts, yes. But it is not fatal."

"I'm not sure the goal is a thinning of our ranks." Reed's cell phone vibrated. He looked at the caller ID, sent Sara to voicemail *again*, and passed the conversation over to the Aussie handler. "Les has a theory."

Les ran a hand through his dripping wet hair and laid it out. "I think the demon might be absorbing the Marks it kills. Parts of the physical body, and also some of the Mark's thoughts and connection to their handler."

The archangel paused. His gaze moved over all three of the *mal'akhs* before him. "What evidence do you have for such a claim?"

"The Infernal knew where I was shifting almost before I did."

"That is hardly proof," Uriel scoffed. "I would call it dumb luck, unless it happens more than once."

"It *will* strike again." Mariel's tone was resigned. "But learning from our failures doesn't sit well with me."

Uriel arched a brow at Reed. "Suggestions?"

"To find it, we need to know how it hunts. I've been considering the similarities between the three kills, trying to find a pattern we can use."

"All three Marks were in remote areas," Mariel said. "Places the Infernal couldn't have simply 'stumbled' upon them."

"All three were hunting an Infernal they specialized in," Les added. "They were in their element."

"All three were under the direction of established, prominent handlers." Uriel's mouth was a somber line. "Handlers with years of experience and information."

Reed believed Les was onto something with his theory, which led him to a horrifying realization . . .

"Eve . . ." he breathed, his gut clenching.

She wasn't safe. She had been paramount in his thoughts at the moment the Infernal had absorbed Takeo . . . and possibly Takeo's connection to Reed. If Sammael knew about her, he would exploit her to the fullest extent. Cain had been a focus of his since the dawn of time and he would seize any opportunity to minimize Cain's effectiveness or turn Cain against God.

The archangel stared at Reed, comprehension dawning in his eyes. "Would he not have gone after her directly? Why come here first?"

"Maybe Kimberly and I had something he thought he could use?" Les suggested.

"Or maybe there's more than one," Mariel repeated. "The Infernal who killed my Mark was much smaller than the one you saw."

"We need to coordinate with the other firms," Uriel said.

"We can start by establishing teams to covertly accompany experienced Marks on remote hunts for Infernals they specialize in." Reed's gaze touched upon Mariel and Les, then came to rest on Uriel. "We can also set a trap to prove or disprove Les's theory."

"How?"

"We can feed the Marks false information and see what happens."

Uriel nodded. "And what if the only way to access that information is through death?"

"It's a chance we have to take. We need to know."

"I agree." The archangel's smile didn't reach his eyes. "You have no qualms. You should have my job."

That was Reed's plan. Not to take Uriel's place, but to join him in the rank of archangel. The creation of a new firm was long overdue. Reed fully intended to step into position as firm leader when the time came. Handling Eve was going to help him do that. By supervising her—and therefore Cain—he would prove that he could handle any task. From the training of new Marks, to the managing of the most powerful Mark of them all.

"I wouldn't go that far," he demurred. "I hate to lose Marks, whether they're mine or not. But casualties are inevitable in war."

Mariel's verdant eyes were sharp and assessing. "You have someone in mind?"

"Not yet. I'll work on that. In the meantime, Eve is in training now. In light of the possible danger, I will shadow her until Cain returns."

"Understandable," Uriel said. "I will arrange a conference call with the other firm leaders."

Mariel pushed gracefully to her feet, her long red hair swaying around her shoulders. She offered a shy smile to Les, who managed to return the gesture despite the grief that shrouded him.

Reed and Mariel left Australia in the blink of an eye. They shifted to Gadara Tower, landing in the subterranean Exceptional Projects Department.

Touching his arm, Mariel said, "Sara is going to be livid when Uriel calls."

"That's her problem."

"And subsequently, yours and Ms. Hollis's."

Reed's jaw clenched. Ambitious, masochistic, and

shrewd, Sara had wanted to head any investigation into the rogue Infernal creature so that she could take the credit for its eventual vanquishing.

"There's nothing to be done about that," he dismissed. "The Infernal has never hunted on her territory. She's in no position to lead an investigation."

"She'll expect that your relationship will give her an advantage."

"We don't have a relationship." They'd never had one. He had been a stud to service her and she had been diverting. Once he realized she would rather sabotage his efforts to advance to archangel than help him, he'd ended the affair. However, although she didn't love him, she didn't want anyone else to have him either.

Mariel studied him carefully. "Has Sara seen you with Ms. Hollis?"

"No."

"You better pray she never does."

His mouth curved. "You've never seen me with her either."

"I've seen you without her, that's plenty."

Reed caught her elbow and led her down the long hall, away from the traffic and Infernal stench that distinguished the lobby area. Eve said the E.P.D. reminded her of noir films. He could see the resemblance in the muted lighting, inlaid glass doors, and smoky air.

"What are you going to do now?" he asked.

"Pay attention to all the orders that come down and protect my Marks. I'll skip a call before I send one of my crew to get slaughtered."

"Uriel isn't one to delay."

"Thank God. And you? Are you leaving to join her now?"

Reed kept his face impassive. “After I grab a few things.”

“Be careful.” Her tone told him she wasn’t fooled by his nonchalance.

He pressed a kiss to her temple. “You, too.”

“My worries aren’t even half of yours,” she muttered. “You’re on shaky ground, my friend. I don’t want to see you fall.”

Walking toward the elevators, Reed thought of Eve and suspected it was already too late. God help him.

“God help us all.”

CHAPTER 7

Monterey was a chilly, foggy town in the morning. The gray sky and thick, misty ground cover added to the somber mood of the training area. Lined up shoulder-to-shoulder with the other Marks, Eve gazed warily at the view beyond Gadara, who stood before them. Peeling paint, broken windows, and haphazardly leaning structures formed a dystopian city occupied by rotting mannequins and junkyard cars.

"Welcome to Anytown," the archangel said in his luxuriant timbre. "Where anything can happen."

He was smiling and looking far too anticipatory for Eve's taste. His attire of khaki green sweat suit emblazoned with "Gadara Enterprises" was overly casual in her estimation. She had never seen him so laid back, and the skeptical side of her brain wondered if he expected to be camped out here for a while.

For her part, she'd dressed in comfortable jeans, T-shirt, and sweater jacket. On her feet she wore what she now considered to be necessary footwear—combat boots. All of her pretty heels and sandals were stored away. She missed them, but she valued her life more than her fashion sense.

"As Ms. Hollis so heroically demonstrated last night," Gadara continued, "vanquishing a target is only half the battle. First, you must confirm that you have acquired the correct Infernal before proceeding. That is the focus of today's training exercise."

"Was that the plan before last night?" Ken asked.

"Why do you ask?"

"I wantae ken if our training was goosed because Hollis and Molenaar were scrapping like a bunch of haddies."

"She attacked me!" Molenaar cried.

"This particular assignment was scheduled for later in the week," Gadara conceded. "But this is a simple rearrangement, not a replacement. You will not be deprived of anything, Mr. Callaghan. I promise you that."

Ken leaned forward and looked down the row at Eve. His expression clearly said he wasn't pleased. She smiled and waved. He wore all black today—black jeans, black turtleneck, and black ski cap. On someone else the outfit might have been too stark and slightly intimidating. Ken, however, looked like he'd stepped out of the pages of *GQ* magazine.

"This exercise is designed to simulate actual field conditions." Gadara began to walk down the line, inspecting each Mark. "In this scenario, you are hunting a rogue faery."

"What is the alleged crime?" Edwards asked.

"You are not concerned with *why* you are hunting, Mr. Edwards. That is something you will rarely know."

"Got it. Sorry."

Gadara held up a black armband, which he produced out of thin air. "For training purposes, you will wear these directly over your marks. It holds a thin metal pad that will heat up when in proximity to a similar band worn on your target."

"The smell of the Infernal will not be enough?" Romeo asked.

Laughter swelled through the group.

"If there was only one, yes. But when will you be in an urban situation such as we are staging today and have only one Infernal in the area, Mr. Garza? Today's exercise would not be a very realistic simulation with only one demon present."

"So there's more than one," Eve murmured.

"Of course. In addition to your target, there are other Infernals within the designated training area. Some are working in collusion with the demon you hunt and they will try to distract you. The others are simply bystanders. Later on in the week, we will also be training alongside an Army platoon, which will add mortals to the mix and force you to work without arousing suspicions. But in the beginning, you will be focused on hunting your designated target among a group of Infernals."

"Well," Ken said, grinning. "If our bands burn, we'll know what tae do."

"It is not quite that easy, Mr. Callaghan. You will see how fear alters your judgment and goads you to act rashly. That is the reason we train Marks so extensively. You must learn to ignore your terror and work through it."

"What does the winner get?" Richens asked.

"You will succeed or fail as a team, which leads me

to the rules of engagement. Number one: take pains to avoid wounding your fellow Marks. Anxiety fosters careless mistakes."

"Yeah, Hollis." Laurel blew a bubble with her chewing gum, then popped it. "Watch out."

Eve looked at her and rubbed the space between her brows with her middle finger.

"Are you flipping me off?"

"Ladies, please." Gadara shook his head. "You may save each other's lives one day."

"How much time do we have to catch the Infernal?" Romeo asked.

"This is not a timed assignment. We will remain at the training site until the Infernal is captured." Gadara moved over to the nearby tent and picnic table. He set his hands on one of several large coolers resting on the tabletop. "There are sandwiches and drinks here, if you need them."

"We should begin now," Claire said. "I have no wish to be out here after dark."

"It's morning," Izzie drawled. "There are eight of us. We will not be out here long."

"Will we be given weapons?" Ken asked.

"To a certain extent." The archangel swept his hand in a wide swath before him. A tarp covered with various knives and pistols appeared on the ground at his feet. Eve bit back a smile. The twinkle in his eyes told her he was thoroughly enjoying the free use of his celestial gifts.

Ken frowned. "I dinnae ken."

"Injuries inflicted with these items are survivable. The bullets are rubber and the knife blades are short to ensure shallow wounds. So whether or not they will be of any use to you remains to be seen."

"What's the point, then?" Richens muttered. "A bloody mug's game. That's what this is."

"Rule of engagement number two: this is *not* a hunt to kill. The Infernals work for me, so refrain from overzealousness. Some of you will strike first and ask questions later. It will take time to learn how to suppress your instincts long enough to use mental reasoning."

"I thought learning to trust our instincts was the point," Edwards said.

"When you are frightened and something lunges out at you, what is the usual instinctive response?"

"Fight back," Izzie said.

"Or run," Claire offered.

"Correct. But you are marked, Ms. Dubois, and you will not flee. The mark will have filled your veins with adrenaline and you will thirst for blood. And if it was a mortal who happened to be in the wrong place at the wrong time? Someone who is as frightened as you and fighting for his life, mistakenly believing you are the enemy? Instincts are blunt instruments; reasoning minds are sharp."

Silence weighed heavily over the group.

"Any further questions?"

Eve spoke up. "What would you consider a successful mission?"

The archangel smiled. "Since the goal of this exercise is discovering that answer for yourselves, telling you would defeat the purpose. I can tell you what I would consider to be failures: the injury of one of you, failure to cooperate among yourselves, or the injury of one of my Infernals. There are more, but those are the outcomes I would find most disturbing."

Ken rubbed his hands together. "I'm ready to go."

"Excellent. Chose your weapons. One per person, please."

Eve watched the others pick over the selection. Izzie and Romeo both selected knives. Edwards picked a revolver. Molenaar went for a 9mm, as did Laurel after rejecting all of Romeo's varied suggestions. Claire liked the Glock. Ken went with brass knuckles. Eventually, only Richens and Eve remained. The others moved with Gadara over to the tent area to be outfitted with their armbands.

"I hate this," Richens muttered. "Why did I have to get a field assignment? Why didn't they put me to work doing something I'm good at?"

"You're asking the wrong person." Eve studied what was left to choose from—a couple of knives, a revolver, a 9mm, a telescoping baton, mace, and a taser.

"Take a gun," she suggested. "A knife requires proximity."

"Right, then. You take a knife. If the Infernal gets through you, I'll shoot it."

Eve glanced aside at him. "Are you kidding?"

"Hey." His boyish features took on a sullen cast. "I'll be analyzing the scene for clues. If you watch my back, we'll get done a lot faster. Brain and brawn, remember?"

"That might work if you knew anything about faeries. Since you don't, you're no better off than me. Is Edwards watching your back, too?"

"Edwards is a pain in the arse."

"Not interested in being a bodyguard, eh?"

"He's still griping about you. He thinks Cain is going to blow his top and kill us if something happens to you."

Her brows rose. "What would you guys have to do with anything bad happening to me?"

"My point exactly! If anything, Cain should appreciate that you had colleagues."

"I'm sure Edwards would have preferred it if Izzie had said yes," she trawled, "instead of me."

"Screw Edwards." He scowled. "I'd never work with Seiler."

"She says differently."

"She's loony." Meeting her gaze directly, Richens reiterated. "I didn't ask her for a damn thing. I didn't like her before and I like her even less now, the bloody liar."

"How would she know what you were up to?"

Although she asked the question, Eve found herself believing him. He seemed sincere. Izzie . . . well, she had seemed sincerely insincere, which was honest in its own way.

"Maybe she was in the kitchen when you and I were talking. I don't fucking know." He ran a rough hand through his short hair. His hooded sweatshirt was black and had "Killer Rabbit!" screened across the front along with an image of a predatory hare attacking a medieval knight.

Eve's mouth curved.

"What the hell is so funny?" Richens snapped, his compact frame vibrating with anger.

Her smile faded. She'd forgotten about his quick temper. "Your shirt."

Dropping to a crouch, Eve selected the 9mm. She checked the magazine, then straightened and walked away.

"Hollis! Wait."

But she didn't. She joined the others just as Romeo

volunteered to outfit the class with the armbands. They had come to McCroskey with a skeleton crew and every Mark was expected to pitch in when he or she could.

Romeo's gaze met hers, so dark she could see why Laurel would want to drown in him. "Come here."

Eve shoved her gun into her waistband at the small of her back, then shrugged out of her sweater and presented her arm. He attached the band directly over the Mark of Cain and double-checked it for a tight fit. It was slender, maybe a quarter of an inch wide, just enough to cover the eye in the center. The intricate triquetra and circled serpents remained visible.

"How does that feel?" he asked, his voice velvet smooth and seductive.

"Fine." She looked at him, noting his heavy-lidded stare. Izzie had called him a gigolo and Eve could see how she had come to that pronouncement. With his slumberous eyes, fit physique, and accented voice, he fit the "Italian Stallion" image to perfection. Eve could believe a woman would pay for his sexual favors.

"Flex," he ordered.

Complying, she fisted her hand and tautened her biceps. The band tightened, but didn't become prohibitively uncomfortable. "Still fine."

"*Buono,* go wait with the others."

Eve grabbed her sweater off the picnic table bench. "Need any help with yours?"

He tugged up his T-shirt sleeve, displaying his band. "No, *bella.*" A faint smile curved his mouth. "Thank you for asking."

"No problem."

Laurel walked up and set her hand possessively on Romeo's waist. "Hi, babe."

"*Cara mia,*" he greeted.

If looks could kill, Eve thought as she walked away. Laurel was the jealous type, apparently. Having experienced the green-eyed monster herself the night before, Eve understood. But Laurel and Romeo were such an odd couple. There appeared to be little true affection between them. Theirs was a liaison created by circumstances, which was fine if that worked for them. Eve wasn't going to dwell on it. She had her own difficulties to deal with.

She rejoined the group. They waited at the start of the street that led into the training area. Once again, she looked over the visible area. A female mannequin wearing a sun-bleached and tattered coat stood on a nearby corner, her wig askew and flapping in the salt-tinged breeze. She was pushing a carriage that was missing a wheel. The smell of mold and decay permeated the air and emphasized the sense that time forgot this place. The tableau made Eve's stomach churn.

"Can you think of how the insides must be?" Izzie asked, drawing abreast of her.

"We'll find out in a minute."

"I can't wait." The blonde palmed her blade with obvious familiarity. Her pretty face was fully made up with darkly rimmed eyes, pale powder, and purple lips. The palette was oddly beautiful on a woman so fair. She still managed to look dainty, despite the spiked collar around her neck. "I visited California once before, for Knott's Berry Farm's Halloween Haunt. I went three nights. It was great."

"Good for you."

"You do not look excited."

"Not my cup of tea." Which was a total understatement. She kept picturing *The Texas Chainsaw Massacre* in her head. It didn't give her the warm fuzzies.

Izzie's voice lowered. "You have killed an Infernal before. What was it like?"

"You just . . . do it."

Eve thought about the water demon she vanquished. He had been trying to kill her. His umpteenth attempt, which made him officially a nuisance. She had been terrified, but something inside her reared up and fought back. She was still astonished that she succeeded. She was also surprised that she wasn't haunted by her actions. Fact was, she would do it again.

Izzie snorted. "That is all you can say? Only 'do it'?"

"Yep."

The sudden apprehension Eve felt wasn't due entirely to the creepiness of the fake town. A lot of it had to do with the eagerness of the others in her class and her lack of the same. Ken was pacing in his impatience to start. Claire had a camera with her, as if this was a sightseeing event and not training for murder.

"Those things take dodgy photos," Laurel said, walking up with Romeo and Richens.

Claire shrugged. "I won't jeopardize my good camera."

"What do you need one for?" Eve asked. When Marks and Infernals were in their element, they didn't show up on film. They functioned on a different plane altogether. Eve assumed that was why her mother couldn't see the Mark of Cain on her arm.

"Posterity."

"You should take one now," Eve suggested, trying to find the same enthusiasm the others exhibited. Maybe posing for a group picture would foster solidarity among them. It certainly couldn't hurt. "Of all of us."

Claire gestured to Sydney, who stood nearby in full black urban commando garb. "Will you take the picture for us?"

Everyone lined up into two rows—men kneeling in the front, women standing in the back. Claire asked Gadara to stand to one side. The result was an assemblage reminiscent of an elementary school class photo.

Yanking up her poplin sleeve, Claire said, "Show your armbands, *s'il vous plaît.*"

The group posed with funny faces and proudly presented biceps wrapped with the armbands. The mood was festive.

Which made Eve wonder why she felt as if something was about to go horribly wrong.

"*You've reached Evangeline Hollis. Leave a message, and I'll return your call as soon as I can.*"

Alec terminated the connection with a quick tap to his headset, then he applied more pressure to the accelerator. The black convertible Mustang's 300-horsepower engine rumbled with pleasure, hurtling the sleek sports car along Highway 17.

"You're going the wrong way," Giselle said.

He tossed her a dry glance.

As they passed a freeway sign, she pointed at it. "You're going north."

"I know where I'm going."

"Gadara headquarters is in Anaheim. To the south."

"Do you have a point?"

Giselle frowned behind her new five-dollar sunglasses. They'd purchased more appropriate clothes for her at a truck stop—shorts, a tank top emblazoned with *California,* flip-flops, and a kerchief to wrap around her head.

They were cruising with the top down. Hot wheels, beautiful day, wrong girl. Alec would say two out of three wasn't bad, but he missed Eve too much.

And his girl wasn't answering her cell phone.

He knew she was in training, but after their conversation the night before, he needed to talk to her and make sure she was feeling better. He also needed to ease the sense that something was off, and only the sound of her voice could do that.

"You promised to take me to safety," Giselle argued.

"No. You asked me to take you with me. I've done that."

She pivoted in the seat. "We can't go north!"

"Why not?" Alec kept his hands relaxed on the steering wheel, but inside he was still and watchful.

"Because it's too dangerous."

"You'll have to give me more than that."

"Where are you going?"

"I'm hunting." He glanced aside at her. "Don't be coy."

"I'm not coy, damn you. I'm scared."

He knew that much was true; he smelled the fear on her. "Tell me why."

"Tell me you're not going after Charles Grimshaw."

Alec smiled. "I'm not telling you shit. The sharing between us only works one way."

"That's not fair!"

With a quick glance at the rearview mirror to check for traffic, he eased diagonally across the second lane and pulled to a stop on the shoulder. "If you don't like the rules, get out."

Her features altered into the enraged mask of her Infernal soul. "You're a dick."

"You're right."

"You need me."

"You wish."

She crossed her arms. "You have no idea what you're up against."

Cars and trucks roared by, shaking the Mustang on its wheels and stirring exhaust in the slightly chill air.

"Make me care," he challenged. "Tell me why I should."

"Do you want to die?"

"Not gonna happen. I've known Charles for years."

"No one knows the Alpha, not really."

"Don't talk in riddles."

Her too-slender fingers fidgeted with the hem of her shorts.

"Okay." He backtracked. "What does Charles have to do with you?"

Mares and wolves weren't known to associate. They were too different; one a physical aggressor, the other a mental marauder.

Giselle chewed her lower lip, her eyes darting over their surroundings, running in the only way she could—mentally. Alec was more than alert now. There was no doubt she wanted to reveal only the amount necessary to stem his questions.

"I don't have time for this," he snapped.

"If I tell you everything here," she whined, "what leverage do I have to get you to take me back to Anaheim?"

"You have no leverage. I need your blood, that's it. Obviously, I don't need you alive to get it."

"I'm running from Charles," Giselle blurted. "I need to get *away* from his territory, not drive *into* it."

"Does he have anything to do with what happened last night?"

"Start driving south and I'll tell you."

Alec's mouth curved. "Nothing you can say will get me to turn around. I have business to attend to and until it's done, everything else takes a backseat."

She looked prepared to argue, then her gaze met his and she knew it was pointless. "If you won't listen to me, will you listen to Neil?"

"Who is Neil?"

"The vamp who staked himself."

He recalled the events of the night before. *Servo vestri ex ruina.*

"Save myself from ruin?" he scoffed. "I'm getting a tan; Neil's dead. He should have taken his own advice."

"Save yourself from *destruction,* you idiot. And trust me, if Destruction gets a hold of you, you'll be dead, too."

Alec tossed his arm over the back of her headrest and pushed his shades up with the other hand. He stared at her with cold eyes. "Want to rephrase that?"

She pouted. "Sorry."

"Start from the top."

Giselle groaned and collapsed back into her seat. "Can we talk about this in Anaheim?"

Knowing they would attract the California Highway Patrol if he stayed on the shoulder too long, Alec faced forward and eased the car back into traffic. He pulled off the freeway at the next exit and into the parking lot of a gas station/convenience store. From the sudden gleam in Giselle's eyes, he knew she thought their stop was a good sign, which just showed how different the reasoning was between Infernals and Marks. Alec knew who ran the show in his world. He had been given an order by God. Ignoring it was not an option. Demons, on the other hand, were all egomaniacs. None of them wanted to admit that Sammael ruled the roost in Hell. They all preferred to delude themselves with the thought that Sammael's commands were optional and they followed them because it was fun.

"Okay." He slid the manual transmission into first gear, pulled up the emergency brake, and turned off the engine. "What is Destruction?"

Giselle's mouth took on a mulish cast. Her arms crossed.

Alec opened the driver's side door and unfolded from the seat. Rounding the trunk, he reached into the passenger side and plucked her out. She hadn't worn a seat belt—against California law—and he hadn't cared enough about her well-being to enforce it.

He returned to his side of the car and slid behind the wheel. "See ya."

"You are not leaving me here!" she protested, her lips white. "You need my blood."

"I also need my concentration, and being pissed off at you affects that." He reached for the ignition.

"Destruction is Sammael's pet."

Pausing, Alec glanced over at where she stood. "His *pet*?"

"A hellhound, but unlike anything you've ever seen before. It's a hybrid of demon and Cerberus, nephilim and Mark."

His jaw tightened.

Giselle's shoulders slumped and she looked even more gaunt, which he hadn't thought possible. "Sammael has been working on a new breed for centuries. None of them were viable; they all died."

"Except for Destruction."

"Right." She pulled the door open and dropped wearily into the seat.

"Was it the Mark blood that made the difference?"

"Yeah. Mark blood regenerates; it held all the parts together."

Holy shit. They were using Marks to create new demons. "What does Charles have to do with this?"

"Charles was the key. He's the Hound Whisperer. Sammael was able to keep the mutt alive, but he couldn't train it."

"Use a canine to train a canine."

Charles was one of the most powerful Alphas in the world. He ruled his pack with an iron fist. He was also wily enough to stay under the radar, which enabled him to expand his territory with only minor interference from Marks. He might have continued to grow in power, if he hadn't sought revenge for the death of his son by killing Eve in the Qualcomm Stadium bathroom. And now this.

"What does this have to do with you?" he asked.

"Once Sammael saw how successful Charles was in training the beast and how destructive it was, he wanted more of them. The hound is powerful and ravenous." Giselle's eyes turned fever-bright and she began to pant, her body thrumming with excitement. "If there were enough of them, they would wipe you all out. Every single Mark and angel. Every archangel. Even God. They're unstoppable."

Alec growled low, disgusted by her joy. "Answer the

fucking question. What does this have to do with you?"

The glazed look of pleasure faded from her expression. "Every Infernal from the Oregon border down to Seaside, California, was tasked with feeding the growing pups. They take decades to mature, and they eat. And eat. And eat." She growled. "Why do you think I look like this? You try getting a plate of food and only eating ten percent."

"They're feeding *from* you?" he asked, incredulous.

"Like I said, ten percent is our share. That's why Neil and the others checked out. Sammael gave strict orders—no leaks of the Lebensborn-2 program. If we're too weak to fight off a Mark attack, we are to take ourselves out of commission before we're captured. I thought Charles would back me up when I argued against that, but I was wrong. He's hot and a great fuck, but I'm not going back to Hell for anyone or anything. Especially not for a guy who thinks I am just a disposable piece of ass."

Lebensborn. Alec's fists clenched. Sammael considered the Holocaust his greatest masterpiece, his trial run for Armageddon. That he would revisit the horror, even in name only, made Alec fit to kill. "I've never met an Infernal willing to commit suicide."

"You've never met an Infernal with Destruction on his tail," Giselle retorted. "Charles warned us that if we returned to Hell as a traitor to the program, Sammael would make us pay. When the choices are to get ripped to shreds by a hellhound then tortured by the Prince or to kill yourself and wait in the earthbound queue, suicide is the lesser of the two crappy options."

"You didn't follow through."

"Thanks to you." She smiled. "What are the chances

that you would come along? Cain of infamy, the only Mark powerful enough to give me a shot at staying on Earth. It has to be fate."

Alec's gaze lifted heavenward. He never knew at moments such as this whether he was following a divine plan or just monumentally cursed to always step into shit. Perhaps this was all part of an elaborate punishment for his machinations to resurrect Eve. If so, he would consider the price worth it.

"Are the puppies still with Charles?" he asked.

She nodded. "That's why we want to drive in the other direction. They're housed in a kennel dead center of a gated, wolf-only community. You're good, but you aren't *that* good."

Alec turned the ignition. "Was that a dare?"

Giselle paled. "No! I didn't mean it that way."

He backed out of the parking spot and headed toward the northbound onramp. Brentwood was an hour away. "I've never been one to turn away from a challenge."

Raguel. The archangel needed to be brought up to speed. Then, Alec would grill Giselle to formulate a plan of attack. And when he found a private moment, he would touch base with Eve and make sure she was okay. As long as she was doing fine, he could manage the rest.

"This isn't a challenge, you idiot!" Giselle screeched. "This is a kamikaze mission. We. Are. Going. To. *Die*."

Alec grinned, then opened the throttle.

CHAPTER 8

Eve hated horror movies. She didn't believe she had ever watched an entire one. Usually she had her face buried in her hands or she left the room. Her best friend, Janice, refused to sit next to her during slasher flicks and boyfriends quickly learned that it was safest to stick to blow-'em-up action films. She loved to watch stuff explode, but creepy music and waiting for mass murderers to pop out of closets was too much suspense for her.

Too bad Richens hadn't figured that out yet.

The Mark lagged behind her, as if she would be of any help at all during a surprise attack. He also exacerbated the problem by stage-whispering all manner of provoking statements, like: "Did you see that?," "What was that noise?," and "Do you smell anything?"

Thankfully, Edwards held his tongue, bringing up the rear with a silent stride. They were searching through the ground floor of a three-story building that was dressed as an office unit. It was the tallest building in Anytown and perhaps the most inhabited by vermin. Roaches climbed gray walls and rats dashed across the retro-patterned linoleum. A worn mannequin with a broken face staffed the receptionist desk, its dead eyes staring blankly. Eve shuddered and tried not to look at it. Her overactive imagination made her feel as if she was being watched with malicious intent.

Morning light spilled in through the windows, many of which were broken. Shards of glass shimmered on the dusty floor and crunched beneath their booted feet. Outside, the cries of seagulls filled the air with a mournful cacophony.

"This would have worked better at night," Edwards said gruffly. "We're open targets in the daylight."

"Gadara says fifty percent of hunts are conducted during the day." Richens snorted. "I'll be asleep then."

"You can't sleep through a call." Eve's tone was wry. "The mark burns like hell."

"I can sleep through anything."

No point arguing. He'd figure it out soon enough.

"Ow!" he screeched, lurching into her.

She stumbled. Her armband heated to burning, defeating any need to ask him what his problem was. From the outside, Ken whooped a joyful war cry. A smile curved her mouth, and Eve pivoted to face her companions. "Too bad you're not asleep."

Richens glared.

Edwards hissed, "How can you joke at a time like this?" He spun around wildly, his posture hunched and his revolver up.

Eve sniffed the air. "The Infernal isn't near enough to smell. Yet."

"It's around here somewhere."

Richens looked at Eve with wide eyes. "Now what? Is this how it happens in the field?"

She nodded. "Your handler will also communicate with you, either in person or with some kind of telepathy."

"Crap." Edwards's jaw tautened. "I don't want someone poking around in my head."

"You'll appreciate it when the time comes." Eve thought of Reed and how she sometimes leaned heavily on his support. He calmed her in times of stress, though he was often miles away. It was a bond of some sort. A connection. And it was screwing with her equanimity. She was a one-man woman. At least she always had been.

A hot, spice-scented breeze wafted over her. It was stronger than usual, more forceful. *Reed.* Either he was close in proximity or their tie was strengthening. Both possibilities gave her a tingle of apprehension. He was responding to her, letting her know that he knew she was thinking of him. How much of her emotions did he feel? How deep into her thoughts could he go?

Richens set his hand on Edwards's wrist, pushing it—and the gun—down. "Put that away before you hurt someone." He glanced at Eve. "So what now?"

"We hunt." A flutter tickled her tummy at the words. The feeling was a mental trick, like sympathy pains. She wasn't brave or kick-ass. Tracking and killing evil beings from Hell scared the shit out of her.

"Lead the way," Edwards said, sketching a mocking bow and gesturing her forward with a wide sweep of his gun hand.

"No way."

"What the hell are you here for, then?"

Her shoulders went back. "I led the way in here. It's someone else's turn now."

"Don't be a baby, Hollis," Richens said.

"Screw you," she retorted. "Be a man."

"We're scared," he whined, reminding her that he was barely past his teens.

"So am I. If you wanted a fearless leader, you should have tagged along with Ken and his brass knuckles." She was glad they hadn't. It was doubtful that anyone else would have teamed up with her, and the thought of searching through the creepy fake town alone made her nauseous.

Edwards stilled. "*You're* scared?"

Eve growled. "Of course I'm scared! Why wouldn't I be? Four weeks ago the most stressful thing I faced was fitting a client's wish list into her budget. Now I'm lucky to survive the day, between the Infernals that Cain pissed off in the past and the ones I'm annoying right now."

Sighing, Edwards's features softened. He patted her awkwardly on the shoulder. "I'll take the lead."

"Someone do it," Richens snapped. "Before one of the others bags our faery."

"It's not a race," Eve reminded, wondering how a petulant narcissist had come to be selected as a Mark.

"The hell it isn't. We're talking about our *souls* here, Hollis. I'm playing to win. Besides, if this was a group effort, wouldn't we all be together instead of wandering around separately?"

Edwards shrugged. "He has a point. Okay. So we'll search this building, then move on if we don't find anything."

Starting out tentatively, they began with the bottom floor and worked their way up. As they opened the stairwell door to the uppermost landing, the scent of Infernal drifted into their nostrils. Edwards held up one hand, slowing them to a halt. He made eye contact with both of them and placed a finger to his lips in a gesture for silence.

Richens rolled his eyes and mouthed, *We're not bloody idiots*. Then, he pushed Edwards over the threshold and into the hallway.

Edwards made a strangled noise and brandished his revolver with terror-goaded carelessness.

Eve marveled at their dynamic, whatever it was. Richens was a kid. Edwards was middle-aged. Why he deferred to the younger man was a point that inspired much speculation.

Richens peered around the jamb, his head swiveling to get a 180-degree view. Eve put her foot to his ass and kicked him into the hallway.

What's good for the goose . . .

"Mind out!" he shouted, stumbling into Edwards, whose weapon discharged into an overhead fluorescent light fixture with a thunderous boom. Plastic and glass rained down on the two. They cursed in unison, lifting their arms to shield their heads. The report echoed through the once-quiet floor, killing any hope of a stealthy entry.

"Oops." Eve vacated the stairwell behind them, unable to watch Edwards's obvious fear and not join him. "Sorry about that."

"Are you *insane*?" Richens barked, pointing his gun at her.

"No, but I'm beginning to think you are." He didn't appear to be frightened at all. More like curious, watchful. Like a spider.

"What is going on out here?"

They all turned their heads to find the source of the clipped female voice. They found her down the hall, standing in the doorway of an office. She looked to be in her midfifties, her silver hair restrained in a chignon and her mouth a grim line. She wore a business suit in gray—a knee-length skirt and matching jacket. She reeked of rotting soul.

Her gaze dropped to the three guns pointed in her direction. "I am ringing the authorities." She pivoted on her heel and slammed the door.

"Maybe we should shoot her," Richens suggested.

"She's not the one," Edwards said. "My armband isn't hurting."

"Yeah, but she might call the faery and warn her we're coming."

"True."

Eve waited for her armband to signal a proximity warning. After a long moment, she shrugged off the possibility, opened the stairwell door, and left. Hurried footsteps followed . . . *and* approached.

"Where are you going, Hollis?" Edwards called out, tripping down the stairs after her.

She slowed on the second-floor landing and raised her hand in a gesture for silence.

Edwards drew abreast of her, his gun hand trembling.

Richens paused two steps above them. "We left a witness behind."

Eve glared at him. "We're not vigilantes. She's not the target and that means we don't take her out."

Clutching the handrail with white-knuckled force, she shot a quick glance down the center of the spiraling staircase. A flash of platinum caught her eye. She straightened quickly.

Izzie.

"Everyone heard the gun go off," she said. "They'll all come running to this one location."

Richens smiled, catching on. "The faery will see that we're all distracted."

"It would be the perfect time to move," Edwards finished.

"Right." Eve turned back. "Let's go."

In unison, they raced up the stairs. They burst onto the rooftop and ran to the edge, their booted feet crunching atop the gravel. Without discussion, they spread out, taking in the view of the city beneath them. As they'd anticipated, Marks rushed toward the building from all directions. Izzie was already on the premises. Claire was still a few blocks away. Romeo and Laurel appeared a few moments later, both looking suspiciously disheveled.

"Freaks," Edwards grumbled, voicing Eve's thoughts. She couldn't imagine that there would be any clean, nonspooky places in Anytown to indulge in some nooky.

"Where's Callaghan?" Richens asked.

"Maybe he's already in the building," Eve suggested, keeping a few feet between the lip of the roof and the toe of her boots. None of them raised their voices despite the distance between them. With their mark hearing, volume wasn't necessary. "I would expect him to be first."

"He certainly wouldn't be last. That's Molenaar's place."

"I see him." Edwards's voice was low, filled with curiosity. "But he's not coming this way."

Eve and Richens joined him. They watched the blond Mark slip furtively along a shadowed wall a couple of streets down, then turn a corner and disappear from sight.

"He's tracking," Eve murmured.

"We have to follow him without alerting the others," Richens said.

Her brows rose. The rest of the class was crawling all over the building now. "And just exactly how are we supposed to do that?"

He gestured over his shoulder. "There's a fire escape over there."

Eve froze. "Very funny. How old is that thing? How many years has it gone without maintenance?"

"How many hours do you want to spend in this shit heap?" he countered. "We could be celebrating by noon, if we bag the faery now."

"No way." She retreated even farther from the edge.

"Why are you so—?" He gaped as comprehension dawned. "You're afraid of heights? Crap. Is there anything you're *not* afraid of?"

"You. I can take you. Don't push me."

Edwards laughed.

Richens scowled. "Come on, Hollis. Get over it."

"It's not a contest. Let's get the others and do this right." Foreboding weighed heavily in her gut, a sort of sixth sense she'd had her whole life. Right now it was ringing the alarm loud and clear.

"No way. They're idiots. We were the ones smart enough to have a workable plan."

She backed up. "I'm not risking my life for your ego."

"Risk it for your soul, then."

Eve snorted. Frankly, she wasn't hanging off a rusty fire escape for that.

When she didn't budge, Richens made an impatient

gesture and set off toward the fire escape. Edwards hesitated a moment, then followed. Eve didn't waver. She left the roof and took the stairs. Gripping the railing, she hurtled down the three flights, passing Claire with a brief wave. Izzie was nowhere to be seen.

Eve hit the sidewalk at a run, but despite her speed, Richens and Edwards were at least a block ahead of her. Just as her brain kicked its way past her competitive drive and asked, *Why are you so into this?*, the mark kicked in, too, pumping the heat of the chase through her veins and urging her into a swifter gait. There was no labored breathing, no throbbing pulse. The lack of physical stress allowed feelings of euphoria and omnipotence to take precedence, inspiring false courage and confidence.

"I'm just watching out for them," she muttered to herself, skidding around a corner in time to see a glass door swinging from recent use. "Good Samaritan and all that."

The building was long and squat, its exterior a shiny silver metallic reminiscent of a 1950s Airstream trailer. Above the entrance, a crooked and faded sign read Flo's Five and Diner.

Eve went in with gun drawn, hissing as her armband burned her skin. Cracked and torn red vinyl booths lined the wall beneath the many grimy windows. Plastic food on plates decorated tabletops and the counter. Two mannequins in pink and white uniform dresses stood at the coffeemaker and the register, respectively. Lifting to her tiptoes, Eve peered through the opening to the kitchen but saw nothing at all.

Had they run out the back?

She continued cautiously, one step at a time. Her next step hit the ground wrong and she lost her footing, skidding atop something on the ground. Grabbing for the back of a barstool, she nearly fell as it swiveled under her grip. She glanced down, saw that she'd slipped on an armband, and guessed that Richens had lost his short temper over the annoyance.

A shout followed by a crash rent the air.

A dark shape flew past the food service window. Eve dropped to a crouch. A hand touched her biceps and she caught it, yanking hard. Claire tumbled into her lap. The Frenchwoman shrieked at the same moment pots banged wildly against each other. Clamping a hand over Claire's mouth, Eve strained to hear.

"Let him go, lovey," Richens cooed.

"Make me, darlin'," purred a sweet feminine voice.

Claire tensed.

With a narrowed look of warning, Eve pushed Claire up to a kneeling position. *Go around back,* she mouthed. The Frenchwoman nodded and crab-walked awkwardly to the front door. Eve waited until she was gone, breathing in the smell of mold and dust, her emotions fluctuating from excitement to dismay.

Part of her was enjoying the hunt.

You're losing your mind, she told herself, crawling the length of the counter to its end. Peeking around the corner, she saw the aluminum swinging door to the kitchen. The quilted surface and round glass window were covered in grime. Through the two-inch gap at the bottom, Eve searched for shadows that would betray movement on the other side, but all she saw was darkness. She moved closer.

We could be celebrating by noon, Richens had said.

Who was the faery holding hostage? Ken? Edwards?

There should be three Marks in there. Where was the third man?

"Come any closer," the faery said, "and he gets it."

"He 'gets it'?" Richens laughed. "What rubbish."

"Shut your mouth, Richens!" Ken gasped. "This knife is jaggy."

Eve paused a moment, surprised to learn that it was Ken who was captive. She was further astonished when she pushed the swinging door open a couple of inches and took in the enfolding situation courtesy of her nictitating lenses.

Richens stood with his back to her. Two yards in front of him, Ken was kneeling. Behind Ken, a portly and kindly faced woman with gray hair hovered gracefully, supported by impossibly tiny wings.

It was one of Sleeping Beauty's faery godmothers; cherry red cheeks, pastel dress, and pointed hat included.

Unsure of whether to laugh or freak out, Eve surveyed the rest of the kitchen. It was staged as if the owners had walked outside for a short break. Pots and pans sat on the stove, knives and cutting boards littered the island. She looked for Edwards and found him prone on the floor, unconscious. Her feelings of unease increased. The sight of an unmoving body on the filthy ground was just too realistic for her tastes.

How far would this simulation go? What was the best way to bring it to an end?

Ken's eyes were wide, his neck arched away from the blade pressed against his skin. "What do you want?" he bit out.

"You're coming with me, toots." The faery smiled and the result was so sweet-looking and innocuous, Eve had a hard time reconciling it with the reality of the knife in her chubby little hand. "We are going to slip out the back and make our getaway."

"You're not going anywhere." Richens's voice held a chilling amusement. "I'll shoot him before I let you walk out of here."

A dark cloud moved over the faery's features, briefly revealing the horror of her demonic soul. An Infernal could never be tamed or trusted. But they could be understood. They were similar to infants—self-centered, impatient, ravenous for attention and stimuli.

The faery made a *tsk*ing noise. "You should have crossed over to the dark side, sugar. You would have made a great Infernal."

Eve took aim and shot Richens in the ass.

He screamed like a girl. The gun fell from his hand and hit the floor, firing a bullet into a cast-iron skillet hanging on a pot rack above the stove. The bullet ricocheted, squealing through the air and waking Edwards, who bolted upright. His upthrust head smacked the underside of a cutting board whose edge protruded beyond the lip of the island. The knives atop the board leaped into the air. They spun and twisted, then fell to the counter in a deadly riot. They skidded across the surface as a single writhing mass, hitting a small metal canister and sending it toppling over the side. It struck Edwards on the crown of his head, dumping its contents over him before rolling to the floor with a resounding *gong*. The resulting cloud of flour billowed outward, expanding in unison with Edwards's choked curses.

Ken tossed the startled faery from his back, sending her careening into a tailspin. She crashed into the overhanging rack, her "Oh, shit!" muffled by the stockpot that fell from its perch and dropped over her head. She toppled to the floor with a substantial thud, landing still as death.

Richens was still screaming. Ken lunged to his feet and hit him with a perfect right hook. The Mark crumpled to the floor beside the faery, knocked out.

"Arsemonger," Ken muttered.

His gaze met Eve's. She looked at Edwards, who resembled Casper the Friendly Ghost or an uncooked corn dog, depending on the turn of his head. His eyes were two blinking black holes in an otherwise white face, his mouth a round "O" as he stared at the two prone bodies on the ground.

Eve's brain caught up to the series of events.

The screaming hadn't stopped. It had just moved outside.

"Claire," she breathed.

She jumped over the unconscious bodies and sprinted out the service door. For a split second, her nictitating lenses hindered her sight, then she retracted them with a deliberate blink.

Claire stood in the center of the narrow alley, her beautiful features frozen into a mask of terror. Her mouth was wide and a hideous wailing poured out. Her eyes were locked on a spot beyond Eve's shoulder, and madness stirred in the cerulean depths. Eve turned her head, her gaze following the Frenchwoman's line of sight.

She choked, then stumbled, the world spinning. Ken's tall form emerged from the unlit kitchen, his head turning to align with theirs.

"Holy mother of God," he gasped.

Pinned to the exterior wall of the diner was Molenaar's body. Arms splayed and hands affixed to the metal facade with iron nails through the palms. Urine soaked his pants and puddled on the crumbling asphalt. His sightless eyes gazed heavenward, his mouth lax and lips spattered with crimson. A circlet of rusted barbed wire hugged his head, completing the sick re-creation of the Crucifixion.

Where was the blood . . . ?

"*Sa tête est—*" Claire doubled over, but no vomit came up, her body too perfect to succumb to her emotions.

It was then that Eve realized Molenaar's head had been severed from his body. It was held in place above his neck by nails staked through his ears.

Terror chilled her fevered skin.

Eve screamed, her fists clenching even as her knees weakened.

A flock of seagulls joined them, screeching to the sky and the God who allowed such things to happen to those who served him.

CHAPTER 9

Reed pulled off Highway 1, the fabled Pacific Coast Highway, at the Fremont Boulevard exit. A moment later his rented Porsche was purring across Fort McCroskey.

He could have been with Eve already if he'd shifted directly to her, but he knew Raguel too well. The archangel would have his students holed up together with no chance of privacy. That was fine for training. It wasn't fine for dealing with the turmoil Reed sensed in Eve.

Through their handler/Mark connection, he felt her alienation from the rest of her class and sensed that she was dealing with it by shutting herself off emotionally. She was running on autopilot and that was dangerous for a Mark. He suspected he'd need to get her away from the strain of her classmates before she would relax enough to talk about what was troubling her. Hence the need for wheels.

The fact that the car was also a babe magnet was a bonus. Eve had been attracted to Cain and his Harley. It wasn't a stretch to hope that she might find the 911 Turbo Cabriolet a turn-on, too. With a top speed just shy of two hundred miles an hour, Reed hoped to open the throttle on both the engine and Eve's stress.

Using his connection to Eve as an inner tracking device, Reed maneuvered across the base. Raguel would want a report on the trip to Australia, then the archangel would try to make Reed leave, which wasn't going to happen. He wasn't going anywhere while there was any hazard to Eve's well-being.

Although he would never admit it, he was still reeling from losing her last week. Seeing Cain broken had only added to the surreal quality of his torment. All his life, he had wanted to see his older brother humbled by something. *Anything*. Yet he'd discovered that losing Eve to accomplish that aim was too high a price to pay.

He had handled countless female Marks over the centuries, sharing a connection with them as deep as the one he shared with Eve, yet she was the only one with whom he'd ever felt so conflicted.

She blamed his fascination on the animosity between him and Cain. She said he was only interested in her because she represented an opportunity to hurt his brother. But they both knew that wasn't true. Reed wished it was. Everything would be so much easier that way.

Rounding a bend in the road, he slowed as he came upon the duplex with the unmarked white van in the driveway. The license frame read *Gadara Enterprises*. Reed pulled into the vacant spot beside it. He didn't need to knock on the door to know that no one was home. He felt the yawning vacancy before he turned off the engine.

Reed exited the car and set off on foot, walking in Eve's wake. As he passed the house, he noted the shattered partition by the entrance of the far side of the duplex. The mess looked fresh and gave him pause.

The first wave of terror hit Reed with enough force to hinder his stride. The second rolled over him like thunder, building in tension until it exploded with such force that he began to run. The leather soles of his Gucci moccasins gained little purchase. He shifted in midsprint and materialized beside Eve.

She was screaming. A quick glance at the building she faced told him why. Reed snatched her close, snapped open his wings, and surged into the air. Airborne, he held her tightly, containing her struggles.

"Shh." His arms wrapped completely around her slim body. "I'm here."

"Reed." She clutched at him, her face buried in his neck, her tears sliding across his skin.

He alighted onto the neighboring rooftop and retracted his wings, but didn't release her. Her fear, grief, and horror pulsed through him in rhythmic beats that left him unable to erect the barriers he used with his other Marks.

And the feel of her . . . the smell of her . . . It had been weeks since he'd touched her.

He had been *forbidden* to touch her.

"D-did you s-see?" She pulled back to stare up at him with tear-filled eyes.

"Yes." He didn't tell her that she would inevitably see much worse.

"I can't do this."

And in that moment, Reed didn't want her to, which screwed up everything—his ambitions, goals, and dreams. They all hinged on keeping her around. And he wanted her again, damn it. His entire body was hard for her.

Along with every-fucking-thing else, he was obsessed. How the hell was he supposed to get over that, if even a dead Mark and her terror couldn't diminish it?

"Help me get out," she begged.

His forehead dropped to rest against hers, which was hot and damp.

Shit. Deep shit.

Her fingertips dug into the muscles framing his spine. "Say something, damn you!"

Inhaling sharply, he slipped into the tried and true lines he always used to calm skittish Marks. "I know this is tough for you. But think of the good works you will do, the people you will save—"

"Like him?" Eve gestured viciously at the alleyway below. "Isn't that what he was told, too? What about his good works? What about the people he was supposed to save? Are they just as fucked as he is now?"

"Eve . . ."

She shoved him away. "Tough for me? That's all you've got to say? Some propaganda bullshit? There is a dead man down there. Without . . . his . . . head!"

"Give me a break, Eve," he snapped, angrier with himself than with her. "I'm trying to help."

"Try harder."

Her lithe form vibrated with her inner turmoil. She was covered in jeans, shirt, and sweater jacket. Her hair was in a simple ponytail that accentuated the exotic tilt of her eyes. Her face was devoid of makeup, allowing the porcelain perfection of her Asian skin to take the stage.

Reed struggled with his attraction to her, a magnetism that started in his gut and worked its way out. Having been surrounded by brunettes for centuries, his first exposure to blondes had spurred a fascination with fair-haired beauties like Sara. Yet here he was, fighting an itch that wouldn't quit over a woman who looked nothing like his "type."

"What kind of training is this?" Eve rubbed her eyes with her fists. "No one said anyone was going to *die*!"

"Accidents happen, rarely. Overzealous and frightened Marks are unpredictable. But never like this. Never murder."

The sky darkened as clouds rolled in so fast they appeared to be on fast-forward. The breeze turned chilly, whipping the long strands of Eve's hair across her face. Reed watched her frame stiffen and her fists clench. He shifted to the edge of the roof and looked down at the scene unfolding beneath them.

Raguel hovered several feet above the ground, his arms and wings spread wide. His head was back, his eyes glowing gold and trained heavenward. His mouth was open in a silent scream. It was a riveting sight, both eerie and beautiful.

As Eve drew abreast of Reed, her hand pushed into his. She leaned over cautiously, her balance maintained by her death grip on him.

"What is he doing?" she asked, her voice ripped away by the furious wind.

"Lamenting. Sharing his grief with the Lord."

"I have something to share with the Lord," she muttered. "A piece of my mind."

Thunder cracked, booming through the dark gray sky.

"Watch it," Reed admonished, squeezing her hand in warning.

"Did the faery do this?"

"Faery?"

Eve pulled wind-whipped strands of hair out of her mouth. "The Infernal we were hunting in this exercise."

"You always blame us first."

Reed turned to face the speaker. So did Eve.

A dour-faced woman with gray hair that matched her gray suit stood just outside the stairwell door. Her laser-bright eyes told him she was an Infernal a second before the scent of her decaying soul did. She was staring at his hand holding Eve's, which seemed to remind Eve of the connection. She tugged her hand free.

Eve shouted to be heard above the storm. "Don't get pissy. It's a valid question."

"Pox on you." The Infernal approached with a pigeon-toed stride that did much to mitigate the intimidating force of her glower. Her details weren't visible, but her accent and haggard appearance suggested that she was a Welsh gwyllion—a demon known for its ability to inspire trust and confidence while leading mortals directly into danger. "We're out here in this dump, playing your idiotic war games, training assassins how to kill our kind. Yet every time something goes wrong, we are the first to be blamed."

A bark of laughter escaped Reed. He couldn't help it. A self-righteous Infernal? Now he'd seen everything.

Eve stared at the gwyllion for a long moment, then

she started forward, her steps deliberate and unwavering. "That's total crap. You're not here out of the goodness of your rotten soul. You're here because you can't be wherever you would really like to be and you want to save your damned hide."

The demon halted and crossed her arms. "That doesn't mean you should accuse us first!"

Pointing toward the alley, Eve asked, "Doesn't that look like Infernal handiwork to you?"

The dourness faded into a broad smile. "It's brilliant, that much is true. So precisely rendered and creative."

"I have a loaded gun." Eve aimed it at the demon. "Perhaps you might reconsider your admiration?"

The gwyllion's merriment faded instantly. "Quite right. Terrible. Only a sicko could have done something so heinous."

"Who?"

"Wasn't me."

"Make a guess."

Reed held his tongue, watching Eve work, noting the stubborn set of her chin and determined glint in her eyes. She didn't know her own strengths, at least not when they applied to her marking. The selfish part of him smiled, thinking that maybe she could manage to accept the calling without becoming jaded and hardened. Maybe she would learn to take pride in her accomplishments and find something worthy in what she was doing, some positive amid all the negative. Maybe she would become a believer and find her faith.

Miracles were known to happen in his line of work.

The wind died down and the clouds separated. In the wake of the abrupt storm, silence reigned. The air was heavy with uncustomary humidity. It was oppressive, reflective of the confusion, horror, and sorrow that permeated their immediate vicinity.

"There are three of us working this training session," the gwyllion said. "Griselda, Bernard, and me."

"And you are?"

"I'm Aeronwen."

"That's . . . lovely," Eve said grudgingly.

Reed grinned. "It's derived from the name of the Celtic goddess of carnage and slaughter."

"Why do these things keep surprising me?"

"I like it." Aeronwen beamed.

"Of course. Griselda is the faery?"

"No, Bernard is the faery. Did you like the godmother glamour? He's so fun like that."

"A laugh a minute. What's Griselda?"

Raguel appeared at the edge of the roof, levitating over the lip and landing beside Eve. He pointed to the shacklike protrusion that shielded the stairs from the elements. Eve's sharp inhalation told Reed that she saw the dragon peering around the corner.

"Great," she muttered. "My favorite type of demon."

"Hello, Raguel," Reed greeted.

"Did she herald you?" the archangel asked.

"No."

"Then why are you here?"

Reed arched a brow in an expression that asked, *Do you really want to talk about that here and now?*

Raguel nodded. "You frightened the others with your abduction of Ms. Hollis."

A shrug was Reed's reply. The other Marks were Raguel's concern.

The archangel's gaze passed over the two Infernals, then settled on Eve. Deep grooves framed his lips and eyes. He could hide them, if he wished, but he chose not to. "What are you doing, Ms. Hollis?"

Eve felt her mouth curve, although she found nothing at all humorous about the mess that was her life.

"Freaking out. Losing my mind. Take your pick." Outwardly she probably looked composed, maybe even serene. But the knuckles of her gun hand were beginning to hurt from the force of her grip and the set of her shoulders was causing a crick in her neck. She was still screaming, even if no one could hear it.

"You should be with the others."

"No, I should be in Orange County. Designing the interior of someone's dream house. Looking out my windows and considering hitting the beach. Reminding myself to get my car washed and speed-dialing Mrs. Basso to see if she needs anything from the store." Her foot tapped rhythmically into the gravel. "But I can't do that, because she's dead. And the poodle is dead. And now Molenaar is dead. I'm sick of people dying around me, Gadara."

"Let me deal with this."

"What are you going to do? Make us pack up our toys and go home?" She made a sweeping gesture with both arms, causing the two Infernals to duck below the arc of the gun. "This is a perfect training exercise. We have something to hunt down and slaughter. You couldn't have planned it better if you tried."

Gadara stared hard at her. It took everything Eve had to hold his golden gaze. He was a handsome and elegant man, but when enhanced by the full force of his divine gifts, he was blindingly beautiful. His dark skin like silk, his features finely wrought by a deft and loving hand. "This is far beyond your limited training, Ms. Hollis."

"So we learn as we go."

"It is against protocol. You know that."

"I also know that it's 'perfectly acceptable to continue a deviation once it has been set in motion.'" She shrugged out of her sweater jacket, switching her gun from hand to hand until the garment fell away from her overheated body. "Isn't that what you said when you assigned me to hunt tengu and travel to Upland before I was trained?"

"If proceeding is the only reasonable course," he added. "Remaining here is far from reasonable."

"I agree with him, Eve," Reed said, his voice smooth and dark. Comforting, even when contradicting her.

Eve tried not to look at him, knowing it would just make her even hotter, but she lost the battle. He stood with his hands thrust into the pockets of his tailored black slacks, his pale yellow dress shirt sans tie and open at the throat. The wind ruffled his dark hair, draping the locks across his brow. Like his brother, he watched her with a predator's stare, hungry and determined.

He held her gaze. If he'd touched her, it couldn't have felt more real. In some ways, the brothers were very much alike. In others, they couldn't be more different. One warmed her with a slow, steady burn. The other ignited a scorching fire.

With Alec the world stilled, external concerns faded away. She enjoyed him as she would a fine wine, with delicate sips and limitless time. With Reed her response was like a runaway train, increasing in velocity until she was breathless and reckless.

Eve looked away, rolling her shoulders to ease the knotting there.

"We are vacating the base," Gadara said.

"What if that was the goal of the attack?"

"Why?"

"I don't know, but it's a possibility."

"A far-reaching one," Reed interjected. "And regardless, it's too dangerous for you to be here."

Gadara continued to watch her intensely. "I have already ordered an investigative team up here. They are far more qualified and are therefore at less risk."

Eve knew she couldn't argue with that. She also knew that doing nothing at all wasn't an option. "Will you let us participate in the investigation from the safety of the tower? Studying evidence or whatever else can be done?"

A hint of a smile touched the archangel's mouth, but she was too upset about Molenaar to chafe over playing into Gadara's hands. So what if she was determined to participate? That didn't mean she was married to the idea of being a Mark.

"I am certain something can be arranged," Gadara said magnanimously.

Reed gestured for Eve to head toward the stairs. "I'll take the class back to the house."

Gadara nodded. "You can record your report and transfer it to my desk."

"I'll be sticking around awhile."

"That will not be necessary."

"You haven't heard my report."

Eve frowned. "You're worried about something else?"

He caught her elbow as she came closer and started to escort her off the roof. "I'll tell you later."

There was no way to avoid inhaling the unique scent of his skin. It was musky, exotic, seductive. It flowed through her senses, creating tingles where she didn't need them and aches where she didn't want them. The heat of his touch burned through her shirt to her flesh. Sweat dotted her upper lip. Her body remembered the feel of his. Craved to feel it again.

Reed glanced at her. She kept her own line of vision firmly on the ground. He opened the rooftop door and she was about to step inside when something long, gray, and quick darted past her booted foot.

Eve yelped. The rat stilled halfway down the stairs. It turned its head, staring at her with teeny beaded eyes.

Are you screaming 'cuz of me? it asked.

A mental shudder rolled through her. The sight of the rodent's long, ribbed tail was revolting. She swallowed back her disgust and asked, "Did you see anything when you were up there?"

Rearing up on its rear legs, the rat made a noise suspiciously like a laugh. *I scared ya. Gotta love newbies.*

She aimed her gun. Reed chuckled and lounged into the stairwell railing.

Take it easy, doll, the rat said hastily. *Where's your sense of humor?*

"What's your name?"

A loud screeching was his reply.

Eve cut him off with a wave of her hand. "Okay, let's call you Templeton."

What kind of name is that?

"A rat's name."

"*Charlotte's Web,*" Reed murmured.

Startled that he would know such trivia, Eve looked at him with a widening smile. "I'm impressed."

Who is Charlotte? Templeton barked.

"Never mind," Eve dismissed. "Did you see anything on the roof?"

Nope. Nada.

"You're lying."

Prove it.

"Come on," she cajoled, firmly squelching the voice in her mind that shouted, *You're talking to a* rat*!* "You had to see something."

It's not true.

"What's not true?" She glanced at Reed, who shrugged and grinned boyishly, the combination briefly distracting her. She cursed her raging libido, which seemed to be fueled by her low-grade fever.

What they say about rats. Templeton's whiskers twitched in a manner that seemed . . . affronted. *It's pigs who squeal, the miserable bastards. They'll do anything for food.*

"I like pigs. They're useful. They make bacon and ham. What have you got to offer?"

Entertainment?

She waved the gun carelessly. "I have to be honest, it's not looking so good for you right now, Templeton. You're giving me the willies, not information."

You'd shoot an innocent rat? Man, that's low.

"Gimme something, then."

Did you see the lip around the roof? It's at least three feet high. I couldn't see shit.

Eve considered that. "What did you hear?"

Struggling. Gurgling. Hammering.

She swallowed hard. "That's not helpful."

Templeton dropped back down on all fours. *Told ya. Can I go now?*

Her gaze shot to Reed. He raised both brows and

straightened. The air around him stirred, causing his scent to waft to her. She changed her line of questioning. "Did you *smell* anything?"

Nope. Nada.

"I don't believe you."

Templeton looked at Reed. *Tough crowd, Abel. You sure she's worth the effort?*

Reed looked at Eve, his dark eyes soft. "She's worth it."

Eve forcibly ignored the physical response she had to his tone and words. "You're a rat, Templeton—"

You're brilliant.

"—which means you have a great sense of smell. You can tell me what kind of Infernal did . . . *that.*"

Templeton shook his head. *I didn't smell anything but Mark.*

Her head tilted to the side. "I could maybe see that if there was blood everywhere, but there isn't any."

Right, doll. So you tell me . . . No blood to stink up the air and a killer exerting himself strenuously, but all I could smell was Mark. How is that possible?

"What are you—" Reed's hand came to rest at the small of her back. She swallowed hard. "Are you saying there wasn't an Infernal down there when Molenaar was killed?"

Seems that way.

The chill in her gut spread. "Then who did it?"

Templeton's whiskers twitched. *That's the question, isn't it?*

"Who was the last person tae see Molenaar?" Ken asked, his gaze raking over the other Marks.

They were waiting in the men's side of the duplex

for Gadara to return from Anytown and the tension was thick as fog. Eve stood on the open threshold between the dining and living rooms. Reed leaned a shoulder into the wall beside her, a causal pose she knew was only a facade. She was unusually antsy, with a simmering need to *move*. The itch to leap into offensive action crawled over her skin like a thousand tiny ants.

The smell of mold and decay in the house was more pronounced now, almost oppressively so. The weak rays of sunlight shining through the windows showcased every flaw the moonlight had concealed: the stained and warped hardwood floors, the crumbling walls, the scuffed baseboards. The air was choked with the proliferation of dust that swirled around them like tendrils of smoke. Eve found herself becoming more agitated by the moment.

Inside her mind, Reed murmured words she couldn't understand in a soothing tone. Their connection was too weak to convey more than impressions, but she got the gist. He wanted her to take it down a notch. She was hot and irritable, and she wanted to cry but her eyes were dry as bone.

"Well?" Ken demanded, looking oddly fierce in his ski cap, like a bank-robbing felon. "The last time I saw him was when we entered Anytown. I went tae the left. I saw Hollis, Edwards, and Richens go intae the office building. Who went tae the right with Molenaar?"

Claire raised her hand. She stood with feet wide and arm wrapped around her waist in a defensive posture that belied the aggressive tilt of her chin. "I did, in the beginning. We separated when I entered a video rental store. He continued without me."

"What time was that?"

"Half past eight?" She muttered something in French. "Maybe eight. What does it matter?"

"What about you?" Ken directed his question to Romeo.

"I was with Laurel."

Ken stared a moment at the pretty Kiwi, who looked chagrined and might have blushed if she wasn't a Mark. "You two make me sick," he bit out.

Laurel blinked, then recovered. "Fuck you, Callaghan."

"Isnae that what he was doing?" Ken jerked his chin toward Romeo. "While Molenaar was losing his head, you two were houghmagandying on a training mission!"

"You didn't save him either," Laurel snapped. "What were *you* doing?"

"Where was Seiler?" Edwards interjected.

"She was following us," Eve said.

"I was not!" Izzie protested.

"You came onto the scene awfully quick," Eve drawled, deliberately goading.

"I am fast. That's all. I do not care about what you are doing. You have problems if you think I would."

"Since you and Richens keep contradicting each other, it's clear that one of you is a liar. Which one of you is it?"

"I am confused," Romeo said, frowning.

Izzie palmed her blade and spoke with dangerous softness. "Do not call me a liar."

Eve crossed her arms. "We don't have time for these games you and Richens are playing. Until one of you admits that you told me a lie, I'm not going to believe either of you."

"Sod off, Hollis," Richens bit out. "My arse still hurts, you know. I told you to pick the knife!"

"I shot you on purpose," she said wryly.

Reed's hand touched her elbow. She caught his frown and shrugged it off.

Ken stepped closer. "What are you talking about, Hollis? What lies?"

"They know what I'm talking about. Let's go back to what happened to Molenaar. Did anyone else notice the lack of Infernal stench around Molenaar's body?"

A stillness came over the group, then a cluster of protests. Eve cut them all off with a wave of her hand. "I understand you were all freaked out. I am, too, but we need to stop thinking about how we feel about this and do something about it instead."

"I didnae smell anything but Mark blood," Ken said.

The others quickly concurred.

"Right." Eve's gaze raked over everyone, searching. "So what does that mean?"

"We weren't paying attention?" Edwards suggested gruffly.

"Or maybe the only thing to smell was Mark. Maybe there was never an Infernal there."

"You accuse one of us?" Romeo cried, dark eyes wide. *"Sei matta! Come puoi dire una cosa del genere?"*

"I have no idea what he said," Laurel snapped. "But I agree!"

Reed's grip on her arm tightened. "Come with me." He dragged her toward the door.

"She is lying," Izzie said with a smile in her voice. "I think it was the faery."

Pausing, Reed faced them. "Leave this matter to Raguel and his team."

"If there's a traitor among us," Richens said, "we have a lot to worry about."

Reed snapped his fingers at the two guards standing watch just outside the front door. "No one leaves."

Without waiting for their acquiescence, he yanked Eve down the steps and away.

CHAPTER 10

Eve stumbled after Reed as they rounded the driveway corner and stepped out of sight. He tugged her around the hedges that separated the duplex driveway from the drive next door and faced her, scowling. "What are you doing?"

"Talking."

"Bullshit. You're instigating infighting on purpose."

"I have a really good reason," she said. "Maybe they'll wake up and smell the stench."

"You aren't in any position to train others."

"This is just a game to them. Richens acts as if we're playing for points and not lives. Ken chose brass knuckles for his weapon. Brass-fucking-knuckles, against Infernals? And Romeo and Laurel were *screwing* for christsakes—*ow!*" She glared at the sky and rubbed her mark through her armband. "That doesn't count!"

Reed's mouth thinned into a disapproving line. "You

should be working together, not fighting among yourselves. You know none of them did it."

"Says who?" she challenged, spoiling for a fight. "We can't rule anyone out. We need to be looking very closely at everything and everyone around us. We can't afford any blind spots."

"Marks don't do shit like this, Eve! They're not capable of it."

"And demons don't exist. Sometimes what we think is an absolute truth is completely false." Eve stabbed a finger viciously toward the house. "They have to step outside of the cocoon they're living in and face facts. You can't trust anyone, and if you turn your back, don't be surprised to find a knife in it."

He growled. "Not the conspiracy theory again."

"Gadara has wiretaps in my condo and cameras on every floor of my building. You think he doesn't have Anytown scoped out?" Eve ripped off the Velcro-secured armband. "We're all wearing these. They're supposed to simulate a call, but I would be willing to bet they have GPS locaters in them and maybe bugs, too."

"Will you listen to yourself? You're nuts, and you're driving me nuts, too. Gadara wouldn't let a Mark *die,* Eve."

"Why? Because he's an archangel?"

"Because losing a Mark during training looks bad," he bit out, his powerful frame taut with frustration. "Really, really bad. It will take Raguel centuries to regain the standing he lost today."

Eve's hands went to her hips. "Then why didn't he stop it from happening?"

A muscle in Reed's jaw ticced. He knelt down to get

the armband. "You're leaping to conclusions based on assumptions. Look—" he straightened and snapped the metal plate of the band in half, "—there's nothing in here. It's solid. Raguel's running on full power now; he doesn't need secular electronics. These are for your benefit. The pressure on your arm keeps you focused and the metal gives Raguel a concentrated area to heat."

"Are you telling me there's no way Gadara could have known about the attack and prevented it?"

"He's an archangel. Not God."

"I don't see how—"

"Do you think he's evil?" Reed demanded, shoving the destroyed band into his pocket. "Is that what this boils down to? You think he watched your classmate getting butchered on a live feed and ate popcorn?"

She rubbed at the bead of sweat that ran down her nape. Said in that manner, it did sound implausible. "No."

"Everything happens for a reason." His voice softened. "You have to believe that."

"I *don't* believe, Reed. I'm agnostic."

"You're a pain in the ass." He caught her face in his hands and tilted it up. With his thumbs brushing over her cheekbones, he examined her. "Shit. You're burning up. Why didn't you say anything?"

"I did say something," she groused, "to both Gadara and Alec. One says it's all in my head, the other says it's just my body adjusting to the mark."

He snarled something in a foreign language. Eve meant to ask what it was but was distracted by the feel of his touch, which cooled her. The scent of his skin filled her nostrils, altering the tension that gripped her from anger to something far more dangerous.

She caught his wrists and tried to pull his hands away. "Uh . . . Maybe you shouldn't touch me right now."

"No wonder you're so combative," he said roughly. "The Novium is on you."

"You sure that's what it is?" Her voice was a whisper, her throat clogged by the images that filled her mind of *him* on her.

"Oh, yeah. No doubt." He released her abruptly. His gaze was sharp . . . and frighteningly fervent. "You're crawling out of your skin. Marks don't reach this stage until much later, but you're primed like a veteran."

Her hand lifted to her face, coming to rest over the spot where he had touched her. The skin tingled and was cooler. "Why?"

"You were made for this work, babe. It's just that simple."

"No, I wasn't. You said it yourself; I wouldn't be here if Alec had kept his dick in his pants."

"I said that to fuck with you and get you pissed off at Cain."

"This isn't me," Eve argued. She couldn't face days on end of this job. She would lose her sanity. "Remember? I'm the one who screams at the idiots in horror movies who grab a weapon and pursue the maniacal killer instead of running for help."

The negating shake of his head infuriated her as much as if he had covered his ears with his hands.

"I didn't commit a sin worthy of being marked," she insisted. "This is all just a monumental fuck-up to punish your brother."

"You know how many mortal women have fucked Cain?" Reed's smile was tinged with malice. "And of those, how many of them have ended up where you are now?"

Her chin lifted. "He loves me. I can be used to hurt him. That's the difference."

"You want to toss around theories and conjecture?" He advanced. "Let's take it further. What if Cain is in this mess because of you, instead of the reverse? I've been watching you, babe. You're a natural. What if you two met because you have the inherent skill to rival him and no one else could mentor you as well as he can?"

"That's r-ridiculous."

"No, that's a possibility." His quiet conviction sent a chill down her spine. "You've survived demons no untrained Mark should have."

Eve took a step forward. Reed's suggestion pounded through her skull like a migraine. Her skin and muscles ached as if she had the flu. Even the roots of her hair tingled with a prickling that maddened her. *Don't kill the messenger,* or so the saying went. But she wanted to. Unease slid sinuously around her insides, hissing like a serpent. "I love how you all conveniently forget that I was *dead* just a few days ago!"

A visible shudder moved through him.

That telltale sign devastated her. With everything around her unfamiliar and hostile, what she longed for most was something familiar. Someone who cared for her.

Her arm lifted toward him. "Reed—"

He turned away, his shoulders set against her. "I can feel the heat of the Novium moving through you. It's making me . . . edgy and agitated."

"I'm sorry."

"I need to stay away from you while you're like this, Eve."

She realized then that her bloodlust was translating into a different kind of lust, which created an entirely new problem on top of all the others. She could fight her fascination for Reed, but not his returning fascination for her. "Does that mean you're leaving?"

"I can't," he said gruffly. "Not yet."

Eve would have asked why, but she had a more pressing question. "What *is* the Novium, exactly?"

Reed looked over his shoulder at her. "A change, similar to the change you went through when you were marked. Over time, a mentor and Mark pair become connected. Emotionally and mentally. They learn to think and move as one unit. When the time comes for the Mark to work alone, that bond has to be severed. Cauterized. Some Marks call it 'the Heat' instead, due the fever that accompanies the process."

"Bond," she repeated, "like you and I share? But I can't feel Alec's thoughts and feelings like I do yours."

"There hasn't been time. Neither of you has been trained. You haven't hunted together. The connection has yet to grow."

"And now it won't?"

He shook his head.

"And what about my connection to you? Will that go away, too?"

"No. It's a rite of passage—similar to leaving a father's household for a husband's. The handler/Mark link grows during the Heat, as does the Mark's connection to his firm leader."

"Gadara."

"In your case, yes."

"Boy, that sure works out for him, doesn't it?" She watched the confusion drift over his handsome features, his train of thought following hers.

"It doesn't work that way. It's not vulnerable to manipulation."

Eve rounded him so that they faced each other again. The transition was akin to stepping out of a cool house into sweltering desert heat. Her temperature shot up to an alarming degree, making her dizzy. "Tell me how it works."

His gaze was as hot as she was. But when he spoke, his voice was calm and sure. "A Mark is trained. Then exposed to missions. They witness deaths and battle various Infernals. They absorb information from their mentors. Somehow, that combination eventually sets off the Novium."

"Okay. Let's see." She started counting down on her fingers. "I've been exposed to missions. I've witnessed deaths and battled various Infernals. And I have a romantic relationship with my mentor. Good enough?"

"You're forgetting time."

"Maybe it's not so much time as it is a buildup," she speculated. "I've had everything thrown at me at once, then I was killed and resurrected, which has to mess with a person, right?"

"Right, which exonerates Raguel."

"Not necessarily, since he's the one who sent me on the missions to begin with. Plus, he's been suspiciously stubborn about acknowledging my present condition."

"There's so much more to this than that, such as how you met Cain and how you were killed. Raguel didn't have a hand in any of that."

"I'm not saying he orchestrated this thing from the very beginning, but once he realized how it had been set up, he could have manipulated things from there. If I'm more connected to him than I am to Alec, it benefits him exclusively."

Growling, Reed ran both hands through his thick hair. "What do these paranoid delusions have to do with your classmate dying?"

Eve studied him, noting the fine sheen of perspiration that glistened on the skin of his throat. She would guess it was no more than fifty-eight degrees in Monterey today, but they were sweating as if it were double that temperature. If she concentrated hard, she could feel the morass of thoughts and emotions roiling within him.

"Answer me, Eve!"

She shook her head, trying to dissipate the ethereal connection to him that was making it hard for her to think. Instead she lost her balance and fell into him. Jolted by the collision with something so hard and solid, she gasped and clutched at him. The sudden surge of cooling relief she felt was so astonishing and so welcome that she sobbed her gratitude.

"Babe . . ." His arms tightened around her and his lips pressed to her sticky forehead.

She stammered over her dry tongue, "How l-long does this l-last?"

"The Novium usually begins during a hunt," he murmured, "and ends with the kill. A few days, usually."

"Days!" Her nails dug into his skin through his shirt. "It hasn't even been one yet and I'm sick of it."

"This is supposed to happen in the field, where it actually helps a Mark by imparting confidence and fearlessness. Without the culmination of a kill, I don't know how long it will last, and since you're restrained, all that energy and bloodlust has nowhere to go."

It was going somewhere all right. To intimate places on her body. The familiar and longed-for sensation of his embrace only exacerbated her condition. "Touching you helps," she whispered.

"It's killing me."

Her hands moved of their own volition, unclenching and resting flat against him.

Reed stiffened. "Don't do this, Eve. I'm not a saint."

"I'm not doing anything." She was barely moving, arrested by the volatility between them.

"You're thinking about things you shouldn't be. You're a one-man woman."

"There's just one of you."

He moved too fast to register. His fist captured her ponytail, arching her back. She found herself wrapped with him, mantled by his powerfully aroused body. There was no denying that he was hard for her, not when she could feel nearly every inch of him against her.

Armani and steel. Elegance and brutal passion.

Desire burst across her mark-regulated senses, exploding across her nerve endings and leaving her shaken. She groaned into his hovering mouth, her nipples hardening and thrusting into his chest.

"You're playing with the wrong brother." His lips moved against hers, his words so softly spoken they were menacing.

"I'm not playing with you," she whispered, repeating the words he had once said to her.

Reed's tongue followed the line of her cheekbone, then dipped into her ear. "Then, what are you doing?"

Eve swallowed hard. "I g-guess I'm . . . coveting."

He cupped her buttock with one hand and ground his erection against her. The lewd gesture was so patently Reed, it made her weak in the knees. "You can't covet what belongs to you."

Reed was deeply pained by the admission, she could feel it. That only made his feelings more precious to her.

How was it possible for her to love Alec, yet want Reed so strongly? However her affection had grown, it needed to stop. Alec had killed Reed—*again*—for touching her the last time. She couldn't put any of them through that twice. It wasn't fair. It hurt people she cared about. It made her not like herself. She wasn't a cheater; she respected herself and her partners too much.

"Remember what I told you in the beginning?" His voice was low and gruff, the words breathed into her mouth. "You're a predator now. Predators like to fuck. That's all this is."

"Don't lie. Not about this."

His tumult was palpable and added to hers. She felt safe with Alec; she felt far from it with Reed. The fact that fear pushed her forward instead of urging retreat scared her. *What if he's right about me? What if killing things is what I'm meant to do?*

No, she refused to believe that being a Mark was her destiny. She *couldn't* believe it, because if she did, it meant that all of her childhood dreams and hopes had to die. There would be no fairytale wedding, no possibility of a family. Everything and everyone she loved, the very aspects of her life that made her who she was, would grow old and leave her life. Who would she be then? Someone she didn't know. Someone she might not like.

"Don't count on me to put on the brakes, Eve. I'm selfish. I won't say no to a prime piece of ass."

She couldn't stop the smile that curved her lips. "Isn't that what you're doing now?"

His mouth took on a mulish cast. "I don't want you like this. I've seen the show, I know how it ends."

"It was a good show." Really good. Reed was rough, edgy, wild in a way she never expected to like, let alone crave. The fact was, the mark . . . Novium . . . *whatever* . . . didn't make her want him. It only lowered her inhibitions enough to free her existing attraction.

He nipped her lower lip, then licked across the spot to soothe the sting. "Come to me again when you're not strung out with the Heat. You'll get a different answer."

"Reed—"

"Enough." Tilting his head, his mouth slanted across hers, taking her breath until she grew faint.

His fist in her hair tightened, arching her further backward, forcing her to mold into him. Her scalp ached with the pressure, the pain intensifying until she whimpered in protest and writhed. The prodding of the gun into her lower back was the final injury that pushed her over the edge.

She stomped on his foot and wrenched free, stumbling a few feet away. "You're hurting me!" she accused.

Reed wiped his mouth with the back of his hand, then adjusted the prominent bulge in his slacks with impatient movements. "Look what you've done to me. Look what you *keep* doing to me, you fucking cock tease."

Eve blinked, shocked by the vehemence of his attack. And the justification behind it. "I'm sorry. I—"

He cut her off with a glare. "Cain's the one getting

laid. That means he's the go-to guy for your crap, not me. I want to fuck you, not carry your baggage."

"Jesus," she breathed, wincing at the resulting burn from the mark. A bucket of ice water couldn't have doused her lust faster. "You know I feel like—"

"—you haven't had sex in three weeks? Join the club, Eve. Don't expect sympathy from me."

A hand touched her elbow. She jerked in surprise, her head swiveling to see who joined them. Gadara's gaze moved over her, pausing on the labored lift and fall of her chest and her clenched fists.

"Ms. Hollis," he murmured.

The tension rushed out of her like water down a drain, fleeing her body at the exact spot where the archangel touched her. Eve was suddenly chagrined and emotionally exhausted. Still aching and slick between her thighs, she nevertheless was now capable of coherent, rational thought.

"Walk it off, Abel." Gadara's order resonated with divine command.

Reed spun on his heel and left them, the leather soles of his shoes thudding angrily upon the cement drive and sidewalk. It took everything Eve had not to chase after him. The set of his shoulders told her so much about his mood. She'd backed him into a corner, then wounded him. Her frustration turned inward.

"You should be inside with the others," the archangel said. His irises were an iridescent gold rimmed with obsidian black. He was so beautiful it hurt to look at him. "Our plane will arrive within the next two hours. We will need everything packed by then."

"I don't want to leave."

His brows arched.

"I need to be here," she continued. "I can't go. You might not want to admit it, but the Novium is on me."

Gadara stood silently, eerily composed in the face of the day's events.

"There has to be something I can do here that we can both live with," she persisted.

"It is too dangerous. I prefer your original suggestion to assist from the sidelines."

"I don't think that's going to be possible. Not in the shape I'm in."

"We can resume training next week. A hunt conducted under controlled conditions should suffice—"

"*Next week?* I can't stay like this for—"

The rhythmic thumping of an approaching bass beat halted Eve's tirade midsyllable. Her head turned toward the sound, her eyes catching sight of the pea-green van that turned the corner. It was followed by a white sedan, which in turn was followed by a red pickup truck. The procession slowed, then pulled into the driveway of the duplex directly across the street.

"Is that your investigative team?" she asked, her gaze riveted on the exiting occupants of the vehicles. They seemed far too rambunctious to be long-standing Marks. They tumbled out with whoops and excited chatter.

He stepped forward, taking an almost protective position in front of her. "No."

"Then, who are they?"

"Good question."

"They're fresh faced," she noted. "Maybe a college study group? Biology or chemistry, if all that equipment they're unloading is any indication."

"No one is supposed to be here while we are."

Glancing aside at Gadara, Eve registered his alertness. His sweat suit wasn't capable of softening him completely, not with his ramrod-straight posture and elegant bearing.

"Did you tell whoever's in charge that we're clearing out today?"

"Yes." He returned her gaze. "But the military rarely moves quickly when civilian requests are involved. We began talks for this year's training two years ago. I fail to see how they could have granted permission to a new group in so short a time."

Eve started across the street. Every step was a relief. She needed to walk it off, too.

"Ms. Hollis." The archangel's tone was admonishing. "What are you doing?"

"Saying hi to our new neighbors." She looked down the road toward Anytown, which was within walking distance. Far too close for mortal comfort.

As she approached the new arrivals, Eve caught the attention of one of the girls—a somber-looking brunette with black-framed glasses and orange camisole. The girl elbowed the lanky man next to her, gesturing toward Eve with a jerk of her chin. He turned with a frown that dissolved into a smile when he saw Eve. He had unruly brown hair, a peach-fuzzy goatee, and slumberous hazel eyes that were emphasized by the olive-colored T-shirt he wore.

"Hey," he drawled, sauntering down the drive to the sidewalk.

"Hello." She extended her hand. "Evangeline Hollis."

"Roger Norville." He lifted her hand to his lips and kissed the back. "What's a babe like you doing in a place like this?"

She was taken aback by the line, thinking it was too

cocky for such a laid-back guy. "I'm teaching a class on interior design."

The answer rolled off her tongue as if it was her idea, but she knew it wasn't. She didn't have to look behind her to know Gadara was watching and listening through her . . . and compelling safe replies into her brain. Mind rape, but it had its uses.

"In this dump?" Roger's brows rose. "No amount of decorating is going to fix these homes."

"Interior *design*," she corrected. "How spaces are laid out."

"Oh, gotcha. Sorry."

"No problem. How about you?"

He released her hand and shoved his hands into the pockets of his brown corduroy jeans. "We're going to be filming the next episode of our show here."

Eve frowned. "Show?"

"Ghoul School." Roger stilled when she just stared blankly. "On Bonzai. The cable channel."

"Sorry." She shrugged. "I'm not familiar with it."

He beamed, his vaguely smarmy countenance changing to one more genuine. "That's good news."

"It is?"

Roger laughed. "Forgive the corny pickup line. I thought you recognized us."

She smiled, but was bemused.

"Chicks like geeks and television personalities," he clarified, "but not sleaze."

Eve laughed softly. "Whatever works."

He gestured toward the brunette. "Linda, come meet Evangeline. She's teaching an interior design class across the street."

Linda walked over, her lips curved shyly. She was so short, the top of her head barely reached Roger's shoulder. Her attire was deceptively casual at first glance, but closer inspection revealed a penchant for pricey designer pieces and her bob hairstyle was cut with expensive precision. "You must be part of the group we're supposed to steer clear of."

Roger nodded. "Right. Evangeline, this is my girl, Linda."

"Please, call me Eve," she corrected. She felt Gadara in her mind, sifting through her thoughts and leaving new ones behind. To her knowledge, he had never been able to do that before. Considering how new the Novium was for her, he seemed able to leap right in and make use of it without any trouble.

"So, what's *Ghoul School*?" she asked, the thought coming from Gadara. "If you don't mind my asking?"

"We're a paranormal investigative club based out of Tristan College in St. George, Utah. For a while, we were putting our investigation videos up on YouTube, but someone from the Bonzai network found us and gave us a weekly slot."

"Paranormal investigations?" She glanced back at Gadara. "Like *Ghostbusters*?"

"The opposite, really," Linda said. "We don't go into an investigation hoping to find something. We go in hoping to disprove it. We're skeptics."

"You're hoping to disprove something here?"

"At the request of the commandant," Roger said. "She granted permission for another show—*Paranormal Territory*—to investigate a few months ago and they suggested that areas of the base are haunted. She appreciates our more scientific approach. Basically, she wants a second opinion."

"That's fascinating." In a wholly alarming way, considering Molenaar's tragedy just hours ago.

Roger draped an arm around Linda's shoulders. "Are you a skeptic, Eve?"

She shook her head.

Linda grinned. "We've found a believer."

"I wouldn't call myself that," Eve said dryly. "But there are unusual events and situations—"

"Beings?"

"—that are unexplainable."

"Want to come with us?"

Roger shot a startled look at his girlfriend.

Linda's returning glance was mischievous. "Don't look so surprised. Eve's interior design expertise could prove useful. Plus the contrast between her belief in the supernatural and our skepticism would make for great television. She'll reinforce *Paranormal Territory*'s position on the hauntings; we'll debunk it. Gently, of course."

"Ms. Hollis." Gadara's voice poured over the three of them like warm water. It affected Roger and Linda immediately, bringing an enthralled look to their faces.

Eve made the introductions and rehashed the information the archangel had already heard through eavesdropping.

"My brother is a big fan of yours, Mr. Gadara," Roger said, shaking the archangel's hand. "He's a house flipper who wants to be like you when he grows up."

Gadara's smile was a thing of beauty. "Real estate can be wonderfully lucrative."

"That's what he says. Of course, he needs to learn how to budget first. So far he's managed to barely break even."

"Tell him to detach himself from the project. It is business. No more, no less. He should not approach the assignment with his own desires and needs in mind." The archangel looked at Eve, but she already understood that he was talking to her as much as to them.

"I'm impressed that you would take time out of your schedule for a class," Roger said. "The waiting list for that course must be years long. Maybe I could get my brother on it? I forgot his birthday last month."

"It is a private class, given to select employees."

"Lucky employees." Linda smiled. "So . . . would you be interested in roughly thirty minutes of fame? It's an hour-long show, but commercials and setup eat up time. We would love to have you along. We've never had a celebrity guest before."

"I am hardly a celebrity," Gadara protested, but Eve sensed he enjoyed the thought.

"You're very nearly a household name," Roger countered. "As well known as Donald Trump."

"Your presence would boost our ratings," Linda cajoled. "Plus, it's fun."

Gadara smiled boyishly. "Where are you investigating?"

"Anytown."

If Eve hadn't been looking for his surprise, she might have missed it.

Archangels are brilliant actors.

Startled by the new voice, Eve's gaze darted to find the source. A deep bark brought her attention to the Great Dane leaping from the passenger seat of the red pickup. A pretty redhead exited from the driver's side and called out, "Don't bark at the neighbors, Freddy."

Freddy rolled his eyes, then dipped his large head in a bow to Gadara.

"You have a dog," Eve said.

"Yeah." Roger snapped his fingers, and Freddy padded over. "Animals have keener senses. When the viewers see that Freddy is bored, they know nothing paranormal is at work."

Obviously, I'm a brilliant actor, too.

Eve winked at him.

Gadara cleared his throat and looked suitably regretful. "We are utilizing Anytown at the moment."

"No worries," Roger assured. "The commandant warned us. We film at night, so we won't get in your way."

Curious to see how he would maneuver his way through this new curve, Eve watched the archangel closely.

"Hang on." Linda pulled away from Roger and ran back to the van. She dug into a duffel bag resting on the threshold of the open sliding rear door, then returned with a DVD case that she extended to Gadara. "Here's the episode of *Paranormal Territory* that was filmed here at McCroskey. Take a look at it. We won't start filming until midnight. Hopefully that will give you plenty of time to consider it."

Gadara accepted the video, then made their excuses. Eve waved to Freddy before falling into step beside the archangel.

"We can't leave them here alone," she said.

"Clean-up is progressing as we speak, and I will speak with the lieutenant colonel again."

"Going to put the persuasive whammy on her?"

"I will simply suggest that she delay them until we are completely cleared out."

"Shouldn't we catch whoever killed Molenaar before we say we're done here? We can clean up and go, but that doesn't mean the killer won't be left behind."

"You no longer believe the culprit is one of your classmates, Ms. Hollis? Or me?"

She also had concerns about the Infernals working for him, but she'd keep that to herself for now. "I never said it was any of you."

"Not directly, but the implication—the suspicion—is there."

"Okay. That mind-pillaging thing is just plain creepy. If I have something to say to you, I'll say it. Please don't dig around in my brain."

"It is concern for you that motivates me."

"Really? And that's why you decided to ignore the Novium that's tearing me up?"

Stopping by the Porsche, the archangel faced her with narrowed eyes. "Tell me how you think I can best help you."

Eve's fingers touched the trunk, seeking a connection with the vehicle in lieu of Reed. The car was sleek, expensive, and dangerously fast. Just like the man who drove it. "They invited us to go with them. I think we should. We could protect them."

The archangel shook his head and handed her the DVD. "Let me speak with the colonel before we consider that. In the interim, go inside with the others and help them pack. Make sure that we are prepared to go."

She took the video. "The girls' side is done and ready to load."

"Excellent. Now concentrate on the provisions and equipment."

With two guards still in Anytown and two always on point with Gadara, that left only the Marks to do the grunt work. "All right, I'll play along," she said, disgruntled. "For now."

"And stay away from Abel," he added. "He needs to cool down some, as do you."

Eve shot him a wry glance. "So you finally admit I'm running a fever?"

His mouth thinned, briefly reminding her of her dad's style of silent chastising.

She shrugged it off and headed toward the house.

Reed stood in the shade of an oak tree and watched as Eve ran her fingers over his car as if it were a lover. Her mind followed suit, returning to musings of him and her confusion over her attraction. She loved his brother but she wanted him, too. In ways she had never wanted anyone else.

His jaw clenched so tightly it ached.

I covet you.

The words should have been his, not hers. And if she settled into her fate as a Mark, he would have numerous years with her. A blessing, if he was able to head a new firm and snag her for his team. Or a curse, if she remained in love with Cain even after their mentoring relationship was over.

I want to fuck you, not carry your baggage.

The truth mixed with a lie. He wanted everything, which pissed him off to no end. If his brain hadn't been scrambled by her Heat, he would have pulled her into an abandoned home and pinned her to a crumbling wall. He would have pounded himself into her until neither of them could breathe, think, or walk. He would have spilled every drop of his lust into her writhing body, thereby deepening the ethereal connection between them. He also would have irrefutably checkmated Cain by severing their connection before it had a chance to fully form. Eve might have hated him afterward and hated herself for giving in to the desire she didn't understand, but he would've had her in every way that mattered.

But his brain had fried when she laid her feelings on the line. Without a driver behind the wheel, his gut had taken over and fucked it all up.

I want to fuck you, not carry your baggage.

He was such a dick. He'd felt how deeply the words cut her and had relished her pain because it mirrored his.

He could have had her body, but taking her while under duress wasn't enough. He wanted her sober, cognizant, and fully willing. No remorse, no regrets.

"*Hello.*"

Pulled from his thoughts by the greeting, Reed dragged his gaze away from Eve to find the pretty blonde with the dark fashion sense approaching. Her wrists and throat were hugged by spikes and leather, her palms were covered in fingerless gloves, and her legs were wrapped in black-and-white-striped knee-high socks.

He used to seek out women like her—light-haired women with harder-than-usual edges. He'd considered them his type.

His head tilted slightly in silent acknowledgment.

The blonde's gaze followed his previous line of sight and came to rest on Eve, who stood talking with Raguel.

"If it's any consolation," she said, "she's not accessible to your brother either. He has been ringing her cell phone all morning."

"It's not," he said gruffly. Another lie. If there had to be a gulf between him and Eve, he wanted the same distance between her and Cain.

Then why did you let her go?

"Perhaps I can help you."

He turned, leaning his shoulder into the tree. "In what way, Miss . . . ?"

"Call me Izzie." Her stained lips curved in a come-hither smile. "In any way."

Reed knew the invitation had as much to do with Eve as it did with him. Rivalry, perhaps. Or jealousy. Catty girl crap. He wanted to shut her down just for that, just to choose Eve's side. He didn't. Eve wasn't celibate, why should he be?

His gaze dropped to the blonde's lips. "You have a pretty mouth, Izzie."

She nodded, comprehending what he wanted. She turned around and led the way. He followed. Once he dealt with his raging hard-on, he might manage to hold himself together until Eve was safe and he could once again put distance between them. They couldn't keep butting heads. He'd gambled a great deal in order to help Cain resurrect her. He couldn't afford to wreck all of his plans by alienating her beyond repair.

Sparing one last look over his shoulder at the driveway, Reed found that both Raguel and Eve were gone. The Marks would be clearing out soon. Eve would be squired away to safety. Class would end, the blonde would be assigned to a mentor, and he would never see her again. No harm, no foul, no complications.

That didn't stop him from feeling like shit.

CHAPTER 11

"Don't leave me like this! What if the maid comes in?"

Alec smiled down at Giselle, who wrestled futilely against the handcuffs that secured her to the pipe beneath the hotel room sink. "I'll put the Do Not Disturb sign up."

"Cain! I'll scream, I swear. They'll call the cops."

He bent down and tugged the handkerchief off her head.

"No!" she protested. "I was just kidding. I didn't—*Mmphfff . . . !*"

He secured the gag with a tug and stood, stepping clear of her kicking legs. "Don't wear yourself out. When I get back I'll need some blood from you, so you should save your strength."

The metal links of the cuffs were muffled by the pipe insulation used to protect the legs of wheelchair-bound guests. Still, Alec shut the bathroom door and turned on the television as added camouflage. Then, he grabbed his black leather messenger bag and crossed into the adjoining room. He shut both connecting doors, then moved to the desk set against the opposite wall. He withdrew the various components of his satellite videophone, but paused to hit redial on his cell phone before assembling them.

The line rang three times. He was about to hang up when Eve's voice, breathy and filled with relief, answered. "Alec!"

"Angel." Concern straightened his spine and canceled his plans to chastise her for not answering his other calls. "Is everything all right?"

"No—"

"Are you okay?"

"Yes, but—"

"Are you hurt?"

"No, but Molenaar—the Stoner—is dead."

"*What?* How?"

He listened to her explanation with a growing sense of urgency. "I want you out of there," he said when she finished. "Right now."

"That's Gadara's plan. We're packing up as we speak."

He knew her well enough to pick up the stubbornness underlying her tone. "Don't fight him on this, angel, although I can't imagine why you would. Sounds like just the sort of thing you would want to avoid."

"No shit. Where's my scaredy-cat sense of self-preservation when I need it?" She sighed. "I've been told I'm going through the Novium. It's making me bitchy."

Alec stilled. It was impossible. It was years too soon.

"I would take that with a grain of salt," he said

gruffly. "Raguel doesn't have enough experience with the Heat to make that diagnosis."

"Well, your brother agrees with him."

"Abel is there?" His concern for her safety turned into something baser, an emotion that was darker and more selfish.

"Yes. He has something going on with Gadara. I don't know what it is."

Alec was more concerned with his brother having something going on with Eve. She shouldn't be so susceptible to the Heat so quickly. By design, the Novium helped train Marks to overcome their lingering fears so they could achieve successful independence. Eve hadn't been marked long enough to be affected, plus they hadn't attained the sort of bond he'd seen in other mentor/Mark pairings. If she went through the Novium now, not only would he lack a vital part of the experience he hoped would help him advance to firm leader, but he would also miss the opportunity to bind Eve more tightly to him.

With a growl, Alec moved to the bed and sat. It was time for another argument with God about the return of his *mal'akh* powers. Eve, bless her, was somewhat of a disaster magnet. "Are any of the other students showing signs?"

"I have no idea." Her tone was weary. "They're argumentative, and Romeo and the princess are still screwing like rabbits, but other than that . . . ? I don't know what to look for."

"They're not important. Just take care of yourself." If it was only Eve, he would have to seriously consider if her acclimation was being manipulated. And if so, who was responsible.

"Take care of myself how? I feel like shit, Alec. As

if I have the flu. Isn't the mark bad enough? Why does my process have to be so out of whack with the norm?"

"Angel . . ." Fuck, he should be with her now. She shouldn't be alone. And she damn well shouldn't be anywhere near Abel, whose connection with her would strengthen while his waned. "I'm guessing the Stoner's death triggered your Heat early. Maybe you're being affected so strongly because you've already been on a hunt."

"That's what I told Reed. This sucks. I'm not a dog; I shouldn't feel like a bitch in heat."

"It's not like that."

"You're not the one going through it, Alec," she argued. "Trade places with me, then tell me how it feels."

Inhaling sharply, he forced himself to remain seated and not break speed limits back to Monterey. Not for the first time, he damned the fact that he was as untrained in his role as she was in hers.

"I hate being clueless," he growled, shoving a rough hand through his hair. "This whole situation is fucked all to hell. Everyone's got their thumb in the pie and we're stuck cleaning up the mess."

"No one's finger is in my pie," she said dryly. "And sadly, I'm disappointed about that. The Novium is making me horny. How insane is that?"

Alec stilled, considering. He'd come across all types of mentor/Mark pairs over the years. Romantically linked teams were rare, but they did happen. One Mark had sworn that the best sex of her life had come during the Novium. She'd wondered whether it was melancholy over the end of her mentor relationship that had made the sex so hot or whether it was due to the Heat itself. Either way, the Mark had said her emotional attachment had strengthened during that time despite the imminent end to the training bond.

And Abel was there with Eve . . . Damn it.

"I wish you were here," she said in a small voice. "I don't know what to do with myself. I feel like a stranger in my own skin."

There was something he could do for her from this distance, one way to ensure that she didn't fall into Abel's greedy hands like a ripe, juicy apple. "I don't have to be with you to help you."

"Talking helps. But honestly, that's the last thing I want to do with you right now."

"All action. My kind of girl." Alec piled the pillows against the headboard and made himself comfortable. He pictured Eve in the grip of lust—her eyes glassy with need, her lips red and parted on gasping breaths as he pumped hard, fast, and deep into her.

With his voice low and thick, he asked, "Are you alone?"

Her hesitation told him that she registered the change in his mood. "No. I'm with the others, helping them pack up the equipment."

"Can you find someplace where you will be within a safe distance but far enough away to prevent anyone from overhearing you?"

Eve's breath caught, then was exhaled in rush. "I think so."

"Then get there. Quick."

Raguel unfolded from the back of his bulletproof Suburban and slipped on a pair of sunglasses. Before him stood the headquarters where the garrison commander, Colonel Rachel Wells, oversaw the nuts and bolts of what was left of Fort McCroskey and the adjunct installations.

He had called ahead and she was expecting him, but the tone of her voice had warned him of trouble ahead. Debunking the ghosts was important to her for a reason he had yet to discern. But her motivation was moot. He would *persuade* her to postpone the filming of the ghost-hunter show long enough for his team to purify the area. A few days, at most, were all he needed.

Montevista exited the front passenger seat. With practiced movements, the guard straightened the fit of his navy blazer, effectively concealing the bulge of his shoulder holster and gun. From behind dark sunglasses, the Mark scanned their surroundings with a sweeping glance. "I can't stand feeling vulnerable."

"You have the strength of an army in you."

"Flattery won't save you if we're attacked by whatever butchered Molenaar today. You and the students should be on the move as we speak, sir."

Raguel brushed a careless hand down his dress shirt. The time for leisure was over and his change of attire reflected that. "Charles Grimshaw will circle us for a while before he strikes again. He just wanted us to know he was here, hunting."

Montevista looked at him. Although the Mark's shades were dark enough to be impermeable to mortal eyes, Raguel's enhanced vision saw through them as if they weren't there. The Mark was clearly taken aback. "Grimshaw did this? How do you know?"

"Molenaar was hunted by an animal. He was targeted because he was the weakest and slowest member of our group. And the manner in which he was killed was a message, one guaranteed to reveal the sender."

"What is the message?" Sydney asked. She was a petite blonde, less than five feet tall. Delicately feminine, she downplayed her fragility with a severe chignon, starkly cut pantsuit, and button-down dress shirt. Like Montevista, she wore dark shades and her right ear was wrapped with an earpiece that kept her connected to the rest of his security detail.

"He intends to cut off God from the people—hence the decapitation of a crucified man—through those who are lacking and vulnerable."

Montevista's hazel eyes narrowed consideringly. This was why Raguel trusted him with his life. The Mark examined everything. "How is that Grimshaw's signature?"

Raguel moved to the walkway that led to the headquarters entrance. On the lawn to the left, a bronze statue celebrated a person or event rather than the hand of God who guided all. He looked away, noting instead the number of cars in the parking lot and the proliferation of uniform-clad soldiers scurrying like ants around the various buildings.

"Charles once told me that Infernals are not an accident. He claimed they were created by design and our time here on Earth is merely a test. Survival of the fittest, he said. One day, only the strongest and wiliest will remain. That is who God seeks, he claims. Not the most faithful, but the most ruthless."

"What do you think, sir?" Sydney asked.

"I think Charles lost his originality with age. His actions are not motivated by survival of the fittest; they are spurred by his own misplaced grief and self-recrimination. Nearly everyone blames God when they lose a loved one. I expected better of him."

Montevista's face took on a stony cast. "The loss of a child is something you could never understand unless it happened to you."

Raguel was well aware that Montevista—a former police officer—had approached the acquitted murderer of his six-year-old daughter and fired six rounds from his service revolver straight into the man's heart. One for each year of her life. It was why Montevista was marked.

"The Lord gave," Raguel murmured, "and the Lord hath taken away."

"Job 1:20–21," Sydney offered.

"It's a brutal test even the most pious fail." Montevista's voice was tight. "A demon like Grimshaw didn't stand a chance."

"Perhaps that was the point." Raguel reached into his pocket for his beeping cell phone. He withdrew it and read the text message from Uriel.

Satellite conference @ 18:00 EST.

He checked the time and exhaled harshly. It was just past noon. He still needed to speak with Abel, who would explain what happened in Australia. Going blind into a meeting with the other archangels was not an option. There were very few things he disliked more than discovering that he knew less than his siblings.

Once he learned all he could from Abel, Raguel would send him away. The *mal'akh*'s appearance so swiftly on the heels of Molenaar's murder had created a volatile situation Evangeline was not prepared for. Later, she would serve God's purpose. For now, Raguel wanted nothing to interfere with his own work with her. He fully intended for her to align with him so completely that she related to him more than she did with Cain and Abel. He could manage them through her. Together, he and the two brothers could form a triumvirate that would ensure his position in the celestial hierarchy. And bringing the warring siblings together would prove unequivocally that he could accomplish any task. Ascension to the rank of *hashmal* wouldn't be far behind.

Raguel's fingers wrapped around the cool metal handle of the door. The entrance to the headquarters was set into the side of the building, shielded by an overhang that kept the doorway in shadow. Free of the sun's glare, the glass was as clear as still water. Even without his enhanced sight, he could see directly through to the twin doors on the opposite side of the long foyer.

The lights were out. Nothing moved. He listened closely and heard only silence.

Montevista rushed in front of him, preventing him from opening the door. Sydney pressed her back to his, shielding him from a possible rear attack.

"Take him back to the truck," Montevista ordered.

"Not yet." Glancing over the Mark's shoulder, Raguel noted the flashing red light on the wall. "Someone set off the fire alarm."

"I don't smell smoke."

"Neither do I." If it were present, he could smell it from a mile away. Literally. "A drill, perhaps."

"I don't like it," Sydney said. "Something's off. I can feel it."

"Sir, if you'll wait in the car with Sydney," Montevista suggested, "I'll investigate and find the colonel."

"Not this time," Raguel demurred. "Under the circumstances, I prefer that we remain together."

Something weighty and cool was pressed into his palm. Raguel glanced at Sydney, who gave a nod. Then, his gaze dropped to the gun in his hand. His lip curled in distaste. Such a blunt and brutal weapon, lacking all elegance and refinery. That he was forced to carry, and possibly use, such an instrument was insulting. Against an Infernal, he could unleash the full force of his God-given power. But against a mortal—a Satanist or possessed soul—he had to restrain himself to inflicting wounds that wouldn't destroy the body or betray what he was.

The restrictions on his gifts chafed deeper every day. To his knowledge, the other archangels were happy with their lot. Uriel loved the ocean. Raphael loved the Serengeti. Sara had earthy appetites. He, however, would leave mortal life behind in an instant to return to the heavens. There was little here that appealed to him. He found it all so primitive. Despite centuries of technological advances, human nature had yet to mature beyond its infantile stages.

Raguel handed the gun back. "I changed my mind. Wait here."

"I don't—!"

He shifted before Montevista could finish the sentence. He winked in and out of every room in the building. Signs that the occupants had vacated in a hurry were prevalent—open e-mail in-boxes on monitors and cold drinks sitting amid puddles of condensation.

Yet it was calm outside. Whatever alarm had been triggered here hadn't alerted anyone beyond these walls. A drill would explain that, but it didn't explain the chill that moved through Raguel. Something was wrong; he simply had to discover what it was.

Pausing his search inside the colonel's office, Raguel glanced out the wall of widows that overlooked the field below. His brows lifted at the sight of the formation on the grass a few hundred yards beyond the building. A hundred or more soldiers stood at parade rest in neat, precise rows.

"What are you doing?" he wondered aloud.

Footsteps thundered up the stairs, the pounding beat echoing through the hallway and reception area.

Sydney and Montevista.

"In here." Raguel's voice came at conversational volume, knowing their enhanced hearing would pick it up. With the casement windows ajar to invite in the breeze, he was hesitant to disturb the ranks below.

The two guards rushed in behind him. Sydney dipped into the adjacent garrison Command Sergeant Major's office, searching for hazards. Montevista took up a position at Raguel's right shoulder.

"Everything okay, sir?"

"So it would appear."

He scanned the visible area, spotting the baseball game taking place on the opposite side of a thick barrier of Monterey pines. Off-duty soldiers at play. What had started out as a gloomy morning had turned into a sunny day.

"Uh . . . Sir," Sydney said from the CSM's office. "There's a disturbance at the tree line. I can't make out what it is from here."

Montevista leaned forward as if doing so would improve his vision. Old habits died hard. "Where? What are you looking at?"

Raguel's gaze honed in on the swaying of a twenty-foot pine. He pointed. "There."

Enhancing his vision, he looked through the trunks

and watched some . . . *thing* struggling. A huge creature, pale enough to glimmer like a pearl even in the shade of the towering trees around it. A creature capable of shaking a mature pine down to its roots.

"What in hell can move a tree that size?" Montevista asked.

Mariel's voice echoed through Raguel's mind, *It was a monstrous beast; easily several feet in height. Flesh, not fur. Massive shoulders and thighs.*

"I believe we have found our mysterious Infernal."

"Or it found us first," Montevista said grimly. "If that's the thing Mariel and Abel are after, what is it doing here and how do we kill it?"

This creature was much bigger than what she had described, but size was moot. The thing in the trees was evil, a being so afflicted in the soul that it tainted the air around it. Its thrashing and writhing sent waves of horror outward in shockwaves. The branches recoiled, their creaking a cry for help that reverberated inside him. Below, the formation shivered in unison. They felt the *wrongness* but were incapable of discerning the source.

Raguel breathed deeply, inhaling the fresh air entering through the window. The faintest hint of sweetness teased his nostrils.

Mark blood.

With a roar only enhanced ears could hear, he shifted through the glass and plummeted along the outside of the building, leaving his cell phone spinning like a top on the office floor behind him. As the ground rushed up to meet him, his wings snapped outward like a flag in a Santa Ana wind. He caught the current and soared over the formation, his upward surge sending a torrent of air across the soldiers. Their hats scattered, twisting and tumbling.

A unified cry of dismay followed him. Blinded by their mortality, they couldn't see his celestial form, but they felt him. Not just in the wind, but in the inner sense that connected them to the heavens. A sense dulled by time and misuse, but still inherent nevertheless.

The beast returned Raguel's war cry with one of its own, a fulsome growl that caused every animal within a goodly distance to sound out in fear, giving voice to the hidden reality of the battle about to ensue.

Accelerating to a speed faster than mortal time, Raguel noted how the world around him slowed. The wayward hats hovered in midair, arrested. Birds hung in midflight. The only thing moving at his pace was the Infernal. The creature broke free of its confinement and leaped out onto the field, felling two trees and leaving a depression in the ground.

It was a flesh-colored mass the size of a bus. The beast barreled toward the unsuspecting formation with a speed that was stunning considering its bulk. It ran on all fours, fists punching into the earth with unrestrained ferocity. The shoulders and thighs were disproportionately gigantic, a grotesque contrast to the smaller head and tiny waist. But the crowning atrocity was its mouth, a yawning cavern lined with rows of yellowed teeth.

It crawled inside my Mark, Mariel had reported. *She screamed and it lunged into her mouth. It disappeared inside her. It should have been impossible. The creature was many times her size . . .*

The falling trees were at the midway point in their

rush to the ground. Tucking his arms close to his sides, Raguel beat his wings, increasing his velocity.

He was one of the holy angels. *He who inflicts punishment on the world and the luminaries.*

But he had no problem kicking the ass of *anything* vile. Sammael had been gunning for him since he was cast from Heaven. Raguel supposed it was time to give his fallen brother what he'd long wanted.

"Out of the belly of Hell I cried," Raguel said grimly, zeroing in, praying for strength and the blessing of God. "And You heard my voice."

So much time had passed since his last battle. Time wasted. Time misused. He'd grown arrogant. Sloppy. And an innocent, untrained Mark had paid the price. Jan Molenaar's soul would now wait in *Sheol*—purgatory—its owner denied the chance to redeem it. Raguel prayed his next act would redeem them both.

The Infernal reared up on its hind legs, attaining a breathtaking twenty-plus feet in height. It screamed with open-throated hatred at the heavens, beating at its chest in an awesome display of power.

Retracting his wings at the last second, Raguel dived into the gaping maw.

Eve was striding down the hallway before her brain fully registered Alec's intent.

Get there. Quick.

Her aching body was galvanized by the purring rumble of his voice, a seductive timbre that even cellular reception couldn't diminish. She hurried through the kitchen and opened the rear door. Richens sat on a folded-up jacket on the lowest step, his head turning to see who joined him.

"Hollis." His eyes and expression were eerily blank. "I need to talk to you."

"Lose Mastermind," Alec ordered.

For some silly reason, it meant a lot to her that he remembered her nicknames. "Getting there," she muttered.

Eve shook her head at Richens in silent negation. *Later,* she mouthed. She jumped off the step and onto the dead grass.

"You just showed up and now you're leaving again?" he groused. "We have to pack."

She didn't bother pointing out that he wasn't doing anything to help. "I forgot something next door."

"That's what Garza and Hogan said . . . before they headed in the opposite direction."

Eve waved him off, unsurprised. Garza was going to get calluses on his dick if he didn't slow down soon.

"You still moving?" Alec asked.

"Yes. By the way, this Novium business is damned inconvenient. I really needed to talk to Izzie. She should have reached Molenaar around the same time as me. But she didn't show up until ten or fifteen minutes later. Where the hell was she?"

"The Novium is never convenient, angel. And you can't do anything about your classmate now anyway. Raguel has you packing and you can't work alone."

"So I'm just stuck being miserable?"

"Your brain is seeking the sensation of a kill, so we'll trick it—temporarily—into thinking you've done that."

"How?"

"Phone sex, angel."

She stumbled over a protruding patch of dead weeds. "Killing demons is orgasmic?"

"How did you feel after you killed the Nix?"

Euphoric. Slightly drunk. "O-kay . . . That's really kinda sick, Alec."

"Hey, they're the bad guys, remember? The scourge of the Earth. Evil incarnate. It's okay to feel good about vanquishing them."

Rounding the backside of the duplex, Eve bypassed the kitchen door and went to the main entrance of the girls' side. It was unlocked and she hurried in. A pile of duffel bags and backpacks rested on the threshold to the dining room, including hers. "Can you go upstairs and ask God for a little help here?"

"You know better than that."

"Can't you try?"

She should be a basket case right now. Traumatized for life and frightened into paralysis. Instead, the memory of Molenaar's death filled her with an aggressive, wild energy. The need to move, to act, to rip something apart was difficult to fight. But a good hard screw would do just as well. That bothered her more than she could say.

"Angel—"

"Why is sex so much a part of being a Mark?" She swiped at a drop of sweat that trickled down her temple. "Sex brought us together in the first place. Then, it was involved when Abel put the mark on me, and again when I went through the physical changes with you. Seems to me that being marked and being a nymphomaniac go hand in hand."

"It's balance, Eve. You're a killer now. You'll wake up in the morning for the sole purpose of murdering something and you will usually go to bed having accomplished that task. Sex connects you to someone. It forces you to give and take intimacy. It keeps you human."

"Balance would be sex one day and hunting the next." She leaned against the living room wall. "Mixing the two is just . . . kinky."

"Sex isn't the reason we hooked up."

She quivered at his rumbling tone. "Liar," she breathed. "It's all we had time for."

"Liar," he rejoined gruffly. "It took us half a second to see where we were headed. Time had nothing to do with it and the sex was a bonus."

Eve would never forget the sight of him on his Harley outside the ice cream store where she worked after school. He'd had her at the first glance. "You made my mouth water," she confessed. "Still do."

"Right now, I could tell you to cool off with a shower and an ice pack. I could tell you to pick a fight with that blonde who has issues with you and knock out some of the stress that way. I could suggest that you slip away and get yourself off without me. But I'm not going to let you do any of those things, Eve, because I need to be your go-to guy." He paused, then, "And I need Abel to *not* be that guy."

Sagging into the wall, Eve knew she couldn't feel any worse. Reed had run like hell, but she couldn't say that without explaining what he'd been running from. And it didn't matter anyway. Alec was a damn good guy and she was lucky to have him in her corner. He wouldn't be there forever, but right now was better than nothing.

"Eve?"

"Gimme a minute. You slayed me."

He laughed softly. "I'm glad you don't need wine and roses."

She wiped at her wet cheeks with her free hand. "You make this all bearable, you know."

"Just bearable? I'll have to work harder."

More than bearable. He made her feel safe and sane. He didn't put her off or undermine her. He treated her with respect when everyone else was manipulating her into cramped corners.

"I miss you like crazy," he murmured. "You're in my head even when I'm sleeping."

"Did you have a wet dream?"

"Damn near. You were lying beside me, naked and hot as hell. I got hard just watching you sleep."

Eve understood that. Admiring him while he was sleeping was a favorite pastime of hers. Sleep softened him in a way nothing else could.

"I pulled you under me and slid into you before you were fully awake. You made those sexy little noises you always make when I'm deep in you. I could almost feel you fisting around me. And the way you can't stop coming . . . Drives me fucking crazy that I can get to you that way."

The images that flooded her mind concentrated the heat of the Novium and dropped it low in her belly. Alec's voice, roughly seductive like velvet, always left her weak in the knees. He was inexhaustible, and his need to get her off until she couldn't take any more had pretty much ruined her for other men.

"I wish you were here with me now," he purred. "I'd strip you bare and lick you from head to toe."

She gave a shaky exhale. "You have an oral fixation."

"Which you love." The smile in his voice sparked an inner quivering.

Alec never did anything in half-measure. Unlike Reed, who rode a woman hard and put her away wet, Alec took his time during sex. He used his mouth first, then his hands. From head to toe, front to back, every curve and crevice. Whispering praise both lewd and tender. Taking hours.

"Are you thinking about my mouth on you?" he murmured. "Are you hot and wet?"

"Are you alone?" Eve locked the front door. The big picture window was covered by a white sheet that let milky light in, but made viewing impossible. It was as private as she was going to get without venturing off to someplace farther away. "Do you have an audience?"

"I'm all yours. Why are you whispering? Aren't you alone yet?"

"Yes, but we're having phone sex, Alec. And I'm inexperienced. It would be embarrassing if someone overheard me. Where's the horse?"

He laughed. "Giselle is handcuffed to the bathroom pipes in the adjoining room."

"Handcuffed? Sounds kinky."

"Stop it. Tell me you miss me."

She sighed. "A lot. Are you naked?"

"Not completely. Just enough to get the job done. I've got work to do, too, but you come first."

"We'll come at the same time," she breathed. "Are you touching yourself?"

"Yes. Are you?"

"Not yet."

"What are you waiting for?"

Her eyes closed against the building ache in her chest. "You."

She'd been waiting for him for ten years. Staying away hadn't spared her punishment, so when she'd been marked he'd come back for the duration. But now that she had him, she sometimes turned him away and sent him home just to prove to herself that she could still live without him. Because one day, soon, she would have to.

"I'm here, angel," he purred. "Hard and ready. I'm in heat, too. Thinking about you always gets me that way."

It was her complete trust in him that gave her the courage to say, "I wish you were in my hands."

"Fuck, yeah. Me, too."

"I want to hold you. I love how soft the skin of your cock is. How thick the veins are. They make you look so brutal, when you're really so tender."

"Trace them with your tongue."

"What?"

"The veins. Use your tongue."

Eve's mouth watered. Alec wasn't the only one to have an oral fixation. What really got to her was how much he loved it. He was so unabashed in his enjoyment, his hands fisting in the sheets or her hair, his voice hoarse as he cursed at her for stripping him down to base animalistic need.

"I love that sensitive spot just beneath the head," she whispered. "I like to flutter my tongue across it just to hear you fall apart."

Alec groaned. "Touch yourself while you're sucking me."

Eve's fingers went to the top button of her jeans and

flicked it open. "It gives me a thrill to know you're so hot for me."

"I'm beyond hot. I'm about to go up in flames."

She imagined herself kneeling over him, holding his fly apart so nothing impeded her working mouth. The fantasy was so real she could hear the slick suction noises. Her hand pushed into her jeans, forcing the zipper pull to slide down.

Suck harder.

Eve lost her balance, sinking into an off-kilter crouch.

It wasn't Alec's voice she heard in her mind; it was Reed's.

CHAPTER 12

Eve's eyes stung with welling tears.

Why Reed's voice? Why *now,* when she was deep into an intimate moment with another man? A man she'd loved for as long as she could remember.

The gun at her lower back shifted dangerously, freed from its position by the loosening of her fly. She grabbed for it, then set it down on the dusty floor beside the luggage, her fingers clenching spasmodically around the grip.

"Damn, that feels good," Alec gasped. "You suck cock as if you were starved for it."

Her mind was inundated with sensation—the rhythmic drawing of a hungry mouth, a tongue flickering, a fist pumping the thick root. It felt as if she was inside his brain, enjoying their fantasy through his senses. Sweat dotted her brow and upper lip. Heat rippled along her skin in a prickling wave, the Novium burning through her in double time, yet she felt closer to him than ever before.

An orgasm hovered just out of reach. Through no physical manipulation at all, she was about to climax from the feel of Alec's pleasure. She cried softly, nearly dizzy from the surfeit of sensual perception. "Please . . ."

"Yes, angel." His voice was sandpaper rough. "Come for me. Let me hear you."

A pained female whimper yanked Eve back from the edge, cruelly halting her hurtle toward climax.

Her eyes flew open. *She* hadn't made that sound . . . could never make that sound with Alec. He was too gentle. Despite the ferocity of his ardor, he always treated her as if she was breakable.

Eve slid from her crouch to a seated position on the floor. A brazen wet sucking noise rent the quiet of the house, followed by a serrated masculine groan.

Unmistakable sounds with an unmistakable cause.

She wasn't alone. And, worse, she wasn't unaffected. The knowledge that a sexual act was taking place somewhere nearby ratcheted up the tension to painful intensity.

Alec growled in her ear, knowing her well enough to pick up on her sudden preoccupation. "Don't stop! Fuck, I'm about to blow."

"Do it," she urged, struggling to her feet. He could come and keep going. It was a gift.

"Not without you. Are your fingers inside you?"

"Yes," she lied. With deliberate steps, she managed to walk carefully to the hallway without her heavy boots giving her away.

She didn't recognize herself. She wasn't a voyeur. In her previous life, she would be hightailing it out of there, not salivating for a lewd peek. Especially of Romeo and Laurel. Part of her brain was revolted by the thought; the rest of her brain was so inundated with Alec's approaching orgasm it couldn't string a sentence together.

"I can't hold off much longer," Alec bit out. "Are you close?"

"Yes." But her answer referred to her proximity, not her orgasmic state. The fellating noises were spilling into the hall from the farthest open bedroom doorway. Another couple of steps and she would be able to look inside.

Eve hugged the opposite wall. The panting and groaning grew in volume, as did the erotic sound of hard suckling.

The couple came into view and she stumbled. Her free hand covered her mouth, stemming the low moan of torment that rose up unbidden. Her chest constricted.

Reed.

He occupied the center of the master bedroom, standing with head back and eyes closed. Izzie kneeled before him like a supplicant, the bobbing of her pigtailed head betraying the enthusiasm with which she sucked his cock. His fingers were shoved into her restrained hair with white-knuckled force, pulling the blonde tresses in a way that caused her pained whimpers. He moved her as he wanted, his hips thrusting at a breathtaking pace. His neck was corded by straining muscles and his handsome face twisted with a carnal grimace of pleasure and fierce concentration.

Eve was bombarded by a dark and cold desire, as if the walls between them had stemmed a tide that the open doorway now freed. His struggle to climax rushed at her like an oncoming tsunami, carrying her back, beating her against the wall.

Ravaged by jealousy and the aggressiveness of the Heat, Eve watched with horrified eyes, understanding that the sensations she had thought were Alec's were actually Reed's. They traveled to her through their growing emotional link, hitting her in real time with Izzie's movements.

But it wasn't Izzie he pictured behind his closed eyelids.

"Angel?" Alec's voice was strangled. "You're fucking killing me. If you were here, I'd have my mouth between your legs, tonguing your clit until you went off for me."

Alec's intrusion triggered an emotional flood—remorse and longing, sorrow and love. It was so potent, it was tangible. The hairs on her nape prickled.

His breath caught. "I can *feel* you."

Reed gasped and straightened. His gaze found her, his lips moving without sound. *I can feel you.*

And she felt them. Both of them, pushing into her, inundating her with their desire and raw needs, seeping into every pore, every memory, every hidden thought. She was bared in a way only a true . . . *possession* could make possible.

Two men. Inside her at the same time.

They swirled around her like billowing smoke, battling within her, shoving at each other like children over a favored toy and inadvertently discovering her tragic fascination with both of them in the process. Triumph and pain, joy and misery, envy and passion, love and hate—the way they responded to the revelation was destroying all three of them.

The roots of her hair grew damp with sweat. Her skin burned as it had when the dragon killed her, a blistering pain she hadn't survived the first time. Alec and Reed were overpowering her, too focused on their endless rivalry to realize how their centuries of memories and bickering were drowning her.

Sucking in air, Eve pushed her hand into her open fly and cupped her sex. The subsequent flare of pleasure and relief was like a beam of light in the darkness. The two men recoiled from each other and she took the advantage, pushed them backward, slipping into them the way they had come into her.

They each wrapped around her, their mental embraces as heated and passionate as their physical ones. But she was divided and untrained, torn by guilt and confusion. She lacked the sheer strength and knowledge required to see into their souls the way they'd seen into hers. Still, Eve tried to probe their minds even as her fingers delved between her thighs. She moaned as she pushed two fingers inside, feeling how hot and swollen she was, how desperate and greedy. Both men growled in unison, feeling her pleasure as she felt theirs.

It seemed as if there was no separation between them. She felt Alec's strong fingers wrapped around his cock, pumping with unrestrained ferocity. She felt Izzie's lips and tongue around Reed, felt the rhythmic suction and drenching heat.

But mentally, she was the deliverer of both forms of pleasure. The two men saw her in their minds' eyes, a revelation that caused tears to blind her.

Eve . . .

Which one spoke, she couldn't discern. The voice was too guttural, too coarse from the knife's edge of orgasm. Suddenly, the hand between her legs wasn't hers. It was theirs. Both of them. Together. Spreading her, stroking her, filling her.

Her resulting climax devastated her, bringing a cry to her lips that was lost in the conjoined roar of their orgasms. In that moment, at the height of pleasure, there was no distinction between them. They were one, a triumvirate of souls. She melted, crying both inside and out, her skin so hot her sweat steamed off it.

It wasn't until the first brutal surge had passed that she realized their transient embraces weren't meant to cherish but to restrain. As she struggled to explore them while the singular connection existed, they bound her tightly. Too tightly. Preventing her from looking deeper. Their history was behind her, an open book. But their futures—their hopes, dreams, and motivations—were beyond, and they wouldn't allow her to see them.

What are you hiding? her two halves asked, their voices an eerie chorus that sent a shiver down her spine.

She lost her grip on her phone. Her marked reflexes kicked in, enabling her to withdraw her hand from her jeans and fumble for the cell within the blink of an eye. As she struggled to make the catch, she took several stumbling steps down the hall before slipping into the guest bedroom where she'd spent the night. Eve held herself flush against the wall, reeling from an encounter she could only liken to a mental ménage à trois.

Gulping in air, she was arrested by the vortex of emotions that swirled through all three of them. Alec was sick with jealousy, Reed was tormented by guilt, and she . . . she felt an all-pervasive confusion.

What the hell had just happened to them?

Inside Eve, something shifted and solidified. Time passed without her registering it. It wasn't until she heard Izzie's quick, light footsteps pass the open doorway followed by Reed's heavier, more arrogant stride that she realized they had finished and were leaving. In her hand, her cell phone vibrated, urging her to answer. *Seven missed calls,* the display read, and she hadn't felt a one. She turned the phone off, shoved it into her pocket, and refastened her jeans.

The comfort of her waistband reminded her—she'd left her gun on the living room floor.

Galvanized, Eve darted out of the bedroom. She was halted by a collision with a steely chest.

"Let go, Reed."

Part of her took comfort in his need to see her. Another part resisted the lying in wait. Perhaps that was all she was to him and Alec, a prize to be won.

He held fast. "It's too late for that now."

Eve opened her mouth to protest, but was silenced by a piercing female scream.

"Shit," she breathed.

"Stay here," Reed ordered, shifting out of the room.

Running to the living room, Eve dug through the backpacks looking for her gun, missing the feeling of safety the weapon imparted.

A shout. This one male, but not Reed's.

She'd have to find the damned gun later. Rushing out the door, she'd just hit the rear lawn when Reed shifted in front of her.

"I told you to stay put," he bit out, his features hard.

"I should be with the others."

"Damn it." He sidestepped into her path when she tried to pass him.

She shoved at his chest with both hands. "Get out of the way."

Reed hesitated, then cursed in a foreign language. He caught her elbow and she increased her pace to a jog to keep up with his long-legged stride. She could feel their physical connection through his senses—the feel of her flesh in his hand, the scent of her perfume, the growing irritation for the yawning emotional chasm between them.

She also sensed Alec. Through her, he felt her interaction with Reed and she felt the way that affected him. The pain and frustration. The fury and bloodlust. She would have expected his emotions to feed into the Novium, but she was cool and calm. Focused on her external problems.

They rounded the corner of the house and the other side of the duplex came into view. Izzie, Ken, and Edwards stood facing the back door, their shoulders set in a way that set Eve's teeth on edge. Sobbing rent the quiet afternoon and drew her attention to Claire who sat crumpled on the ground. The wind blew gently, bringing the scent of sweet Mark blood with it.

As Eve altered her trajectory to skirt the small crowd, her viewing angle changed. The recessed kitchen doorway came into view . . .

. . . as did the disemboweled body that hung upside down from the rafters there. Richens.

"God!" She barely felt the pain of the recriminating mark. Spinning away, she wanted to gag.

"I tried," Reed bit out. "You're too damn stubborn, Eve. You need to—"

Her helpless gaze silenced him midrant. "I-I can't k-keep doing t-this."

Reed caught her to him. His scent was stronger now, more virile. Comforting. Alec reached out to her, too, but she pushed him away. He would worry about her, when he needed to be focused on his own safety.

She didn't understand the connection nor know

how long it would last. It didn't matter. She needed it now and it was there.

"*Mon esprit, c'est perdu, perdu . . .*" Claire sobbed. "*Je ne peut plus rien faire. J'ai perdu toute raison.*"

Eve didn't need to understand French to comprehend that Claire was losing it. The cracking voice and wrenching sobs were heartbreaking. Leaving Reed, Eve crouched beside the fallen Frenchwoman, reaching out a hand out to touch her shoulder.

Claire surged into her arms, rambling incoherent words. "Did you see? *Did you see?* Who could do such a thing to another person?"

"Not who." Reed stood over them, his gaze on the doorway. "*What.*"

Izzie moved closer. Her lipstick had worn off, leaving her looking younger and oddly innocent. "How could this happen? Where was everyone?"

Edwards spoke, his lips white. "Callaghan and I were loading the Suburban in the driveway while Dubois packed up the food in the kitchen. We didn't hear or see anything."

"Where is the rest of your class?" Reed asked, surveying their immediate surroundings.

"I've no idea. Seiler and Hollis took off—"

"They were with me."

A length of silence followed Reed's pronouncement, during which Eve looked at Izzie and caught the narrowing of the blonde's eyes on her. Then, Edwards cleared his throat and said, "Garza and Hogan are shagging somewhere. It's all those two know how to do."

"Where is Gadara?" Ken barked. "We should not be here alone."

Reed pulled his cell phone out of his pocket and turned it on.

"Can't you do that popping in and out thing you do?" Eve asked.

"I'm not leaving you here," he retorted grimly.

Claire looked up, her eyes wild. "We are all going to *die* out here."

"Shut up," Edwards snapped. "The last thing we need is melodrama."

"We're not going to die," Eve soothed, patting her back.

Reed walked a short distance away, his focus on his phone, which beeped a missed call or text message warning.

A growling noise brought Eve's attention back to Ken. He looked ready to blow a gasket. "What good are guards when they cannae stop us from getting killed?"

"We need to forget packing and clearing," Eve said. "I don't think getting out of Dodge is going to solve this problem."

"Aye, we should hunt."

"Bloody hell," Edwards muttered. "You're both daft."

"You are crazy!" Claire's spine straightened. "We should get in the cars and leave this place. Don't look back. Go to Gadara Tower and leave such things to those who know what they are doing!"

Edwards nodded. "I second that. Run like hell. That's the ticket."

"What about the kids across the street?" Eve asked.

"What about them?" Claire shot back. "They are mortal. The Army invited them, they can protect them.

Nothing is going to save *us* other than common sense. God helps those who help themselves."

Ken moved between the corpse and Claire, who was growing more distraught by the minute. "Killing the miserable bajin would do the same."

"Who was the last person to see Richens alive?" Izzie asked.

"I *just* saw him," Eve answered, "about twenty minutes ago." Now she would never know what he'd had to say. That made her indescribably sad.

She had scarcely done more than glance at what remained of Richens's body, but she couldn't forget the sight of him. Strung up by the ankles and wrists like an upside-down starfish. Gutted. His entrails ripped from the now-gaping body cavity and wrapped around his head. Stuffed into his mouth. Blood overflowed from his nostrils and soaked his hair, but it didn't drip. Below him, there was no puddle. Where had the blood gone?

How could this have happened right under their noses? Why hadn't Richens screamed? Did he know his attacker? How else could such an elaborate staging take place on their very doorstep without a sound made?

So many questions and all the immediate answers were terrifying.

"What was he doing?" Edwards asked.

"Sitting on the steps."

"He was lazy," Izzie muttered. "He was always looking for someone else to do his work for him."

Eve shook her head. "You shouldn't speak ill of the dead."

Looking toward Reed, she caught him scowling at his phone. Obviously, he didn't like whatever messages he'd had waiting for him.

Ken's head went back and he growled at the sky. "I didnae hear a thing. Nothing. How is that possible?"

The distant sound of the doorbell caused the group to freeze in place.

"Who's that?" Edwards hissed, looking as if he wanted to bolt.

Eve pushed to her feet. "I'll go look."

Ken came forward. "Allow me."

"Eve?" Linda's voice floated around to the side yard where they stood. "Is everything all right?"

"Shit." She looked at Ken. "I'll stall her. Get him down from there!"

She was running around the corner before she'd finished speaking, nearly crashing into Linda, who was leaning against the side of the house and peering through the sheet-draped window.

"Whoa!" Linda stumbled.

Eve caught her by the forearms and yanked her back upright.

"Where did you come from?" Linda gasped. "One second you weren't there, the next minute you were bowling me over."

"Sorry."

Freddy sat on his haunches beside Linda, his gaze trained at the walkway Eve had just traversed. He whined softly.

"He was barking like mad a little while ago," Linda said, "and looked ready to eat through the front door, which is really out of character for him. Then, we heard the screaming."

"Horrendous wallpaper," Eve improvised. "Some of the fashionistas didn't take it well."

You bullshit good, Freddy said. He looked up at her.

Whatever it was, it came around our pad first and circled the outside.

If her heart could have stopped, it would have.

I think my barking scared it off. I'm sorry I couldn't help your friend. I tried to get out.

Eve rubbed behind Freddy's ears. She would have to question him in depth later. The fact that he'd caught the scent of danger opened another can of worms. A Mark's senses were animalistic in their acuity. Why hadn't the Marks sensed the killer coming?

"Wallpaper?" Linda's dark eyes sparkled behind her black-framed Bulgari glasses. "And here I thought it might be the DVD we lent you."

Eve smiled. "I should share that with the class. It might cheer them up after lime green and orange paisley."

"I like orange." Linda gestured at her tank top. "Can I check out the horror?"

"No!" Eve winced inwardly when Linda's eyes widened. "They hated it so much, they tossed it in the fire."

"Really? That's too bad. And having a fireplace in class? I'm taking the wrong major, I think. Unless Mr. Gadara has a spot for a psychologist."

"How does a psychologist get into ghost hunting?"

Eve's acute hearing picked up the sounds of movement from behind her—rope being cut, grunts of exertion, Claire's muffled gasp followed by more sobbing. The knowledge of what was happening kept Eve on edge. She pushed Alec and Reed to the far corner of her mind, shutting off the view of Richens that filled Reed's vision.

"Unfortunately, parapsychology isn't yet a widely

accepted course of study, so I settled for the closest thing."

"*Para*psychology? Wouldn't that make you a believer?" Eve gestured toward the girls' side of the duplex. "Come inside."

Unfortunately, that side lacked the food and refreshments that would have helped break the ice.

Linda fell into step next to her. With a quick side glance, Eve reconfirmed what she'd noted before. Linda's hair was beautifully, perfectly cut. Her camisole was silk and her leather sandals were Manolos—identical to a pair Eve had at home. The girl was wealthy, but attending a small college in Utah. Eve doubted the production company paid enough to keep her in style, especially considering the lack of a professional camera crew. Had she been born into money? If so, what fueled the desire to hang out in dumps like this with other students far below her social class?

The questions weren't goaded by curiosity. Eve had to learn what Linda's hot buttons were and which ones would get the college kids to pack up and go home.

"I love what you've done with the place," Linda said when they entered the house.

Eve wrinkled her nose. She didn't know whether it was a trick of the mind or not that she still smelled Reed in the empty space. She looked again for her gun, knowing that its presence would be difficult to explain, but it wasn't visible from a cursory inspection.

"I can imagine how cute these homes were once upon a time," she said. "The bones are here—the hardwood floors, the picture windows, even the sea-foam-colored tiles in the bathroom are worth keeping. But neglect has done a number on them, I'm afraid."

"And the bugs." Linda shuddered. "These homes should be condemned."

"I'm really surprised they put you up here instead of in the guest quarters."

"Billeting for guests is on one of the annexes; they don't have anything here at McCroskey. And they don't take pets."

"Gotcha." Heading toward the kitchen, Eve crossed her fingers and hoped there wasn't anything lying around that would incriminate them or arouse suspicions. She was relieved to find only an ice chest in the spot where a refrigerator should be.

"Are you leaving?" Linda asked.

Eve turned and found the brunette looking down at the pile of backpacks and duffels. "Gadara would like to," she admitted, "but I'm still hoping to talk him out of it. I think we still have a lot to learn here."

"Well, I hope you stay, and I hope you'll come with us tonight."

"Problem is," Eve said with regret, "if we stay longer, I don't think you'll be able to film in Anytown."

"We'll just have to work something out," Linda said determinedly. "We have to leave tomorrow for the Winchester Mystery House. We've been granted permission to film some night footage there, but only tomorrow night. Who knows when we'll be back out this way? And honestly, I know having Mr. Gadara on the show would boost ratings. Television is all about ratings, you know. We're not getting rich off *Ghoul School*, but it does fund things we would otherwise have to forgo."

Moving to the sink, Eve washed her hands using the foaming hand wash she'd put there the previous evening. She ripped a paper towel off the roll by the sink, then faced the cooler. She approached it cautiously, unable to stop imaginings of decapitated body parts inside.

"You look like you're expecting something to pop out of there," Linda teased.

Freddy padded over. *I'm ready. No worries.*

Eve winked at him. "This cooler wasn't here earlier. Who knows if the cheese is moving or the bologna has gone bad."

I'll take them.

"Is bologna ever good?" Linda queried with an exaggerated shudder.

I think it's delicious.

"I like it fried." Eve pushed the lid open the rest of the way and peered inside. A variety of beverages, both canned and bottled, were nestled in a soup of melted and semimelted ice. So was a small bag of Styrofoam bowls. Leftovers from the long road trip the day before. "There's soda and water. Are you thirsty?"

"Water would be great."

Ditto.

Grabbing three bottles and the bag of bowls, Eve knocked the lid back down with her elbow and handed a water to Linda. Then, she filled a bowl and set it down on the floor for Freddy.

"So, when will you know if you're staying?" Linda asked.

"We're waiting for Gadara to get back from a meeting with the post commander."

There was a pause as they all drank, then Linda said, "Honestly, this place gives me the creeps."

"You hide it well."

Isn't she a gem? The others freak out, but not Linda. She's always got it together.

"I'm left-brained," Linda explained. "My imagination is dull and boring, so I don't think about zombies chasing me or mass murderers leaping out of dark corners. I don't believe locations can be haunted by those who once occupied them. People once lived here, and now they don't. It's just that simple. That's why the vibe from this place really bothers me."

"You say that," Eve smiled to soften the sting of her words, "but if you didn't believe at all, why would you dedicate so much time to researching the validity of other people's claims?"

"I don't believe, but people close to me do."

"So you want to prove them wrong?"

"I want to help."

"I'm intrigued." And hopeful that there was an exploitable hot button in the story somewhere.

Linda set her half-full bottle on the counter. "Do you have any siblings?"

"A sister."

"Are you close?"

Eve nodded. "She's younger, but she married before me and has two beautiful children. She lives out of state, so I don't see her as much as I'd like to, but we talk often and she sends lots of pictures."

"That's wonderful."

"And you?"

"Only child. But I had a best friend who was like a sister to me. We were inseparable until after high school. I was all set to go to college; Tiffany joined the Army."

"Brave girl."

"Practical. Her parents died when she was young and joining the military was the only way she was going to get college money." Linda sighed. "When word came back that she was killed in action, I was devastated. My grades suffered. I dropped out of school. My boyfriend and I broke up. Everything fell apart."

"I'm sorry."

Linda accepted the condolences with a grim nod. "Have you lost someone close to you, Eve?"

"I recently lost my neighbor, who was also a dear friend."

"Then, perhaps you can understand how difficult it was to learn that Tiffany wasn't dead at all."

Eve frowned. "You lost me."

"It was all a great big cover-up, including a letter from the Department of Defense and a military-provided funeral service." Her voice hardened. "I should have known something was wrong when they couldn't produce a body."

"Why would the government fake her death?"

Freddy moved from his spot by the cooler to sit at Linda's feet. She stroked the top of his head with a distracted rhythm. "I don't know for sure why they did it, but my guess is that she was exposed to some whacky chemicals out in the desert. Something that really messed with her head and they didn't want us to find out about it because of the scandal that would ensue."

"But you figured it out?" Eve suddenly had an inkling of what she must sound like to Reed when she went off about Gadara being shady.

Linda nodded. "My parents took me to Europe in the Spring, hoping the change of location would help my grief. We weren't there a week before I spotted Tiffany at a bakery in Münster, Germany. I called out her name, but when she caught sight of me, she ran.

I've never seen anyone move that fast until you. Today."

Eve shifted her gaze away to avoid revealing her dawning unease.

"Fact was, Tiff *wanted* us to believe she was dead. Whether she was protecting her grandmother and me, or the government, or all of us . . . I have no clue. It took me a week to track her down after that incident in the bakery. I looked for her everywhere, haunting the neighborhood until I finally spotted her again. She didn't run that time. She knew I wouldn't let it go. I'm too stubborn."

"What was her explanation?"

"She swore she had been chosen by God to save mortals, like Joan-of-fucking-Arc or something. She said there were demons among us, hunting us, and it was her mission to kill them."

Eve reached out to the counter to steady herself. "Yikes."

"That's an understatement," Linda muttered. "She was completely delusional, pointing at normal people and saying they were evil, that she could smell their souls rotting. She saw marks and tattoos on her skin that weren't there. She said I couldn't see them because I'm not one of the chosen."

"Lucky you," Eve said sincerely.

Someone has to fight the good fight.

Eve wrinkled her nose at Freddy.

Just sayin'.

"Tiff could tell I didn't buy a word she was saying. I begged her to come home with me. I told her how much her grandmother missed her. How much *I* missed her. I promised to help her get back on her feet. But she wouldn't budge. She said it was better if she was dead to us, because the demons would hurt us if they thought they could get to her that way. She said the only thing I could do was believe. 'When you believe,' she said, 'then I'll come to you for help.'"

"Wow."

"No kidding." Linda straightened. "I never saw her again after that. We stayed in Germany another two weeks, but she didn't contact me at the hotel, even though I gave her the information. I came back to the States and hired a private investigator to find her, but he never did. Sometimes I wonder if I dreamed up the whole conversation in some sort of grief-induced delirium. Then I remember that I have no imagination. I couldn't make that stuff up. So I've been trying ever since to believe her, or at least give the impression that I believe her. I have a blog detailing our investigations, hoping she'll find it and realize I am trying. I figure the show is another way to reach Tiff, too."

"You're a good friend."

Eve couldn't help but consider her own obligation to Mrs. Basso. Her friend and neighbor had died because of Eve's connection to her. What had she done since then to justify that sacrifice? Nada, aside from making a sorry, half-assed attempt at going through the motions. She was shamed to realize how little she'd done to honor the memory of such a wonderful woman.

Shrugging, Linda said wearily, "I wouldn't go that far. Tiffany always did more for me than I did for her and that hasn't changed. Because of her I began researching paranormal investigations, which is how I met Roger. I think he's the love of my life. And we receive letters every week telling us how much *Ghoul School* helped someone in one way or another. It's very rewarding."

Eve wondered where Tiffany was now. Was she still alive? Was she still marked? "What's her last name?"

"Tiff's? Pollack. Tiffany Pollack." Linda polished off her water and screwed the top back on. "I need to take a nap or I'll be worthless tonight. Thank you for the water."

"Any time." Eve smiled. "Or at least as long as we're here."

Linda hooked her thumbs through the belt loops of her shorts and smiled. With the empty water bottle tucked between the palm of one hand and her hip, she looked like a Wild West sheriff with gun at the ready. "I will be seriously disappointed if you don't join us tonight, you know."

"I'm still working on Gadara," Eve said, "but you can count on me tagging along if you end up going."

Her mind was set; she wasn't leaving McCroskey without Linda, Roger, Freddy, and the rest of the *GS* gang. Not unless she knew—without a doubt—that it would be safe to leave them behind.

"Oh, we're going," Linda insisted. "This is the first time a military installation has requested our services. We wouldn't miss it." Linda did a little victory hop. Then she hugged Eve. "You won't be sorry, and I will be eternally grateful. Whether Mr. Gadara comes or not."

"I can't say I'll be good for anything more than screaming inconveniently," Eve warned. "Anytown gives me the chills in the daylight."

And that was before Molenaar had been killed there.

"I'll protect you from the bogeyman," Linda promised with a wink. "Don't worry."

"Keep her safe for me, Freddy," Eve said, giving the Great Dane a quick rub behind the ears.

He woofed in reply. *Watch your back, too.*

Eve gave him the thumbs-up. Then she followed them into the living room to resume the search for her gun.

CHAPTER 13

Alec was exiting the bathroom when his cell phone rang. He sprinted the short distance to the bed where he'd tossed it. Glancing at the caller ID, he winced.

"Shit." He ran a hand through hair he'd just finished dousing in the sink, an ineffectual attempt to cool off his raging temper. He was ready to kill. Starting with Abel.

The last person he wanted to deal with was . . .

"Sarakiel," he bit out before the phone reached his ear.

"Sorry, *mon chéri,*" Sara purred. Forbidden to use her archangel gifts at God's *suggestion,* she relied heavily on the power of her feminine wiles to make up the lack. "I can hear your disappointment, and I do sympathize. Your brother has not been answering his phone, so I, too, have been waiting to speak with someone."

He really didn't give a shit about Sara's issues with

his brother, but that wasn't something he could say to an archangel arbitrarily. It wasn't her fault that he was infuriated by the distance between him and Eve, and the closeness he sensed between her and Abel. He was confused by the singular connection between all three of them. How common were such meldings? How long did they last? What were the ramifications?

"How can I help you, Sara?" She wouldn't be calling him unless she wanted something.

Sara laughed softly. "Do you know why there is an emergency conference call in a few hours?"

His brows rose. Considering the events of the last two days, he didn't know where to start, and he damn well wasn't going to take a stab in the dark. He liked to keep his cards hidden. "Who initiated the call?"

"Uriel. Who else would have something worthy of bothering all of us?"

"It must have something to do with that new class of Infernal." He didn't bother to answer her question.

Moving to the table in the corner, Alec began connecting the various cords that would power up his satellite videophone. He needed to talk with Raguel about the hellhounds before the archangel spoke with the others and since the archangel was playing his power games and refusing to answer his summons, Alec was forced to reach him the secular way. He also wanted to touch base with Uriel. Uriel would explain what happened to him, Eve, and Abel this afternoon without withholding vital information, as Raguel and Sara were likely to do.

"Yes." She didn't sound pleased. "That is what I suspect, but I was hoping for confirmation."

"Well," he drawled, "I imagine that's why you are having a meeting."

"Do not toy with me, Cain."

"Of course not, Sara. I would never do that." The mark on his arm burned in reprimand for the lie. "Listen, I have my own shit pile to shovel through at the moment, but I can tell you that Raguel assigned Abel and Mariel to investigate the most recent sighting in Australia. That guarantees they're the two most knowledgeable *Malakhim*. If you want to stay one step ahead, you might want to stick close to one of them."

"That might be possible, if your brother ever bothered to answer his phone. Where is he?"

Alec had known Sara would disregard contacting Mariel. The archangel had never gotten along well with other women, even easygoing ones.

"He's with Eve," he replied, knowing what the answer would do to Sara. Hell hath no fury like a woman scorned. While Alec couldn't agree with that statement absolutely, he did concede that the two had their comparative qualities and he wasn't above using jealousy to get his brother out of the way. "Considering the danger involved, he's keeping a close eye on her."

"I bet he is." Sara's voice was tight. "I never took you for a trusting soul."

"I trust Eve." And that hadn't changed. She was certain that she was in love with him, regardless of her infatuation with Abel. While that didn't alleviate the feeling that he'd been sucker punched in the gut by a rakshasa demon, Abel had fucked himself six ways to Sunday by messing around with the blonde. As usual, his brother had no idea how to put someone else's feelings before his own.

"Where are they?"

"Fort McCroskey."

Sara made a disgusted noise. "A dreadful place."

"Lucky you're in France." But not for long, he'd bet.

"Actually, I am on a plane."

His smile turned into a grin. "Where are you headed?"

"California."

Beautiful. "When do you arrive?"

"I have only been in the air thirty minutes." Her frustration at her inability to use her gifts was evident in her disgruntled tone.

She wasn't as far along as Alec would like, but it was better than nothing. Sara would keep Abel on his toes and away from Eve. She would also have a contingent of guards with her. Security was never tighter then when two archangels were in close proximity. Eve would be in the safest spot in the world.

"They were planning on pulling out of McCroskey," he advised. "They should be back in Anaheim by the time you arrive."

"Thank the Lord for small favors. I will check in with you in a few hours. Find out where they will be when I land. And keep your phone on."

"If it won't get me killed." Alec snapped the phone shut.

It behooved him to help her, but he only took orders from God. Presently, his latest order was to kill the Alpha, and that took precedence over everything else—including his need to deal with his relationship with Eve.

If he had his way, he'd be on Grimshaw land by nightfall. He definitely wouldn't have his phone powered on then, although he would have it with him. Charles was the reason Alec wasn't with Eve, so sending the Alpha to Hell had to happen as soon as possible. He certainly wasn't waiting for a call from Sara to get things started.

Pulling out a chair, Alec sat and used his cell to call Raguel, inwardly cursing the unnecessary inconvenience. The phone rang longer than usual, then, "Montevista."

He paused a moment at the unexpected voice. "Where's Gadara?"

"Cain." The relief with which his name was spoken increased his unease.

"Who is this?"

"I'm Diego Montevista, the head of Gadara's security team."

Alec leaned into the seat and asked quietly, "Where is Gadara?"

"I t-think—" Montevista cleared his throat. "I think Gadara is dead."

"Say that again."

"There was a creature here, a beast. It s-swallowed Gadara."

"Impossible!" Alec bolted upright, knocking the chair to the floor. "He is an *archangel.*"

"Yes, I know, Cain. I've lived at his side for years. It doesn't change the fact that he was eaten alive by a . . . a *thing* the size of a tank. I saw it with my own eyes, and I'm not the only one who bore witness." The conviction in the Mark's voice was undeniable.

"What happened to the Infernal?"

"The earth opened up and sucked it down. One moment the beast was there, the next the ground split and it sank into the fissure. There were mortals everywhere. An entire company of soldiers stood a few hundred yards away, but all they saw was the felling of two trees."

Alec stared at the blank video screen, his chest lifting and falling in its same measured rhythm even as his world spun haphazardly.

An archangel. Dead. He couldn't imagine it. Not like this. Without fanfare or storms from the heavens. Without a shockwave that reverberated through the world.

It was too quiet. Too still. All wrong.

"How long has he been gone?" Alec asked.

"Less than thirty minutes." Montevista exhaled harshly. "It gets worse."

"How the fuck can it get worse?"

"I just got off the phone with Abel. There was another fatality in the class."

Alec gripped the edge of the table, images of Raguel's students sifting quickly through his mind. He reached out to Eve, felt her touch him in reply. Cool and collected. Controlled. She had pushed him aside earlier. He'd thought it was because she was mad at him; now he suspected she just hadn't wanted him to cloud her mind with his worry.

"Chad Richens," he murmured, seeing the scene through her mind's eye.

"How did you know that?" Montevista asked. "Did they call you first?"

"No. You need to get back to the other students."

"I'm on my way now." In the background, a car door slammed shut and an automobile engine rumbled to life. "Gadara suspected Charles Grimshaw of this morning's attack, but I'm not sure this second killing fits the Alpha's MO. Gadara said he would circle us for a while before striking again—"

"Charles thinks he has the upper hand; he's not going to play it safe anymore." And it would only worsen when he learned about Raguel. “Why was Richens alone after what happened this morning?”

“He wasn’t. All of the other students were nearby.”

Yet no one heard a thing, and Eve had been *right* there. Alec considered his options. He could get back to Monterey in a couple of hours . . .

But first he had to understand what he was walking into. Charles wanted *him*. A trap wasn’t inconceivable.

Montevista growled. “I know how bad this sounds, but my team isn’t inept. We’re being ambushed. Stalked. It’s against the rules to—”

“Fuck the rules.” Charles had obviously tossed them into the fire. They would, too. “How did you get Raguel’s phone?”

“He left it behind.”

“Was his confrontation with the Infernal *planned*?”

“Totally. He was gunning for it.”

Alec’s thoughts raced. “Did you check the phone for messages?”

“No.”

“Do it.”

Standing, Alec walked through the adjoining door and headed to the bathroom. Giselle lay on the pile of towels he’d spread out on the floor—still cuffed, gagged, and now deeply asleep. As he watched, she made soft chuffing noises of pleasure. His gaze lifted to the far wall. He’d bet there was a poor soul in the next room, taking a nap and having a doozy of a nightmare. Feeding the Mare.

“Power up,” he muttered to her. “You’re going to need it.”

“What did you say?” Montevista asked.

Alec shut the door quietly. "Nothing. Find anything?"

"A text message from Uriel about a conference call at three o'clock. That's only a couple hours from now."

"Right. I'll be there. Make sure Abel is there, too. Don't let any of the Marks out of your sight, especially Evangeline Hollis. Don't expect her to cooperate either," he said dryly. "Sometimes she does, sometimes she doesn't."

"She's a woman," Montevista said, as if that explained everything. Which it did.

"She's *my* woman."

"Understood."

Alec rubbed the back of his neck and looked out the window at the Mustang parked just outside the door. Hop in, hit the gas. So easy. He wished.

"Cain?"

"Yeah?"

"I don't know what to do." The Spanish inflection in Montevista's voice was more pronounced, deepened by sadness and confusion. "Who should I notify? Who do I take orders from? You?"

"Yes, me. I'll take care of the peripherals."

Whether Raguel was truly gone was debatable. Alec had known the archangel the whole of his life and he had yet to see Raguel do anything completely self-sacrificing. A kamikaze attack wasn't in keeping with what Alec knew. But there was no benefit to what-ifs at this point. The fact was simple: a once-in-an-immortal-lifetime opportunity had arisen. He could step up to the plate and take over the firm for the present, proving he was capable of the position.

But . . . the odds of him securing the necessary

blessings without manipulation were slim, and thanks to Eve's penchant for landing in trouble, he was running out of favors and secrets to exploit.

"What do you want me to do?" Montevista asked.

"Your job is to keep those students safe until you can be extracted. What's holding things up in that department?"

"Hank is flying up here, along with a crew to investigate the earlier slaying. Once they bring Gadara's private plane, we can fly out. I tried to arrange an immediate departure, but the Monterey airport is tiny and none of the airlines had the space to accommodate the whole class on such short notice. Breaking up into smaller groups was just too risky."

"And venturing out in public while you're waiting would endanger mortals. If an attack is coming, you want to be somewhere you can fight back."

"Exactly."

And yet no great battle had been fought for Raguel's life, despite the proximity of a literal—albeit mortal—army. "Why was Raguel near a company of soldiers?"

"The base commander gave permission for a television show to film at Anytown—the place where Jan Molenaar was killed this morning. Gadara hoped to convince the colonel to reschedule."

"Get Abel to follow up with that." A television show. Somehow he'd missed that.

"You say that as if he'll listen to me. I'm only a Mark."

"—who's following my orders. He'll do it. And tell him to answer his phone when I call. I'll get with him in a few minutes, and he sure as shit better pick up."

He checked the clock on the nightstand. Two hours before the conference call.

The mark on his arm burned with vicious intensity, reiterating Sabrael's order to put down the wolf.

Alec scowled heavenward. As if he could forget. He was hoping that killing the Alpha would kill the problem.

But first he had to get over his aversion to blitzkrieg attacks. He was a sniper by nature, choosing to wait for the perfect moment. One strike, one kill. He didn't have that luxury now. The longer Charles was alive, the bolder and more dangerous he would become.

"I'll talk to you at the time of the conference," Alec said. "But if you need me beforehand, you have my number."

"I wish you were here. Protecting an archangel against possible threats is a hell of a lot different from protecting a multitude of untrained Marks from actual danger."

"I promise to get there as soon as I can."

Alec snapped the phone shut. Then he set to work on keeping that promise. Turning with the intent to wake up Giselle, he nearly ran into the giant occupying the doorway between the two adjoining rooms.

"Sabrael," he greeted, only slightly surprised. He blinked, engaging the wash of celestial tears that protected his eyes from the blinding brilliance of the being before him. Sabrael stood in his customary pose—arms crossed and legs spread wide to better anchor him to the ground.

The seraph's piercing blue eyes examined him. "You will proceed with your assignment, Cain."

"You know about Raguel?"

"Of course." Something dark passed over Sabrael's features.

"I'm going to manage the firm in his absence." Alec

never asked for what he wanted, since the answer was always no.

"You are far from qualified."

"Prove it," Alec challenged with a jerk of his chin. "Tell me who's lived with the mark longer than I have."

"Foot soldiers do not advance to generals overnight, regardless of how well they have performed on the battlefield."

"I would hardly call the passage of centuries an overnight occurrence."

Sabrael's head tilted to one side. His unrestrained ebony hair slid over a massive shoulder and the top of a wing like liquid silk. "Perhaps Abel would be the better choice," he murmured. "He is in the thick of things, as they say."

Alec laughed through the clenching of his gut. "Abel won't want the responsibility. He doesn't even keep his cell phone on."

"But he follows the rules."

"Is that what you need right now? With one archangel out of commission, a rogue Alpha with an ax to grind, a rash of slaughtered Marks, and an unknown breed of Infernal on the loose? You want someone who does only what's required and follows the rules?"

There was a length of silence before Sabrael spoke. "I never knew you had such lofty ambitions."

"There is a lot you don't know about me."

"True. Such as, how badly do you want this?"

Inside Alec, frustration and fury raged. He'd played this game before; it kept his hands dirty. "What do you want, Sabrael?"

"I have yet to decide."

"Makes it hard for me to decide, then. Of course, Abel won't give you a damn thing."

A frightening shadow briefly transformed the seraph's features. His bluff had been called and he didn't like it. "I will speak to Jehovah on your behalf. As an *interim* solution."

Alec snorted.

Sabrael's slow smile chilled Alec's blood. "But you will owe me, Cain of Infamy."

"You'll have to take a number."

"Number one."

Pointing a finger at him, Alec said, "Get me the go-ahead first. Then, we'll see where we're at."

"What are you doing?"

Reed watched as Eve bolted up from her crouch. Raguel was gone, two Marks were dead, and she was alone; a state that had led to two Mark deaths already today. To make matters worse, he could feel Cain like a phantom limb. Altogether, his patience was short and his temper shorter.

She spun around, her long ponytail arcing through the air. "Jeez! You scared me."

"What are you doing here by yourself?" he barked. "You should have come back as soon as the girl left."

"I lost my gun."

He wanted to shake her. "I don't give a shit. What's your aversion to a flame-covered sword? You know you can summon one at any time."

The line of her mouth turned sullen. "I'm not so great with swords."

"You killed a dragon with one," he reminded.

"Forget the gun for now and rejoin the others. You're less likely to be attacked in a group."

"What if one of the group is the killer?"

Pausing, he stared at her for a long moment. Then he exhaled harshly. "Enough, Eve."

"Richens didn't make a sound. Perhaps his attacker wasn't perceived to be enough of a threat to elicit a scream or a fight."

"Or the Infernal was a witch, warlock, wizard, mage, or faery who bound his vocal cords."

"Like the faery who participated in the exercise today? The faery who was within several feet of Molenaar when we found him?"

"Your conspiracy theory is mucking things up in your brain. Did the faery stink or not?"

"To high heaven," she groused.

"The Infernals who work for firms have a compelling reason to stay in the archangels' good graces—they can't go home. You know that. You said it yourself."

"It seems foolish to rule them out, though."

He chastised her with a shake of his head. "In the history of Marks, we've never had a rogue Mark in training. After a few years, yes. But not fresh. They're too new to the realities of Celestials and Infernals to decide to go one way or the other. They just float with the tide for a while until they catch their bearings."

"Okay," she conceded. "Hang with me; brainstorming helps me think. So, let's run with the bad guy Infernal theory for a bit. They must be wearing that masking stuff to hide their scent, or Templeton would have smelled them."

"Or the rat was lying."

Eve ignored him and went on. "There was no residual smell around either of the bodies. With that level of brutality, the killer would have to be worked up. Blood pumping, soul rotting . . . maybe they cut themselves. I saw a forensic show on television where they said most knife wielders injure themselves. In any case, the scene should have stunk at least a little if it was really an unmasked Infernal who did it."

Reed felt himself smiling, despite the events of the day.

"You're laughing at me," she accused.

"No. I'm congratulating myself. You're going to be a great Mark, babe. If you don't get killed first." He gestured toward the front door. "Speaking of which, we should be tossing these ideas around with the others. Just don't get them all riled up this time."

"Alec says sometimes you have to shake things up," she grumbled, "to see what falls out."

"Everyone has been shaken up enough." And it was about to get worse. Somehow, he had to tell them about Raguel without inciting total pandemonium. The Frenchwoman in particular seemed fragile.

She nodded. "You're right. We have work to do, too. Garza and Hogan are missing, so we should—"

"Romeo and the princess are back. Looking rumpled and slightly worse for wear."

"Maybe there's something in the water. Seems to be going around."

"Could be. Toss a little aphrodisiac in the food, get everyone so horny they're too busy getting off to fight back, and *wham*! Take 'em out. Brilliant Infernal strategy."

Eve snorted. "You're a riot."

"It was your idea. And where did you come up with those nicknames?"

"Don't you know?" She stared at him. "You were in my head."

And what an experience that had been. He had no idea how other women's brains worked, but he knew he liked the way Eve's did. It was convoluted and slightly twisted—as he'd come to accept as the norm for females—but regardless, it functioned with what he considered to be the perfect mix of creativity and common sense. She also had the hots for him. Not just the horny kind of hots, but the deeply rooted type of fascination that could lead to something that scared the shit out of him.

"I was interested in other things at the time."

"Hope you enjoyed the view," she said testily. "I got nothing out of you, besides a swift kick in the ass."

He hadn't had a choice. He couldn't allow her to see his ambition to ascend to archangel. And her role in that. "Sure you did. You're so attuned to me now, you have no defenses. I walked right up to you and no alarms went off."

"It's called distraction." But her frown belied her words.

"You wish that's all it was."

She blew a stray strand of hair out of her face and looked adorable while doing it. "Why can I still feel you and Alec in my head?"

He was still reeling from the experience. He had a picture of Cain in his mind, one built by a lifetime of association. Yet Cain, as seen through Eve's eyes, was not the same. "Hell if I know. I've never heard of anything like it."

"Well, someone has to know what happened and how long it will last."

"Yes. And I intend to find out. In the meantime, let's rejoin the others. We have a lot to discuss."

Eve scrubbed both hands over her face. “I feel naked without a gun.”

The statement would have sounded melodramatic coming from most people, but Eve had spent a few hours of every week for the last few years practicing her aim at a Huntington Beach shooting range. As a single woman, living alone, she’d felt as if she needed the added protection. Reed was more inclined to think her senses had picked up on the Infernal undercurrents, even if her brain hadn’t yet been trained to catch on. She was made for this work.

He gestured toward the door. “We’ll ask the others if they’ve seen it.”

“Ugh.” Eve’s nose wrinkled. “I’d prefer to think it was around here somewhere.”

Reed crossed his arms. “Why?”

“I set it down earlier. You know . . . *before*.” Her gaze moved to the hallway, which was clearly visible from where they stood. “I don’t want to think about one of them seeing . . . hearing . . . I would rather believe I didn’t embarrass myself.”

“You would rather pretend it didn’t happen,” he corrected. “I won’t let you.”

Eve glared. “If you want to remember your tryst with a tart, go ahead. But don’t presume to make that decision for me.”

“A tryst,” Reed repeated wryly, indulging in an inner smile. “With a tart. My . . . You *are* jealous.”

“Fuck you.”

Irritated by his own feelings of guilt, he taunted her by reaching for his belt buckle.

“Whip it out,” she challenged. “See what happens.”

Pausing, Reed assessed her warily. He couldn’t get

a read on her thoughts. "What do you intend to do to it?"

"Did Izzie get the third degree, too?"

"No." His hands went to his hips. "I told her what I wanted. Her opinion didn't matter."

"Yes, that seems to be the only way you like it."

Reed's jaw clenched. She was referring to their lone encounter in the stairwell. He hadn't been able to get in her fast enough. Everything in his way—her clothes and conscience—was disregarded in the intensity of his need.

"It's the way you like it, too," he bit out.

"A one-shot deal." Her mouth thinned to a fine line. "Lucky for you, you found greener grass elsewhere."

It didn't escape his attention that she was starting to sound like Alec. "The grass wasn't greener. It just didn't have a guard dog."

"Don't blame this on Alec. He didn't deserve to be hurt the way he was today."

"He's a big boy, Eve."

She ran a hand over the top of her head and growled softly. "It's one thing to know that what you're doing can hurt someone. It's another thing altogether to feel their pain as if it was your own. Alec really cares about me and I repay him by having a stupid crush on *you*."

Reed struggled to stem cruel words. Damn it, that stung. He could tell her that what happened today wouldn't have been possible if they didn't have feelings for each other, but she knew that already. It was simply easier for her to pretend otherwise. Too bad for her, he was sick of pretending.

"The hurt you felt was your own," he shot back.

"And you love that, don't you?" Her lovely face took on a hardened cast, shutting him out. "It didn't matter to you who you stuck your dick in, but you're gloating that it mattered to me."

"Think how much worse you'd feel if I'd stuck it in you. I did us both a favor." And he was an asshole for doing it. He'd lied to himself about hiding the encounter from her. Her discovery had been inevitable, and some part of him had wanted to get to her that way. To show her how it felt to him, knowing that Cain could have her any time.

She laughed, the sound absent of any joy or humor. "You went to Izzie for *me*? What a great line. Pass all responsibility for your actions to my shoulders."

He grabbed her arm and yanked her closer. "You would have spread your legs in a heartbeat if I'd bothered," he snarled, "and we both know it. But like I said, I've seen that show. I'm waiting for the episode where you come to me."

As short as she was, Eve still stood up to him. Her chin lifted, her shoulders went back. "You don't need me, Reed. You *want* me, sometimes—apparently only when Alec is around to be irritated by it—but that's as far as it goes. I won't give up what I have for that."

Reed pushed her away. "Then you should be really damn happy I played the gentleman today. Lord knows I didn't do it for me."

Reaching into his pocket, he withdrew his cell phone and turned it back on, keeping his gaze on the illuminating face rather than meeting Eve's wounded and furious gaze. Due to Sara's frequent calls, he had powered up his phone only long enough to call Raguel. He had no one to call now, but the act of playing with the damn thing gave both him and Eve the chance to cool down. They needed to work together on this, not bicker about what couldn't be changed.

His phone beeped as it woke to full operation, but there were no waiting messages. That bothered him more than a full voicemail box. Sara was more inclined to escalate her attempts than to give up.

Eve acted as if she were focused on dusting herself off. "Let's go."

"Listen." Reed looked at her. "I don't know how long these residual connections between us will last."

"We can't get rid of them soon enough for me," she muttered.

"You're starting to use some of Cain's phrasing, and we've established that we can feel each other's emotions. That could be disastrous for all of us, if we don't get it under control."

"How so?"

"If Cain is gung-ho in his hunt for Charles, you could feel the same recklessness."

Her frown altered into raised brows. "And if I feel fear, he could feel it."

"Right. Which means we need to keep you even-tempered and focused while he's hunting Grimshaw." Not for his brother's sake, but for Eve's. If she was inadvertently responsible for crippling Cain in battle, she would never forgive herself.

"Then you should probably know," she began with a determined glint in her dark eyes, "that if Gadara can't get the base commander to delay those kids across the street, I'm going with them into Anytown tonight."

Reed froze. "You are *not* going back there."

"We can't leave them here alone!"

"Raguel is dead, Eve."

Eve stumbled back as if struck. He'd meant to break

the news with more tact, but her pronouncement took him off guard.

"Abel." A grim masculine voice broke the heavy silence.

Reed didn't move his gaze from Eve, but she glanced at the door, her eyes wide like a deer caught in headlights.

"Montevista," she breathed. "Where is Gadara?"

The guard replied unflinchingly, "In the belly of an Infernal."

Reed studied the Mark, taking in the man's stocky build and jaded eyes. There was a calm, steadfast air about him that inspired confidence. Reed could see why Raguel had relied on this Mark for his safety.

Eve's lower lip quivered. "What happened?"

Montevista explained, visibly weary as he spoke. He looked at Reed when he was done. "Cain wants you to turn your phone on so he can call you."

Reed glanced down at his cell, understanding now why he'd turned it back on to begin with. He was still connected to his brother in some way. He glanced at Eve, who seemed not to notice his dismay. She might be the conduit, but if so, she didn't feel the information passing through her.

"What type of Infernal was it?" Eve crouched and began digging through the duffel bags again.

"I have no idea."

She looked at Reed. "Was it your mystery demon?"

"The description is the same," he said.

"We need to go back to that copse of trees and see what's there that might help us go after Gadara."

Montevista exhaled harshly. "You don't believe he's dead?"

"She doesn't believe anything," Reed growled, still stinging.

Eve glared at him. "Gadara doesn't strike me as the type to commit suicide. Isn't suicide a sin?"

"Murder defies God's command," Montevista answered. "Suicide is self-murder."

"So it's doubtful Gadara would do it, right? He must have had a plan."

"We can hope, but how would he know how to deal with a class of Infernal we've never heard of before?"

"*We* haven't, but maybe *he* has. It's the first time he's seen it right? Maybe he recognized it."

"I doubt that," Reed said. "Mariel and I described the creature very clearly."

"I'm just tossing out ideas." Eve finally gave up looking for her gun and stood. "We also have to take into consideration the setup you walked into—fire alarm set and Infernal restrained outside. If they'd wanted the soldiers dead, they would have killed them before you guys got there."

Montevista looked at Reed. "Was she a cop?"

"Interior designer."

"She's pretty good at this for a novice."

"Enough to be dangerous," Reed agreed.

"Hey!" Eve pushed his shoulder, which didn't budge him at all. "I'm right here."

He shrugged. "You're here. Whether or not you're right remains to be seen."

"You agree that the culprit is probably Grimshaw?" Montevista asked.

"If Gadara and Alec think so," she said, shrugging, "I'll follow their lead."

"That's a first." Reed's jaw set. "But you're not going back to Anytown. That's not debatable."

"It makes sense that it would be the Alpha," she continued, ignoring him. "He's the only demon we know of who has openly declared war on us."

Montevista tensed. "He has?"

"He's already killed me once."

"He has?" Running a rough hand through his close-cropped hair, Montevista cursed in Spanish.

"And we're not having a repeat performance," Reed said grimly, "which is why you're not going to—"

His phone rang, interrupting his words. As he pulled it from his pocket, the muffled tune of his "Jessie's Girl" ringtone became crystal clear. The caller's name glowed on the screen.

Cain.

Growling, Reed lifted the phone to his ear. "What?"

"Fuck you, too," his brother retorted. "Has Montevista reached you yet?"

"Yes. And we're busy."

"Have you arranged to meet with the colonel?"

Reed's jaw clenched at the impatience in Cain's tone. It didn't help matters to see Eve and Montevista huddled together in conversation. "That's none of your damn business."

"It's absolutely my business, since I'm heading Raguel's firm in the interim."

"No fucking way." *Raguel's absence had created a firm vacancy.* Shit. He should have made that mental leap earlier. His focus was still on finding Raguel, not replacing him. Once again, Cain was ahead of him, knocking him out of the running before he even had a chance to play.

"Yes way, little brother." Cain's tone was so smug, Reed wished he was nearby so they could talk with their fists.

"Then shift over here and deal with the colonel yourself!" Reed hung up, his mind whirling.

Cain's *mal'akh* gifts had been curbed. He couldn't shift from one location to another in any celestial way. His wings were clipped and discolored a dark, inky black. Why would *he* be given the power to rule a firm when he couldn't be trusted with an angel's gifts?

It was so unreasonable, Reed couldn't believe it. Cain was a nomad, a wanderer, a sociopath. Aside from Eve, Reed couldn't recollect anyone whose feelings Cain had put before his own. How could he be charged with the safety of millions of people?

And why in hell did he sound so damn pleased about it?

CHAPTER 14

Alec briefly considered redialing his brother, then thought better of it. Abel would need to digest the state of affairs for a while. The dig about shifting was a knee-jerk reaction. All the archangels were stripped of their powers except for seven weeks of the year. They managed without them; so would Alec.

He dialed 4-1-1 instead and requested the phone number to the commandant's office. A few minutes and connections later, he was told that the colonel had left for the day and wouldn't be available until tomorrow.

"Shit." He needed a Plan B. After considering his options, he called Hank.

"Cain!" The coarseness of the answering voice was reminiscent of Larry King, yet Hank's true gender was a mystery. An occultist who specialized in the magical arts, Hank was a chameleon, changing form and gender to suit the client. The only things that never changed about Hank was the flame-red hair and head-to-toe black attire. Those were staples.

"To what do I owe the pleasure of your call?" Hank husked.

"Death and destruction."

"Sounds like my kind of party." Hank made a choked noise, then shouted, "Be careful loading that box! The contents are irreplaceable."

"Where are you now?"

"At the Monterey Municipal Airport in Northern California. Raguel called me up here. I had to bring my equipment, so I was forced to fly. Can't expect Marks to understand how important my gear is. If I left it to them, they'd break everything in transit. Even loading up the rental van seems to be too much for them."

Alec considered Hank his favorite Infernal. In the dozen centuries or so since Hank joined Raguel's team, the demon had proven to be extremely helpful. "Who's with you?"

"Two investigators from the Exceptional Projects Department and two guards."

Alec exhaled with relief, then explained the situation as it now stood.

"I know," Hank said. "I felt it the moment Raguel was gone."

"How?" After noting the complete lack of celestial reaction to Raguel's disappearance, Alec was more than startled to hear that an Infernal had sensed what no one else appeared to.

"We've been working together a long time. He bonded with me just as he has to all the Marks who work for him."

Alec reached a hand out to the wall, bracing himself against what he considered to be an earth-shaking revelation. "Do all Infernals working for archangels bond with their firm leaders?"

"Sure. Why not?"

Holy shit. Infernals bonding with archangels. Sharing information. Seeing how each other's minds worked.

Shaking off his astonishment, Alec went back to the original point of his call. "When you get to McCroskey I need you to report all of your findings to me in real time. Don't wait for an official report."

There was a short pause, then, "Have you stepped into Raguel's wings?"

"In a manner of speaking."

"You give orders like an archangel, my friend. But you do not sound like one."

Archangels had a unique resonance to their voices that inspired both awe and capitulation.

"Roll with me on this," Alec said.

"As you wish. I look forward to seeing your lovely girl again."

"Keep her out of trouble for me, will you?"

"And away from Abel?" Hank purred. Working for the good guys didn't mitigate the innate desire Infernals had for chaos and conflict.

"That, too. Call me when you know something."

"Will do."

Alec hung up and headed into the adjoining room's bathroom. He stood over Giselle and called out, "Wakey wakey."

The Mare didn't budge.

Alec turned on the faucet. He filled his cupped palms with the flowing water, then dumped the whole of it on Giselle. As she sputtered and lurched into a seated position, he backed up swiftly. Her attempt to swipe at her eyes was arrested by the handcuffs, resulting in a yanked arm and a string of muffled bitching.

He crouched beside her and pulled the gag down to hang around her neck. "Sweet dreams?" he asked, smiling.

She glared at him through wet, spiky lashes. "What did you do that for? I wasn't finished."

"Yeah, you were."

"You suck, Cain," she grumbled. "Totally suck. Get me out of these cuffs."

"I need you to draw a layout of Charles's compound. You gonna give me a hard time?"

The petulant curving of her lips changed to a bright smile. "Does this mean I don't have to go with you? I'll draw you the best map ever. Then I'll just wait here for you to finish and we can drive—"

"I need some blood, too."

"—down to Anaheim and—" Giselle's blue eyes widened. "My *blood*? After you chained me to a bathroom sink? You've got to be—"

"Okay." Alec pushed to his feet with a dramatic sigh. "Have it your way."

"Where are you going?"

"To get my knife. If you don't squirm, it might not scar too badly."

"Wait!" she called after him, the handcuffs rattling against the pipes. "Let's talk about this some more. You didn't give me a chance to think. You can't wake a girl up in the middle of a meal and expect her to be fully coherent."

He stood just outside the door with his back to the wall, smiling.

"Cain! Damn you," she complained. "Didn't your

mother teach you any manners? This is not the way you're supposed to treat guests!"

Backtracking, he kneeled at the sink and pulled the cuff keys out of his pocket. "When you're an uninvited guest, all bets are off."

He released her and stood.

Giselle rubbed her wrist, then she held out her hand to him for assistance gaining her feet. Her blonde hair was a mess from both the handkerchief and bed head, but the look was a good one on her. "This floor is hard and cold."

"If you hadn't wiggled so much, you might have been somewhat comfortable."

"You shouldn't cuff people to pipes!"

"Don't make me gag you again."

"You are really not a very nice person."

"Says the demon who gives people nightmares," he retorted.

"I have to eat!"

Alec preceded her out of the bathroom. He went to the nightstand and withdrew the hotel letterhead from the drawer. Setting it on the tabletop along with the provided pen, he said, "Draw. Now."

"Go. To. Hell." But she plopped onto the edge of the bed and caught up the pad. Her hand began to push the pen across the paper. "It's a gated community. I don't see how you're going to get past the guards. You stink."

Alec opened the backpack he'd set on the other bed and pulled out a bottle of body wash. The contents had already been laced with an anticoagulant. He just needed some Infernal blood to add to the mix.

"You're going to fix that." He faced her.

Giselle's eyes dropped to the syringe in his hand.

Her mouth fell open. "Uh . . ." She swallowed hard. "I'm afraid of needles."

"It will only pinch a minute."

She shook her head violently and stood. The pad dropped to the floor. "You don't understand. The sight of blood makes me vomit."

Alec's brows rose. It figured that he would end up with the one demon who had a gore complex. "You don't want to find out what happens if you puke on me."

"Then don't stick me with that! What kind of sick torture is this?"

"You know damn well what I'm doing." He gestured to the bed with a jerk of his chin. "Sit down."

"Can't we have sex instead?" she suggested, setting her hand on her hip and trying to look seductive. "You'll smell just as nice, and it's less painful."

"For you maybe. Now sit."

Giselle opened her mouth, but the look on his face must have warned her off. She dropped back onto the bed and held out her slender arm, turning her face away.

Alec kneeled and said, "I'm good at this. It'll be over before you know it."

She kept her head turned. "People only say that about things that last forever."

"Count to twenty." He secured the tourniquet. As always, he took a moment to absorb the similarities between them—the beating hearts, the pumping blood, the fragile shell of their skin.

"*Ett, två,*" she began, shivering as he tapped the inner fold of her elbow with his fingertips, "*tre, fyra—*"

Alec slid the needle into a plumped vein.

Giselle screeched and jumped to her feet. Her knee

struck him in the chin, sending him toppling backward into the neighboring bed.

He started to laugh, then pain lanced his brain like a white hot poker. Clutching his head, he yowled in agony.

She screamed, too, then smacked him on the shoulder. "You scared the shit out of me! What are you doing yelling like that?"

Falling onto his side, Alec curled into the fetal position.

"Oh, please," she muttered. "Drop the drama. I barely touched you."

Acid pumped through his veins, eating its way through his system from the inside out. Tears burned his eyes and his throat clogged.

"Are you serious?" Giselle prodded him with her foot. "Cain. Are you bullshitting me or not?"

Alec's back arched and his frame tautened like a bow. He writhed in torment, his bones altering with such alacrity he felt as if he were being ripped apart.

"You're not kidding," she breathed, standing over him. "I really did a number on you."

If he lived, he was going to kill her.

"This could save my ass!" Giselle clapped her hands. "I can tell Sammael that I didn't return to Hell because I had a shot at knocking you out of commission! This is perfect. I'll be a hero. Charles is going to be sick with envy. A Mare taking out Cain of Infamy. Who'd have thought?"

He grabbed her ankle and squeezed. Hard.

"Ow!" She yanked her leg free. "You're hurting me in your death throes."

Heat pooled in his belly, scorching and heavy. It began to radiate outward, lengthening his limbs and extending his fingers and toes. Pulled like a victim on a medieval rack, Alec was ready to pray for death when he felt Eve moving through him. As solid as the pain and just as intense. Phantom arms embraced him, calm and cooling. He struggled into her, grasping at the ethereal feel of her as a drowning man would a lifesaver, dragging her into the anguish with him.

Alec. Her voice. Filled with worry and growing alarm.

Eve began to panic as she sank deeper into his pain, but he couldn't release her. His instinct to survive was too powerful.

His body began to convulse and Giselle screeched. She leaped over him and rushed to the door.

"Stay."

It was his vocal chords that created the sound, but the voice wasn't his. What he heard was deeper, darker. *Resonant.*

Giselle froze with her hand on the knob.

Insanity lapped at Alec like waves of dark, cool water. He sank beneath the surface with Eve in his arms, his body a prison of torment.

Cain!

Alec jerked at the sound of Abel's roar—a reverberating bellow of fury in the still darkness of his mind. Eve resumed her struggles with renewed vigor, reaching upward with flailing arms and gaining purchase. She was ripped from his embrace and pulled away, too far to reach her despite Alec's clawing attempts.

Like a firefly in the darkness, she flitted away. He followed her upward through the suffering of his body, then through the more painful ache created by the knowledge that she was connected deeply enough to his brother to be stolen away.

Then his misery was gone as quickly as it had come.

Peace enveloped him, soothed him, relaxed every muscle and tendon, loosened the fist of heartbreak that tightened his chest.

His eyes flew open. The ceiling was lowering to him.

No, he was rising toward it. Levitating.

The roaring of blood in his ears faded to the background and pitiful sobbing filled the gap. He straightened from his prone position, his feet aimed toward the earth, his head pointed toward the heavens.

Shrugging off the lingering tension with a roll of his shoulders, Alec's wings burst free. His feathers were black as night—as they had always been—but now tipped with gold.

"My life sucks," Giselle cried, drawing his attention. She sat crumpled by the door, her lovely face wet with tears.

Alec smiled, reveling in the power that flowed through him like an electrical current. His feet touched down on the carpeted floor and he stood a moment, soaking up the flood of knowledge that poured into his consciousness. What was most pleasant, however, was the tranquillity he felt. His emotions no longer ruled him. In fact, he scarcely felt them at all.

"Sammael will never take me back now." Giselle sniffled and scrubbed at her running nose. "I've turned Cain of Infamy into an archangel."

Eve jolted as the doorway between her mind and Alec's slammed shut with violent finality. Drained and devastated, her knees gave way, but she was caught by strong arms and held tightly. The scent of Reed's skin drifted across her nostrils and brought her back to herself.

Her back was to his front, his lips at her ear. She blinked and recognized the interior of the girls' side of the duplex.

"What the fuck was that?" Montevista's gaze darted between both of them. "One minute we're having a conversation and the next, you two are off in some kind of zombie trance!"

Gasping, Eve's hand lifted to her shirt. She'd half expected to find it dripping wet, but it was bone dry. The sensation of floating on an inky sea had seemed so real . . . And mind-breakingly terrifying.

"Something *awful* just happened to Alec." She broke free of Reed's hold and faced him. "We have to find him."

Reed's face was set into an unreadable, yet ominous mask. His dark eyes were cold, his lips hard. "He almost killed you."

Hearing the words said aloud was a shock to Eve's system. Although their connection had felt that way, she couldn't believe that had been his conscious intent. "He would never hurt me."

"He's not the same person anymore, Eve."

She frowned, fighting off the lingering fuzziness in her brain. "What do you mean?"

Reed's jaw tensed, then, "He has been promoted to archangel."

"Huh?" Dread sank like a heavy stone in her gut. "How is that possible?"

"Raguel is gone. Alec was tapped to step into his shoes."

"Alec?" Her arms wrapped around her middle. "How do you know . . . ?"

"He told me," he bit out. "He's never given a shit about anyone in his life, and now he is responsible for caring for thousands of Marks."

Eve had no idea how she was supposed to react. What did this mean? What would happen to her and Alec now? She pulled out her cell phone and speed-dialed Alec.

Sydney called out from her position on the stoop. "A van just pulled up."

Outside, an automobile horn honked twice.

"Reinforcements?" Eve asked, frowning when she reached Alec's voicemail.

A cell phone went off, its ringtone a Paul Simon song that Eve couldn't quite place. Montevista dug into his pocket and withdrew a sleek silver smartphone.

"That's Raguel's," Reed noted.

"Yes, it is." The phone fell silent. However, the caller ID was apparently still visible on the face, because he said, "Hank's here."

Eve hurried toward the door. Just as her foot stepped over the threshold, she paused, causing Montevista to bump into her from behind. She tripped but caught herself on the partition that framed the back of the cement porch step—the twin to the one she'd tackled Molenaar through on the boys' side.

"Are you all right?" the guard asked, frowning. "Maybe you should take it easy."

"Where are the Infernals?"

He blinked. "Which ones?"

"The ones Gadara brought with him. The faery, the dragon, and the gwyllion. And whoever else there might be."

"It's just the three. The faery can work with any glamour."

"Where are they now?"

"They're staying in a house around the corner." He gestured in the direction of Anytown.

"Why aren't we using them?"

"We are. They're helping my team with the bodies."

The mention of "bodies" made Eve shiver inwardly. "What are they doing with them?"

"Field autopsies."

"You brought equipment for that?"

His look was wry. "That's why we're using the Infernals."

"Gotcha. Where is this happening?"

"In Anytown. Lots of space, no public access, and it's near the scene of the first attack, which was still being examined at last check-in."

Reed brushed past them and headed out to the driveway.

"Have you looked over the area yourself?" she asked.

"A cursory inspection, but my job is to stay with Gadara." A cloud passed over Montevista's blunt features. "My job *was* to stay with him."

Eve touch his biceps gently, imparting silent comfort. She still didn't know the whole story about what happened to Gadara, but she would be there when it was explained to Hank and could catch up then. With that in mind, she started moving again. Montevista fell into step beside her.

"What are you getting at?" he asked.

"I would imagine you're going to head over there soon."

He glanced at her. "There's no way Cain or Abel is going to allow you to go back there."

"Can you really tell me that it's safer here than there? Especially if you're there and not here?"

His mouth curved. "Not really, no."

"See? Don't worry about them. I'll get them on board," she assured. "If they let me check out the area now and we keep it under surveillance afterward, I'll have no problem making my regrets to the *Ghoul School* team."

"I can't wait to see this. Can you tell me why you're pushing this so hard? You know we're all doing the best we can to figure out what's going on."

"I just feel like I'm missing something, and I can't let it go until I know what it is."

He bumped her shoulder with his. "Good Marks always follow their guts."

They reached the driveway where Ken, Edwards, and Romeo were helping Hank—whose sole contribution to the effort appeared to be dire warnings—unload a variety of wooden crates from the back of a black van. Izzie, Lauren, and Claire sat in the shade of an oak tree on the edge of the driveway. Their attention was divided between something they watched on Claire's laptop and Hank's appearance, which altered from a buxom, beautiful, Jessica Rabbit–type redhead in a Morticia Addams dress and a tall, well-built, red-haired hunk—depending on the gender of the person he was speaking to. The transformations were fluid and instantaneous. A blink and they would be missed.

As Eve approached, Hank caught sight of her. Altering to the masculine form, the occultist moved toward her with a wide smile and leisurely stride. He was dressed in a black dress shirt and black slacks, the severity enhancing the red currant color of his hair.

He held his hands out to her, studying her with both pleasure and curiosity. "Lovely Eve, so good to see you again."

She placed her hands in his. She always got the impression that he enjoyed her as a scientist enjoyed experiments. "Hi, Hank."

The Infernal paused, head tilting to the side as he read her. "Cain has altered. Advanced. Blossomed. You don't like it."

"That's not true," she protested, deciding that she really hated how people were just popping in and out of her head. "I don't understand it. I'm hoping you'll explain it to me."

Ken cursed and Hank spun around, morphing into the red-hot female before he'd completed the rotation and shouting in a masculine growl, "Be careful with those! Please."

"What have you got in here?" Edwards gasped, limping under the weight of a smaller box. "An elephant?"

"Must I do everything myself?" Hank muttered. Holding a hand aloft, Hank's fingers snapped and the box was gone from Edwards's hands.

Without the weight to balance his contorted pose, the Englishman toppled over. "Bloody hell! If you could do that the whole time, why didn't you?"

Hank faced Eve again, as a man. "Novices are so tiresome."

"I'm a newbie."

"You are unique."

Uniquely plagued with bad luck. She visually searched the area. "Where did the box go?"

"Into the house." Linking their arms, Hank started toward the men's side of the duplex.

She glanced over her shoulder at Montevista. "Don't leave without me."

The guard gave her the thumbs-up.

As she and Hank passed the girls, Eve asked, "Do you know what they're doing?"

"Watching a video they found in the kitchen."

Eve frowned. "A video?"

"A television show about ghosts here at the base."

"Oh . . . right."

"I can't tell you much about Cain's advancement," Hank went on. "To my knowledge, no one has been promoted to archangel in the history of . . . well, in history. Period."

"Great."

"You worry that you've lost him."

She shook her head. "I worry that he's lost himself. I was with him—in him—when the change happened. I don't know how anyone can live through pain like that and still be the same person. I could feel his . . . *soul* separating from his body."

"He did not lose his soul, Evangeline. It has simply connected more fully with God. Sammael is known for his ability to lure the weak to worship, but he has yet to achieve the level of expertise that God enjoys."

"Are you saying that God is *luring* Alec away from me?"

Hank smiled. "He can make Cain happier without you. You bring turmoil. God will give him peace."

"Peace."

"It is easy to entice someone to have sex, yes? Sammael does it every minute. It's much more difficult to convince someone to forsake it, *forever,* yet God manages to do that regularly. With the strong, not the weak."

Eve tried to picture Alec—the most virile man she knew, along with Reed—forsaking sex. "Uh . . . I don't think that—"

"—Raguel is dead?" The sparkle in Hank's pale blue eyes told her that he knew what she'd intended to say. "You're right, I don't."

They reached the porch, and Hank surveyed the damaged partition. They had cleaned up the destruction as much as possible, but it was clear that things were not what they should be.

The front door was open to facilitate the moving of the boxes. Hank entered first, which made Eve wonder if Hank was a woman or just clueless about etiquette. Moving directly to the largest crate, Hank circled it. "It isn't by chance that the number of archangels has been immutable," he murmured.

"No, I wouldn't think so."

He looked at her, smiling. "I love that you aren't naïve, you know. Makes you much more interesting."

"Thanks. You're pretty interesting yourself." She gestured at all the crates. "Can I help you with any of this?"

He pointed to three crowbars propped up against the wall by the door. "There has to be a balance. Just as the kings of Hell are still alive and well, so are the archangels. They both make a great show of protecting themselves, because they don't want to insult the other by making it too easy."

Eve grabbed a crowbar and picked the nearest crate, which was chest height. "Like nuclear weapons in the Cold War? The United States and the Soviet Union spied on each other, lied to each other, and were prepared to blow each other up, but in the end, no one wanted to tip the balance. The cost was too high."

"Exactly."

"But," she tugged on the crowbar, venting her frustrations with physical exertion, "Alec might remain an archangel, regardless of what happens to Gadara?"

Hank's arms crossed over the top of a crate. "Maybe. He could be demoted back to *mal'akh,* which would create more issues to deal with. It's easier to adjust to an improvement in one's circumstances than it is to taste success and slide backward into failure."

Pushing down on the bar with all her might, Eve pried the top open amid a cacophony of protesting nails. "Can you find out who or what killed the two Marks with this equipment?"

"I can certainly give it my best shot. I take it you don't want to talk about Cain anymore?"

"I want to talk *to* him." She managed a half-smile to soften any sting her words might cause. "Although I appreciate what you've shared so far."

She dug through the sawdust that filled the box and withdrew . . . a lampshade. A child's lampshade with a cartoon theme featuring stars and moons. Her brows raised and she looked at Hank.

Blushing, Hank explained, "Frame of mind is as important to success as tools."

"I'll go with that." Which brought home the fact that her frame of mind had been skewed all day. She needed to slow down, take some time alone, and rehash everything she knew about the events with a fine-tooth comb.

Her phone vibrated in her pocket. Hoping it was Alec, she was in such a rush to get it out that she nearly dropped it. But the name on the display was *Mom.* Eve briefly considered sending the call to voicemail, then thought better of it. She needed a hefty dose of reality right now. Her old reality, not her new one.

"I have to get this," she said to Hank. "I'm sorry."

"Don't be. I will still be here when you're done."

"Hi, Mom," she greeted, while moving down the hallway for privacy.

"Your dad just told me you called yesterday. Is everything good?"

Eve winced, but said, "So far. We're busy, but that's to be expected."

"Is Alec with you?"

"No, he's away on business." Not for the first time, she felt what it might be like to live a normal life with Alec. She grieved for that imaginary life when she allowed herself to think about it.

"And Reed?" Miyoko asked. "Is he there?"

"Yes."

"Strange. There is something wrong with Alec that he puts up with that."

Eve smoothed her brow with her fingertips. Her skin felt damp and hot, which worried her. "I would think there was something wrong with a man who interfered with his girlfriend's job."

"Jobs don't last forever," her mother said. "Marriages do."

Unwilling to touch that with a ten-foot pole, Eve looked into the first bedroom as she passed it. It had been completely cleared out. "Is there anything exciting happening with you?"

"Just my children giving me gray hair. Sophia got another tattoo. Two of them."

"Really?" Eve's sister had been fond of tattoos when she was a single girl, but she hadn't indulged in new ink since her marriage. "What did she get?"

"Cody and Annette's names wrapped around her ankle."

"I think that's sweet, and the kids might think their mom is really cool for doing something like that." She went on to the next room. The master bedroom had only a couple of sleeping bags and duffel bags left in it, bearing witness to the interruption of Ken and Edwards's efforts to pack up the vehicles. Richens's laptop case was set neatly atop his bag and a shaving kit that resembled a camera case was set on top of that.

Camera.

"Don't sound so happy about it," Miyoko complained. "I hope you never get one."

Eve thought back to the conversation they'd had a few days ago when she'd thought her mother noticed the Mark of Cain on her arm. Instead she'd learned that the mark wasn't visible to mortal eyes. "I'm not planning on it, but never say never."

"Evie . . ." her mother said in her best warning tone.

"I have to go, Mom."

"What did you call for last night?"

"I was lonely." Eve pivoted and left the room. "Now I'm busy, so I have to run."

"Eh. You call me later, then."

"I'll try. Love you." She hung up and noted the time on her cell phone. It was almost two. Barely enough time to get what she wanted.

Rushing down the hallway, she waved at Hank as she passed him. She nearly ran into Ken as he backed up the steps with a crate that was steered by Montevista on the opposite end. She jumped off the porch and ran around the back of the house to the girls' side where Claire and Sydney were just returning.

"I need your camera," Eve said to the startled Frenchwoman.

Claire seemed confused for a moment, then her face cleared. "*Bien sûr* . . . of course."

Eve waited outside while Claire retrieved the camera.

"You'll have to hurry with whatever photos you want to take," Sydney said. "Cain is adamant that we clear out of here immediately."

"Did he call?" Eve looked at the phone in her hand. No missed calls.

"He's in the driveway talking to Abel."

Eve looked down the walkway toward the drive, but the angle was bad and she couldn't see anything more than the driver's side of the white van.

Claire stepped out onto the porch with the camera in hand. "There is a lot of room left in the memory."

"That's fine. Thank you!"

Grabbing the camera, Eve took off at a run toward the driveway.

CHAPTER 15

Reed was debating whether punching his brother as an archangel would have different consequences than knocking him out as a *mal'akh* when Eve rounded the duplex corner at a flat out run. His fist stayed clenched, but his biceps relaxed. The look on her face was enough to stay him. She could tear into Cain much more effectively than he could.

Hank was in the house with the rest of the ill-fated class, using their labor to set up his equipment before they left for the airport. Reed wished the occultist was present for this impromptu visit from Cain, just to see if his reaction to his brother's new incarnation was unique or not. Montevista was the only Mark, aside from Eve, who was present, and he just looked relieved. He was a Mark after all, and they thought Cain was the best thing since sliced bread. The heavy artillery was here and all would be well.

"Alec!"

His brother turned and smiled at Eve's enthusiastic greeting. "Hello, angel."

Eve skidded to a halt a few feet away, her lovely face marred by an uncertain frown. He greeted her as one would a friend, not as a lover he had craved deeply over a decade's separation.

"How are you?" she asked, watching him approach with concerned eyes.

"I'll be better after you've been moved to safety."

Cain didn't sound like himself, his resonant words spoken at a slower tempo and slightly clipped. He also didn't look like himself, his eyes rimmed with gold, his caramel-colored skin luminescent. In his jeans and tank, Cain took the position of archangel to another level. Reed knew that level was now beyond Eve's reach.

"Are you okay?" she persisted. "How are you feeling?"

"I'm fine." As he brushed stray strands of hair from her face, Cain's smile was kind. "Are you packed?"

Reed leaned back against the front of the Suburban and crossed his arms, watching with avid interest. In the past, the two had been combustible together. Now, he'd call them lukewarm at best.

"Yes, I'm packed," Eve answered, "but I'm not ready to leave."

"Because of the crew across the street?"

She nodded.

"I've arranged for them to stay overnight on Alcatraz, but the offer is only open tonight. The last ferry leaves at ten to seven, so they'll need to leave quickly if they want to go."

"Wonderful," she replied, but her tone was flat. The look in her eyes was confused, wary. Her fingers clenched and released against her thigh. "Have they been told already?"

"I was hoping you would take care of that."

"Okay." She backed away, then stopped. "The Alpha . . . ?"

"Not yet. After this."

"Don't leave until I get back. Please."

Reed knew how much it cost her to say that—Eve was not the type of woman to cling to a man—but with the detachment his brother was displaying, it was a valid concern.

Montevista stood poised to follow her. Cain moved first, closing the small gap she had created between them. He gripped her by the biceps and stared down into her upturned face.

"The conference call is in less than an hour's time, and I still have to deal with Charles."

"What's wrong?" she whispered. "I can't feel you anymore."

His lips pressed to her forehead. "Things have . . . *changed,* angel. When everything here is resolved, we'll talk about it. There's a lot I don't know or understand. I'll have to find answers before I can give them to you. I need some time to do that. Can you give me that?"

Eve gave a jerky nod.

Reed was fairly certain she had just been kicked to the curb. From the wounded look on Eve's expressive face, she thought so, too.

Her shoulders went back and her chin lifted. "Be careful."

"Don't worry about me." Cain released her and stepped back. "Take care of you."

Recognizing a golden opportunity when he saw one, Reed straightened and said, "I'll go with her."

"I'll go," Montevista offered. "You're needed here."

"Quite the opposite actually." Reed smiled. "My entire reason for being here is Eve."

"Don't you have something to tell me about your trip to Australia?" Cain asked with narrowed eyes. That was the only sign that he was affected at all by Eve's departure and Reed's offer of accompaniment.

Reed watched Eve reach the other side of the street, then glanced around to ensure privacy. "We think the Infernal grows with every attack," he said in a low tone. "The one in Australia was considerably larger than the one Mariel first saw and the one that attacked Raguel was even larger than that."

"You don't think it could be more than one?"

"Maybe, but Les—the Australian handler—watched the creature increase in size after it destroyed his Mark."

"All right. Thank you." Cain looked away, dismissing Reed altogether.

Shock threw Reed for a loop for a half minute. He almost told Cain about the Infernal's suspected ability to absorb its target's thread of awareness and connection to the handler. But in the end, he wanted to join Eve more than he wanted to give his brother any advantage in the upcoming conference with the other archangels.

Heading across the street, Reed reached the front door of the *Ghoul School* duplex and knocked. One dog bark and a minute later, the door opened and revealed a pretty redhead in a pink and purple sundress.

"Hi." She grinned, checking him out.

"Hi. I'm looking for Eve."

"He's with me," Eve called out.

The redhead held out her hand. "I'm Michelle."

"Michelle." Reed lifted her hand to his lips. "Reed Abel."

She stepped back and waved him in. He entered a dormlike space filled with an inflatable sofa, a few folding lawn chairs, lots of cardboard boxes, and a couple of air mattresses. The air was redolent of insecticide and nacho tortilla chips.

Reed offered an all-encompassing wave and took note of the various occupants in the living room—a brunette in glasses shared the couch with a goateed guy in corduroy slacks. Another guy in jeans and white T-shirt was snoring from his spot on a nearby bed. A brown Great Dane paced the perimeter of the room, while Michelle pulled up a lawn chair and offered it to him. He declined the hospitality with a shake of his head and a grateful smile.

Eve made the introductions, then continued with her interrupted conversation. "So there you have it. We're really sorry about the inconvenience."

"Hey," Roger grinned, "We're not going to get upset about a shot at Alcatraz at night. We've been signing up for the lottery there for two years now, but never get in. And even if we did, there's no guarantee we'd be allowed to film there."

"I'm not sure," Linda said. "We were asked specifically to come out here to McCroskey. I hate to burn that bridge."

"I'm certain the invitation will be reextended," Reed reassured smoothly, celestial *persuasion* resonating through his tone. "Gadara simply wants to make some small restitution for imposing on you. He hadn't expected that we'd be using the area in the evening, too."

"That's very nice of him," Michelle said, her eyes dazed.

"What the heck can you all do at night, anyway?" Linda asked.

Reed's brows rose. The brunette seemed unaffected.

"Lighting," Eve improvised. "Exterior and interior."

"Linda doesn't like spontaneity," Roger explained, "but I'm excited. Alcatraz at night isn't an inconvenience."

Linda frowned. "We'll have to talk it over and let you know."

Reed looked at Eve. *Tough cookie,* he thought.

Her mouth curved. *I like her.* Aloud she said, "Well, let me know what you decide. But don't wait too long. It's a two-hour drive from here, without rush-hour traffic."

"I really want you to participate in an investigation."

Reed was taken aback by the fervor with which Linda made her pronouncement. He had assumed Eve was pushing herself to go along with them. He hadn't realized she was facing pressure from the "ghost hunters."

"I'll take a rain check." Eve smiled. "I promise."

A few minutes later, Reed was standing on the sidewalk next to Eve and they were both staring at the Mark duplex across the street. From the outside view, the place was still and quiet. Everyone was inside, all the vehicle doors were closed, all the equipment packed away.

"I'm going to Anytown," she said. "Coming with me?"

He looked down at her, noting her stubborn chin and challenging gaze. "I can stop you."

Her lips pursed. "Why?"

"Safety?"

"Right now, there are three of Gadara's Infernals, two guards, and two investigators working in Anytown. If you come, I'll have a guardian angel, too. A veritable army."

Reed seized the opportunity. "You'll owe me."

Eve paused, then crossed her arms. "Owe you what?"

He looked at her hands with their slender fingers. Certain she'd had a camera in hand when she set off toward the *Ghoul School* house, he asked, "Where's your camera?"

"I left it inside."

"Want to go back and get it?"

"Want to stop changing the subject? What will I owe you? It can't be sex."

"Why not? Maybe that's exactly what I'll want." Might as well lay it all out there. He didn't want her saying later that she had no idea what she was getting into.

She snorted. "You didn't want it from me a short while ago."

"And you didn't hesitate to get it on the phone with Cain," he countered. "We both found substitutions for what we really wanted."

"You can't even compare the two. They're not even in the same ballpark. I care about Alec. You—"

"And that makes you better than me?" he challenged, cutting her off. "I'm an asshole for blowing off steam with someone who doesn't give a shit about what I do, but you're on the high road for using a guy who cares about you?"

"I wasn't using him!"

"Bullshit." Reed scrubbed a hand over his face. "This is all jealous bullshit."

Snorting, she said, "Jealous? You flatter yourself."

But her mind filled with images of him with the blonde—some were memories and some were made up in her head. She was torturing herself by imagining him doing things he hadn't done. He couldn't appreciate her possessiveness because it was driving her crazy. Some women could live with sharing. Eve wasn't one of them. Remorse slithered inside him, then fury.

His arm shot out and caught her nape, yanking her closer. With his nose touching hers, he whispered, "Your jealousy has got nothing on mine. I feel it every time you come. *Every* time. Think about that for a minute."

Reed licked across her lips, then released her. "So maybe I'll want you to wash my car in a bikini," he bit out, "or cook me dinner. Maybe I'll want you to answer my phone for a week or wear a particular outfit. Or maybe I'll want to fuck you senseless. I'm not sure. But whatever it is, you have to do it willingly."

Her shoulders went back. "You're a pig."

He grinned wolfishly. "You love it. And Cain just kicked you to the curb so you have no obligation there."

"He did not!"

"Okay, if he didn't—nothing sexual. If he did, all bets are off." His confidence rattled her further, he could tell. But he knew a Dear John speech when he heard one and he had no problem using it to get back in her pants.

"You're asking for a hell of a lot for a quick look around an abandoned town," she complained.

He stepped one foot into the street as if to cross over. "Take it or leave it."

"If I leave it and go anyway?"

"Try it. I dare you."

A wicked light lit up her brown eyes. "Fine. But I want more."

"Babe," he drawled, "you could barely handle what I gave you last time."

"I need you to track down a European Mark for me."

"Who?"

"Never mind who. Will you do it?"

Reed held out his hand, "Deal."

Eve shook on it, then took off without him. "Come on, then."

He quickly fell into step beside her. "Do you know what you're looking for?"

"Not really." She glanced aside at him. "But I'll know it when I see it."

He reached out and caught her hand, linking their fingers together. "I want you to tell me what you think about the new Cain."

Her grip tightened. "I liked the old Cain better."

"That's it?"

"I've got bigger things on my mind at the moment, Reed."

He sifted through her thoughts, trying to see if there was more she wasn't telling him. There wasn't. So he pressed on, hoping to milk the situation for all it was worth. "You can only be truly in love with one thing, Eve. Cain is so focused on Jehovah he doesn't have room for you now, and look how much happier he seems to be."

Reed didn't tell her that he longed for advancement even more, thirsted for it like a vampire thirsted for blood. What a relief it would be to lose his fascination for her. How much easier his life would be if he weren't thinking about her all the damn time. But he thought about the ramifications as they related to Cain, not to himself. If Eve was in his head, she would misunderstand his thoughts on the matter.

"That's a lie," she said, her gaze trained straight ahead.

"Excuse me?" *She couldn't be that good at reading his mind . . .*

"The only-loving-one-thing part. And Alec doesn't look happy, he looks brainwashed. Lifeless."

He almost asked her if she'd ever loved two people at once, but he bit back the urge. Damned if he'd get hopeful over something that was temporary by necessity.

"How are you feeling physically?" he asked, noting that she was still sans the sweater jacket she'd discarded earlier. It was probably a balmy day for the locals, but for a Southern California gal it had to be chilly. The air moved briskly around them, smelling of salt and sea.

"I'm trying not to think about me either."

"How's that working out for you?"

"Not as great as I'd hoped." She looked at him with a rueful smile. "How about you?"

While Reed really wanted to address *her* issues, he was willing to go first . . . and pick her brain through their connection in the interim. "I'm worried about Raguel. It's easier on us to believe that he knew what he was doing when he went after that Infernal, but we're just guessing. If he's truly gone, we are in deep shit."

"You don't think your brother will be a good firm leader?"

"I . . . I doubt it. He's been a loner a long time and

he's been disconnected from the mark system since its inception."

"You've been anticipating the creation of a new archangel for a while," she noted, rifling through his brain in his moment of weakness. "You wanted the job."

"No," he lied, training his thoughts to follow as if he were speaking the truth. "I think a new archangel should be familiar with all aspects of the system, like I am. You misread me."

"Hmm . . . but you do think there should more than the seven archangels? Did I get that part right?"

"The world has exploded from a population of two to a population of billions, yet the number of archangels hasn't increased."

"Makes sense. So even if Raguel comes back, Alec could stay the way he is."

"Yes."

"I would need a new mentor, then."

"Yes. You could also, possibly, be reassigned to a different firm."

Eve didn't say anything to that, but then she didn't have to. He felt her distress as if it were his own. He squeezed her hand.

They reached Anytown. Reed took in the view he had missed in his first visit to the training area. The mannequins in various states of disrepair were especially effective in creating an atmosphere guaranteed to set trainees on edge.

"Once a coveted community," he intoned in mimicry of an announcer's voice, "Anytown has suffered a steady decline in recent years and is now in dire need of revitalization."

"Totally." Her nose wrinkled. "This place creeps me out."

"That's the point. Every time I come here, it's deteriorated further, but it's been a mess as long as I've known of it."

She slowed, then stopped. Facing him, she asked, "McCroskey isn't considered an international tourist destination, is it?"

Reed laughed. "No. Unlike Alcatraz, which has tours almost daily, the McCroskey tour is an annual one."

"So, would you find it strange for a foreign national to have visited McCroskey?"

"Depends. But for the most part, yes. I would find that noteworthy."

Eve nodded and resumed walking, but at a slower, more contemplative pace. "Edwards said that he's been here before."

"Any details?"

"Not really, but he did say there were a lot of bugs here. He called the place a 'dump,' I believe. Said it was overgrown and crawling with vermin."

Reed's brows rose. "You can't tell that from the public areas."

"Right. When we first got here, I remember thinking that it wasn't what I expected. It was clean, well maintained. I told Alec I thought the troops probably missed this base." She glanced at him. "So how would a Brit know its state of disrepair?"

"A Google search would probably reveal that."

"But it doesn't explain why he's been here before."

"Right."

They turned a corner at the end of the main street and Reed saw the diner up ahead.

"Izzie's been to California before, too," Eve said.

"And she showed up to training with a gun, against Raguel's orders."

"Izzie?"

She stared at him. An image of the blonde who'd sucked him off popped into his brain.

"Oh . . ." He winced. "That didn't look good."

"No, it didn't."

Reed quickly changed the subject. "Are you thinking Edwards is involved in some way?"

"Honestly, I really can't see how he would be involved. I've trained alongside him for three weeks and there's nothing even remotely Infernal-like about him."

"And remember, the masking agent wears off. At some point or another, an Infernal in your class would've reeked."

"Izzie, though . . . There's something going on with her. I just can't put my finger on it. She gives me the evil eye a lot."

Reed smiled wryly. "She's probably jealous. You're smokin' hot. Makes me hard just to smell you."

"Eww." Eve smacked him. "Don't be crude."

They paused at the end of the alley where Molenaar had been killed. The Mark was long gone. Since he'd been drained of blood before being pinned to the wall, there was very little left behind to proclaim that a soldier of God had died here. A couple of holes in the wall, that's it. Two men and two women occupied the narrow space. Two in black—Raguel's guards—and two in navy blue jumpsuits with the initials E.P.D. on the back—the investigators from the Exceptional Projects Department.

A female guard caught sight of him first. "Abel."

"Draw any conclusions?" he asked, leading Eve closer with a hand at her back.

The nearest investigator glanced up. He had a lanky frame, gray hair, and intelligent green eyes. "We're still collecting evidence, but the jaggedness of the wound edges suggests that the head was severed with a physically wielded blade."

"Because magic would have left a clean slice, like a laser, right?" Eve asked.

"Right. There are also contusions on the wrists and ankles. Our attacker was hands-on with this killing. But preliminary tests show no signs of Infernal blood. Usually in knife attacks, the assailants injure themselves. The hilt becomes slippery with blood and their grip slips."

Reed smiled, remembering Eve saying something similar earlier.

"How do you test for Infernal blood?" Eve queried.

"By spritzing the area with holy water. Even the smallest trace will sizzle and steam. It doesn't have the wow factor of luminol," he said dryly, "but it works the same."

"I have a question," she said. "When we first discovered the masking agent, we learned that it was Charles's in-laws—a mage and a witch—who had cast the spell that helped create the Infernal mask. Hank said it was the combination of mage and witch, male and female that allowed the mask to work on all Infernals, regardless of classification or sex."

"Right."

She pointed at Reed. "He killed the mage, but we never found the witch. Could she have found a new partner, someone who could alter the spell sufficiently to make it longer lasting?"

The investigator scratched his head. "Doubtful. I think it's more likely that the intimate relationship between the original pairing made the spell potent to begin with. Unless she's fallen madly in love with another mage or wizard, any other combination would lack that edge."

"I agree."

The voice came from behind Reed, forcing him to turn his head to see who was speaking. Hovering at eye level was a tiny blonde pixie in a minuscule green dress. Bernard. In a Tinker Bell glamour.

Reed scowled.

Eve leaned forward to look around him. "Hi, Bernard."

"Hey, toots. What a day, eh?"

"Has it only been a day?" she asked, weariness evident in her tone. "Seems like an eternity."

"Let's take a closer look," Reed said, dismissing the Infernal.

She shook her head. "No, thanks. I saw enough earlier. I'll just hang out here with Bernard."

"I thought the whole point of coming to Anytown was to check things out."

"I wanted to guesstimate the time it would take to get from the video store—where Claire last saw Molenaar—to here. When you're done, we'll walk the various routes and see if we can get an average timeline."

"We'd appreciate it," the investigator said. "When we were called out here, it was for one scene, not two. We're understaffed."

Reed looked at Eve. "Give me a second, then we'll go."

She winked at him, a playful gesture that rocked

him back on his heels. She took hits, but kept on trucking. That trait made him admire her, and that admiration was leading them both into dangerous territory. Especially now that Cain had apparently stepped aside.

He'd traversed half the distance between Eve and the murder site when his cell phone vibrated. He pulled it out and looked at the caller ID.

Unavailable.

He turned the power off and shoved it back into his pocket.

Prolonged exposure to darkness destroyed minds. Prisoners who were sent to "the hole" in prisons usually emerged disoriented and senseless. Even *He Who Inflicts Punishment on the World and the Luminaries* felt claustrophobic dementia flirting with the edges of his mind, and he had only been in the belly of the beast for a few hours at most. But then a prison "hole" would be preferable to the gore he was presently stewing in.

If he was forced to fight now, Raguel would be at an undeniable disadvantage. He'd been cramped into the fetal position for hours, cocooned in his wings to protect his flesh from acid, lacking water and sitting in a waist-deep pool of Mark blood. The beast purred and cavorted gaily, inundating him with noise and nauseating jostling. Raguel definitely wasn't at the top of his game, and that would worsen the more time passed.

But Sammael would make him suffer for as long as possible. Not only for retaliation purposes, but because his freedom would come at a steep price.

By the time the vessel within which he waited finally cried out its agony and collapsed, Raguel was ready to claw his way out. Light pierced into the obsidian darkness with a sword's blade. It seeped in while the blood poured out, the exchange courtesy of the downward slice through the beast's torso.

Raguel was borne into the depths of Hell in a gush of crimson, his body emerging through the widening gap in the Infernal's gutted belly. He skidded along the hot stone floor, until the blood pool became too shallow to carry him further.

"Brother," Sammael greeted, his deep purring voice laced with malice and fury. "You owe me a dog."

Raguel rolled to his belly, then pushed up onto his hands and knees. His brother came at him in a blur of red wings and black velvet, kicking him in the gut and wringing a cry of pain past his lips. Raguel was returned to his back, gasping, but when the next attack came he was ready. He yanked his body to the side when Sammael's cloven foot stomped down toward his face. Raguel's wings burst free, spraying blood and launching him upward. He didn't achieve sufficient height to fly, but he did regain his footing.

Facing his brother with scarlet-stained feathers, Raguel struggled to stay upright without swaying. The air was sweltering, the stench of decaying souls cloying when mingled with the Mark blood seeping from the freshly killed Infernal.

They seemed to be alone in a vast receiving room. The appointments were impressive—the vaulted ceiling with a replica of Michelangelo's *Fall of Man,* the mosaic stone floor, the white marble walls, Corinthian columns, and the massive throne positioned beneath a chandelier that levitated and moved with Sammael.

Statues of various historical figures—such as the Marquis de Sade, Hitler, and Stalin—decorated symmetrically placed alcoves that lined the walls. The room was the size of a football field, yet the Prince of Hell did not appear dwarfed by it. In contrast, Raguel felt small and helpless.

He studied Sammael carefully, looking for any sign of the brother he had once known. Possessed of awe-inspiring beauty, Sammael had hair dark as ink, golden skin, eyes a brilliant green, and a mouth designed to lure the faithful to sin. The Angel of Death. He had once been the most favored archangel, trusted with the meting of punishments and the overseer of two million *mal'akhs*. Raguel had once admired and envied Sammael. Like Cain and Abel, Sammael did everything wrong while Raguel did everything right, yet Sammael had been loved in a way the other archangels had not.

"A clever way to get what you wanted." Sammael gestured to the fallen hellhound with a graceful wave of his hand.

"Desperate is more apt."

"How did you know Havoc could only die by an Infernal's hand?"

"I did not know."

Sammael's smile was icy. "You took a chance hoping I would save you rather than let you die and spark the war. Patience is not one of my virtues. Perhaps I am ready for Armageddon."

"I had no choice. Your beast was set on killing hundreds of mortals." Raguel widened his stance for better balance and shook out his wings.

Sammael smiled . . . and circled him. "With your blood-soaked wings you resemble me now, brother.

Perhaps you will consider staying. I would love to have you."

Raguel laughed without humor, sidestepping to maintain the gap between them. He kept his gaze on his opponent, but he was always completely aware of his surroundings. Demons never played fair; they didn't see the point. Winning was all, so an ambush was not only likely, but expected. A sudden apparition or a trapdoor. "Perhaps *you* will come home with *me*."

"Impossible. Father and I have fundamental differences in our views."

"Creation versus destruction," Raguel murmured.

"Coddling versus challenging."

"Generosity versus selfishness."

Sammael snorted. "Arrogance versus acceptance. We complete each other. Yin and yang."

"Up and down."

"It is not so bad here, is it?" A warm, seductive chuckle rumbled up from Sammael's chest. "You look so disappointed. Did you think I was pining for His good graces? Did you believe the mere chance of begging, groveling, and giving up all autonomy would have me crying in relief?"

"I am autonomous." Raguel coughed, choking from the heated air.

"Within the limits of a system I created here on Earth. Where would you be without me?"

It was a testament to Sammael's charisma and powers of persuasion that Raguel could almost believe that his brother was happy in this mire he'd created for himself. But Raguel couldn't shake the memories of the man Sammael had once been. A man like Cain—capable of dark acts, but for a just cause. "I am certain that I have yet to see the best of your hospitality."

"True. But we can rectify that," his brother purred, his eyes sparking with malevolence.

Raguel carefully extended claws from his fingertips, keeping his hands tucked behind his thighs. He couldn't kill his brother. Not because he was restrained by sentimental reasons, but because Sammael had powers that terrified him. Still, he would not go down without a fight. "Why set the trap you did today?"

Sammael *tsk*ed softly, twice as horrifying because his magnetism was enough to lure even the most frightened of souls like moths to a flame. Even a painful death was no deterrent. "Does that seem like my style to you, Raguel? Do you remember so little about me?"

"Nothing stays the same. Change is inevitable."

"Not for Father. He never learns. Never grows."

They were circling each other, each move perfectly gauged. Sammael could be fully human in appearance, but he chose to wear hooves for effect. Each clopping step he took was like a gunshot in the quiet. There was no doubt that he was the predator and Raguel was the prey.

"Why?" Raguel asked again, wondering why his brother seemed unconcerned about the death of his pet. Fact was, Havoc had been an unmitigated success, and if it was true that it was vulnerable only to an Infernal's hand, then its loss should be a lamentable one to him.

"It was a transgression, a show of cockiness by a lower-level demon flush with his first successes."

"Are you losing control of your domain?"

"Never." The word was spoken with such vehemence it reverberated through the room around them.

The door at the far end of the chamber opened and Azazel entered. The archdemon had been Sammael's lieutenant forever. He bowed before his ruler and waited to be acknowledged.

"You will see for yourself," Sammael said, his focus still on Raguel, "since you will not be leaving. I cannot kill you . . . *yet,* my brother, but I can keep you. And I shall."

"My liege," Azazel murmured. "Forgive the intrusion. I bring news of importance."

Sammael's growl echoed through the vast space. He turned his back to Raguel and stormed away, his form changing as he moved into that of a fully realized man in Tudor-era hose with waistcoat, doublet, jerkin, and gown. His hair was long, past his shoulder blades, and it moved as a separate entity. Lifting and shifting as if caressed by a breeze. But the air was sulfuric and stagnant here. Oppressive.

The Prince of Hell took his throne, lounging with long legs extended and arms draped over the thick, carved wooden armrests. He was majestic, and as graceful as a feline. "What is it?"

Azazel approached. Aside from similar height and build, he was as opposite from Sammael as opposite could be. His hair and eyes were white, his skin like ivory. Dressed in breeches and doublet of silver and blue, he looked as cool as the snow . . . in a place as hot as Hell. "Cain has been advanced to archangel and placed as head of the North American firm."

Raguel stumbled, the room suddenly spinning around him. He had been gone only hours . . .

His gaze shifted wildly, his brain struggling to catch up with the ramifications. He saw the dead beast on the floor; its massive body lying on its side, its opened gut still oozing gore. Its legs were sprawled, its male genitalia clearly visible.

He froze.

Why have reproductive organs? *Unless it had a mate . . . ?*

"See how easily you are replaced?" Sammael gloated with a triumphant smile lighting his darkly beautiful face. "Discarded and forgotten. Expendable. Where is the love and loyalty Father promised you all of your life?"

Raguel spread his wings for balance as the room began to spin. *Did no one find and recognize the clues he'd left behind? Did they think he was dead to them . . . lost forever?*

Why Cain, of all the Marks? Once again, Jehovah favored one who was far less than perfect. Raguel would not have chosen him as his successor.

"What are your orders?" Azazel asked.

"Orders?" Sammael made a careless gesture with a flick of his wrist. "I have none."

"None?" The archdemon glanced at Raguel.

"My brother's presence does not hold my tongue. This is cause for celebration, not alarm. Cain is removed from the field. Raguel has learned how little he means in the grand scheme of things." Sammael stroked his chin thoughtfully. "However, it does me little good to keep Raguel if it is believed that he is dead. The word of his capture can be spread, of course."

"And quickly," Azazel added.

"Yes. But I think it might be more effective to return him to a world in which he has lost importance. I will have to consider the matter further." Sammael's malice-laced smile was riveting. "You can always choose to stay of your own accord, brother. I welcome you with open arms."

"Never," Raguel spat.

Sammael snapped his fingers and Raguel found himself contained in a cage suspended over the fiery pits of Hell. Smoke, ash, and heat billowed upward and wrapped him in a cocoon of torment. But what was worse was the dead space inside him that he hadn't noticed while consumed by fear.

For all of his life, his mind and heart had been filled with a steady influx of orders from the seraphim, reports from handlers and mentors, and the occasional comment from Jehovah himself—new assignments for his Marks, reports and receipts, commentary and encouragement. It had sounded like the faint buzzing of hundreds of flies, a steady hum that was the rhythm of his existence. The beat to which he marched, the tempo of his heart, the cadence of his life. The sudden awful silence within him was like a yawning black hole.

Discarded. Forgotten. Expendable.

Raguel sank to his knees and cried.

Azazel approached his prince, his face schooled to impassivity so as not to give away his surprise. He would not have expected his liege to act so boldly in regards to the archangel Raguel. Terror and temptation were expected. Torture and imprisonment were not.

He looked at the fallen hellhound and shook his head at the loss. "The boy is a loose cannon. He is a danger to us all."

Sammael smiled. "He thinks he is invincible and who can blame him? He was at ground zero in an explosion that took out an entire city block, yet he lives to cause more trouble."

"I request permission to kill him."

"Kill him? He walks among Marks as one of them. The glamour he wears is so perfect none suspect him. If he pulls this off, he will prove that we are being too cautious."

"He is an abomination," Azazel said. "I would celebrate that fact, if he were not also an idiot."

"When his time comes, you may have him." The prince stood. "In the meantime, we have many successes to relish. Our position has not been so favorable in a very long time."

Azazel shifted with unease. "Will you keep Raguel, then?"

"No. I will hold him only long enough to despair and doubt his faith. The rest he will do to himself, because of jealousy and resentment. It is more fun that way."

"Cain's advancement could be quite a coup for you," the lieutenant agreed. "You might consider telling him the truth."

Sammael laughed. "I am still waiting for his mother to do the honors."

"After all these centuries? I doubt she intends to."

"The time will come," Sammael said, his gaze dreamy and his thoughts on some future Azazel could not see. "When it does, all Hell will break loose. What a day that will be, my friend. What a day."

CHAPTER 16

Alec didn't shift directly into the Grimshaw compound. Instead, he paused at the convenience store across the street and studied the main entrance from a safe distance. He breathed with concentrated steadiness, willing his system to become accustomed to his long-repressed *mal'akh* power to shift from one location to another.

From the exterior, the Charleston Estates gated residential community looked like many others. A fountain occupied the center of a circular drive. A guard station stood at the entrance. A tall stucco fence surrounded the entire perimeter, providing privacy for the homeowners inside. Mature trees dotted the winding streets, providing shade and an exterior appearance of tranquility. While the developer's brochure listed some upscale amenities—tennis courts, a helipad, and a concierge house—there was nothing to proclaim it as the domain of the Black Diamond Pack. But every single resident was a wolf under Charles's command.

It was ingenious, actually. An ideal way to keep tabs on his subordinates . . . and to ensure that secrets stayed secret.

Like the Lebensborn-2 program.

Thanks to Giselle, he had a fairly thorough map of the community in his mind. The Mare was frightened by his transformation to archangel and equally wary of what would happen if he were to be captured with the motel room key on his person. She would not fare well if Charles found her in the possession of Cain the Archangel. It wasn't a risk she was willing to take, so he trusted that the map she drew him was as correct as she could make it.

The question now was whether he should go to the kennel first and kill the hellhound pups, or whether it would be wiser to take out Charles, then deal with the Alpha's mess. He glanced at his watch. It was quarter after two. Forty-five minutes until the conference call. This might have to be a reconnaissance mission. Get the lay of the land. Get out. Come back later.

But he'd much prefer to strike during the day when the wolves least expected it, when they were at their laziest and most vulnerable. Maybe he would blow off the conference call instead. The other archangels weren't expecting him. It might be better to allow them time to adjust to his new role.

The sooner he finished this task, the sooner he could return to Eve. That was still his motivation, although it was a conscious decision rather than an emotional compulsion.

He felt her. Tangibly. As if she stood beside him with her hand in his. But in reality it wasn't his hand she was holding, it was Abel's. He felt no personal response to that, a lack of reaction that made him feel like a stranger in his own skin. Worse yet, in lieu of his own feelings, he felt Abel's—a brutal, covetous, consuming lust for Eve that fed off Alec's connection to the hundreds of Infernals under Raguel's command. The ties to the demons were thready, but what he did absorb was cool, dark, and very seductive.

Alec could only conclude that just as the Novium found a loophole around the lack of physical response, his brain was finagling around the lack of emotional reaction. It was telling him that Abel's feelings for Eve were *his,* not his brother's.

In short, he was screwed.

Instead of the peaceful disassociation archangels enjoyed, he felt the frustration and lust that were Abel's. Mixed with the confusion and heartbreak Eve was experiencing, Alec was suffering like a teenager with a megadose of pubescent hormones.

It wasn't supposed to be this way; archangels were serene. But Eve's Novium was throwing a wrench into everything, along with the fraternal bond between him and Abel, her affection for both of them, their pressing desire for her, and the triumvirate of mentor/Mark/handler. The whole morass was completely unique, creating an environment that fostered an anomalous connection that had to be addressed as soon as possible. With the overwhelming influx of information pouring into him from both the seraphim and Raguel's Infernals, Alec didn't have the energy left over for . . . angst. He felt as he suspected schizophrenics might, with hundreds of voices in his head telling him what to do and when to do it, while his own mind was telling him that Eve was still important to him no matter how he felt. Or didn't feel, as the case may be.

Archangels weren't supposed to experience romantic

love. With everything else they dealt with, they weren't equipped. They were kept detached by the hand of God, which is why they were discouraged from using their powers. The restriction was the most efficient way of cultivating the sympathy for mortals and Marks they would otherwise be incapable of feeling. But they had an advantage he lacked: they didn't know what they were missing. It was easy to turn down something when you'd never had it. Far more difficult to resist something you were addicted to. While he didn't feel the urge for a fix any longer, he still remembered what it felt like to be high and the sensations filtering in from Abel and Eve kept the memories potent.

"Eve."

He wanted to reach out to her, but was afraid to. The connection to the Infernals had . . . awakened something. Like a hidden coiled serpent unwinding from its den and making its presence known. Alec was forced to feel Eve's turmoil without the ability to comfort or explain.

Until he finished here.

Alec supposed he could assign a Mark to the task of killing Charles now that he was no longer a Mark himself, but he didn't. Charles had killed Eve because of him. He would, therefore, be the one to avenge her.

The kennel was where he decided to start. He could use the death of the pups as psychological warfare. Fear of Sammael's retaliation would knock Charles off his game and give Alec another advantage. With luck, that would add a layer of unrest to Charles's last day here on Earth and added torment when he returned to Hell.

Alec shifted to the far side of the building, which

was built off of the red-tile-roofed community center in the very heart of the compound. Children played in the nearby Olympic-size pool. Adults basked on white plastic loungers in the sun. It was a demon's paradise and its existence was one of the reasons why Charles's wolves were so loyal to him. It was also a warning to Alec—everything breathing within a two-mile radius wanted him dead with a vengeance.

Reaching the rear double doors, which were made of reinforced steel, Alec attempted to shift inside and was prevented by a ward of some sort. He would have to get inside the old-fashioned way.

He tried the levered handle and found it unlocked. He was slightly surprised, despite how difficult it would be for anyone with a nefarious purpose to get this far without detection. A camera was trained at the doorway, but it wouldn't register him. Secular technology was good, but it wasn't capable of registering beings functioning on a different plane, such as archangels using their full powers. Which meant it was there to catch Marks and mortals. The question was—was it catching them going in, or running out?

A sense of foreboding tightened his jaw. He depressed the handle with his thumb and the lock gave way without a sound. He cracked the door to look inside and was immediately assailed by the sweet odor of Marks and the cacophony of multiple creatures protesting their confinement.

The building was soundproofed.

Peering through the narrow slit between the two doors, Alec took in a long hallway that made an uninterrupted line to the other side of the building. A stocky wolf in human form stood an arm's distance away with his back to him. Alec waited for the guard to scent him. When the wolf pivoted and attacked in half-form with claws and canines extended, Alec jerked the door open and lunged for the guard's throat. His fingers dug into the flesh, piercing through it. Fisting the trachea, Alec ripped it free. The wolf fell, unable to voice a sound and paralyzed, his life's blood spurting from his carotid in thick, powerful pulses.

In full wolf form, he would have turned instantaneously to ash. *For you were made from dust, and to dust you will return.* In half-form, the process took longer and was sometimes incomplete, leading to semiburned bodies that mortals attributed to spontaneous combustion.

Alec waited for the welcome and familiar rush of bloodlust to heat his veins and thicken his muscles. It didn't come. The absence was excruciating, like blue balls from fucking without the resulting orgasm. Loving Eve and killing Infernals were the only things in his existence that brought him pleasure and both had been taken from him. He understood now why the archangels were so ambitious. What else did they have to live for?

Dropping the remnants of the throat onto the man's chest, Alec stepped over him, finding a modicum of relief by siphoning his frustration through to the Infernals connected to him.

Cages lined either side of the hallway. The walls were windowless, whitewashed cement block and the ground was polished concrete liberally scarred with claw marks. Small trenches were dug into the juncture of the exterior walls and the floor, with steadily flowing water running the length like a river.

Driven into a frenzy by the scent of blood, the beasts snarled and leaped into the bars without regard for their own safety. A quick count told him there were a dozen of the creatures, each one at least five feet tall. Fleshy and lacking fur, they had thickly muscled shoulders and thighs, and tiny midsections. They panted like dogs, but ran like apes, their hands fisted and punching into the concrete floor. The more excited they became, the sweeter they smelled. Like Marks.

Alec yanked open a glass door that protected a wall-mounted display of shotguns. He would rather not use his newly acquired archangel powers, if he could help it. The force required to kill an Infernal would send out a ripple that would be easily detected by the adult wolves sunning themselves just beyond the door.

Alerted by the ruckus, another wolf in human form emerged from a room at the end of the hall. She charged Alec, growling with a fury that incited further frenzy from the caged beasts. The bitch altered to canine form midstride and leaped. Alec shifted to a position behind her and fired, severing her spinal cord at the nape. Reduced to ash that exploded outward, the bitch's remains dusted the creatures in the nearest cells. They grew rabidlike in their mounting hysteria, slamming into the bars with such force they rattled the anchors and filled the air with clouds of debris.

Pumping another round into the chamber of the shotgun, Alec began searching the rooms of the building, looking for further threats. In the end, he didn't find anyone else, which wasn't a great surprise. Giselle had said the pups took decades to mature, plenty of time for security to grow lax. Since the Infernals hadn't been caught yet, there was no reason for them to believe they would be now.

What he did find of interest was a rolling metal cart protruding from the doorway the second wolf had appeared from. Its shelves were covered with a dozen five-gallon-size aluminum bowls filled with a putrid stew. Giselle had said she kept 10 percent of her meals; the rest went to feeding the pups. Which meant the contents of those bowls—and the puppies' stomachs—was an amalgamation of evil from an assortment of Infernals.

He looked again at the beasts that were creating a racket that was capable of shattering mortal eardrums. Those that were close enough to the dead wolf at the rear door were extending their long tongues to lap at the widening pool of blood. Those that were too far away continued to beat themselves against their cell bars.

Alec lifted the shotgun to his shoulder, pushed the muzzle between the bars of the nearest cage, and squeezed off a round. It was a dead-on hit to the temple. The bullet went clean through and embedded in the wall on the other side. The beast sat and growled, the picture of forced docility. It looked at Alec with a malevolent gaze. There was no visible wound.

"Shit." Adding a prayer to the mix, he shot the Infernal again, this time between the eyes. The beast became even more accommodating by sliding into a prone position. Same result—no injury and an embedded bullet in the cement block.

The guns were behavioral tools.

"How the hell do I kill you, if I can't even hurt you?"

One of the other hellhounds was lying on its belly, licking at the wolf blood that was creeping beneath the bars. Its tail was protruding from the cage into the hallway. Crouching, Alec used a trick Eve had taught him and summoned a flame-covered dagger. He pressed it against the appendage. It was like pressing against solid stone. There was no penetration, no scorching. The creature snarled and glared at him, but was otherwise unaffected.

"Fan-fucking-tastic," Alec muttered, sending the blade back with a flick of his wrist. It had been centuries since he'd run across an Infernal he didn't know precisely how to vanquish.

He was about to abandon the kennel and make Charles tell him how to kill the damned things when he noted that the tail he'd touched was damaged, its end chewed off and healed raggedly. Pivoting, Alec looked at all the hellhounds, noting that some had torn ears, while others had scars on their limbs.

So . . . they weren't completely impervious to injury.

They were caged separately. Fed separately. But clearly at one point they hadn't been. Were they vulnerable only to each other? Or were they just protected against Marks?

Alec moved to the dead wolf, whose corpse was beginning to smoke. One arm in particular was nearly severed, the elbow area having melted into a gory puddle. Gripping the wrist, he picked it up and carried it back to the distracted hellhound. He crouched and hammered the severed hand downward, claws first. They sank deep into the tail, causing the beast to leap away with a furious roar.

"Gotcha." Alec grinned. He couldn't kill the dozen with one clawed hand, but he had a better idea.

He returned to the office he'd searched earlier. Via the computer, he quickly acquainted himself with the kennel setup. Each cage floor was hydraulic, lowering to an underground dog run set up like a maze, with each pup segregated from its siblings by cleverly placed walls. A set of drawn schematics pinned to a corkboard above the desk showed that live bait was occasionally brought in for hunting and training. The kennel doors could be opened remotely for cleaning while the pups were below.

Alec smiled. "I love it when a plan comes together."

He left the office. Moving to the metal meal cart, he pulled it completely out of the doorway it protruded from and wheeled it down the hallway. The beasts went wild. He paused by the first cage and lifted a bowl.

"*Requietum.*" His voice resonated with command.

All the Infernals immediately quieted and sat, waiting. There had been other commands listed in the office, but the rest of them were only useful if you wanted something hunted. The pups eyed him with obvious malice, obeying him only because they were instinctive creatures that wanted nothing so much as to eat.

Shifting with lightning speed, Alec entered the first cage. He dumped the contents atop the Infernal's head and shifted back out. Rinse and repeat, all the way down the line. The last two were the hardest, since the first few were screaming in protest by the time he reached the end.

Spattered with the noxious meal, he shifted back into the office and locked the door. With a quick downward wave of his hand, he removed all traces of puppy food from his clothes. Then, he hit the release for the cage locks. The subsequent collision of powerful bodies was like listening to eighteen-wheelers crashing on the highway at top speeds. Alec grinned and text-messaged Abel—*Not going to make the con-*

ference. He cc'd Raguel's phone, too, since Abel was unreliable about using his.

Outside the office door, the screams were deafening.

"Ten minutes." Eve looked at Reed, who was rubbing the back of his neck. "*If*—and that's a big 'if'—Molenaar was walking at a slug's pace, and Claire is right about last seeing him at eight-thirty."

They stood outside the video rental store where Claire had last seen Molenaar alive. They'd occupied the same spot a half dozen times over the course of the last forty-five minutes and the conclusion was undeniable.

"That's not enough time," he said, "to cross the distance from the store to the alley, pin him up, then mutilate his body . . . Not while using bare hands. Magic . . . maybe."

"So, how did the killer gain time?"

He shot her a bemused look. "Good question. She did say the time could be closer to eight."

Eve shook her head. "Not possible. We entered Anytown at eight."

Reminded of the ticking clock, she glanced down at her watch. "We have to head back. It's five minutes to three."

"Did you get what you needed here?" His fingers circled her wrist.

"Yes, I'm all set." She wondered if he noticed how often he reached for her, both mentally and physically. Luckily, their physical connection seemed to short-circuit the mental, which afforded her some privacy, but she wouldn't have bitched even if it hadn't been convenient. Right now, she needed to be touched.

To say she was smarting from Alec's personality transplant would be the understatement of all time. Eve had a few absolutes in her life—her parents would always be married, her sister would always be wild, Janice would always be her best friend, and Alec would always be madly in lust with her. The loss of one of those made her doubt the others, which in turn made her wonder if there was anything she could count on at all. Silly to pin so much on the affections of one man, but there it was.

"Are you sure?" Reed insisted. "No coming back?"

"I'm sure." They hadn't examined every crack and crevice of Anytown, but an exhaustive search wasn't necessary. She didn't have the same feelings of dread she'd had at the start of the exercise, a familiar cloud of foreboding that had hovered over her from the very beginning of training. All this time, she believed the sensation of being disliked and an outcast in her class had been externally generated. Now she understood that disquiet came from inside her.

"Unless the *Ghoul School* team decides they want to stay," she equivocated. "Then we'll have to revisit."

He nodded, apparently satisfied with that. "They think this place is going to be lit up like Times Square. I doubt they'll decide that's conducive to filming eerie-looking night vision footage."

"I don't know. Linda isn't doing this as a lark." She related what the young woman had told her earlier.

"This Tiffany person," he began when she finished. "She's the European Mark you want me to check up on?"

"Yes." She glanced up at him and felt her stomach clench. He was boyishly handsome when he smiled, but when he was somber, he was devastating.

"Why? They can't be reunited, babe. Not unless Linda gets marked."

"Don't say that," she admonished. "I don't expect that Linda will ever know what happened to her friend, but she'll be all right. She's got Roger to lean on when she needs to, and a calling that gives her purpose. It's Tiffany I worry about. I think if she knew about Linda's blog and the show, maybe she'd find some comfort in knowing how much her friend still loves her."

"Marks are cut off from their old life for a reason."

"You promised."

Reed shook his head. "That was before I knew what you wanted the information for. Rules are rules."

"Hey, I don't know what you want from me. There's a lot of ground to cover between wild gorilla sex and washing a car."

His slow smile made her toes curl, not exactly a convenient thing when walking in combat boots. "True."

She didn't really believe sex would be the forfeit or she never would have agreed. Reed wanted her to come to him on her own. Since he wouldn't take her during the Novium, he certainly wouldn't take her for a bet.

"It's not as if Linda's actions are covert," she argued. "Her weblog, episodes of the show, their website, the website of the network . . . It's all public domain."

"So let the Mark find it—or not—on her own. If you're claiming inevitable discovery, allow her to discover it inevitably."

"If you renege on our deal, I'm free to do the same."

He growled, looking so disgruntled she couldn't help but find humor in it despite her worry over Alec.

"Hey." She bumped her shoulder into his. "Just say the deal is off and you're free."

"So you can sucker some other poor soul into trouble with you?"

"You're claiming selfless motivation?" She laughed. "That might have more impact if you weren't blackmailing me."

"You started it by dragging me here."

"You would have come, regardless," she countered. "I just got myself invited."

She was pretty sure she could have swayed Montevista, if she'd had to. At worst, she could have proceeded without him, which would have forced him to tag along for safety's sake. But she was much happier to have Reed with her. Despite his rough edges, she enjoyed his company, and while he was a risk to her in many ways, he was also protective. Sometimes.

They passed the boundaries of Anytown, then reached the street. Turning left, they headed toward the duplex.

"You just barrel through everything," he grumbled, "rules be damned."

"Break the deal." Her voice was low and taunting. "I double dog dare you."

Reed met her gaze with narrowed eyes. "Not on your life."

His look promised all sorts of wicked consequences and a fission of attraction moved through her.

Eve shrugged it off by necessity. "I don't understand what you and your brother are fighting about." Or why she had to be stuck in the middle.

"What does Cain have to do with anything?" he snapped.

Growing cautious at his harshness, she replied carefully, "You tell me."

He stopped and faced her, his back to their destination. Blocking her way. "Explain your convoluted female thought process to me."

"Can't you read my mind?"

"Not without screwing up my own."

"If I'm going to be the rope in your tug of war, shouldn't I know what the war is about?"

He gave her an aggravated look. "What does Cain have to do with finding this Tiffany person?"

"You obviously don't want to find her for me," she explained, "but you want our little agreement more. I have to think that has something to do with Cain. You don't seem like the type of guy who breaks the rules arbitrarily."

And a bet with her was arbitrary, no doubt.

Reed's lips thinned and a vision of her bent over his knee popped into her head. "When I do something with you because of Cain, I'll let you know."

"Spanking isn't my thing, caveman." She crossed her arms. "And I'm not talking about you and me. I'm talking about you and Cain."

"You can't say it's not your thing until you've been spanked properly." He caught her elbow and pulled her toward the duplex.

"We were having a discussion," she protested.

"No, you were prying."

"Alec said it had something to do with a woman."

Reed stared straight ahead. "On the periphery."

"And the fact that you are both interested in the same woman now doesn't signify?"

"Not anymore. Now there's just one of us interested."

He glanced at her. "Note that Cain's defection didn't affect me at all. What does that tell you?"

"That you don't think he got over me that quickly either."

"He's an archangel, babe. Archangels don't feel love like you know it."

"Are they celibate?"

He laughed. "Hell, no. They can even feel fond of a lover, like an owner with a pet. But love . . . that is reserved for God."

Eve sighed. Until she spoke with Alec at length, in private, she wasn't jumping to any conclusions. "So get back to the origins of your fight with your brother."

"Get over it, Eve."

"Were you ever close?"

Shrugging, he said, "My mother says we were once, but I don't remember it."

"Your mother *says*?" Not past tense.

The wry smile he shot her was a knee-weakener. "She'll tell you all about it when you meet her. Like most moms, she loves to share embarrassing childhood stories."

Eve was too stunned to reply. Alec and Reed . . . with their mother. The singularity of meeting the Original Sinner had nothing on the thought of seeing the two potently virile men she knew with their mom.

As they neared the house, they spotted Linda and Roger outside with Freddy. Linda waved, then crossed the street.

"Hey," she said, smiling. "We all talked it over and we've decided we're going to stick around tonight. We tried reaching the commandant, but she's gone for the day. If we had gotten a hold of her and she agreed to let us come back, we would have headed up to Alcatraz. But since we couldn't reach her, we feel like it is best if we stay. All we have is our reputation. We need to protect it."

Reed's hand settled at Eve's lower back, intensifying the rush of his thoughts in her mind. He wasn't at all happy with the turn of events.

"Completely understandable," he said. "And admirable. But Eve's been called away and won't be available to join you tonight."

Setting her boot heel on his toes, she shifted her weight to that side. *You're an ass. You could have at least talked to me about it first.*

You've been there, done that, he countered, pushing her off his foot with a firm but gentle hand. *No more.*

Why not? If it's safe enough for them, it's safe enough for me.

Not as safe as Gadara Tower.

I won't argue that, but I can speak for myself.

"I haven't decided," she said to Linda, smiling, "whether I'll be leaving or not."

Reed's fingertips tickled her spine. "She's needed in Anaheim."

"Tonight?" Linda asked, frowning.

"No," Eve said.

"Yes," Reed interjected.

Eve shot him a warning glance. "We'll have to discuss it."

"Okay." Linda looked warily between them. "Let me know. We're going to head over there around midnight. You should be mostly done with whatever you're doing by then, right?"

"Sure," Eve said.

"Doubtful," Reed qualified.

Linda returned to Roger and Freddy, who were cavorting in the empty driveway. Freddy in particular was rambunctious in a way that was out of character with his behavior so far. Eve's gaze narrowed on him. He caught her looking and settled down.

Reed led Eve back to the house. They went to the men's side, where Hank had set up shop. The occultist was seated at a folding card table that was serving as a makeshift desk. In the guise of a man, Hank's gaze met Eve's.

"Your friends across the street left—"

"—something here for me?" she asked, cutting him off.

He eyed her for a moment, then nodded. "Yes."

She accepted the compact disc he held out to her. Their fingers touched and he read her, seeing more than she wanted him to. But also what she needed him to see.

"Interesting," he murmured. "Let me know what you find out."

She stared at his red hair, thinking of the last redhead she'd talked to. When Hank pulled away, she caught his wrist.

His brows rose. "Clever girl."

"Will you do it?"

Hank smiled. "Yes."

Reed moved over to the kitchen, where Montevista had set up a satellite video phone. Eve wondered why they didn't just use a webcam, but that question would have to wait until later.

Moving down the hall, she returned to the room where she'd seen Richens's laptop earlier. It was still there, as were all the rest of the men's bags. She closed the door and sat cross-legged on the floor. It only took a couple of minutes to power up the laptop, then she slid the CD into the drive and waited for the photos on it to load.

Her sister had once told her that she'd hacked a disposable digital camera and used it multiple times on vacation. Eve didn't ask Sophia how it was done, but she'd asked the *Ghoul School* kids if they knew. Michelle was familiar with the process, so Eve left Claire's camera with them.

The photos began to appear on screen, thumbnailed within some type of photo editing software. Eve skipped over the two of Gadara Tower, and also the ones taken of Monterey Bay and the entrance sign to McCroskey. She clicked directly on the last known photo of Molenaar and Richens, the one taken that morning before they began their excursion into Anytown. With bright eyes and big smiles, the group was arranged like an old elementary school class photo, with two rows of students—men at the top, women at the bottom. Raguel stood regally to the side, his elegance undiminished by his gray sweat suit. The students had all pulled up their sleeves, displaying their armbands for posterity.

Eve blew up the photo and examined each student carefully.

"Bingo," she whispered.

Her mother hadn't been able to see the mark on her arm, because it was undetectable by mortal eyes. Secular technology was also unable to register them. So when Eve's eyes discovered the edges of the mark peeking out around the silver plate of a student's armband she knew she'd found what she had secretly hoped she wouldn't—a fake Mark, hiding in plain sight. Only it wasn't whom she had suspected. It was worse.

Everything fell into place.

"Sneaky. But I caught you."

She heard footsteps thudding atop the hardwood floor of the hallway. Hitting the eject button on the disk drive, Eve closed the window for the photo software and folded the laptop shut. She scrambled to her feet just as the door opened and he walked in.

"Hollis. What are you doing in here?"

Eve tried to appear nonchalant. "Just checking my e-mail." But mental images of the corpses of Molenaar and Richens flashed incessantly and something must have shown on her face.

His friendly mien changed. His lip curled and he snarled like a wolf. Another Mark appeared behind him.

Eve feinted to the right, then bolted left, shouting for help. He lunged, tackling her to the floor.

Her skull hit the hardwood and the lights went out.

Reed stared at the text messages on the screen of Raguel's smartphone and felt his stomach knot.

KIEL, SARA—13:08—1K

On my way. Will arrive at LAX early tomorrow A.M.

Ask Abel to turn on his phone.

He growled. There was so much shit piled on him right now, he could barely breathe through it. Cain was running through his brain on the periphery, using his experience to deal with the influx of information from the seraphim and handlers. It kept Reed edgy and infuriated. Why hadn't he been selected for advancement, when Cain obviously wasn't capable of functioning without his help? "Montevista, I think—"

A yelp from Eve at the rear of the house stiffened his spine to the point of pain. Midpivot, a deluge of information poured into his mind, a confusing disjointed morass that made him stumble.

He was in motion before his brain fully understood why, rounding the makeshift dining table and bolting toward the hallway. His shoulder bumped into Hank's, who was also responding, and his heel was clipped by a pursuing Montevista. They were nearing a bottleneck when Eve stepped out to the hallway from one of the bedrooms. Seeing the stampede, she winced and looked sheepish.

"Are you all right?" Reed barked, hating the fear that gripped him.

"I'm fine."

"What are you screaming for, then?"

"Uh . . ." She shifted nervously. "Big spider. Huge."

Montevista exhaled and leaned into the wall. "You scared the crap out of me, Hollis."

Hank's voice came low and somber. "Anything I should know?"

She frowned at him for the length of a heartbeat, then her face cleared. She smiled. "No. Nothing."

He nodded and walked away.

"You slayed a dragon," Reed said, curious enough to probe her thoughts but finding her as calm as if she were dozing, "but freak out over a *spider*?"

"I told you it was big," she said defensively.

He released his tension with a frustrated exhale and

caught her elbow. "Come on, then. Show me where it is and I'll move it outside."

He reached for the doorknob.

"No!" She stayed him with a viselike grip on his wrist. "I'm over it. Forget it. Really."

Reed stared for a long moment. "You sure?"

She nodded. "Yes, I'm sure."

That worked for him. He had enough to worry about without adding spiders—big or not—to his list. Like preparing both himself and Eve for Sara . . . If it was possible to do anything more than brace themselves for the impact. "The conference call is about to start. You coming?"

"Wouldn't miss it," she said, smiling.

They headed back to the dining room.

CHAPTER 17

It seemed like hours before the kennel finally fell silent. Alec pushed up from the wheeled, black-leather office chair and shifted into the hallway. The destruction in the main area was plentiful. Blood and tissue covered every surface. Very few of the pups remained in recognizable form. Most were in pieces. Only two were capable of movement—a faint twitch of a tail and an ear. They'd be dead within minutes due to copious blood loss.

Alec tried to shift into the underground dog run, but was prevented by more warding. He could shift freely once he was inside, just as he was able to shift within the kennel. It was the gaining entry part that caused trouble.

Returning to the office, he activated the hydraulic lifts in the cages and shifted to the nearest one. He was lowered into the maze, his nostrils flaring at the scent of death and decay that permeated the space. He moved carefully through the vast underground complex, which was dimly lit and cooler than the kennel above. The walls here were metal, the ductwork-covered ceiling low, and the floor more polished concrete. He cursed when he found a liquid nitrogen tank where embryos were being stored.

"I don't want to know how Charles got the goods to make those," he muttered to himself.

He searched the lablike room and found a heating element. Five minutes later the various cans that held the embryo straws were sitting in a deep metal tray set atop the hot plate. Alec wasn't going to take the chance that they might be rescued. The last thing the world needed was a legion of rampaging, ravenous, indestructible-by-Marks hellhounds running around. He would rather burn the place down, but until he killed Charles, he didn't want to risk any smoke signals. In this case, literal ones.

Satisfied that he'd crippled the breeding operation, Alec took the subterranean tunnel that led to the garage of Charles's castlelike home. Because the structure was built atop a small rise in the center of the community, the Alpha was both cushioned from his enemies and able to view the extent of his domain.

From the exterior, the home was majestic and lovely. Gray brick covered the exterior, which was distinguished by two turret-shaped corner staircases that connected the three stories. A large, rolling green lawn and imitation gas lamps lining the driveway gave the home a storybook quality. A coat of arms featuring a black diamond decorated the space above the front double doors. There was nothing to tell mortals that a demon ruled from here, quietly biding his time until he could attempt to destroy the world.

Pausing a moment, Alec took time to appreciate his

situation. While there were plenty of mortals filtering through the gated community—postal workers, gardeners, pool cleaners, baby-sitters, and the occasional police patrol—it wouldn't have been easy for him to get this far as a Mark. And getting to the pups? That would have been impossible. Yet Jehovah had given him this task—a task he'd needed an archangel's gifts to accomplish.

The Lord worked in mysterious ways . . .

Alec shifted into a lower-floor guest bathroom. The stench of rotting souls was overwhelming in the house, as was to be expected. Every pack member traversed the halls here on a regular basis and Charles—an unmated wolf—was known for his insatiable appetite for sex, which kept a large quantity of women in the house.

That was why Alec started in the master bedroom.

The private domain of the Black Diamond Pack Alpha suited a wolf. Wood paneled walls, tan carpet, and forest green drapes gave the impression of the great outdoors. As Alec expected, two women lounged there, naked and decorated with details that betrayed one as a witch and the other as a wolf. A console at the foot of the bed was raised, revealing a hidden television. They were too busy giggling over a talk show to notice him standing in the shadows of the unlit sitting room. Charles was absent.

Alec kept moving, shifting from room to room, growing more uneasy by the moment. Aside from servants, the home appeared to be empty. Where the hell was everyone? When an Alpha was in residence, his home was usually crammed.

Pausing in the office, Alec searched the desk but found nothing of note. Just rosters, dues spreadsheets, mating and birth records—the tools of a healthy pack. So he returned to the bedroom, shifting to a seated position atop the console television with his legs dangling in front of the screen. He spread his ebony wings with their gold tips and waved at the naked ladies.

The women screamed.

He knocked out the spiky-haired blonde with a single burst of lightning from his fingertips to her chest. He leaped atop the brunette and covered her mouth with his hand. She stared up at him with wide, horror-filled hazel eyes. Every infernal with the most basic of training knew who he was on sight.

"Howl," he warned darkly, "and I'll stab you through the heart with a flame-covered silver sword. Nod, if you understand."

She moved her head in the affirmative, her tousled curls tumbling around a pretty face.

"Where's Charles?" He removed his hand.

"He left."

"You should try telling me something useful," he murmured. "Like where he was headed."

"I don't know, Cain. I swear. He left in a hurry."

"Why?"

"Whatever the reason, it has to be important. When he's in full rut, nothing can drag him away."

"What was said to get his attention?"

"Devon, our Beta, said he had an important phone call. Something about Timothy."

"Who's Timothy?"

"His kid." She swallowed hard. "The one you killed."

Alec's gaze narrowed. "Did you overhear the call?"

She pointed to the sitting room. "He took it in there. I couldn't hear him, but he wrote something down.

Then he dressed and grabbed a change of clothes. That's all I know. I promise."

An Infernal promise was worth about as much as used toilet paper, but the smell of the wolf's fear was potent. If there was anything that passed as truth with Infernals, it was that they'd do anything to save their own skin.

"How long ago?"

"Twenty minutes, maybe."

Touching her neck, he sent a surge of power through her that rendered her unconscious. He leaped from the bed and moved into the next room. There was a small writing desk with an old-fashioned corded phone. A blank pad of paper and a pencil waited for the next note or message, while a desk lamp sat unlit and oddly placed, as if it had been shoved aside hurriedly.

He picked up the pad and pencil. Rubbing the tip of the lead lightly over the page, he revealed the imprint of the prior messages.

Right at commissary
Right on Pvt. Mitchell
Left on Garrison Way
White van, black Suburban

Directions to the duplex where Eve was staying. Why? The consensus was that Charles was responsible for the terrorizing of Raguel's class. If that were true, why would he be jotting down Eve's location as if he didn't know it? And why would that information, which he should have already had, cause him to leave two willing women in bed?

Alec shifted back to the motel. He freed Giselle, whom he'd once again cuffed to the sink. "Come on."

She scrambled to her feet and ripped the gag from her mouth. "Is he dead?"

"Not yet. But the pups are."

"All of them?" Her tone was both awed and horrified.

"Yes."

"Oh, man . . ."

A surge of alarm struck him, a rolling wave of emotion from Eve that halted him midstride. He reached out to her, but the sensation was gone as quickly as it had come, leaving behind a quiet, peaceful stillness.

"Hurry up," he bit out, urged to haste by the mystery.

"Where are we going?"

"Monterey." He returned to the bedroom.

"Yay!" She clapped. "That's south. We're finally getting somewhere."

"Don't get too excited." He touched her and tried to shift to the other room, just to see if he had the skill to move them both. He made the trip. She didn't. He shifted back, cursing.

Giselle's eyes were lit with amusement. "Doesn't work on Infernals. Our cooties don't travel well with angels."

"I'll have to leave you here, then." He glanced at the clock. It was shortly after four. "The way things are going, we might all be dead soon. You should go do something you always wanted to do before you croak."

"Ha! Archangels can't die. And you're not getting rid of me. Cain of Infamy turned into Cain the Archangel, and I had to be in the vicinity when it happened. I'm half dead already. At least with you I have a chance of saving the other half."

Alec pulled the car keys out of his pocket and set them on the dresser. "Archangels aren't invincible."

"Might as well be," she scoffed. Then a stunned silence permeated the space between them. "Wait a minute . . . Something happened to one of them, didn't it? Which one?"

"You can head down to Anaheim. I'll let them know you're coming."

"That's why you're an archangel now, isn't it?"

He pulled out some cash and set it next to the keys. "Grab everything that's here and take it down with you. I don't want to have to come back here, if I can help it."

"Cain, damn it! Talk to me."

He moved into the adjoining room and took a last look around, praying that he wasn't forgetting something. With the enormity of information passing through him—from the handlers underneath him and the seraphim above him—he was barely keeping his own thoughts straight.

"Are you a *machine*?" she cried. "Don't you care at all about what this means? I'm not ready for the world to end yet."

"Can anyone ever be ready for it?" he retorted, aggravated by her outburst.

Giselle skirted him and got in his face. Hands on her slim hips, she demanded, "What about that woman you were talking to on the phone last night? I heard the tone of your voice. She's special to you. Do you care about what the end of the world means to *her*?"

Alec paused and exhaled harshly. Examining his feelings for Eve was like trying to see through fogged glass. He knew they were there, could see the shadows and shapes, but the details were lost to him. It was similar to being served his favorite dessert and discovering he had no appetite.

"Yes," he said, honestly. "I care about what happens to her." There was more than sex and love involved in his feelings for Eve—respect and admiration, affection and nostalgia. The best days of his life had been spent with her. Being an archangel didn't change everything.

She nodded. "Okay, then. Tell me what's going on, so I can help."

He related the bare minimum required to bring her up to speed, while simultaneously reaching out to Eve. She seemed to be . . . napping. She was presently a blank slate, hovering in the space between consciousness and REM sleep. He frowned, wondering if the panic he'd felt from her a moment ago had been part of a dream. Having never shared a connection like this with anyone before, he wasn't certain how they worked. He reached out to his brother and found him unconcerned about Eve beyond what Alec would expect.

Abel expelled him forcefully. *Stay out of my head, Cain, before I find you and kill you.*

Alec gave the mental equivalent of flipping him the bird.

"Wow." Giselle sank onto the bed. "I can't guarantee I'll be any help, but I will sure try."

His brows rose. "What happened to the Mare who thought we were on a suicide mission?"

"She hooked up with an archangel. Kinda changes the odds, you know."

"Pack your stuff. We leave in five."

The conference call was anticlimactic. Raguel had, of course, been absent. His replacement was a no-show. Sara had a poor connection. It was decided to postpone the bulk of the conversation until all seven firms could be represented.

Reed left the crowded interior of the duplex in favor of the driveway. He was trying to figure out a way to keep Eve out of Anytown short of tying her up, when a low female voice drew his attention.

"Hey."

He turned his head and watched the blonde—Izzie, the Goth girl—approach. She had her fingers shoved into the teeny pockets of her black skirt and her eyes were half lidded.

"Hey back," he replied.

"I hear Cain was around earlier."

"You didn't miss anything."

She shrugged. "I've met him before."

"I'm sorry."

A smile teased the corners of her pretty mouth. His gaze rested there, his thoughts returning to what that mouth had done to him earlier. The memory had as much impact as remembering to get his hair cut—convenient and good for the vanity, but not necessary. He wished he could say that about Eve.

"It was not so bad," she said. Her gaze locked with his. "In fact, it was very good."

Reed froze, absorbing the innuendo with growing unease. Her accent was Germanic. "You're from . . . ?"

"Germany."

"Sarakiel," he growled.

"I was marked by one of her team, yes."

"When?"

"A few weeks ago. I arrived in California the day class started."

"And which firm will you be attached to when class is over?"

Her smile widened. "This one."

He rubbed the back of his neck. In the normal order of things, Izzie would have had anywhere from one to seven weeks to settle into her new country and firm. She would have been assigned housing, given a vehicle and a bank account, shown around the city, and had a tour of Gadara Tower *before* starting training. In some cases, Marks were transplanted to their new firms, then found themselves back in their home countries for training if that's the way the schedule fell. But following that bit of protocol would not have placed Izzie in the same class with Eve.

Nothing was coincidence. Sara had known of Izzie's past and put it into play against Eve. Izzie's selection was the hand of God, but using her as an irritant . . . that was pure Sara.

"You are not happy about this," Izzie murmured.

"Why would I care?"

"Sara believed you would be pleased. But then, I do not think she knows how you feel about your brother's girlfriend."

He kept his face impassive, despite her dig.

"You called Eve's name," she continued, "when you came."

Screw beating around the bush; he didn't have time for it. "What do you want?"

"The same thing you do. Cain away from Hollis."

He laughed. "Did no one tell you that Cain has been promoted to archangel? He's incapable of giving a shit about either of you."

"I do not need him to care. I just need him to give me an orgasm." Her lashes batted coyly. "You and I can help each other."

Seeing the similarities between Izzie and Sara, fury

filled him. With his wings spread wide, Reed lunged across the distance between them, his face contorted with the rage of angels. He caught her by the throat and lifted her feet from the ground. Her eyes were like saucers in her pale face, her stained lips parted in a bid for breath.

In a terrible voice he warned, "You forget your place. We are not equals."

"I d-did not m-mean—"

"Keep your distance from Eve. You will do nothing to her. *Nothing*." His free hand lifted and cupped her face, his thumb pressing into her lips and smearing her purple lipstick along her cheekbone. "Or you will answer to me."

Her hands wrapped around his wrists. "P-perhaps *you* w-will answer t-to Sara . . ."

His grip around her neck tightened.

"Abel." Montevista's sharp tone snared his attention. "What are you doing?"

Reed tossed Izzie to the grass that bordered the driveway. She puddled, but he knew she wouldn't stay humbled for long. He faced the guard, schooling his features into a less frightening mien. "It seems Ms. . . . ?"

"Seiler," Montevista provided grimly.

"It seems Ms. Seiler has too much time on her hands. Perhaps you have something you can occupy her with?"

Montevista nodded. "Come with me, Seiler."

Izzie stood and straightened her skirt. Her slow smile with its ruined lipstick was macabre and served as a warning to Reed. Like Sara, life was all about the game to her—the maneuvering, the planning, the winning. Cain was a prize to be won and Reed had played right into her hands by joining his brother as a notch on her belt.

Retracting his wings, he turned away. Shit. Sara being here would only add to the tension. Cain was out of commission, but the obstacles in Reed's path hadn't diminished; they'd just changed. And women were much sneakier than men.

He looked at the house across the street, returning his attention to the most pressing problem. The redhead—Michelle—had come outside with a camcorder. The Great Dane and the Scottish Mark—Callaghan, the Ken doll—stood nearby. She appeared to be filming the neighborhood, whether for the show or for fun, he didn't know. He was concerned, however, by Callaghan's presence. The class was supposed to be in the house, helping Hank with the processing of evidence. Observing the many duties of the Exceptional Projects Department was part of training. Why wasn't Callaghan participating?

Reed shook off the thought. Eve's paranoia was filling him with suspicions, too. Fact was, Callaghan was a man and Michelle was pretty and possibly available. In the Mark's shoes, Reed would think that making out with a hot redhead was more fun than hanging out with Hank and his potions, too.

Sensing Reed's stare, Callaghan looked up and waved. He said something to Michelle, then walked over.

"Montevista asked me tae keep an eye on them," Callaghan explained when he reached Reed. "So they dinnae wander off."

"She's cute."

Callaghan grinned. "Aye, that she is. She wanted tae

see Anytown now for some daytime filming, but I think I talked her out o' it."

"Where are the others?"

"In the house."

Reed made an aggravated sound. "This whole thing is fucked all around. We don't have the time or resources to baby-sit them."

The unmistakable sounds of gagging preceded the abrupt appearance of the French Mark—Claire, the fashionista—lurching from around the corner.

She paused at the sight of them, swallowing hard. "I never thought I would wish for the ability to vomit," she said.

"What's wrong?" Reed's gaze lifted to the side of the house she'd emerged from.

"The E.P.D. investigators are examining R-Richens's body." She bent over and clutched her knees, inhaling and exhaling carefully.

The urge to puke was all in her head, but like the Novium, knowing the cause didn't make the phantom feeling seem any less real. Reed sympathized. He wasn't fond of cadavers either, especially grisly ones.

"I have to leave," she said. "I hate this place."

"We're trying," he murmured, also sympathizing with whichever handler ended up with her. She was going to need a lot of help acclimating to the mark.

"I hated him, too," she said.

"Who?"

"Richens. He was an asshole."

"Aye," Callaghan agreed.

"And now I feel terrible to have thought about him in that way," she muttered.

Reed smiled.

"How much longer do we have to stay?" she asked.

"As soon as they go," he gestured across the street with a jerk of his chin, "we can go."

"What do they want?"

"To prove or disprove that there is paranormal activity in Anytown."

"Where is a tengu when you need one?" she groused.

Reed paused, considering. A sense of déjà vu washed over him, as if he was meant to think of the idea that popped into his head. "Good idea."

"Excuse me?"

"Why wait for them to figure it out for themselves?" He looked at Callaghan. "Let's go with them now. We'll rig something to give them the proof they want, then there won't be any reason for them to stay."

"They dinnae want proof of it," Callaghan said. "They're here tae disprove."

"I watched the video they gave Hollis," Claire said. "Mostly it was nothing for the first half an hour or so. Then they went to the video store and there was a shadow that looked like a DVD case floating in midair."

"Perfect. So we give them a reasonable explanation for what the other crew saw and they're done here."

"Can I accompany you?" Claire asked. "I cannot go back in that house. Not now."

"Where's Hollis?"

"Helping Edwards. He is worse than me. He liked Richens."

"And Hogan and Garza?"

"Hogan is fine with the corpse. Better than the rest of us. Garza accompanied Hank back to Anytown. He had to carry the equipment."

"Let's keep Hollis out of this." Eve was safer

surrounded by her class, the guards, and the E.P.D. investigators than she was anywhere else.

"Callaghan." Reed looked at the Scottsman. "Offer to accompany the ghost hunters to Anytown, then lead them around to the video store. Claire and I will go on ahead, and set things up."

"Will do." Callaghan set off across the street.

Reed turned his attention to Claire. "Are you ready to go?"

She nodded. "I'm ready."

"Good. Let's get—"

A wolf howled. A long, drawn out cry followed by excited yips.

The rapid whirring of an approaching helicopter's blades shouldn't have bothered Reed, not considering the number of military installations in the area. But the wolf—far from indigenous to the area—sounded almost . . . *joyful* at the sound. Welcoming. Its tone set off alarms. Reed listened to them.

"Callaghan."

The Mark turned back. "Aye?"

"Get the redhead in the house, and keep the rest of the kids in there."

The urgency of his tone brought a gleam to Callaghan's eyes. The Mark nodded grimly and stepped up his pace.

"I will go with him," Claire offered. "At least there are no dead bodies in their house."

"Yes, go. No one comes in or goes out until I say otherwise."

She took a step forward, then looked at him with blue eyes wide behind her trendy black-framed spectacles. "I'm scared," she whispered.

He reached out to her, touching her shoulder in a

silent offer of comfort. "You can do whatever needs to be done. God would not have chosen you otherwise."

Seemingly reassured, she jogged after Callaghan.

Reed pivoted on his heel and strode toward the house.

CHAPTER 18

Eve woke to a dull throbbing at the back of her head and a phantom shiver coursing down her spine. The howl of a wolf had woken her. Had it been a dream, or reality?

She wiggled, trying to find a more comfortable position. Instead, she realized she was strapped to a wobbly metal chair with her wrists bound behind her. A gag was in her mouth, the knot of which was pressing hard to a sore spot at the back of her skull. She must have been nearly brained during the attack, otherwise the mark would have healed her by now.

Groaning, she willed her foggy mind to catch up with her circumstances. She sat in near darkness, light filtering in through two thin vertical cracks on either side of her. She extended one leg, trying to gauge the amount of space around her. It connected with hollow wood that swayed outward, briefly allowing more light to enter. She tried to rock backward, but discovered a wall behind her.

She was in a closet with sliding track doors. The kind of closet that was in the McCroskey duplexes.

Was she still in the home Raguel had arranged for? Or had she been moved to a vacant one? Where was everyone else?

Eve focused on her superhearing, but registered only her own breathing. Then it came again, unmistakable and chilling—a wolf howling in what sounded like victory.

A whirring in the periphery of her consciousness grew in volume and she recognized it as an approaching helicopter. There was no reason to put the two together, aside from her instinctive belief that they were connected.

Follow your gut, Alec had said.

Using her feet, Eve worked the closet door over in small but regular intervals. Her mind was working as well, reaching out to Reed and Alec, then recoiling as pain lanced through her skull. She moaned into the gag, wishing her hands were free so she could check the back of her head for the stake that had to be driven through it.

How the fuck was she going to get out of here? She tried again to connect to either of the brothers. Same result. Pain intense enough to make her fear unconsciousness.

She needed a knife. And a new brain, because the one she had was killing her.

Feeling completely hypocritical, Eve closed her eyes and asked—as nicely as she could under the circumstances—for a sword. Frankly, she would prefer that such things were provided without her begging or that she could get a gun instead, but she knew the drill. The Almighty preferred the biblical flame-covered sword for a dash of drama. Flashy intimidation was one of his fortes.

She hadn't told Reed earlier when he asked, but truth was, she was always surprised when her request for the weapon was granted. She believed that one day the Almighty would turn his nose up at her and say her lack of faith had tried his patience one too many times. The possibility didn't inspire confidence.

Thankfully, this time *wasn't* the time when God left her to the wolves. The sword materialized in her hand. Actually, it was more like an envelope opener. She almost dropped it, but retained it with a fumbling grasp and a muffled scream. Even as it burned through the rope around her wrists, it scorched and blistered her flesh. The smell reminded her of dying in a men's bathroom at Qualcomm Stadium and strengthened her resolve.

Damned if she'd let these fuckers kill her again.

The rope gave way and Eve dropped the knife. She pulled her sizzling hands into her lap and felt the blood rush into the extremities with sharp tingles. The damage repaired before her eyes, the ruined flesh dropping away like torn gloves, leaving unmarred skin behind. The pain faded away at a much slower rate, but Eve pushed it aside. She didn't have time to focus on herself. She had to know where the rest of the class was, and she had some Infernal killing to do.

Tugging the gag from her mouth, Eve sucked in a deep breath. She stood and bumped her head into the underside of a shelf. Cursing, she froze, wondering if anyone had heard her. Wondering if it mattered.

The dagger continued to burn on the floor. She could stop it by sending the blade away, but she didn't. There was more than one way to call for help, and she'd use the old-fashioned smoke signal just as well as preternatural means. As the varnish melted and exposed the vulnerable wood beneath, smoke began to tendril upward. Pushing aside one of the closet doors, Eve rushed out and found herself in the bedroom where she'd been knocked out. She also found the mauled and lifeless corpse of another classmate.

A scream was trapped in her tightening throat.

Behind her, the drywall caught fire and burst into flames.

Etheric projection was never easy. The concentration required to be in two places at once was always draining. Fortunately, the rush inherent in the hunt and subsequent kill energized. Without that, there was no way to have maintained the duplicity this long.

In less than an hour, they would all be dead.

What a coup! Just weeks ago, all had seemed lost. All *had* been lost—killed, destroyed, ruined. Then, exactly like a phoenix emerging from the ashes, the hopes and dreams of every Infernal had arisen from the remnants of the Upland masonry.

Since that night, they had achieved more than any demon ever dreamed was possible. They had lived with an archangel, spoken face-to-face with both Cain and Abel, mingled among the most traitorous of their own kind, and through it all they remained undetected.

The entire balance of power had shifted now. They could do anything, go anywhere. Soon, Abel would be in Hell. He'd killed Malachai at the masonry. He deserved to suffer the torments of the damned. He deserved to watch Evangeline Hollis die to see what it was like to lose someone he cared for.

But that was not to be . . . yet. Sammael planned to use her. One day, though, she would be expendable, too. And the next time she died, they would be certain it was irreversible. They would sever her pretty head and impale it on the gate to Sammael's palace for all to see. They would be heroes, revered and feared in every corner of Hell.

In less than an hour, they would have it all.

From the singular vantage attained by hovering over the ghost hunter group, it was easy to see that Callaghan was destined for greatness. He studied the nearly empty living room with narrowed eyes, his enhanced senses picking up the anomalous etheric body hovering over him and the others. He was the only one to notice; even the rambunctious dog seemed oblivious to the malevolence waiting to strike.

The redhead in the pink and purple dress studied photos of Anytown. "These dummies are creepy looking."

"Psychological warfare," the brunette in orange said from her seated position atop an ice chest. "They could easily replace those mannequins, if they wanted to. But then they'd lose the freak-out factor inherent in having them decayed and riddled with vermin."

"I love it when you talk dirty," the goateed man at her feet drawled. "Makes me hot."

"Roger." The brunette poked his thigh playfully with a pedicured toe. "I can only imagine how much worse the place looks at night, with shadows thrown into the mix. I can see why *Paranormal Territory* would get psyched out enough to think they saw something here. But I researched the area thoroughly. While it's a training ground for both military and local law enforcement, there have been no deaths or unfortunate accidents here."

"We should have gone to Alcatraz," Roger muttered.

"We were asked to come here," the brunette said, sounding exasperated. "It would have been fucked up to take off just because we got a better offer."

The sound of an approaching helicopter grew uncustomarily loud and snared the attention of everyone in the room. Callaghan, in particular, widened his stance as if preparing for battle.

"Why does that chopper sound like it's flying directly over us?" the redhead breathed, her arms wrapping around her middle.

"I am certain that is normal for a military base," Claire said, but the quaver in her voice ruined any chance of her words soothing.

They were completely clueless. It was all too much fun.

The brunette stood and moved to the front picture window. "It does sound awfully close. Almost like it's going to land."

They were too distracted to notice when the doors and windows were sealed, both with secular locks and a containment/warding spell. No one could come in, and no one could get out. There would be no escape.

Within the hour, they would all be dead . . .

The men's side of the duplex was abuzz with activity.

Richens's pale cadaver was splayed on a collapsible gurney. Two E.P.D. investigators bent over his remains, probing into the gaping wounds to collect evidence and reach some helpful conclusions.

There had been a lot to like about Richens—

selfishness, arrogance, lack of remorse, the way his intestines had gushed out of his body like fat, slippery sausages. A shame he'd been marked. With his fondness for half-truths and manipulation, he would have made an amusing court jester.

"Hey." One of investigators looked up with a smile, which faded when she saw the bloodstains on his clothes. "What happened to you?"

Laurel turned to face him, her pretty glittered face changing from welcoming to concern. "Oh no! Are you hurt?"

With Havoc home with Sammael, there was no longer any need to save the Mark blood to feed the hellhound with. And with the Marks' deaths imminent, there was no more reason to hide who he was. He would greet the Alpha with his war paint on—the evidence of his kills dripping from his muzzle and claws.

He took in the room's occupants with a sweeping glance. Two investigators and two female Mark trainees—Seiler and Hogan. Three guards and Montevista were locked outside. Callaghan and Dubois were across the street. Hank—the only possible fly in the ointment—was occupied in Anytown, along with two more guards. They all expected the threat to come from without rather than from within.

He made a show of stumbling as if wounded and was caught by Laurel's soft, pale arms. She was sexy, susceptible to manipulation, and blessed with a ravenous juicy cunt. Just the way he liked his women. She'd spread her legs every time he snapped his fingers and in doing so, had spread her Mark scent all over him.

"Let her go, Garza."

Hollis's voice momentarily took him aback, then a

slow smile curved his mouth. What few weapons they'd brought with them were packed in the Suburban and Hollis's skill with a sword was mediocre, at best. He had every confidence he could take her.

Deliberately keeping his back to her because he knew nonchalance would rattle a newbie Mark, he said, "Make me, *bella*."

"Bugger off," Laurel snapped. "Find your own man."

"You cannot have all the men, Hollis," Seiler intruded.

Women. They were their own worst enemy.

"He's not a man," Hollis retorted.

Laurel tossed her hair over her shoulder. "Uh, I think I would know if he wasn't."

"You should sit this one out, Evangeline," he said, glancing over his shoulder. "The Alpha is here now. In just a few minutes, this will all be over."

"It'll be over *for you,*" she corrected.

She stood at the mouth of the hallway, her dark eyes hard and wrathful, her fists clenched. But her frown gave her away. She knew he wasn't a Mark, but she didn't know who he was or remember their history together. She couldn't recognize him through the glamour.

"What the fuck are you talking about?" Laurel demanded. "Why do you have blood all over you, Antonio? And why are you squeezing me so tight? I can't breathe."

His smile widened into a grin. "The better to kill you, my dear," he whispered for her ears alone.

Gripping Laurel tightly to him, he set his hands on either side of her spine and extended his claws, ripping deep into her liver and kidneys. She would have screamed if he hadn't restricted her chest. She looked at him with horror-filled blue eyes, her lips lovely as they parted to expel her last breath. He inhaled it deep into his lungs like a lover's kiss.

His animal senses picked up the whistle of a blade, and he jerked to the side to narrowly avoid the flame-covered dagger aimed at his head. "You suck," he taunted Hollis.

A rapid volley of blazing knives shot toward him. He dropped Laurel's corpse and ducked.

Spewing a stream of German, Seiler tackled Hollis.

Regaining his footing, he took on his wolf form and lunged for the nearest investigator. His teeth perforated the jugular before they hit the hardwood. Sweet, syrupy blood gushed down his throat, and he growled with open-throated triumph.

Pounding came to the door and the guards yelled for entry. The cacophony created a unique and provocative requiem. It made him want to howl with joy, so he did.

Seiler and Hollis continued to fight like hissing cats. The second investigator withdrew a pistol from beneath her lab coat and aimed. The fired bullets pierced excruciatingly through fur and flesh, but the mask mitigated the silver that would otherwise slow him down. Finally, the gun clicked repeatedly with no report. Realizing the magazine was empty, the investigator screamed.

He vaulted forward and took her down for the kill.

In the "ghost hunter" house, the sound of panicked shouting in the neighborhood lured everyone to the window. The group stood shoulder-to-shoulder as a unit, exposing their backs as they watched the guards across the street scurry like ants.

"Why can't they get in?" the brunette asked. "Look at them. They're pounding on the doors and windows."

"I should be there," Callaghan said, tension gripping his powerful frame.

"Go," the redhead said. "They need you."

He shook his head. "I gave my word tae stay here."

"We're fine," the brunette insisted. "We'll just—Wow!"

"What the hell?" Roger's tone was awed. "There are at least a half dozen of them!"

Wolves. Big ones. Running from the direction of Anytown in a cohesive pack. A large wolf with a white diamond patch on the forehead led the group.

The Alpha was here. After three weeks, the time had finally come. She had hated him once. Detested him for raising her grandson as a wolf rather than the mage he was. Her only child had died giving birth to his son, and Charles repaid her memory by ignoring Timothy's magical birthright. She had done everything in her power to turn Timothy against his father, but now she looked to Charles as the deliverer of her vengeance.

"Ready to die?" she asked sweetly.

They turned and faced her. Callaghan scowled. "What?"

She smiled and killed the dog first, throwing a ball of pure, icy evil that the stupid creature chased and bit into. It screamed and rolled to its back, legs sticking upright and jerking quite dramatically.

"Jesus, Claire!" the brunette cried. "What the hell did you throw at—?"

Shedding the glamour of the Frenchwoman, Kenise revealed her true form. Then, she went after Callaghan.

She hit him with enough force to lift him from his feet and slam him through the nearest wall, embedding him in the drywall. He hung splayed like a starfish, his black turtleneck smoldering right between his pectorals. A direct hit.

That left her with the mortals, who stood frozen with shock. She smiled and rubbed her hands together.

She struck Roger next, knocking out the kids in order of threat level. The men first, then the girls. But when she turned to the brunette, the redhead lunged at her, toppling her to the floor.

Stunned by the unexpected attacked, Kenise began to laugh. A mortal taking on a witch? It was comical. Then, the redhead pushed up and smiled a cat-with-cream smile that chilled Kenise into silence.

The pink and purple dress changed, turning to black as if afflicted with a spreading ink stain. It swept over bare arms and legs, turning into long sleeves and floor-length skirts. The strawberry-blonde tresses lengthened, the hue deepening into a darker, richer shade of red. The pretty features morphed from fresh youth to stunning, bewitching beauty.

"Evangeline was right," it murmured, in a gravely male voice so at odds with the highly feminine appearance. "She swore the traitor would come after the college kids if they were given the opportunity."

Kenise gaped, her brain arrested in midthought by utter surprise.

The rapid clicking of canine paws turned her attention and her head. Her eyes widened at the sight of the Great Dane, who changed midstride, growing in height into a lumbering dragon. "Cain's woman is a smart cookie," it rumbled.

Roger pushed up from the ground, dusting himself off. He sighed over the gaping hole in his chest that went clear through to the other side, then altered into a faery of such blinding beauty Kenise was enamored with the sight of him. Tall and lean with pale blond hair, pointed ears, blue eyes, and a winsome smile, the prince was the most gorgeous creature she had ever seen. "I was certain the empty driveway and house would give us away," he said. "You're dumber than you look."

The gravity of her situation sank into her stunned brain along with the horror sinking into the very marrow of her bones. Three Infernals. There was no way for her to fight them all off. She would have to appeal to their dark side and pray to Sammael that they could be lured home.

A groan came from the wall and Callaghan slowly roused. "'At wis a helluva dunt tae my heid."

"How . . . ?" Kenise gasped, feeling her hopes die. She might have had a chance if only Infernals were present, but with a Mark around it was a long shot convincing them to return to the fold.

"We protected him with warding. Couldn't leave him hanging out to dry," the dragon explained in his guttural voice. "We like him."

"What should we do with this, Aeronwen?" the redhead asked, looking at the brunette while gesturing to Kenise.

"Let's train the Mark how to vanquish witches." The brunette's glamour fell from her like a shrugged-off cloak, revealing a gray-haired woman in a gray suit. A gwyllion. Incapable of creating her own glamour, which meant one of the others had created it for her while wearing his own.

Four powerful Infernals and a Mark. She had no chance. None.

The faery shifted into the guise of Pinocchio's Blue Fairy. "I agree. No need to let her go to waste."

"I don't smell you," Kenise managed through dry lips. "Any of you."

The redhead's smile lacked even a semblance of warmth or humor. "Did you think you were the only one who could create the mask? Once I had the materials, the rest was simple. Of course, I admire your pioneering spirit. The mask was very clever."

"You are a traitor to your own kind!"

"My kind?" The gwyllion stepped forward. "My kind is those who want to keep me alive."

"Sammael would take you back," Kenise said quickly. "You have insider knowledge he desires."

"You presume to speak for Sammael?" the faery asked quietly. "You *are* stupid."

The redhead stood, removing her not-inconsiderable weight, but when Kenise attempted to regain her feet, she was restrained. With just a single snap of the faery's fingers, her arms were splayed and palms staked into the hardwood in semblance of a crucifixion. Screaming, she fought the magic and broke free, only to be repositioned just as quickly as the first time. She continued to struggle until exhaustion set in.

Murder by numbers. There were too many of them. Infernals who had used her own creation against her. The plan had been perfect. Brilliant. They would have gotten away with it, if it hadn't been for that meddling Evangeline.

"We can do this all day," the faery drawled. "Or we

can just get on with it and you can rejoin your dear Malachai in Hell."

Malachai. Her spouse, lover, partner-in-crime. His contribution to her spell had made the mask possible . . . and it had cost them his life by Abel's vengeful hands.

"Go help the others," the redhead said to the dragon. Her gaze moved to the gwyllion. "Bernard and I will commence training."

Callaghan came forward, shaking off the drywall debris. "I'll ask fer explanations later. Right now, I just want tae know how to kill this bajin."

Kenise closed her eyes and thought of Malachai.

CHAPTER 19

What the fuck is the matter with you?" Eve shouted, yanking on Izzie's hair. Smoke was roiling down the hallway, churning through the air like a tidal wave, clogging her throat and burning her lungs. Somewhere in the house, a window shattered.

"What is—" Izzie gasped for breathable air, "the matter with *you?* Attacking Garza—"

Gaining her knees, Eve yanked the blonde up by her hair and pointed at the wolf presently devouring the investigator's throat. "Does that look like Garza to you?"

Izzie froze. Eve hauled back and socked her square in the jaw, knocking her out. She dropped the blonde back onto the floor and struggled to her feet, screeching when she was hauled upward and clasped back-to-front to a steely frame.

"Did you have to hit her?" Reed asked, his lips to her ear. He was scorching hot, as if he were giving off a great deal of energy.

"Yes, actually, I did."

His hand fisted between her breasts and ripped something from around her neck. Instantly, a surfeit of emotion poured into her—his and Alec's. As soon as they reconnected, Alec shut himself off like a spigot, but Reed's mind latched onto hers with something akin to desperation.

She looked down at his hand and in his palm saw the Sigil of Baphomet amulet—the official insignia of the Church of Satan, a symbol adopted by Sammael himself because he thought its design was clever. Reed dropped it, revealing a smoldering burn in his palm.

Her gaze returned to the wolf, who lifted his head and leered at her with his bloody, gaping maw. The pounding on the door stopped. A moment later the sounds of battle rang out in the yard—growling and barking, shouting and cursing. Screaming.

"Get Izzie out of here," Eve said, tensing for her own fight.

"I'm not leaving you in here with him."

"And I'm not leaving Izzie to the wolf, even if she is enough of a pain in the ass to deserve it."

"Shit." He released her. "Two seconds."

She felt him collecting Izzie behind her, followed by the soft breeze that accompanied his shifting away.

"Can you take me in mortal form?" she goaded the wolf. "Or do you need to be in animal form to win?"

The wolf shifted before her, taking on the shape of a ghost she recognized. At least he should have been a ghost, considering she'd killed him once already. Recognition hit her hard, followed by an immediate chill down her spine.

"You," she said.

"Me." He smiled.

Eve's heart dropped into her stomach. How was she supposed to kill something that wouldn't stay dead?

"You're going to break the steering wheel if you don't ease up." Giselle shouted to be heard over the roar of the Mustang's powerful engine and the surrounding freeway traffic.

Alec glanced at his white knuckles, startled to see a visible sign of tension he didn't feel. He forced his grip to relax. They flew past Gilroy, weaving through cars as recklessly as possible.

Forty-five minutes to Monterey. But then it should have been an hour and a half to Gilroy. He'd cut that travel time almost in half.

He was changing lanes between two cars when Eve hit his brain like a ton of bricks, blackening his vision and thrusting his head back against the headrest. Swerving, Alec lost control of the Mustang, the car fishtailing and skidding recklessly.

Giselle screamed. Car horns blared. Tires squealed.

Jerking the steering wheel, Alec fought to keep the sports car on the road. Vehicles flew by all around him. It was only by the grace of God that they reached the shoulder of the highway without hitting another car. Yanking on the emergency brake, he maneuvered the Mustang into an abrupt, violent halt just an inch shy of a guardrail.

"Jesus fucking Christ!" Giselle shouted, gasping. "What the hell was that?"

He unhooked his seat belt. "I have to go."

"*What?*" Her hand whipped over and caught his. "Go where?"

"To McCroskey." His gaze met hers. "He's there already. He flew."

She stilled. "Oh, shit."

Alec pushed open the door and climbed out. "Just keep driving south and follow the signs."

"To where?"

"Wherever. Anaheim. Mexico. Hell. You might end up there anyway within an hour or two."

Her jaw tightened and she crawled over to the driver's seat. "I'll meet you there. Don't get yourself killed."

He was already gone.

Eve stared at the teenage son of the Alpha and wondered how he could look the same, yet different. She'd guess he was sixteen. Seventeen at the most. His hair was still a mop of dark waves that fell to his shoulders. He still had a weak chin, and a pouty, sullen mouth. But his hazel eyes were colder, more barren than before. Soulless, and drowning in malice and bloodlust.

He was also buck naked, which gave her the willies. Pubescent boys had never been her thing. She'd kept her virginity until she was almost eighteen, then she gave it to Alec. A virile, potent *man* . . . several centuries her senior.

The pounding at the door resumed, Reed shouting words she couldn't understand. His near-panic, however, was palpable and gave her courage. The wolf was using his magical side to keep Reed out.

I'm coming, Reed thought grimly. *You stay alive until I do.*

No worries, she said with pure bravado. In truth,

she was scared nearly witless. A wolf with magic. Just what she'd always wanted.

In response, Reed bolstered her the best way he could. The mark on her arm began to tingle and burn, pumping celestially enhanced adrenaline through her system. Her senses honed, her muscles thickened. Permission granted to kick some demon ass.

"He can't come back for you, you know," the wolf murmured, circling around Richens's corpse. "I've locked us in a warding/containment spell."

"Great. No one to interfere while I kill you."

"For years," he continued, "I couldn't control my wolf or my magic. Now, thanks to being cooked in Mark bone and blood meal, I can control both."

As understanding dawned, Eve exhaled in a rush. He'd been locked in with the kiln in Upland when it exploded—a kiln that had been stuffed with all the ingredients to make the Infernal mask, including Mark blood and bone meal, which were remarkable for their regenerative properties.

It's how they made the hellhounds, Alec said.

Hellhounds?

I'll explain as soon as I get in there.

Alec was outside with Reed. Her heroes. Unfortunately, it looked as if she would be stuck saving herself. Against a wolf with magic. Without a weapon she was proficient with.

She sidestepped in opposition to him, keeping him directly across from her. At least the gurney hid the lower half of his body from view, although it kept Richens's mutilated cadaver a bit too close for comfort. She tried not to look. "I really don't give a damn about your existential angst or your shitty childhood," she retorted. "All I care about is how to kill you so you stay dead."

Smoke tumbled across the ceiling, black and gray, like specters on the hunt. In the rear of the house, the fire ate through wood and drywall with gleeful cackling. To make things worse, she was facing a hybrid who had a lot more experience than she did, despite his youth.

"Aw, gimme a break," he teased, as if they were friends or people who liked each other. "I don't want to kill you. I want to turn you over as a gift. You're not a believer anyway. What does it matter which side you're on?"

Eve choked on smoke. "You're k-kidding."

"I'm going to get a car out of my dad for this." His dead eyes brightened at the thought. "A Porsche like the one in the driveway. The bitches will love it."

She'd love to run him over with it, the little bastard. She tossed a flaming dagger at his right side just for the hell of it, then followed it up with another to the left. When he ducked away from the first, the second nicked him on the shoulder. Then it smashed into a jar of something on a crate behind him that exploded into flames. The ignited liquid splattered on him and he cursed, tamping the fire out with swats of his hands.

Eve raised her arms in triumph, relishing the wild aggressive energy the mark was pumping through her veins. "Yes!"

"Stupid whore." His lips curled back from his teeth.

"Asshole," she countered.

He feinted to the left, then the right, trying to psych her out. She laughed instead. It was a shaky, rather unconvincing sound, but it was still a shock to hear, which was the point. Sometimes bullshit was all a Mark had to keep the tension even.

The wolf growled and shoved the table at her, prompting her to jump back. Richens's body tumbled to her feet.

Then she realized she had a weapon after all—his temper. She'd seen it before, the last time they met. When she provoked him, he'd become careless and violent. He'd run straight into her roundhouse kick and gotten his dumb ass knocked out.

The house is on fire, Alec said.

No shit? I thought it smelled like barbeque.

You're *going to be barbequed,* Reed snapped, *if you don't get the hell out of there.*

From the ruckus outside, she guessed they were brawling. Hopefully against the Infernals and not with each other.

Bummer, she thought, *I was hoping to hang out here awhile. It's so pleasant and—*

Eve! they shouted in unison.

"You should have dropped the glamour before you killed Laurel," she said to the wolf, "let her see what she's been fucking the last three weeks. Or were you afraid to?"

"I'm not afraid of anything! I've done what no other Infernal ever has."

The smoke began to thicken and lower from the ceiling, swirling around their heads and blistering their breathing passages.

"She said you sucked in bed," she went on. "No finesse. But the Antonio glamour was hot enough to make it bearable. Wonder what she would have thought if she'd seen that you're just a kid."

"I'm not a fucking kid!"

Eve opened her mouth to continue, but he threw a bluish glowing ball straight into her sternum. The impact lifted her feet from the floor and slammed her into a crate the size of a refrigerator. She crashed through plywood and into sawdust, the room spinning from the force of the blow.

"Is that all you've got?" she wheezed. "No wonder Laurel was bored."

He leaped across the overturned gurney and landed in a crouch. "You should have heard her begging for it," he snarled. "She couldn't get enough."

She squirmed free of the crate and fell to her knees, sucking scorching, ashy air into beleaguered lungs. The mark helped her to heal fast, but it didn't make her invincible. At least there was less smoke closer to the floor. "So you say . . . but that's not what she told me."

His fingers and toes lengthened into claws. The skin across his back rippled with fur, then returned to skin. "I'll show you," he growled, stalking forward. "I'll fuck you till you scream."

The ground fell away. Eve found herself levitating a foot above the hardwood floor, then slammed backward into it, splayed. Magic stayed her. She couldn't move more than her head, fingers, and toes. Fear coiled insidiously through her gut, despite the steady pumping of adrenaline and bloodlust through her veins.

The wolf came closer, half boy and half beast. He was leering, his eyes triumphant, his cock hard.

Eve laughed softly, knowing she was either going to succeed beautifully or fail miserably. "Do your worst," she taunted. "With a dick that small, I won't even feel it."

He pounced, altering into his wolf form midleap.

She waited, holding off until the last possible moment, shaking like a leaf and grateful she couldn't vomit.

As if in slow motion, he came at her, hovering over her. His mouth was wide, his teeth bared.

"Now," she whispered, crossing her fingers that she wouldn't be denied. A flame-covered silver sword appeared in her hand, facing upward and ready.

He speared himself cleanly, the blade sliding through fur and flesh like a hot knife through butter. A horrendous howl turned into a sick gurgling. As the magical hold he'd had on her released, Eve rolled, taking the top. She lurched to her feet, yanking the blade free and swinging it downward with all her might. The instant the tip hit hardwood, both the severed head and body disintegrated into ash.

"Eve!"

"Angel."

She spun to face the two men who charged into the house. Freed from the necessity of watching the wolf, Eve took in the state of the house. Fire licked along the walls from the hallway, rushing toward the fresh air introduced through the front door. The blaze she'd started in the living room had spread to the kitchen. The whole house creaked in protest, shuddering at its impending collapse.

Alec reached her first, snatching her up and tossing her over his shoulder. The sword clattered to the floor.

"Time to go," he muttered.

The next instant she found herself by the Porsche, disoriented and barely breathing. Around her was chaos. Twin piles of ash dotted the lawn, as did the bodies of two Mark guards. Two wolves fought with those who remained standing. The dragon was acting as cover for the Marks, spewing fire according to the directions shouted from the gwyllion, who stood on the roof of the van.

"Is he d-dead?" she gasped, clinging to Alec as the sky swirled madly above her. "Is the wolf really dead this time?"

Reed's voice came clipped and furious, "I'd say so."

"Are you sure?" she persisted. "We burned him up before and the son of a bitch came back."

Alec pressed his lips to her forehead and released her. "Ash is ash, there's no coming back from that. Can you get Montevista out of here?"

Eve blinked. "What?"

He gestured to the passenger seat where the guard laid crumbled, his black shirt glistening wetly, his throat torn and gushing. If he were mortal, he'd be long dead. As a Mark, he was damn close to it. Defenseless and vulnerable.

Reed pressed keys into her palm. "Go."

A piercing howl rent the air. They turned their heads, saw a massive wolf on the front steps. It stared at them with bared teeth and glowing red eyes. The white diamond on its forehead told her who it was, but she asked anyway, "Is that Daddy?"

"Get the fuck out of here!" Alec yelled, his wings snapping free with such force, Eve was plastered to the hood. Reed joined the fray, the two brothers launching forward, intercepting the wolf, who charged at her full-bore while flanked on either side by two wolves.

Black and white wings, powerful masculine bodies, ferocious beasts . . . She was arrested by the sight. The eternal conflict between angel and demon. The battle cries and howls of pain. The smell of fire and ash, of blood and urine.

"Hollis . . ."

Montevista's weak voice snapped her back to reality. Eve slid off the hood. She leaped over the driver's-side door of the open convertible and hopped into the seat. She turned the key in the ignition and the powerful engine roared like a dream. She squealed out of the driveway in reverse, running over an attacking wolf in the process.

Gripping the stick shift, she slammed the transmission into gear and punched the gas. She adjusted the rearview mirror, trying to see the fracas behind her. Montevista yelled in terror. Eve's gaze shot forward and she screamed, too. She stood on the brake. The Porsche's rear end fishtailed wildly, the car skidding down the street passenger side first . . .

. . . straight for the house-size, flesh-colored beast thundering toward them.

The car juddered to a halt.

"Fuck me," she breathed, then coughed as her lungs burned. Was that the hellhound?

Turn around and run, Alec bit out. *Only Infernals can kill it.*

Wasn't that just really damned inconvenient?

She looked back at the blazing house and the two winged men who circled low over it, combating the wolves that poured out of a widening hole in the ground. Satan was sending reinforcements. They couldn't deal with the behemoth from Hell on top of that. No way.

One wolf broke free of the melee and raced toward her, foaming at the mouth and lathered at the throat. The Alpha.

Eve restarted the stalled car and spun around, hurtling toward the wolf with the same reckless intent he displayed. If it was just a game of chicken between a canine and a car, she'd know who would win. But against a werewolf . . . She gripped the steering wheel tighter and shifted gears in rapid succession.

A foot away from impact, the wolf leaped onto the hood, his massive claws piercing through the metal. He roared at her through the windshield, his red eyes wild and filled with evil. He lunged headfirst into the safety glass, shattering it.

Fucking A.

Downshifting, Eve yanked the steering wheel hard left and spun the car back around, skidding across the empty street and hitting a curb. The bump dislodged the wolf, who slid across the hood and almost fell off before gaining purchase at the very nose.

She gunned it, putting the Porsche through its paces as she accelerated toward the approaching mega-Infernal. Zero to sixty in less than four seconds.

"This might not work," she shouted at Montevista.

"Go down in a blaze of glory," he said back.

"Give me your gun."

Montevista pulled the weapon free of his thigh holster and racked it, then handed it over. She aimed and fired through the wolf, the Glock autoloading and discharging again and again and again. The sixth bullet widened the hole in the Alpha's shoulder and pierced through the other side, hitting the hellhound. Covered in werewolf blood, the bullet penetrated the beast's hide. Eve continued to fire, punching through the back of the wolf to injure the hound with nearly every shot.

The hound screamed in fury and lunged. Eve punched the gas. With the Alpha as a hood ornament, she hit the beast head on. The wolf's head sank muzzle-first into the hellhound's belly before he disintegrated into ash. The Infernal bellowed, then exploded, spraying Eve and Montevista with a deluge of gore.

Unable to see, she ran the Porsche over a curb and crashed into an oak tree. The air bags deployed and her head slammed forward into the pillow, then back into the headrest.

The world came to an abrupt stop.

Eve groaned and looked at Montevista. He was slumped over the dash, eyes open and sightless. Crying, she tried to open the driver's-side door, but was unable to.

Strong arms plucked her out. She fell into Reed's embrace with a sob of relief. "He's dead. Montevista's dead."

The arms that held her were shaking. "You're fucking nuts, you know that? Absolutely insane. What the hell were you thinking?"

Thinking? Her brain had stopped working when Alec beamed her out of the house. "I—"

A massive explosion shook the very ground they stood on. Looking around Reed's shoulder, she saw flames from the duplex shoot toward the heavens. Another enormous *boom!* had her ducking her face into his chest.

Then her feet left the ground and they were moving. "What—?"

"Gasoline," he bit out, tossing her over his shoulder as Alec had done.

Eve smelled it then. Her head lifted to watch and found Alec fast on their heels. They were barely across the street before the Porsche went the way of the house, erupting into a billowing inferno.

Reed put her down and stared at the destruction with an arm around her shoulders. Alec drew abreast of them and took a position on the other side of her. The light of the twin blazes set him aglow, burnishing him in a way that made her look twice.

"You okay?" he asked.

She patted herself down, searching for any spots of soreness or grotesquely protruding bones. "I think so."

An unknown blonde in shorts and a tank top came running toward them. "Un-fucking-believable!" she shouted.

"Do we know that person?" Reed asked.

"You do now," Alec replied, sounding resigned. "Meet Giselle, the Mare."

"She just ran over Sammael's dog!" Giselle yelled, clutching her head.

A blazing chrome wheel rim rolled toward them and came to a shuddering stop at the curb.

"And destroyed another expensive car," Alec said.

"And blew up another building," Reed added.

"What does that matter at a time like this?" Eve snapped, fighting to stay upright. Everything around her was spinning like a top, and blood and tissue were dripping from her hair and clothes.

"If I think about how this place got this way," Reed muttered, "I might go stark raving mad."

The Porsche collapsed to the ground with a loud groan. The passenger door popped open and Montevista's charred body tumbled free.

Eve thought she might pass out. Then the body got up and walked toward her, and she really did.

CHAPTER 20

"I am impressed with your performance, Evangeline."

Eve stared at the stunning blonde at the end of the conference table and felt uneasy. The way Sarakiel said her name was . . . creepy, as was the intensity with which the archangel watched her.

They sat in one of the conference rooms in Gadara Tower. In addition to her and Sara, both Reed and Alec were present, plus Montevista and Hank. On one of the walls, a bank of video screens aired feeds from the offices of the other archangels. Five impossibly beautiful faces stared at her, watching her with the same intensity as Sara. It took every bit of self-control Eve had to sit still and not wiggle nervously.

Two days ago it had seemed as if Armageddon was here. Today they were drinking tea from a Victorian-style tea service and recapping the events that constituted the worst training disaster in Mark history.

"What made you think of the photographs?" Sara asked her.

"I needed proof," she explained. "I suspected there was a traitor in the group after Reed and I established a timeline for Molenaar's murder. Since Claire is the one who provided the benchmark and she didn't have an alibi, I thought of her first. It wasn't until I saw the picture and realized Rome—*Garza* had a visible mark, too, that it hit me: he was the one who volunteered to put the armbands on everyone. Probably because he didn't want to risk either his grandmother or himself getting caught."

"You did not see this when you read her, Hank?" Michael asked, his voice as resonant as a harp. Eve kept her eyes downcast, unable to look at him without quaking. As gorgeous as he was with his dark hair and brilliant blue eyes, he was also terrifying. There was something . . . lethal about him. A darkness in his eyes that hinted at volatile, frightening depths. If someone told her that he was Satan, she'd believe it. As formidable as Raguel and Sara were, they seemed almost friendly in comparison.

"The last time I read her was before she saw the photos," Hank said. Presently in the guise of a man, he lounged with studied insouciance and offered the occasional supportive smile to Eve. "I knew she suspected someone and I followed her plan to assume the guise of the ghost hunters, but I was clueless as to the identity of the Infernals until after they attacked."

Eve waited for someone to ask why Alec and Reed didn't know, considering their insight into her mind, but no one did.

They don't know we're tied together, Alec said.

She looked at him. He sat at the opposite head of the table from Sara. While Sara was dressed faultlessly in a blood-red pantsuit, Alec was wearing his own classic attire of worn jeans and a fitted T-shirt. His hair needed a cut and deep grooves rimmed either side of his mouth, but neither detracted from his appearance. He was still hot as hell.

His dark eyes narrowed slightly. *We're keeping that information hidden from them—for now—but we're going to have to figure out how you hid information from* us.

She'd hidden her thoughts on purpose. They so firmly believed that the mark system was impenetrable by Infernals that they'd refused to listen to her. But . . . maybe she wasn't supposed to be able to hide her thoughts from them?

"It was Hank's penchant for red hair in all his guises that gave me the idea," Eve offered, earning a wink from Hank.

"How did the Infernals get into the class to begin with?" Uriel asked. He seemed to be the most laid back of the archangels, but that didn't make him less forbidding.

"As near as we can tell," Alec said, "they were watching Sara's firm. When the real Antonio Garza and Claire Dubois became marked, Timothy and Kenise took over their identities. Once they were in training, Timothy's sexual activities with Hogan kept him smelling like a Mark. Kenise wore glasses that had porous arm sleeves soaked in a concentrate of Mark blood proteins. Her beauty supplies were also laced with it. The masking agent was continuously administered through their watches, which had reservoirs on the underside."

"There is more to identity than mere appearance and smell," Sara said defensively.

"If we assume that Les Goodman's theory is true,

they probably used the hellhounds. The hounds absorbed Garza and Dubois's memories, which they passed on to Timothy and Kenise. Because the two Marks had yet to be assigned to a handler, they didn't have the ability to send out a herald. There was no way for anyone to know they were dead."

"Refresh my memory," Raphael said. "Why do we wait until after training to assign Marks to handlers?"

"Because it's a pain in the ass otherwise," Reed said. Dressed in a three-piece Versace suit, he put everyone in the room in the pale—except for Sara, who eyed him with obvious hunger. Eve tried not to think about how that bothered her. "The trainees were sending out heralds during exercises, distracting the handlers unnecessarily and putting other Marks in danger."

"There could be more imposters," Eve mused.

Everyone looked at her.

Sara shook her head. "Once they graduate and establish a connection to a handler, they would be discovered."

"But how much damage can be done in the interim?" Gabriel asked. His unshakable demeanor reminded Eve of Raguel. Both archangels projected the appearance of having an inner core so solid it made them unflappable. The others seemed more capricious. "We should test every untrained Mark to be certain."

"Montevista." Remiel's voice flowed through the room. "How are you feeling?"

The guard straightened. "Better than ever, actually."

The archangel turned his gaze to Hank. "Can you explain what happened? Why is Montevista with us today?"

"The same thing that happened to Grimshaw's son,"

Hank replied. "In a nutshell: high heat combined with the masking agent. There are other factors involved—animal DNA, a spell or two—but that's the gist. The hellhounds were made viable by using a similar Mark blood/bone mixture as the Infernal mask, so when the hound's blood splattered over Montevista and the car exploded, it created a situation not unlike the kiln incident."

"Only Jehovah should have the power to preserve life," Michael said in a tone that made Eve want to hide under the table.

"Do we have any idea how many of the hellhounds are in existence?" Sara asked.

"One. A male. Eve killed the bitch. I took care of the pups. That leaves only the sire."

"Have we heard anything about Raguel?" Uriel asked.

"No," Reed answered. "Nothing."

"Perhaps he is dead."

"Jehovah would have told us if that was true," Alec countered.

Frankly, Eve thought it was pretty fucked that God didn't tell them how to get Raguel out, but that wasn't a discussion she was going to have in present company.

"I've got something." Eve reached for the cell phone Montevista obligingly pushed her way. She flipped through the menu until she came to the ringtones, then she played the default one. When it finished, she said, "When I first heard the tune, I recognized it as a Paul Simon song—my mom's a big fan—but I couldn't place the name. Now, I know it's 'Jonah.'"

The group stared at her.

"'They say Jonah was swallowed by a whale,'" she sang softly, "'but I say there's no truth to that tale . . .'"

More silence.

"Didn't Jonah survive in the belly of the whale and come out unscathed?" she prodded. "Can't be a coincidence, right? I'm always told there's no such thing."

Montevista nodded. "Blows me away that you caught that."

"Thank you, Ms. Hollis," Gabriel said. "We will take it from here."

Take it where? Would they go as far as Hell?

Raphael moved on. "How many of Raguel's trainees are left?"

"Three." Alec's fingertips drummed into the tabletop. "Hollis, Callaghan, and Seiler."

"They will have to join the next class." Raphael bent his dark head—only Sara and Uriel were fair-haired—to read something on his desk. "Which will be Michael's."

Eve swallowed hard.

"I can pick up where Raguel left off," Sara offered. "Since I am already here."

Shit.

The curse came from both Reed and Alec simultaneously, which took Eve aback. But the other archangels readily agreed.

"Thank you for your input," Sara said, looking at both Eve and Montevista. "You are both dismissed."

They stood and left the room. Eve didn't look back. She didn't have to. If Reed or Alec had anything to say, they'd do it in her head, not with their expressions.

"We live to fight another day," Montevista said, winking at her.

Eve reached out and gripped his hand. "I'm glad."

Oddly enough, she really was.

Cap and gown. Eve never thought she would wear them again. Yet here she was, walking across a stage with diploma in hand and a crowd of fully fledged Marks applauding madly. The day was clear, warm Southern California perfection. The setting sun's rays fell like a benediction through the skylight of Gadara Tower onto the crowd in the atrium below. It was late Sunday afternoon and the office was closed to the public.

Eve stepped down from the stage and a tall, dark figure intercepted her.

"Congratulations." Reed's voice was a purring, seductive rumble. He was always exquisitely dressed, but today he seemed especially so. His graphite gray suit was set off by a pristine white shirt and robin's egg blue tie. His hair was both the perfect length and perfectly styled. His scent was subtle but addictive, luring a woman to lean closer to get a deeper whiff of it. The outer civilized trappings were so deceptive. Beneath them was a primitive man with very rough edges. But she rather liked him that way.

She pulled the cap off her head. "Thank you."

"Have any plans tonight?"

In her heart of hearts, she had hoped Alec would get in touch with her, at least on this day. But she hadn't seen nor heard from him since they spoke at the meeting with the archangels more than a month ago. Considering that they lived next door to each other and their condos shared a wall, she could only conclude that he was avoiding her. Her parents assumed they'd broken up. Eve figured his failure to appear at her graduation was proof of that. "No. No plans."

"Care to go out to dinner?"

"I would love to."

Reed had stayed away, too, although mentally, he'd been there. Rumor had it that there was history between him and Sara, which kept him at bay. Those whispers had prompted Eve to keep her head down the last four weeks of class, which actually hadn't been difficult, considering how intensive training was. While it wasn't said implicitly, there was the sense that they were preparing for more than just regular Infernal hunting. Eve hoped they were gearing up to go after Gadara. She still believed he was alive somewhere, waiting for them to come and get him.

"Give me a minute," she said, "to get out of this robe."

Half expecting a crude offer of help, she was surprised when he simply nodded. "My car is out front. Meet you outside?"

"Okay . . ." She sensed that something was different about him today. He was more somber, perhaps. More serious.

Eve hurriedly dropped off her cap and gown in an anteroom. She retouched her lip gloss and adjusted the straps of her black satin dress. Pausing, she took in her appearance—the strappy heels she hadn't worn in so long they made her feet hurt, the dress that was a size too big now that she was exercising so much, the silver hoop earrings that would be a hazard in a fight. She'd given herself leeway today, figuring she had earned the right to dress up and be normal. Especially in the safety of Gadara Tower. Now she was grateful that she looked edible (if she did say so herself) because for once, she complemented Reed instead of looking like a charity case.

She found him in the circular drive, sans coat, leaning against the passenger door of a silver Lamborghini Gallardo Spyder. The top was down, his shades were on. Together *mal'akh* and machine made a lethal combination. Her breath caught at the sight of them.

He stared at her for a long, taut moment in which she was certain he undressed her mentally. She could almost feel it through the bond between them—the whisper of his fingertips against her skin as he pushed her straps aside, the press of his lips against her throat, the low groan of desire.

But it wouldn't be that way at all. That was Alec's style. Reed was rough and tumble.

"A guy can change," he murmured, opening the door for her.

Eve smiled as she slipped into the seat. "Who says I want you to?"

He took her to Savannah on the Beach on Pacific Coast Highway, not too far from where she lived. They sat by a window, but she didn't enjoy the view of the water. She was too busy studying him and trying to figure out what he was thinking. He seemed pensive, which didn't jibe with a celebratory dinner.

"So," she began, breaking the silence, "do you always take your graduating Marks out to dinner?"

Reed's lips pursed, then he shook his head. "They don't get assigned to a handler until a week or so after graduation."

"To what do I owe this honor, then?"

There was a drawn-out pause before he said gruffly, "Today was the day you finally decided that you're single."

Wow. Okay. "Is this a date?"

"Yeah . . . Am I doing it wrong?"

It took a moment for her to realize he was serious. An internal shiver moved through her. She shouldn't be surprised that an actual date wasn't part of his repertoire. He was the kind of man who picked up a woman just by giving her "the look." Hell, that's how he'd picked *her* up. Next thing she knew, she'd been in the stairwell of Gadara Tower getting the ride of her life.

She leaned back in her chair. "You're a little tense." She'd tell him to drink a little, but mind-altering substances had no effect on celestially enhanced beings. The body is a temple and all that.

"Loosen me up, then."

There he was, Reed's internal caveman. "Should I sing and dance?"

"I've heard you sing, so no thanks. But dancing? Depends. Will it be exotic?"

"Pig."

He reached over and caught her hand. "Show me how not to be, I'm willing to learn."

"Where is this leading?"

"A sanitarium, if you keep trying to blow yourself up. Beyond that . . ." He shrugged. "Hell if I know."

"I'm not ready," she said honestly.

His dark eyes were amused. "Neither am I. But I'll keep taking you out, you'll keep dressing like that, and we'll enjoy the ride. Wherever it goes."

Eve took a deep breath and jumped in. "Okay. Deal."

It was with great relief that Eve slipped off her heels in the elevator. The image of Reed standing by his car in the subterranean garage of her condominium complex was indelibly etched into her mind. She suspected it would follow her into her dreams. Alec had once looked at her with similar hunger. It was hard to get over wanting to be wanted like that.

The car reached the top floor and the doors opened with a soft *ding*. Padding out to the hallway, she came to an abrupt halt. Alec sat on the floor in black jeans and leather motorcycle jacket. His back was to the wall between their two condos and his long legs were stretched out into the hall.

He stood when he saw her. "Hi."

She just stared.

"You look . . . amazing," he murmured.

"You look different." Darker, leaner, his hair a luxurious mane of black silk that tumbled around his broad shoulders. Still had the golden sheen of an archangel. And the distance between them yawned wider than ever before.

He nodded, waiting.

"Why are you out here?" she asked, gesturing at the length of the hallway.

"I'm waiting for you."

"You could do that in your condo."

"I wanted no distractions from thinking about you."

Convoluted reasoning, but then . . . when had she ever really understood him? The man was a mystery.

Eve didn't mean to sound resentful when she said, "I graduated today."

"I was there. Congratulations. I'm proud of you."

"I didn't see you."

"I saw you," his lips thinned, "leaving with Abel."

"I haven't heard from you in a month."

Alec came toward her. "I've been traveling. Researching what happened to us."

"You could have called. E-mailed. Written a letter."

"Yes." He reached her. His hand lifted to tuck her hair behind her ear. "At first, I thought it was best to stay away from you."

"You're not my mentor anymore?"

"Not while you were in training."

"And now?"

He exhaled harshly. "There's something . . . in me, angel. I didn't know it was there until I became an archangel."

She frowned. "Something *in* you?"

"I can't explain it, other than I want to keep it away from you."

Eve sighed. "What do you want me to say to that, Alec?"

"I want you to say that you'll let me try and fix this."

"Fix what?"

"You and me."

Stepping around him, she headed toward her condo.

"Eve?" He followed.

She unlocked the multiple dead bolts that had once given her a feeling of safety. Setting her shoes beneath the console table by the door and her purse on top of it, she looked at him standing in her doorway. "How do you feel about me?"

He didn't misunderstand. "Confused. Detached."

"You don't love me anymore?"

"I *want* to love you." His deep voice was low and fervent. "I remember what it felt like to love you."

Her head ached. "I think you need to figure out what you're doing with your life, before you try and do me."

Alec stepped inside and shut the door. "What means more? When someone wants you because they can't help it? Because of hormones or some chemical reaction in the brain? Or when they want you because they choose to want you? Because they make the conscious decision to want you?"

She groaned. "You're too fucking complicated."

"We'll start slow," he suggested, stepping closer and moving in for the kill.

"Like what?" she asked, suspicious.

His smile made her toes curl. "A ride on my bike along the coast. That slow enough for you?"

Eve's gaze narrowed. Far from innocent, a ride on his Harley would put him in her arms and between her legs. The gleam in his eyes told her he was thinking the same thing.

"Only if I'm doing the driving," she said.

He hesitated, well aware that she was talking about more than the bike.

"Otherwise, no deal," she pressed.

"Fine. Deal."

Her tummy fluttered. Where had she heard that before?

For a second she wondered how this would work. Even now, she could feel both men in her head bristling at each other with their backs up. Then she gave a mental shrug. They all knew what was going on. They were all adults. Mostly. And she was a one-man woman. They would both be at arm's distance for a while.

The moment she thought it, she felt how well *that* went over.

Smiling, she headed down the hallway to change.

AUTHOR'S NOTE

For some it will be clear that Fort McCroskey is based on the former Fort Ord, an Army base on Monterey Bay, California. I fictionalized it to free me creatively. The Defense Language Institute and Naval Postgraduate School, however, are very real. DLI not only trains some of the best and brightest military personnel in the world, it also holds some of the most vivid memories of my life. My father-in-law attended to learn Vietnamese for the Marines. Years later, I attended to learn Russian for the Army. And years after that, my sister attended to learn Arabic for the Air Force. How times change.

Many languages are taught at DLI, all in the continuing mission to keep the United States military the most formidable in the world.

God bless our troops.

APPENDIX

The Seven Archangels

These are the names of the angels who watch:

1. Uriel, one of the holy angels, who presides over clamor and terror.
2. Raphael, one of the holy angels, who presides over the spirits of men.
3. Raguel, one of the holy angels, who takes vengeance on the world of the luminaries.
4. Michael, one of the holy angels, to wit, he that is set over the best part of mankind and over chaos.
5. Sarakiel, one of the holy angels, who is set over the spirits, who sin in the spirit.
6. Gabriel, one of the holy angels, who is over Paradise and the serpents and the Cherubim.
7. Remiel, one of the holy angels, whom God set over those who rise.

—*The Book of Enoch 20:1–8*

The Christian Hierarchy of Angels

First Sphere—Angels who function as guardians of God's throne

- Seraphim
- Cherubim
- Ophanim/Thrones/Wheels *(Erelim)*

Second Sphere—Angels who function as governors

- Dominions/Leaders *(Hashmallim)*
- Virtues
- Powers/Authorities

Third Sphere—Angels who function as messengers and soldiers

- Principalities/Rules
- Archangels
- Angels *(Malakhim)*

Abbreviated Playlist *(in no particular order)*

"Blitzkrieg"—Metallica
"Symphony of Destruction"—Megadeth
"Like a Dog Chasing Cars"—Hans Zimmer and James Newton Howard
"Voodoo"—Godsmack
"Ghost Riders in the Sky"—Spiderbait

More extras at www.sylviaday.com

Read on for a preview of

EVE *of* CHAOS

Sylvia Day

writing as S. J. Day

Available from Tom Doherty Associates

A TOR PAPERBACK

CHAPTER 1

Evangeline Hollis watched with clenched jaw as a kappa demon served *yakisoba*—Japanese pan-fried noodles—to her mother with a broad smile. Eve guessed that the ratio of mortals to demons at the Orange County Buddhist Church's annual Obon Festival was about fifty-fifty.

After three months of living with the Mark of Cain and her new "job" as celestial bounty hunter, Eve was resigned to the reality of Infernals mingling undetected among mortals. However, she was still surprised by the number of transplanted Japanese demons who had come out to play at the festival. There seemed to be an inordinate amount of them present.

"You want some?" her mother asked, holding out the plate. Miyoko had lived a mostly quintessential American life in the United States for thirty years. She was a naturalized citizen, a converted Baptist, and her husband, Darrel Hollis, was a good ol' boy from Alabama. But she appreciated her roots and made an effort to share the Japanese culture with her two daughters.

Eve shook her head. "I want *yakidango*."

"Me, too. It's over there." Miyoko set off, leading the way.

The festival was contained within the gated parking lot of the temple. To the right was a large gymnasium. To the left, the temple and school complex. The area was small, but still managed to hold a variety of food and game booths. A *taiko* drum was elevated in a *yagura* tower overlooking a space that would later showcase Bon Odori dancers. Children competed to win prizes ranging from live goldfish to stuffed animals. Adults hovered over displays of trinkets and homemade desserts.

The Southern California weather was perfect, as usual. A balmy seventy-eight degrees with plenty of sunshine and very few clouds. Adjusting her sunglasses, Eve relished the kiss of the sun on her skin and breathed in the scents of her favorite foods.

Then a foul stench wafted by on the afternoon breeze, assaulting her nose and ruining her rare moment of peace.

The putrid smell of rotting soul; it was unmistakable. It was a cross between decaying flesh and fresh shit, and it amazed Eve that the Unmarked—mortals lacking the Mark of Cain—couldn't smell it. She turned her head, seeking out the source.

Her searching gaze halted on a lovely Asian woman standing across the aisle from her. A *yuki-onna*—a Japanese snow demon. Eve noted the Infernal's white kimono with its delicate *sukura* embroidery and the detail on her cheekbone that resembled a tribal tattoo. In truth, the design was the demon's rank and it was invisible to mortals. Like the Mark of Cain on Eve's arm, it was similar to mortal military insignia. All Infernals had them. The details betrayed both which species of damned being they were and what their rank in Hell's hierarchy was.

Contrary to what most theologians believed, the Mark of the Beast wasn't something to be feared as the start of the Apocalypse; it was a caste system that had been in place for centuries.

Eve's mark began to tingle, then burn. A call to arms.

Now? she asked with a mental query, exasperation clear in her dry tone. She was a Mark, one of thousands of "sinners" around the world who'd been drafted into service exterminating demons for God. She was expected to kill at the drop of a hat, but her mother was with her and they were at a house of worship.

Sorry, babe. Reed Abel sounded anything but. *You're in the wrong place at the right time. Her number's up, and you're closest.*

You've been singing that tune all week, she retorted. *I'm not buying it anymore.*

She'd been vanquishing a demon a day—sometimes two—for the last several days. A girl needed more than just Sundays off when her job was killing demons. *Why am I always closest?*

Because you're a disaster magnet?

And you're a riot.

Reed—aka Abel of biblical fame—was a *mal'akh,* an angel. He was a handler, a position that meant he was responsible for assigning hunts to a small group of Marks. It was a lot like skip tracing. The seven earthbound archangels acted as bail bondsmen. Reed was a dispatcher. Eve was a bounty hunter. It was a well-oiled system for most Marks, but to say she was a squeaky wheel would be an understatement.

Dinner tonight? he asked.

After that wisecrack, cocky bastard?

I'll cook.

She followed her mom, keeping an eye on her quarry. *If I'm still alive, sure.*